WHAT WILL BE

EVE PEARSON

For Claire

1998

Lucy added the final swirl of icing to her daughter's cake. It actually looked quite good. She'd never been a skilful baker but on this occasion she'd done herself proud. Always good to go out on a high.

She looked to her sous-chef who was eyeing the icing bowl with great anticipation. 'Go on then, you can lick it. It is your birthday after all.'

Like a faithful dog which had finally been permitted to move, Erica leapt at the sticky bowl, grabbing the wooden spoon with gusto. Icing squeezed through her small fingers.

Lucy felt tears threatening and turned her attention to the sink full of washing up. It wouldn't do to cry.

She'd known for years exactly how today would play out, but actually living it was proving more difficult than she'd imagined.

She filled up the cake pan with hot soapy water and steadied herself.

'Mummy?'

'Yes darling?' Lucy turned to find her daughter had acquired a dripping beard. She laughed and grabbed a cloth to clean the child's chin.

'Today's been the best,' Erica said between wipes.

Guilt clenched Lucy's stomach. She smiled despite herself, putting on the show she had perfected over the years, but the words caught in her throat. Finally, she kissed her daughter's head and mumbled "good" before returning to the sink.

'Do we really have to wait until tomorrow to eat it?' Erica whined as she prodded at the cake on its stand.

'Of course darling, it's for your birthday party.' She turned off the tap, having second thoughts on her decision. Glancing at the clock she did some quick maths before turning on her heel. 'Grab some plates, I'll get a knife.' Lucy would be dead in three hours, four minutes and thirty-two seconds. A final slice of cake with her daughter wouldn't hurt.

PLEASE GOD. *Forgive me for what I'm about to do.*

Present Day

Friday. Ten past three.

Erica Hutchinson fiddled with her phone, trying her best to distract herself.

Five minutes 'til the bell.

She was standing at the school gates beside an excited huddle of mums, waiting to pick up her daughter. The other parents were chatting – groups of three or four discussing what their plans were, who was looking after the kids this holiday, what they were doing this evening. The usual.

She was being anti-social but it didn't bother her. The truth was she knew none of these people, aside from recognising a few regulars from her coffee shop and the mums of Georgia's best friends. Idle chit-chat with a bunch of women she had little in common with didn't appeal. It had been a long day at work, she just wanted to get Georgia and go home.

A roar of laughter erupted to her left, stealing the focus from her phone.

Four minutes 'til the bell.

A knot of excitement was forming in her belly. The October holidays were tantalisingly close. She'd taken a week off work and the fun would start tonight. The plan was to take Georgia to McDonalds then enjoy a duvet night on the sofa. Bliss. Even the likelihood of watching a film she'd seen a thousand times didn't dampen her spirits. Why were kids obsessed with watching the same thing over and over? Every princess looked the same. Never mind, she'd sneak a glass of wine later to make it bearable. Maybe she'd keep the bottle going after G went to bed – she was off work after all.

She eyed the school's door and willed time to go faster. To the side of the door stood a customer from work, their eyes locked for a brief second so she forced a half smile. She was almost surprised to find it returned. Most wouldn't say hello – it wasn't personal though, it was just the way her job was. They'd talk non-stop in the confines of her shop but step outside and it was radio silence. What would they say if they knew the truth? Everyone has secrets though; the occasional skeleton they'd prefer to keep hidden.

More laughter to her left – someone was on fire today. *Two minutes 'til the bell.*

What would Georgia bring home tonight? Surely they wouldn't have done any proper work on the last day of school?

She had G's latest drawing pinned up in the kitchen. 'Gran told me to draw this for you,' she'd said, handing it to Erica like it was a sacred manuscript. The pair were talking more often, Georgia's gift getting stronger the older she got. Erica had known straight away her daughter was like her mother. They shared the same eyes – one blue, one brown – a common sign of their hidden talent. She'd hoped it could be forgotten like her own abilities, but her luck was out on that. *Was it ever in?*

Georgia often drew, but Erica hadn't stopped thinking about this particular picture. There were three figures with a house and tree; written beneath were the words MUM, GEORGIA and FUZZ.

'And who's Fuzz? Mum's handsome boyfriend?' Unlikely, but conversation called for it. She assumed it was meant to be a person, it had arms and legs, but the rest of it resembled an unruly mass lacking any features. G had really gone to town with the black scribbles.

'Don't be silly. That's Uncle Fuzz.' Georgia pointed to where a head presumably was. 'Gran says he has thick black hair and a hairy face. That's why we call him Fuzz. It's a nickname.' Her tone suggested that Erica was beyond help for missing such an obvious fact.

'An uncle? How cool, I can't wait to meet him.' Erica smiled; she wasn't going to argue with her mother's prediction. 'It'll go up on the fridge straight away, thank you.' She kissed Georgia's head.

Erica was an only child and, after the email she'd received from G's father, it was obvious his family wanted nothing to do with them.

Still, her mum's cryptic messages were never wrong. A typical mother's move – dead eighteen years and still managing to find her men to live with (even if it was just on the fridge). Why couldn't they be happy as a duo?

Personally, Erica considered the case closed. There was more to worry about than her mother's rudimentary predictions. The less said about them the better.

The school bell jolted Erica back to the present and children began to stream out. Energy levels in the playground multiplied tenfold. She couldn't wait for Georgia to come running out and give her a big hug. She lived for G's cuddles, even more so now her daughter was eight. It wouldn't be long before the kid was too cool for stuff like that, especially at the school gates where her friends could see. Erica wasn't ready to move on any time soon. *Tough luck kid, get used to it.*

She stepped aside and let a few younger kids run by, high as kites. They'd been doing crafts. Glitter shimmered over unidentifiable objects (*a smiling paper plate, who knows?*), and was plastered over their hands and sleeves. Hopefully Georgia hadn't been involved in anything similar; Erica didn't want anything like that anywhere near her car, never mind in it.

The majority of kids were out now, but there was no sign of Georgia. Erica scoured the crowd, going on tiptoe to get a better look; she must have missed her. It's tough to get a good vantage point at five foot three so she conceded and wound her way to the front door. There were steps; she could get a better look.

By the time she made it to the front there was barely a trickle of children leaving. Panic hadn't set in yet, but her gut instinct was turning sour. Perhaps Georgia had needed the toilet, she reassured herself.

Erica was at the foot of the steps when Georgia appeared, a teacher by her side. 'Someone's not feeling very well,' Mrs Mills said. But Erica could already tell.

Georgia never got sick, so her internal maternal alarm bell was ringing at full volume. In fact, she'd never had a single legitimate sick day in her life. Any time she'd been off was for quality mother-daughter skiving excursions. You had to maintain the pretence of being a normal child, so why not throw some adventure in for good measure?

Today though, Georgia's face was ashen. It looked like she was finding it painful to walk, and her usually bright eyes were reduced to a dull glaze.

Pétur was searching for 170 Hope Street. He'd spent twenty minutes going up Wellington Street before realising the building numbers didn't even go up that high and he was on the wrong road.

Why was everything so similar here? The long, straight, block-like streets had confused him no end since he arrived in Glasgow a week ago.

He'd much preferred Edinburgh, in terms of navigating anyway, but the city had been a little too busy for him. Too many tourists (a silly observation, he was one himself). Aberdeen? He could take it or leave it. However, his favourite area had been Fort Augustus and Loch Ness. Ok, it wasn't a city, so it was unfair to draw the comparison but, after nearly two months travelling around the country, it was there that had won him over. He'd walked the Great Glen Way from Inverness to Fort William and spent most of his time watching the canal. It was mesmerising to see the locks filling and emptying, allowing the boats to pass through. A truly magnificent feat of mechanical engineering.

The irony of this wasn't lost on him, given how much he hated water. It was amazing how much faith one could put in a safety barrier. Either that or the hypnotherapy he'd endured in Reykjavik was actually working and he owed his friend nearly three thousand Króna. He wouldn't be jumping to conclusions just yet, he wasn't one to lose a bet so easily.

He reached the next intersection and stood, confused. A signpost above him pointed in the direction of Glasgow's Central Station but he still wasn't sure where he currently was. Should he head back to the city centre and start again, get his bearings? It was only a five-minute walk away.

'You alright? You look at bit lost,' a stranger said, stopping in front of him. The Scots were a friendly bunch, no denying it.

'Just looking for Hope Street.'

'You're on it,' the man said, pointing at the street sign above the law firm opposite. He placed a hand on Pétur's shoulder before heading on his way. 'Take care, pal.'

Now to find 170. God, he missed his phone, he wouldn't be this lost if he'd had it. There was no way he was paying extortionate data fees abroad though.

Pétur took a chance and turned right since he was already on this side of the road. Going left would mean crossing and he'd just missed a green man. 180... Then nothing. Why didn't shops want to advertise their building numbers? A nail bar, a bridal shop, a dry cleaners. Nothing was standing out to him.

The problem was that he didn't know what he was looking for. He only knew the street and number – it could be anything.

He stopped, confused again, and weighed up his options. An idea struck him – if he counted down from 180 he could make an educated guess at the numbers. 180, 178, 176, 174, 172, 170: that would make it the dry cleaners.

He took a deep breath and crossed the road.

'HELLO, CAN I HELP YOU?' the sprightly woman behind the counter asked.

'Erm, yeah. I'm here for a meeting...?' His voice trailed off, unsure. This looked a lot like a real dry cleaners. Then again, Reykjavík's Chambers had a coffee shop on the bottom floor.

'A meeting? This is a dry cleaners.'

Was this a test? He didn't know. She looked genuinely perplexed.

Pétur studied her face, looking for any clues to confirm if this was part of the act. She eyed him back like he was crazy. Perhaps he was.

'I think I've got the wrong place...?' he asked, his voice rising just a little to turn his uncertainty into a question.

She didn't say anything as he walked out. Either she was used to strange people in her shop, or he'd failed the test. No going back.

He stood at the shop door. *What to do?*

Next door seemed busy for what looked like a run-down building.

He moved position to get a better look, pretending to be lost again. Not difficult, seeing as he actually was.

It was an impressive building despite looking on the verge of collapse. At least eight storeys high with an elaborate mix of architecture, more boarded windows than he could count (including six striking bay windows down the entire left-hand side), and a hexagonal turret at the top. It looked like a modern-day castle.

Two busts jutted out from the masonry as if keeping a lookout east and west, (*the founding fathers?*) and a huge coat of arms hewn from stone loomed out from the middle of the second floor. If it hadn't been for the wire mesh covering the entire building, giving it a run-down look, you might guess this was a place of great importance.

One, two, three more people disappeared inside. What's the harm in trying? He followed the last lady in.

It was dark and smelled of piss. This must be right, why else would these people be here? *Could be a crack den,* his inner voice mused.

He made his way down a corridor littered with empty beer cans and plastic bags. The paint was peeling off the walls and kids had broken in at some point – CHRIS IS A BAW BAG was sprayed along the length of one side. Poor Chris.

At the end, flush against the wall, was an elevator door. Funny, he hadn't noticed it when he first came in. It hadn't escaped the graffiti but managed to look out of place.

He squeezed into the already full lift. That was easy.

'In the right place son?'

He'd spoken too soon. An unassuming man in a suit was eyeing him, blocking the elevator buttons.

'I've just transferred here,' he lied.

The man didn't look convinced and continued to size him up.

'Prove it,' the man said.

'Vivat lupi. Vade retro Satana,' Pétur recited while placing a hand over his heart, being careful to position his fingers correctly.

God, please work. I need to meet her.

He'd learnt the Scottish motto from a friend in Australia. He'd never been to any meetings here. Hell – he'd never even been inside a Chamber.

'Put your hand on the scanner then,' the man said, stepping aside to reveal the elevator's panel.

He hadn't accounted for this place being so fancy. A guard maybe, but nothing like this. The suited man stared as Pétur racked his brains for a way around the situation.

A stern-looking woman pushed her way from the back of the lift and put her hand on the scanner, too quick for the man to react. The elevator lurched into action.

'I've got no time for this today, Alan. He knows the allegiance, let's go.' She glared at Pétur and slipped back to her original spot.

Pétur fiddled with his necklace, a nervous habit he was barely aware of. His hand instinctively reached under his collar to massage the thin leather cord.

The ride seemed to take forever, but five floors later they were released.

He expected to step into an equally run-down room but it couldn't have been more different. The corridor was a hive of activity, with crowds of people mingling and talking. It looked like a sombre office party.

Past the throng, he could see pristine dove grey walls lined with regal portraits, plaques and banners. It was an explosion of pride and allegiance – not to mention a few well-positioned pot plants.

His elevator accomplices rushed past him as he took in his surroundings. The stern woman was in front of him, smiling, not so stern after all. He'd been standing still, face frozen in wonder.

'New here?'

'Yeah, only been here a few months.'

'Where's the accent from? Somewhere Scandi?'

Iceland, he nearly replied, on autopilot from his time working in Melbourne's bars. 'Sweden.'

'Well, we'd better hurry up. You can sit with me if you like.'

She was off. He struggled to keep up as they moved through the crowd, filing through a large set of double doors. Oak with gold handles he noted, very fancy.

THE HALL DIDN'T FAIL to impress either. Pétur gawped upwards at the intricate red and gold laurel leaf ceiling roses above him. It was beautiful. The walls showed the Scottish Pack dynasty: a grand display of painted portraits, no expense spared. Swathes of velvet hung from above, creating lavish crimson drapes. At the front was a simple stage; empty apart from a wooden podium taking pride of place in the centre and a projector screen displaying the Pack's coat of arms on the wall behind. The place reminded him of an extravagant apartment he'd once visited in Venice.

It was packed so the woman led them to stand at the back wall. Judging by the number of seats set out, the organisers hadn't been expecting so many attendees. Angry grumbles could be heard rippling through the crowd.

It wasn't long before the oak doors were hauled shut, much to the dismay of those trying to get in. The place was full to capacity. Pétur realised he'd been lucky to get in.

An automatic hush descended as a tall, paunchy man with a well-groomed beard took position behind the podium. His beard was thick and a rich brown, it even had a shine to it. Did the man dye it? Pétur could never get his to look like that. He stroked his own chin; Pétur's effort could only be described as patchy. A small bald spot on his chin was particularly upsetting.

The man had an air of arrogance that made Pétur's skin crawl. He seemed cocky, vain – pompous even – and all before he opened his mouth. Pétur could only imagine what it would be like to hold a conversation with him. It had to be a requirement for Pack Leader, how else could you silence a room of five hundred people merely by stepping on stage?

'Vivat lupi. Vade retro Satana,' the man said, hand over heart. The crowd echoed him.

Tobias, Pétur assumed.

He scanned the crowd, hoping with every fibre of his body to see who he was really here to meet. There was no sign of her. No doubt she'd be seated up front with the rest of the Pack leader's family. There was a hierarchy here – he might not even be allowed to talk to someone as high up as her.

It had been complete chance he was in Scotland when he'd heard the news, and even luckier that he was en-route to Glasgow at the time.

Scotland had always been on the cards as his next adventure and, when work wasn't forthcoming at home, going travelling seemed the natural choice. He'd heard so much about the country from a friend of his girlfriend in Melbourne. *Ex-girlfriend*, he corrected himself. A year on and he still thought of her in the present tense, despite how she'd treated him. When Pétur fell, he fell hard.

The country didn't disappoint, there was so much packed into the small space. He was sad his trip was coming to an end; there was much more to see.

Tobias's voice took him back to the here and now.

'Thank you for coming today. As you are aware, today's meeting was only meant for your regional Pack reps but of course, I can understand your concern given the situation. I will do my best to quash any fears you have.' The man's arrogance carried into his voice. A slow, patronising drawl that made you hang on every word. It was annoyingly deep and silky.

A projector clicked and the coat of arms changed to a table of statistics.

'I'll cut to the chase. There's no point avoiding what we're all here for.' Tobias paused, psyching himself up. 'We are still in the midst of another outbreak. As of today, from the first reported death on the eighth of February, ninety-eight Pack members have lost their lives – over seventy of those being children.' Audible gasps erupted from the crowd. 'That's more than double the 1991 outbreak total already.' More gasps. 'As some of you will know, there were only around three and a half thousand of us left in Scotland at the start of this year.'

Research had told Pétur Scottish Pack numbers were a third of what they were thirty years ago, not even enough to fill half the seats of a small football stadium. One more outbreak like this could wipe out the future generation, and they'd be extinct.

He continued, 'The previous outbreak was self-limiting. We had hoped for a similar timescale, some of you might remember that outbreak only lasted four or five months, but we're far from being out of the danger zone after eight months. Although,' he added with a slight smile, 'the number of new cases is slowing.'

People were now crying; a man to Pétur's right hugged the lady beside him as she wept.

The projector clicked again and a list of precautions flashed up.

'While we work hard to determine what's causing the virus and continue to search for a cure, we urge you to take all necessary precautions.' He turned to face the screen, reminding himself of the steps. 'Do *not* drink *any* tap water. Only drink the bottled or treated water we provide.'

Murmurs spread through the crowd, stopping Tobias's flow.

'I know some of you have heard rumours our supplies may be running out. I am sorry to say this is true.' The woman by Pétur was now near-hysterical. 'We are working on importing from Europe and stocks should be replenished soon.'

Tobias checked the board again, hushed conversations carrying on in the crowd. He waited, hands on the podium, like a disgruntled headmaster.

Silence returned.

'If you're drinking any untested bottled water, fizzy drinks or alcohol, make sure they were produced before this year.' He paused, his face serious. His eyes scanned the crowd. 'Lastly, know the signs. The best thing you can do is come straight to us if you or your child have any of these symptoms: sudden nausea, pain in the feet or hands, unexplained tingling in the limbs or a hardening of muscle.'

Phones were being taken out of pockets to snap pictures of the screen, taking notes.

'This disease is getting stronger. Why? We don't know. What we do know is,' he took a dramatic pause, 'it's a death sentence. I have to say it because it's true. No one has ever recovered.' He leaned on the podium, closer to the microphone to emphasise his next point. 'Rest assured brothers and sisters I will lead you to the other side, we will beat this. Vivat lupi. Vade retro Satana.'

Tobias's face dropped as the oak doors flew open, the unlucky few who were leaning on them tumbling out of the way. In flew a fraught-looking blonde woman, a limp child cradled in her arms.

Pétur knew before she even opened her mouth to plead for help that he'd found who he was looking for.

PÉTUR SURRENDERED to the fact he wouldn't be sleeping any time soon. He rubbed his eyes, adjusting to the hostel's dim light. A shriek of laughter erupted in the corridor, followed by the thunder of footsteps – young travellers causing mayhem and mucking around. Thank God he'd plumped for a single room. The noise was no better but at least he could lock the door and be alone.

He rolled on to his back and let out a sigh, his eyes focusing on the strip light overhead, tracing its outline against the grubby-looking ceiling. He had earplugs in his bag but couldn't be bothered searching for them. To be honest, the noise was a welcome distraction.

The vision of Georgia lifeless in her mother's arms consumed his mind again. He couldn't shake it. His instinct had been to help but he'd known better than to out himself in the crowd. Instead, he'd hung back, making a clean exit when it was obvious he couldn't do anything.

Now, he regretted the choice.

He rubbed his eyes again, trying to clear his head.

Going to the Chambers had been a huge risk. Anyone could have seen him for who he really was and who knew what the consequences would have been. It didn't bear thinking about.

An hour had passed but the sickness in the pit of his stomach remained as strong as ever. He had to find a way back, a way to get to her. He couldn't come this close and throw the opportunity away.

He'd never been a quick thinker, and the idea that he could have simply hidden in the rabbit warren of the Chambers and bided his time had only come to him in the last hour. *Stupid, stupid, stupid.*

A squawk of raucous laughter outside his door forced him back to the present.

He reached for his phone, clicking the screen on. Just after four thirty.

He had to go back.

Pétur slipped his necklace on and the black mass that had been festering under his bed returned to its fleshy prison inside him.

E rica couldn't remember arriving in the city centre, never mind carrying G up to the medical bay at the Chambers. She'd found it empty, a note on the door saying the attending doctor was at the Pack meeting. A meeting Tobias had failed to tell her was even happening. No surprise.

It was a twisted whirlwind of action, climaxing in being told to give the doctor space and wait outside the treatment room. Tobias had lingered at first. For a brief second Erica thought he was there to comfort her. Despite their history she'd assumed (or rather, hoped) things would be different. Could a man really be that cold towards his own flesh and blood? She was oblivious to his icy treatment now, used to it after all these years, but still the thought had appeared at the back of her mind in a moment of sheer desperation.

The notion was quashed, as her uncle was now nowhere to be seen. She sat alone, holding back tears in the bleak hospital corridor.

'You can come in now,' the doctor said, his sudden appearance making her jump.

'How is she?' Erica asked, getting to her feet.

'Stable.' His face changed, his best attempt at appearing sympathetic. He didn't need to speak. She knew, of course she did, but she'd clung to the outside chance she was wrong. Life was just a game of possibilities and percentages after all.

'She has it, doesn't she?' Erica didn't really want to know – as if not hearing the words would delay the inevitable. He was going to tell her anyway; but it could at least be on her terms.

He answered but Erica didn't hear what he was saying after the dreaded 'Yes'. The world was closing in. Her legs gave way and she slumped to the floor, grasping at the cold plastic chair. She was sobbing but couldn't remember the moment when the tears stopped simply threatening and transformed into an angry torrent. She was no longer in control.

The doctor crouched beside her, awkwardly squeezing her

shoulder: unsure if he should be touching a patient's relative, caught out by the instinct to comfort.

'Is there anyone I can call for you?' he asked.

She swallowed hard a few times, giving herself time to catch her breath. 'No. There's no-one. It's fine.'

He squeezed her shoulder again for good measure, gauging what he ought to do next.

'Do you want to see her?' he asked, hooking an arm under hers to help her up. He didn't need to hear an answer to know it would be a yes.

'Is she...?' she began.

'She's still awake, yes,' he answered without her finishing. How many times had he gone through this emotional freefall over the last eight months? What an awful thing to have to witness over and over again.

He led Erica to Georgia's room, his arm supporting her all the way.

She paused at the door.

'Gimme a second,' she said, freeing her arm to wipe the tears away with her sleeve. Georgia shouldn't see her like this.

She sniffed, straightening herself, ready to put on an act. The doctor gave a half-smile teamed with a small nod, letting her know she looked semi-presentable.

'Can you give me a moment alone?' she asked.

'Of course, I'll be back in a minute.'

Her hand hovered over the door's push bar, stalling.

She took a final deep breath before forcing herself to enter the room.

GEORGIA HAD BEEN AFFORDED a private room; presumably it was common practice with virus sufferers. Erica doubted very much that her uncle would have pulled any strings.

There were no windows on this side of the Chambers and the set-up had always struck Erica as odd. The other side of the building was all window: huge things made up of intricate panels, yet this side was monopolised by corridors. The only rooms with a view were the library and Tobias's inner sanctum. That said it all; there was no doubting the Pack's hierarchy.

The lack of natural light made the already sterile room feel even more clinical. The fluorescent light buzzing overhead was unnaturally bright and acted like a spotlight on Georgia's tiny body.

Erica scanned her daughter's small frame; it was lost in the hospital bed, a tiny hump between the sheets.

'Hey darling,' Erica said, perching on the edge of the bed. She stroked G's hand, ignoring the IV line snaking from it.

Georgia's eyes looked heavy as she focused on her mother's face. 'Hey,' she said, her frail voice croaking.

'How're you feeling?' It was a stupid question but it felt natural to ask.

'Ok. The doctor gave me some medicine.'

Erica managed a weak smile. 'Good. I'm glad you're feeling a bit better.'

'Am I going to be alright?' She could hear fear pulling at the edge of Georgia's voice.

She paused, allowing herself a few breaths before answering. What are you meant to say? The truth wouldn't do any good.

'Of course darling. There's nothing to worry about.'

'WE HAVE TO SEDATE HER...IT'S *the best way...the pain will only become worse... Nothing else we can do...*'

After a sloppy 'I love you', that was it. It felt so futile, a huge anticlimax to what would be their last conversation. Only after she was certain Georgia was asleep did Erica let the tears fall.

G LOOKED peaceful despite the breathing mask, her gentle breath like a quiet snore. Erica's head rested on the bed by Georgia's hand, the cover wet from crying. How was this happening to her little girl?

She watched her sleep. How many times had she done this before? From babe to toddler, infant to now; sleepless nights spent by Georgia's bed after bad nightmares; or huddled together in the 'big bed', Erica's arms wrapped around her precious bundle, Georgia blissfully unaware and out for the count as Erica watched on. What a funny thing it was to be a mother – always second-guessing and worrying, even when they were sleeping.

Georgia's eyes fluttered. Do people dream when they're sedated? Erica hoped so. Something pleasant, fun, and colourful. That would be perfect.

'Erica?' A man's voice came from the doorway behind her.

'Yes,' she replied, not taking her eyes off Georgia, scared to move and break contact even though she knew it wasn't the doctor.

He placed a comforting hand on her shoulder and crouched beside her. His eyes were red. He'd been crying too.

'How is she?' he asked, the hint of an accent apparent.

'I'm sorry, who are you?' She swallowed hard and widened her eyes, fighting to hold back the tears. She hated crying in front of anyone. The stranger's arrival had caught her off guard.

He blushed, crimson flushing his cheeks. 'Eh...' He cleared his throat before pulling at his collar. 'I'm Pétur. And, you see, I came here to find you.' He turned to Georgia. 'I'm her uncle.'

'Tobias would hit the roof if he knew another Icelander was there today,' Erica said, her head still resting on the bed.

'He'd be mad then?'

'Oh yeah. He believes in it all.'

'And you?'

'I think I'd be a bit of a hypocrite if I did.' She held Georgia's hands, running her index finger over each nail. So little.

'You knew my brother was from Iceland then?'

'Of course, but it's not like I could jump straight in with a discussion about how you stole our people. I mean, I didn't know what he was.'

He laughed. 'Stole your people?'

'Er, yes.' She narrowed her eyes, a playful wicked grin back despite her tear-stained cheeks. 'Ooh, do we have a nationalist on our hands?'

'No, it's not that but it *was* over a thousand years ago. How else could we populate our island?'

'Time doesn't heal all wounds Pétur.' She smiled again and instantly felt guilty, the smirk dropping. 'Does your father know?' she asked in a near whisper, emotion getting the better of her voice.

'He doesn't know I'm here. He'd be as mad as Tobias.' He sighed, his eyes firmly on the floor.

'It's madness isn't it? To live like that, hating people you don't even know. We should be sticking together. It's not like there's many of us left anyway.' He half-smiled in way of agreement so she carried on despite his lack of input, lowering her voice in case the doctors were listening, 'Who needs us werewolves now anyway?'

It was a valid question but one Tobias would lose his temper over. Not to mention, if he found an Icelandic wolf sitting in his medical bay he'd have a heart attack. The problem, the one Tobias and Pétur's father held on to, had been the Norwegian settlers who'd fancied freshening up the bloodline of their new Empire, so they pillaged Scotland's women on the way to Iceland. What they didn't know was that they were also fusing something very special into their future offspring: werewolf blood.

Adding to the personal upset of having their wives taken, Scotland's wolves could no longer reproduce as easily. Wars were waged. Given the slightest encouragement, Tobias would wax lyrical about the Great War of 1549 with as much enthusiasm as an Englishman talking about '66. Pétur's father favoured the Battle of 1657. Animosity passed through generations with little dilution.

The grudge was the reason Georgia's father wanted nothing to do with them. *And the fact he was an asshole of course.* Why ruin a good grievance in the name of doing the right thing?

Pétur remained silent, lost in thought as he watched Georgia's chest rise and fall. Erica let her eyes linger on her daughter's face.

She'd been smiling and joking as they said their goodbyes this morning. A tear escaped, rolling down Erica's cheek before she stopped it short with the sleeve of her hoodie.

Pétur stood up and, without saying a word, pulled her head towards his body in a soothing embrace. She couldn't contain it any longer and let the tears fall.

HE HUGGED her until there weren't any more tears to cry, comforting her in silence as she let it out. She couldn't remember the last time she'd been held like that. No doubt by her mother after falling off her bike – a silly, tedious, accident to cry over, but Mum would have made a fuss. Her mother wasn't shy of showing her emotion; Erica was told on a daily basis how much she was loved. Kisses and cuddles on tap. *You don't know what you've got till it's gone.* Of course, she was the same with Georgia. How could you not be? In fact G was probably sick to dea–

'This is my fault,' she said, her breath hitching as she attempted to sniff.

'Of course it's not,' he said, bending down and taking her face in his hands. 'Don't say that. You're not to blame.' He stared into her eyes to add weight to his point, his own face wet from tears.

'Bad luck follows me around. It always has.' She pulled away from his hands and lay her head back down on the bed, aware she was a snotty mess, but past caring.

He straightened himself up, wiping his face with the collar of his t-shirt.

'It's funny,' she said, breaking the silence. 'I always find a way to fuck things up.'

He carried a chair over, placed it beside her, and sat down.

'What do you mean?' he asked.

Pétur was a good listener. He had the right kind of face. The sort of eyes that made you want to open up – 'go on, I'm listening' eyes. Big, dark, doe-like things. He only had to look at you for you to know he was paying attention. Usually, this would be annoying. But not today. Today she needed it.

She sat up and rubbed her eyes, her usual steely composure returning. 'It's complicated. Doesn't matter.' She got up and grabbed a tissue from the dispenser, using it to blow her nose before throwing it in the bin. 'I needed her more than she needed me. She would have been happy never knowing I existed.'

She leaned over and kissed her daughter's forehead, brushing a few strands of wavy blonde hair out of the way.

Maybe dad had the right idea.

ALMOST TWO HOURS had passed since Georgia was sedated. The doctor said that, judging by recent patients, she would be lucky to survive twenty-four. The virus was getting stronger, mutating to lay waste to their bodies quicker every time.

If Erica had lifted the bedsheets she would see Georgia's feet and ankles had become calcified, the virus spreading through her muscles from the toes up. Most wouldn't survive it passing their heart, but some unfortunate souls had.

Erica had heard of one man who hadn't come to the Chambers when he fell ill. He was found at home, barely alive but conscious, his body hardened and his eyes permanently open. It made her sick to think of it.

She was grateful that Georgia had been put under, but she'd give anything to be able to talk to her just one more time. It wasn't the same speaking to her like this, it didn't feel right. It wasn't her baby lying there any more.

The doctor returned to check Georgia's vitals. Erica rose from her position draped over the bed. He gave a courteous smile before going about his business. She didn't have the heart to return it.

He noted the numbers from her monitor before producing a long thin torch. He separated Georgia's eyelids and shone the light into her pupil.

'I can't take this,' Erica said, standing abruptly, causing her chair to scrape the floor with a huge screech. She couldn't watch her daughter be poked and prodded. It was a further reminder of the empty shell that had contained her happy, beautiful Georgia just hours before.

Distraught, she stormed from the room.

ERICA SHIFTED in the large armchair, stiff from sitting. She'd made her way to the Chambers' library. Her father's favourite chair sat in the bay window. A bedraggled, much-loved thing, it would never be the comfiest and yet its green leather was worn and cracked where many had chosen to park themselves.

There wasn't much of a view. Just the bricks and mortar of the building across the lane. Had there ever been a view? Maybe. Perhaps. Who knew? It didn't bother her. She wasn't looking anyway.

She had fond memories of sitting on her father's lap here. He called it his Thinking Chair, but even when he was sitting in it to help him think, he was never too busy for a cuddle. Even monsters can have hearts. Looking back, she didn't know why he'd retire here, the same worried expression creasing his brow for hours at a time. Was it the weight of being Pack Leader? She'd overheard him and Tobias bickering over Pack laws more than once. That had to take its toll. Tobias could be a force to be reckoned with.

She hadn't bothered to put any lights on; the moonlight was enough after the harsh lights in Georgia's sick room. She closed her eyes and focused on remaining strong.

PITCH BLACK DARKNESS. Where was she? The ground was squelchy underfoot. A quiet whistling tickled her ears, growing to a low roar like the ocean during a rough storm.

Her vision returned and her mother came into focus. They were on a dirt path in the middle of a thick forest. The pine trees were impossibly tall and loomed over them, blocking the natural light. It could be night or day – you wouldn't know.

I must have fallen asleep.

'Mum,' she said, lunging at her mother for a cuddle. Tears rolled down her cheeks before being soaked up by her mother's jumper. Her big gasping sobs echoed through the trees.

Lucy kissed the top of her daughter's head and stroked her back. 'Tell me about it. Take your time, I'm listening.' God, she'd missed that Aussie accent.

Her sobs evened out enough for Erica to speak and she explained what had happened to Georgia.

Lucy cupped Erica's face and wiped a few stray tears, a futile attempt but appreciated. It was so good to feel her mum's comforting hands.

'Let's walk,' Lucy said, leading Erica off. She threaded her arm under Erica's and pulled her daughter closer, letting her head rest on her shoulder. 'Do you remember when we first did this?'

Erica nodded. Of course she did.

A few days after her mum's death she'd come to her in a dream about Cairnhill Woods, a forest trail not far from their house in Bearsden, Glasgow. But this wasn't where they were now. Erica didn't recognise it at all.

She'd found great comfort in that initial dream – her mum taking the time to explain everything that was going on and what was going to happen in the near future. Lucy had a way with words and a warmth that made it impossible not to feel safe in her presence. Children and adults alike gravitated towards her; you wouldn't meet a more kind soul.

She assumed it wasn't real, it was a dream brought on by the stress of the accident. However, her mum's nighttime visits became more frequent. They were so lucid it was hard not to think there might be a dash of reality to them.

It was confusing for an eight-year-old with no one to talk to (she wasn't to speak to Tobias at the best of times – never mind talking to him about such an absurd notion). Before, she would have turned to her mum...but since the problem was about her, it seemed silly to ask.

Thankfully the meetings continued and Lucy soon quelled the

notion with hidden gifts that could only have been placed before her death, oblivious to Erica until the time was right. Not to mention the premonitions. Erica hated them, dream Lucy liked to give cryptic messages, it was well known in the magic circle that she had the gift of second sight, but why she couldn't just get to the point was beyond Erica. It was always a tedious guessing game where the prize was your future.

In the forest, her mum gave her another comforting squeeze. 'It's going to be fine.'

'They can't do anything mum. Everything's been tried.' The sobs were threatening to return. 'I can't lose her.' That was enough to break the levee and fat tears rolled down her cheeks, causing her breath to stall.

Lucy pulled her close, enveloping her daughter in her arms. 'Sometimes it's a matter of timing Erica,' she explained softly. 'Answers come when you're ready to hear them.'

'Well, I'm ready,' she went to continue but her breath caught in her throat, causing another involuntary sob to escape. She sniffed but it was impossible, her nose was well and truly blocked.

Lucy kissed the top of her daughter's head. 'You know you're a very important and powerful person, I think you forget that sometimes.'

'Me, important?' she scoffed. 'I think you're getting me mixed up with someone else.'

Lucy pulled away and smiled. Warmth filed her eyes, pure love.

'You trust me, yeah?' Lucy asked, holding Erica by the shoulders.

'Of course.'

'Ok, well, I need you to do something for me. I have an idea.'

Erica double-checked the coordinates on her phone. Her GPS had brought her to the Loch Lomond Visitor Centre in Balmaha, some twenty miles north of Glasgow. She doubted her mother's directions. She could see nothing of interest and no sign of a cabin. Judging by the map, Loch Lomond was behind her and to her left was a steep hill covered in a dense maze of trees. A Forestry Commission sign hinted there was a designated woodland walk to enjoy if the mood so took you.

She'd heard plenty about Loch Lomond when she was little but never got the chance to visit. The National Park was teaming with fairy activity – some would argue it was the heart of Scottish Fairyland. It was a place Erica had always wanted to explore, it was just a shame she was here under such awful circumstances.

Sitting in her car with the rain lashing at the windows, it seemed impossible to think anything lived here – never mind fairies. She'd driven to the back of the car park and turned her headlights off. It was eight o'clock and pitch black; should any adventurous souls be out here she hoped they wouldn't miss a bright orange Jeep in the dim light of the car park. Getting her car dented was the last thing she needed.

Jump the burn and head straight up the hill was her mum's next instruction. Erica braced her body, psyching herself up to open the door and face the elements. The wind was howling and battering the rain in great noisy pelts against the glass. She wished she'd worn something more practical than her fake leather jacket over a light hoodie.

One last deep breath and she opened the door. Time was of the essence.

Her car door fought back, the driving wind determined to stop her leaving the vehicle. She slid out, letting the gale slam it behind her, intent to carry on regardless, but a fresh blast of rain forced her to turn towards the car, away from the unrelenting shower. She winced at the biting cold attack and attempted to put her hood up twice before giving into defeat. Her ponytail, soaked already, flapped back and forth over her neck while icy barbs of rain stung every inch of exposed skin. Couldn't have been a dry night, could it?

Erica put an arm above her eyes, shielding herself to get a better view of where she was heading. Her mother said if she looked straight up the hill she should be able to make out the cabin. All Erica could see was darkness.

She started up the gravel path and into the woods, the crunch of her trainers barely audible above the howling wind. Her mother had told her to look out for a tree with fairy markings. She couldn't miss it.

Erica was a good hundred yards along the path when the car park's comforting lights disappeared. It was eerie to say the least, her phone doing little to light anything beyond the narrow path. A shiver ran down her spine as a sense of unease chilled her to the bone. She'd seen enough horror films to know this was not a good start to her journey. These woods could be hiding all manner of nasty types. *Be brave Erica, keep going for G.*

With each step, darkness overpowered the light a little more.

Stopping to squint into the surrounding woods, Erica's eyes could only make out the silhouettes of tree trunks, faint grey barbs that moved with each blink. What else lurked beyond the reach of her vision? Deciding that using her phone torch was nigh-on pointless, she cupped her hands together, one on top of the other. Erica lifted her right palm to reveal a dazzling orb of white light, which grew in size and brilliance as her hands parted. When it was the size of a football she moved her right hand to join her left below and guided the orb above her head. It bobbed in the wind but was safely anchored. She rarely used magic so blatantly outside the safety of her own flat but, given her location and the weather, tonight could be an exception.

Now she could see better but there was still no sign of a cabin. She had to continue with blind faith.

Her mother had told her about an old friend, Bill Hammond. It seemed odd that her mum had never mentioned Bill before, despite saying they were close. However, from what Erica was told, Bill was a capable wizard, almost on a par with Lucy's level of power, so she didn't think twice when her mum suggested she visit his cabin. Lucy had warned it wasn't simple to reach but, with time running out, it was worth the risk.

The tree appeared as she rounded a corner, its branchless trunk standing like a huge splinter at the edge of a small clearing. It had seen better days, its bark flaking and sparse, but the markings were clear – three dinner plate-sized circles shone a bright white, as vivid as a neon sign, telling her this was the place to cross.

Leaving the safety of the path didn't daunt her now she had the comfort of a personal spotlight. The small burn was easy to hop, even in skinny jeans. Erica landed with a sharp intake of breath as she sunk into mud, the wet muck oozing over both feet and into her white Converse trainers. It wasn't long before she could feel it between her toes.

Erica missed the sturdiness and predictable footing of the path as she waded through bracken on the other side of the stream. As she neared the base of the wooded hill, the bracken became more dense, completely hiding the spongy ground below. A rare memory floated to the surface – paddling in the sea with her father. She'd touched something slimy with her foot and had to be carried to the safety of the beach. *No surprises here please, there's no one to save me this time.*

The hill's thick canopy of trees provided welcome relief from the torrential rain, which now sounded like ball bearings on a tin roof, but the ground was still slippery underneath her newly-brown shoes. As she climbed the steep incline, Erica had to be careful to make sure her footing was solid, having to hold on to trees and rocks for better purchase. Bracken continued to keep the ground's terrain a secret, spare a few clearings of copper-coloured pine needles.

The wind rattled through the trees making them groan and creak. It sent out a low hum as it whipped between the trunks. *I should be on the sofa with a glass of wine.* A fresh deluge of rain battered the leaves above, reminding her that plans never work out how you hope.

Once or twice there was a flicker of light at the top, only for it to be blacked out by swaying branches. Was it the moon or something more?

It was taking an age to climb, zigzagging her way up the steep embankment, and she made slippery mistakes as she cut corners to save precious time, losing her balance only to be rescued by a fortuitous branch on more than one occasion.

Higher up, the forest became more dense. It wasn't long before the orb's light was only able to illuminate a few trees close by. Erica would be the first to admit she was scared. Fearing what she'd find around the next winding corner, each time she peeked round the trees Erica saw only dramatic shadows drop on to the trunks behind, which did nothing to relieve her rising panic. Thankfully they were tall thin pines – not wide enough for anyone to hide behind. Still, facts don't help calm an alert imagination when no one else knows where you are.

She was now certain there was a light at the top of the hill and aimed herself in its direction. It wasn't the brightest light, at best a candle, but it was a light.

She heaved herself up an outcrop of rock, her jeans getting the better of her now they were soaked. The ice-cold rain that drenched her hood was spreading down her back, making a sticky, sweaty mix which clung to her with every move. Hands on knees, she allowed herself a pause to catch her breath. A drip ran down her brow and off her nose. Rain or sweat, who knew?

Not long to go now. Looking up the hill, Erica felt her muscles freeze and air catch in her lungs. The dim light from the cabin had become stronger. Erica could now see that it wasn't branches blocking the light, but a *thing* pacing, a thing which looked suspiciously animal-like. And a big animal at that. It was hard to see an exact shape as bushes and trees obscured its lower half.

What large animals do you get in Scotland? It wasn't a deer: it had no antlers and was too bulky. It wasn't a fox: far too big. And it wasn't a badger: they were way too small.

Her knowledge of Scottish wildlife was spent. *Shit.* Do you get bears or wolves in the wild? She was sure she'd read about a reintroduction of something in the past. *Don't be fucking stupid, Erica.*

Regardless of species, an animal of some sort was there, moving from side to side like it was trying to get a better look at her through the trees.

It dawned on Erica that she was a werewolf scared of a woodland creature lurking in the dark. Given the chance, she could Turn into a towering, four-foot-high, jet-black wolf and fight whatever it was.

But she didn't want to have to Turn tonight, not to fight; she didn't have the energy or time. She'd been away from Georgia for nearly two hours and wanted to get back.

Instead she reached up, cupped the orb and, with one brisk motion, sent it in the direction of the animal like a slow-moving boomerang. Trying to get a better look, she squinted, but the creature moved out of sight, startled by the sudden charging light. The orb returned to above Erica's head. She waited with bated breath. Her heart hammered against her chest as she craned her neck to check for signs of life. The wind howled, the rain continued its ferocious beat, and blood pumped in her ears. Ahead, the trees were empty once more.

Happy the animal had been spooked enough to move on, Erica marched forward.

She crested the hill and came into a clearing. The rain didn't feel as heavy now – either that, or she was too wet to notice. In the near distance she could make out a small wooden cabin. It took her a second to realise that the light had gone out and the building was standing in darkness.

It was protected by Fairy magic, the tell-tale white halo of shimmering light surrounding its edges. To the vast majority of people, it would've looked like Erica was staring at empty grassland.

There are three types of non-fairies in this world: those who can see fairy magic, those who cannot, and those like Erica, who can both see and practice it. It's rare for a non-fairy to be able to create her own fairy dust, but it was one of the many abilities she'd inherited from her mother.

With caution, she crept to the cabin door, keeping an eye out for whatever animal had been lurking. Thankfully the land was level here and free of bracken. There were few hiding places for a big beast like that.

She readied herself before knocking; sweeping away the wet hair that was plastered to the side of her face, taking a deep breath, and adjusting her jacket. Another drip ran off her nose.

She knocked.

No answer.

She banged again. 'Please, Bill, I saw your light on. It's me, Erica, Lucy's daughter. My kid is ill, I need your help.'

Silence.

She was going to start pleading again when a small hatch opened, high up in the middle of the door. A bright light was poked out and directed at her face, forcing her to put an arm up to shield her eyes.

'Erica?' said a man's voice.

'Yes, Lucy's daughter.' She looked to see who she was talking to but the glare was too strong. 'Sorry, can you not point that at my eyes?'

'Oh, God, sorry,' he said and extinguished it; the hatch suddenly becoming a square of black nothingness.

'My daughter's sick and my mum said you could help. Can I come in and explain?' Silence again. 'I'm sorry to turn up like this when we haven't met before,' she added, thinking she'd offended him.

'Bill hasn't lived here for ages. I'm sorry.'

'What? No! But he has to.' The hatch began to close, making Erica lunge forward. She slammed a palm against the rough wood. 'No, please. Do you know where he is? My daughter's going to die if I don't find him.'

It stayed ajar as if the person on the other side was thinking, but a sliver of darkness gave no hints to the cabin's occupant. She stepped back, not wanting to intimidate him. He was her only hope.

It felt like an age before it opened again.

'Did you say you were Lucy's daughter?'

'Yes.'

For God's sake please help.

'I can give you directions to Bill. Do you have a pen and paper?'

'No but I've got my phone.' Silence. 'Please, I'll take a note of them here,' she said, taking her mobile out.

'He's in Callander, 141 Glenmidden Road. Not far from the garage.'

'Thank you. What's your name sorry?' she said, wanting to thank him.

There was no reply. Instead, the hatch snapped shut and he was gone.

E rica studied her face in the car's rear view mirror.

It would seem that coming down the slope was a lot harder than going up – especially when you're in a rush after wasting forty-five precious minutes. Three-quarters of the way down she'd lost her footing and skidded a good metre or so. Her right arm took most of the force but her face made contact with something; a jagged bush by the feel of it.

Her lip was split, cheek grazed and eyebrow cut. She looked like she'd been in a boxing match. *Erica 0 : Bush 1.*

There was no time to dwell. She undid her hair and ran her fingers through a few times – it was sodden but it would dry a little on the drive to Callander. The rain outside was still heavy; every so often the breeze would pick up and batter the torrential downpour against the car in a machine gun-like shower. This was not a night for driving.

She turned her windscreen wipers on, ready to go as soon as her phone found Bill's address. Her signal was patchy here and it was taking an age to load. The mechanical swipe of the wipers acted like a metronome marking wasted seconds. Her heart was going doubletime.

Erica pinched at her collar, attempting to air out her t-shirt. It was soaked through and stuck to her skin. She had half a mind to strip off for the drive; anything would be better than how uncomfortable she was feeling now.

She fought the urge to call Pétur. There was no point in losing valuable battery life just to be told what she already knew: no change in Georgia or, more likely, she was worse.

A notification she'd been dreading popped up on her phone screen: 20% battery remaining. *For the love of God, don't you die on me.* GPS was draining what little battery she'd started on, but if she could just get to Glenmidden Road she could bluff her way back to Glasgow.

Erica dismissed the notification and willed her phone to load Bill's address.

Please.

Please.

Please.

The screen sprang into action, the blank grid becoming a sea of green and brown with a red pin in the centre. She couldn't hide the smile on her face as she stabbed at the 'directions' button. Forty minutes. Forty minutes to get to Bill. Jesus, that was ages.

She turned on the ignition and flipped on the lights, no time to waste.

Her heart sank.

In front of her car stood a man, naked from the waist up and only a few feet away in the bushes. His arm was in front of his face, protecting his eyes from the sudden light. He was frozen, caught in surprise. She could make out his bulging tattooed bicep and towering stature as her wipers cleared the unrelenting rain from her windscreen. He was a big bastard.

How long had he been standing there, watching her? Her heart was beating with great hammering thumps against her breastbone, threatening to burst through at any moment. She stared, unable to do anything else.

His brain caught up and in an instant he was moving. The man's eyes were fixed on hers as he lumbered forward, pushing through the shrubbery as he created a direct path to her car. He looked determined.

Erica's own mind clicked into action and she rammed her gear stick into

reverse. He ran at her; she was zooming backwards and he was lunging forwards, holding eye contact. The car screeched around to face the car park exit. With a grating crunch, Erica shoved the car into first as the man grabbed at the door handle just inches away from her. He held on as she made off. For a second it looked like he was coming along for the ride but, as the car picked up speed, he was forced to let go.

Erica checked her rear-view mirror as she sped away. Darkness had swallowed the man's silhouette and there was no sign of him. She swung on to Balmaha's main road, not bothering to slow down. Realising she'd been holding her breath, with a huge, panicked sigh, Erica allowed herself to pant.

Erica leaned over Bill's toothpaste-stained sink, inspecting her face further. Under the unforgiving bathroom lights, it looked even worse. Her cheek was sore to touch, red and angry, threatening to bruise around the graze. But she wasn't too concerned – it would be gone by this time tomorrow.

The drive to Bill's had been uneventful, thank God. She'd travelled the back roads to Callander with a cautious eye – certain the madman would rush from the fleeting hedgerows at any moment. Who was that man? What did he want? What would he have done had she not put the lights on? Was he planning to rob her? Or worse? She gripped the edge of the sink with scuffed hands, steadying herself. So many questions were swimming around her head, she began to feel dizzy.

When she'd arrived – soaking wet and covered in mud – at Bill's modest bungalow, he'd been just as her mother had described. She was welcomed in like an old friend, no questions asked apart from 'Would you like to change out of those muddy clothes?'

It seemed surreal to be standing in her underwear in a stranger's bathroom but, after the day she'd had, it wasn't out of the ordinary.

After Erica explained what had happened to Georgia, Bill said it might take him a while to get everything together. He suggested she take a shower. He didn't need to ask twice.

Erica further examined the bathroom, relishing her slow pace after the manic evening she'd endured. The house was musty, that classic old person smell. Poor Bill. There was a thick layer of dust on his bathroom shelves and the toilet didn't look like it had been cleaned for months. Did anyone ever visit?

She put on the fluffy dressing gown Bill had given her and headed through to the living room. Erica's wet clothes hung in front of an open fire; she lowered herself into an old armchair alongside them. Piles of stuff were everywhere and anywhere. Bill was a classic hoarder. He had a particular thing for books – most of the clutter in the living room was of the literary variety. Beside Erica's chair sat a tall tower of books with a coaster on top. How had he squeezed so many books into such a tiny cabin?

Erica inspected the nearest stack, interested to see what made Bill tick. This

pile focused on steam trains, in particular a line in North Yorkshire; an obvious favourite since half the books were about it.

Despite the apparent haphazard nature of Bill's book collection, she couldn't help but be jealous. She'd never seen so many in one place, apart from in a proper library. As a child this was the heaven she dreamed of. Books had always been a means of escape. But after moving into Tobias's, they became so much more. Her books were sacred. She devoured them like they were going out of fashion; they were the centre of Erica's world.

The only time she got to read these days, if she was lucky, was on the train to work or before bed if she could keep her eyes open for long enough. Erica had a book in her glove compartment, she could read right now but couldn't be bothered to get up. She needed to sit.

Erica closed her eyes and leaned her head back. She could hear Bill moving in another room, rummaging. She should've asked if she could help, but for now she wanted a minute of rest. Today had been full on.

She was on the verge of drifting off when Bill startled her awake.

'Do you want a cup of tea? Sorry, I didn't mean to scare you.' He was staring down at her with a dazzling grin, his frizzy white hair sticking out at all angles like he'd just woken up. In the bright light of the living room she saw he was wearing a tatty old sweatshirt full of holes, and joggers in a similar condition. You'd think he was an eccentric old man, not a powerful wizard.

'No, no. It's ok. I shouldn't let myself get sleepy anyway. In fact, I'll have a coffee if you have it.'

'Of course, no problem. Or something stronger if you want?' He winked and moved towards the kitchen but Erica put a hand up to stop him. He walked with the aid of a quad cane and, when he'd taken her wet clothes, she'd noticed his hands were clawed. Arthritis she presumed. She couldn't have him struggling for the sake of playing host.

'I would if I wasn't driving, believe me,' admitted Erica, getting up from her seat. 'Don't worry – I'll make it; you carry on with whatever you're doing. You want one?'

'A tea would be lovely.' He turned around on his cane and went back to the other room, swerving the odd book tower on the way. It seemed Bill could be agile when he wanted to be.

Bill's kitchen was also full of books and, come to think of it, Erica realised

she hadn't seen any bookshelves.

It took her three attempts to find the cupboard with the mugs (books and other random crap in there too), but the tea, sugar and coffee were sitting out in caddies. It was hard to negotiate the piles in the small galley kitchen. Finding free space on the worktop was challenging – she didn't want to move anything, it didn't feel right to touch the books. She slotted the mugs between two haphazard stacks and leaned against the counter, waiting for the kettle to boil.

The cooker clock informed her it was eight-forty. She'd been out for nearly three hours; she had to get back soon. Erica fought visions of her daughter lying in a hospital bed – she had to focus on what she came for. Getting upset would only slow her down.

Bill's sink was full of dirty dishes, a good week's worth, and a mound of a dozen or so tea bags sat on its edge. Apart from that, the kitchen was tidy. It was just so full of stuff. She didn't consider herself a clean freak, but this crammed bungalow was making her feel uneasy.

The kettle clicked off and she made the drinks, adding to Bill's tea bag mountain. *When in Rome*, she thought, as she carried the mugs through to his back room.

Erica found Bill hunched over a small table, in a room where the walls were fitted with floor-to-ceiling shelves (she was glad to see he had some). These were crammed with hundreds of books, jars, potions, and other interesting objects. A selection of crow's skulls had pride of place on a stack of fairy magic books. The fairies wouldn't be happy with that juxtaposition. A human skull, yes, but not a crow's.

Nearest the door stood a large display cabinet filled with all manner of glass bottles, every shape and size you could imagine. She read a few labels – magpie tears, crushed raspberries (enchanted), and dried spider venom. On the shelf below were more traditional ingredients – acids, crystals, and various chemicals. She'd never seen such a vast collection before.

Bill had three old books in front of him and was writing with furious determination, referencing between the trio of scriptures as he went. Two small glass vessels sat to his left, full of what looked like swirling cloudy water. Now and again, Erica would see the liquid twinkle, as if the light from Bill's desk lamp was illuminating glitter in the liquid.

Chemistry had been her favourite subject at school, and it didn't take Erica long to recognise the distillation apparatus on the desk. It was a complicated setup; she admired it, impressed that he was able to construct such a thing at home. The base was a two-by-four plank. On the left sat a glass flask above a flame, where a thick dark liquid bubbled away. From there, the vapours rose into a condenser, a long glass vessel no bigger than a decent salami, which transported the distilled liquid into a beaker at the other end. Tiny drops of the shimmering water dripped into a third jar at a steady pace.

She placed the mug of tea beside him but he didn't notice, he was so engrossed in his task. Not wanting to disturb Bill, Erica returned to inspecting his shelves.

Two rows down from the skulls was a homemade desiccator – a chamber used to draw moisture out of an item. She picked it up to get a closer look. It was a simple glass dish, intended for cooking, with another, smaller dish, placed in the centre. Around it were packets of silica gel like you'd find in a new handbag.

'Oh I wouldn't touch that,' Bill said without turning around. 'It's fox urine. Nasty stuff if you spill it.'

'Sorry,' she said, putting it back. She didn't need to add fox piss to her problems tonight.

Erica returned to her cosy fireside chair to sip her sugary black coffee. Her phone had died as she'd arrived, so there was nothing to do but force herself to relax.

FIVE MINUTES LATER BILL APPEARED, cupping three jars and a folded piece of paper to his chest. Erica sprung up and relieved him.

'Now, you'll have your altar kit at home, yes? You'll need that too.'

'I...I don't have an altar kit.'

'You don't?'

'Nope, nothing.'

'Then how do you practice?'

'I don't. Haven't done much since Mum.'

He studied her for a second, puzzled. 'So you have absolutely nothing?'

She shook her head and bit her bottom lip. This was going to be a problem.

'Don't worry, we can fix that. Get dressed and I'll be back in a tick,' he said, shuffling off to another room.

Erica's clothes weren't dry but they were good enough. At least the majority of the mud was gone, so her car seats might not suffer as much (not that it would make much difference now).

It wasn't long before Bill returned with a leather holdall. 'This should be everything you need,' he said, passing her the bag. 'Don't worry about returning it; every girl should have a decent altar kit. Even if it is only the essentials.' He smiled. 'Oh, and I've popped some instructions in too, in case you're a little rusty with setting it up.'

'Wow, thank you,' she said, lost for words at his generosity. 'Can I give you anything for it?'

'What? Oh heavens no. Just promise to come back tomorrow – I have something else to give you but I'll need to look it out. Your mother wanted you to have it.'

E rica drove back via Stirling, fully expecting at least one speeding ticket to land on her doormat in the next few days. It would be worth it.

The traffic suddenly slowed to a crawl near Cumbernauld, about fifteen miles from Glasgow. Her nerves were shot already; she couldn't take it if she was stuck in a traffic jam too.

The cars in her lane ground to a halt. Pulling up behind them, Erica craned her neck to check the inside lane – it was slowing too. *Fuckity fuck fuck.* This was the last thing she needed. She was twenty minutes away from Georgia.

She closed her eyes, letting out a long, slow breath. Nothing was ever straightforward, was it? *Go with the flow Erica. There's nothing else you can do. It'll clear soon, have faith.*

Erica looked at the holdall next to her on the passenger seat. It was tatty and well used – Bill had travelled a lot with it. She guessed he didn't do much travelling these days, not with his bad hip and arthritis. Ageing was scary, but she seldom thought that far ahead.

She opened the bag. As she parted the zipper, a low humming pricked at her ears – *was that one of the bottles?* She dived a hand in, rummaging through the contents, seeking out the source of the noise. Sure enough, her hand encountered the origin of the subtle but unmistakable sound. Whatever was in this bottle was vibrating at a low frequency, like a bee fit to burst with excitement. Erica placed it back in the bag with care.

Would this work? Apart from the buzzing bottle all she could see were candles and other unremarkable objects. It looked likely that the success of this spell would come down to her magical ability. That scared the shit out of her.

She couldn't even remember the last time she'd done proper magic. In fact, she doubted she'd ever done anything of note. Yes, she was a master of the little things, but rudimentary tricks and gimmicks wouldn't get her far tonight.

Her mother, on the other hand...She was a different story. Lucy had a constant stream of visitors at the house. Art teacher by day, magic shaman by night. Guests ranged from fellow witches to fairies, elves and cat sith. Erica had even caught sight of a banshee one day. Her mother was respected and powerful. Any problem, big or small, Lucy would help. She had a spell for everything. Who filled that void now? Whoever it was, Erica could do with their help tonight.

If only she'd brought Bill back with her. He'd be able to guide her. He seemed nice; it was a shame they'd never met before tonight.

As she stared ahead at the traffic, Erica wondered if it made her a bad person that she'd only started this crusade after her own daughter had been affected. It felt that way. If only she'd worked on Tobias's sample last week, she would be ahead of the game by now. Although her lack of witching connections would've still let her down. And why was it all reliant on her? There were others out there who were more capable. The thought of delaying the cure for this long made her feel a bit sick. She didn't want this weight on her shoulders.

Tobias had shown an unexpected – albeit fleeting – interest tonight. Did he have unfounded faith in her since their little chat?

Last week, Erica had been summoned to the top floor. It wasn't often she went to the top of the Chambers. It was Tobias's domain and she was more than happy to keep away, avoiding it at all costs. However, there'd been an odd urgency to his text. It didn't sit right. For a start, this was only the second time he'd summoned her to his office, so something was definitely up, but she couldn't think what she'd done wrong this time.

He'd asked her to research a magical cure. He was practically begging by the end of the conversation, his red cheeks giving away the frustration of stooping to the last resort, hitting rock bottom as Pack Leader.

Erica didn't doubt her mother would have known how to stop it; she was an expert. Being able to recall any spell when needed, Lucy hardly ever had to consult books. Erica used to wish she could do the same, but magic served so little purpose now it would be pointless.

Call her a sceptic, but even the best spells couldn't solve her problems. Why bother? She'd given up on learning incantations a long time ago.

Red brake lights disappeared like flashing dominoes ahead and the traffic edged forward. It was a slow crawl but Erica would take anything she could get. The man in the Corsa beside her looked more agitated than she felt. He was going to chew through his fingers at this rate.

She sighed before resting her head on the steering wheel. *Please God, or whatever you like to be called, if you exist please let this jam clear soon. I need to help my baby.*

Erica turned on the radio and skipped through a few stations. Nothing but high-tempo dance, sappy love songs and metal. She turned it off.

Full of nervous energy, she began to tap impatiently on the wheel. Nine-forty. Time was wearing on; she'd been stuck here for ten minutes. There had to be a way around this traffic. Could the police help? An escort maybe? But what would she say? They'd think she was a nut. She could lie: my wife's in labour. My mother is dying. No. Too close to the bone.

Tears threatened. *You can't cry and drive Erica. Hold it together.*

She needed a distraction or she'd end up crying. Once you get close to that edge, it's hard to back down. If only Quinn was here, she'd be good company. Erica felt bad for not texting as she considered Quinn a big sister more than a friend. She'd be mortified to find out that Georgia was ill and Erica hadn't told her. But how could she?

No need for police intervention – the traffic slowly eased forward again as the bottle in the altar kit started to buzz more loudly. It was almost like it wanted to spill her dirty little secret. She reached over, shoving it deeper into the bag.

Erica had wanted to be honest with Quinn a thousand times. It was hard to be so close to somebody but have to hide such a massive part of you. Sometimes she worried it was obvious that she wasn't being her authentic self. There were strict rules about sharing their world with a Seelie, the non-magic humans, and, for the sake of saving herself from banishment and eternal damnation, she could live with a few lies.

Corsa man's lane sped up a little and he gained a few metres on her. He looked more relaxed, with both hands resting on the wheel. She wished she could say the same for herself.

Sweat was forming on her brow and upper lip. An angry knot of frustration was tightening in her stomach, ready to spring open and break apart at any moment. The queue had to clear soon or she was going to lose it. The she-wolf in her was ready to go on a rampage, not caring who or what got in her way, as long as she got to Georgia.

She took a few deep breaths to calm herself. *They were moving. It would clear soon. Don't worry.* She focused on the positives: she'd be back soon. This was going to work. She trusted her mother and Bill.

But then what? No one had ever recovered before. Would there be lasting complications? Maybe it depended on how far up the sickness had travelled. Erica hoped to God it wouldn't hurt her girl in the long term.

The cars ahead were moving more quickly, some managing to break away from the jam and return to normal motorway speeds. In the distance, blue lights flashed – she was nearing whatever had caused the backlog.

Her dashboard informed her it was just before ten to ten. *I could've been back by now. Jesus. Georgia had better be ok.* She'd been away for so long, it seemed like an age.

The lane had surpassed a crawl and was starting to pick up momentum. After a few minutes she passed the police, and could see beyond the glare of blue lights. Two vehicles had had a run-in; the leading car's back bumper hung skewiff and the rear car's headlight lay shattered on the road. Nothing too serious, but enough to cause ungodly tailbacks.

Two families lined the hard shoulder, joined by police officers. Someone was having a bad night. But, then again, so was she.

After passing the accident she brought the car back up to 70mph. *Not long Georgia, mummy's coming.*

C rashing through the door to Georgia's room, Erica found a sleeping Pétur. Well he had been – he'd jolted awake at her ungraceful entrance. G was the only patient on the ward so she hadn't thought of being quiet, only being fast.

Georgia remained sound asleep, unmoved from where she'd left her. She seemed almost the same, aside from a worrying blue tinge to her lips and skin.

Erica could sense Pétur's confusion over the cuts on her face, mud-soaked jeans, and new leather bag. There was no time to explain.

She pulled the sheets off Georgia and stripped her down to her pants, just like Bill had directed. Erica's hand recoiled as she touched Georgia's leg; it was like she had rigor mortis.

'Got any magic in you?' she asked. 'I could do with a boost tonight.' Pétur shook his head. He was still waking up and couldn't match her sudden explosion of activity. 'Well, go get the doctor then,' she snapped, spurring him into action.

First, she uncorked the jar of shimmering black liquid and set it aside to breathe, as instructed by Bill. Its manic buzzing had become stronger; it sounded like a vibrating phone against the worktop.

She moved to the oils he'd decanted for her, mixing the two remaining jars together, one black and one clear, to form a dark, viscous liquid. She placed the new concoction beside the first and set to work emptying the holdall.

With no time to waste, Erica tipped the bag out on to the nearest plastic seat, its contents clattering across the surface. Her heart raced and she could see her hands trembling as she checked Bill's instructions.

Candles. She needed candles.

She scrambled through the mess on the chair and retrieved three white candles. They were large – the sort you'd see on a church altar or fancy dinner table, not by a hospital sink alongside a clinical waste bin.

Now the hard bit. Charging the candles for their intended purpose, fuelling them with magic. Erica had never done this before, she'd only watched her mother do it.

The situation wasn't ideal; conventionally the process should be a lot more complicated and a hell of a lot more precise. Erica had to work with what little time she had. She certainly didn't have the luxury of waiting for a full moon – unorthodox methods would have to work tonight. Her mother would be turning in her grave if she saw the kit Erica had.

She held the first candle in her trembling right hand and, with the marker pen bouncing along while her hand shook, drew on the rune symbol which Bill had illustrated.

Two more symbols on the other candles. Now it was time to charge.

She grasped the first candle in her left hand and extended her right towards the ceiling, visualising her end goal and the power of her intended Goddess. She could feel the power surging through her, filling her body; she pushed it towards the candle.

She continued the same steps with the remaining candles. *I must look a right idiot.* Anything for Georgia.

Erica arranged the charged candles around the jars on the worktop, laying out her tools at the front of the makeshift altar. Sage for cleansing after the ritual, a metal disc with a pentagram inscribed, and a small crystal she couldn't identify. Her knowledge of magic was rustier than an old nail. She was losing confidence with each step. *Never mind, just push on.*

With a surprising amount of patience and composure, Erica lit the candles, reciting the sacred words under her breath. Satisfied that the correct spirits and Goddesses had been called, she picked up the oil. She checked Bill's instructions to make sure she was applying it to the correct areas. She paused. Double-checked. It wouldn't do to mess up now.

Dipping a finger into the bubbling mixture, she was surprised to find it was freezing cold. Erica smeared the oil on her daughter's forehead, cheeks, chest, belly, and limbs. Georgia looked like she was going into combat, decorated with intimidating war paint and ready for battle. It shimmered on her skin under the bright hospital lights.

Please work.

Pétur arrived at the door with the doctor hot on his heels. It had taken them long enough.

'What the – ?!' the doctor blurted out, lost for words.

'Oh thank God,' she said, turning to the doctor. 'I'm going to need you in a moment.' If this went wrong, she wanted back-up.

She reached for the final jar.

Erica took her daughter's breathing mask off and, carefully tilting Georgia's head back, poured the syrupy liquid into her mouth. G swallowed. Erica's fingertips tingled as the glass lost its energy, the vibration fading. She half expected Georgia to start trembling but she remained motionless. *Was that a good thing?*

She looked to the men in the doorway. Both were standing, mouths agape with no idea what was going on. Pétur's hand was on the doctor's shoulder, steadying himself. They were both white as a sheet, the colour drained from their faces. Erica felt sick to her stomach.

There was no ignoring her shaking hands as she picked up Bill's final piece of paper. Three simple words were written. It didn't seem enough for the task but she had faith. She took a deep breath and gripped Georgia's left hand. It was hard and stiff like a doll's.

Renova Consanoto Potenvirtu

she chanted over and over. Nothing was happening. She closed her eyes, forcing all her

strength into the words, gripping Georgia's hand more tightly.

She was shouting, willing something to happen.

Renova Consanoto Potenvirtu Renova Consanoto Poten –

A blinding white light spread from the centre of Georgia's torso until it was surrounding her whole body, cocooning her. It sparkled and danced around her like the sun's rays reaching through clouds. The light became brighter and Erica was forced to drop G's hand to shield her eyes.

There was a flash and the light enveloped the whole room before vanishing into Georgia as if sucked in by a vacuum.

'What was that?' the doctor asked from the doorway.

'I have no idea,' remarked Erica. 'But it better have bloody worked.' She touched her daughter's hand. It was its normal, squishy, warm self.

ERICA once again found herself draped over Georgia's bedside, but this time a smile was plastered across her face. She just couldn't control it. She'd done it; her baby was going to be ok. Only hours ago she'd been given a death sentence but here she was, now a fit and healthy eight-year-old. It was nothing short of a miracle.

After composing himself, the doctor had confirmed Georgia's vitals were normal. The drugs used to sedate her were still in her system but he assured Erica that, apart from Georgia being a little groggy for a day, there were no signs of lasting damage. He'd backtracked and said he wanted to do further tests tomorrow to be sure but, for now, Erica was happy.

'It's getting late,' the doctor said, his gaze focusing on Georgia. 'I'm sorry to have to do this, but I'm going to have to ask you to leave.' Sensing Erica's reluctance, he continued. 'Get some food. You'll need it. I'm sure we can sneak you somewhere to sleep later on.'

'I'm fine. I'll ju–'

The doctor cut her off. 'Honestly, she's sleeping. Get some food. Or some fresh air at least.'

It was nearly eleven. Pétur looked tired but content. Despite being exhausted herself, Erica knew sleep wouldn't come soon. She was running on adrenaline; too much had happened tonight for her to fall straight into bed.

The truth was sinking in. She'd pulled it off – how had she managed it? If only her mum could see her, she'd be so proud. She was more powerful than she realised.

'Is there anywhere close we can get some food?' Pétur asked, standing up to stretch his back. 'I'm starving.'

Food sounded like an excellent idea – a walk and some fresh air were what she needed to calm down before giving in to sleep. Georgia would be fine for a short time. Food and then straight back, it wouldn't hurt. 'I know just the place. You'll love it,' Erica said, stretching her own aching muscles.

'It's one of my favourites,' she said, as they made their way into a bar called Max's. It was a Glasgow institution, best-known for its amazing American-style food and famous 'chicken in a basket'. Pétur was intrigued to discover what 'chicken in a basket' actually was.

Being a Saturday night, the small bar was busy but Erica spotted a free table and grabbed it, asking Pétur to get the drinks in.

With its high roof, raised seating area, and long dark wood bar backed by a ceiling-high mirror displaying shelf after shelf of liquor, Max's wouldn't look out of place in a Western.

Pétur placed the drinks in front of Erica before sitting down. 'The good Sauvignon, like you asked for.'

'Thank you,' she replied, closing her eyes as she took a sip, a smile creeping on to her lips. She must have needed it after the day she'd had. 'Actually, can you let me out? I must look a right mess. I'm going to pop to the loo and freshen up.'

He did as she asked, repositioning himself on the bench where Erica had been, getting a better view of the large TV to his right. The tables were close together – a little too close as he found himself sitting on the woman next door's coat. He mouthed *sorry* as he pulled it out from under himself. Its owner didn't seem to notice.

The TV was showing a cookery show. Heaped plates of chips flanked burger stacks. The presenter had a head of spiked blond hair – Pétur was sure he recognised him but couldn't remember his name. The amount of food on screen made him feel a bit sick.

Five minutes later, Erica returned looking refreshed. 'Made a friend in the toilet and she took pity on me, lent me some makeup.'

'You still look like you've been boxing.' Her lip was healed but the top of her cheekbone was sporting a dark bruise and the remains of an impressive graze.

'Eh, excuse me. You're meant to say how wonderful I look. "What a transformation Erica",' she said, mocking his accent.

'That was rubbish,' he replied, although he thought it was cute that she'd attempted it.

'It was a bit, wasn't it? Points for trying? It's been a hard day.'

'You ok?' he asked, attempting to be sympathetic.

'Yeah, just knackered,' she sighed. ' But I don't think my trainers are going to make it.' She lifted her foot, showing off the mud-stained shoe. 'And I don't even want to think about my car. Still, it could be worse.' She smiled, making light of today's nightmare.

'It's a nice car. You don't seem the type.' Pétur's comment was verging on cheeky but he took the risk. He was learning that she was far from the typical girl he'd first thought she was. Appearances could be deceiving.

She laughed. 'What? The type to like nice things?'

'City girls like you don't usually have cars like that.'

'City girls like me? You're digging yourself a hole, Pétur.' She savoured her wine. 'I needed a new car. I spotted it secondhand. I wanted one so that's what I got.' She wasn't giving much away.

'Fair enough. Nice choice too.' He did love Wranglers, but wouldn't have gone with the same colour choice. A sleek black would have been nicer.

'If we're getting to know each other better, I have a have question that's been niggling me.'

He shifted in his seat; did he look as nervous as he felt? 'Go ahead.'

'What's with the necklace? I saw you fiddling with it in the medical bay. You don't seem the jewellery type.'

'This?' he asked as he pulled it out from under his collar, his fingers finding the chunky pendant hanging from it. 'Just a good luck charm from someone.'

'A girl?'

'No.'

'Shit, sorry – a guy?'

He laughed. 'I'm not gay Erica. It's not a romantic thing. It's purely for good luck.'

She nodded in approval but didn't look convinced.

The bar was busy and it had taken longer than expected for their food to arrive, but thankfully conversation never stopped: they were still quizzing each other over the meal. 'So, my turn,' Pétur said, taking a gulp of beer. 'How did you manage to lure my dickhead brother? He won't even talk to a Scottish person, never mind a Scottish you-know-what.'

'Oh God. That's a long and embarrassing story.' She paused and downed the rest of her wine. 'Short version: I was seventeen, in Ibiza with my friends... You know the type of holiday.' She took a deep breath. 'Basically they dared me I couldn't pull a guy using an accent.' Erica cleared her throat. 'I bought him a stubby, the rest is history,' she said, impersonating a South Australian.

'That's not bad,' he said, impressed. 'A lot better than your attempt at Icelandic anyway. Why the Aussie?'

'That's where my Mum was from. Melbourne to be exact.'

'No way. Have you ever been? I lived there for a year,' he said, getting excited.

'Only once, when I was little. I've always wanted to go back, I've just never found the time to.'

'You should. I loved it.'

'It's top of the list. I'm psyching myself up for the journey with a kid, although it would be ok now she's older.'

The waitress returned, clearing plates away and asking if they wanted more drinks. Erica conceded to one more before she headed back to see Georgia – her smile hinted that she was enjoying the respite after a stressful evening, but she was eager to let Pétur know her mind was still on her daughter. She needn't have worried; he understood the need to unwind, he wasn't going to judge her for not running back to the Chambers.

'So what did you win?' he asked, keeping the mood light-hearted.

'What did I win where?'

'For kissing my brother?' The sentence turned his stomach.

'Oh God, I can't remember.' She paused, thinking. 'A baby?' She laughed.

'So how come we've only just heard about Georgia? Does Tobias have a game plan?'

'That's a tricky one, I'm not sure what Tobias is up to. He'll be planning something though. Speaking to your Dad was out of character.'

'You don't trust him?'

The waitress returned and placed more drinks in front of them.

Erica took a sip of wine before she answered. 'Do I hell. He's a slippery little bastard. That's why I've kept Georgia away from him for the past eight years.'

'What changed?'

'This new outbreak. I thought I'd better register her with the Pack, just in case.'

'You haven't even registered her?' Pétur couldn't hide the surprise in his voice; he didn't know that was even possible.

'Tobias didn't know I had a kid. I mean, it's not like I hid her, but he took so little interest in me that it wasn't difficult.'

'I thought you lived with him? When you were younger, I mean.'

'Only until I was eighteen, then he got his money. He pretty much packed my bags for me. He wasn't going to look after me any longer than he had to.'

'What money?'

'It was in my parents' will – he would get a lump sum if he looked after me until I was eighteen. I wanted to move to Australia and be with my grandparents but he was having none of it. I don't know how much he got, but I'm guessing it was a sizeable amount for him to tolerate me for ten years.'

'How did he not notice you had a baby?'

'I did him a favour and moved out a few days before my birthday. Slept in my car until a friend took pity on me and let me sleep on her couch.'

'That must have been tough.'

Erica forced a half-smile before finishing her wine. 'Can we not talk about this anymore?' Despite the effort to sound normal he could see she was wound up, her balled-up fist under the table an obvious sign.

'Yeah, sure. Sorry, I didn't mean to pry.'

'No, it's ok. It's just stuff I'd rather forget.' She straightened herself, a sudden surge of energy loosening her. 'Let's toast, after today I think we've got a lot to be thankful for.' She thought for a moment. 'To the future. Who knows what it will bring..?'

He raised his glass and clinked hers. 'To the future.'

THEY TUMBLED out of Max's. Time had slipped away, despite Erica wanting to do nothing more than sleep.

'Oh my God, that was so embarrassing,' she said a safe distance away from the bar.

'I can't believe you got chatted up in the state you're in.'

'Oi,' she barked and punched him in the shoulder (hopefully she meant it to be weak, or that was just embarrassing). 'Easy, it's been a hard day.' She looked hurt.

The would-be-Lothario had been in his early forties and was wearing a patterned shirt with messy-rolled sleeves, jeans and dress shoes. She was sure she'd spotted a beaded necklace. *And*, he had a greasy man bun. It was a no from the get-go. He'd sidled up to the table when Pétur was in the toilet and his chat had been horrid. She was out of the bar like a shot as soon as she saw Pétur's head at the top of the stairs.

'Sorry, I shouldn't have said that,' Pétur apologised, thinking she was serious. 'That was harsh. You look good.' He put a hand on her upper arm, his dark eyes contrite. The day had felt a week long, the ordeal they'd been through already feeling like a distant memory. He should have been more sensitive.

'I'm just kidding,' she smiled, laughing at his reaction. 'You've been amazing today. Thank you for staying with G while I was away.'

Between his apology and her gratitude they'd become closer. His hand remained on her arm, their bodies only inches apart.

'It's ok, it was nothing,' he said, his eyes holding a lingering gaze with hers. The cold night air was making him aware of how much he'd drank. It was harder to focus than usual and he didn't know how long he'd been looking at her. She didn't seem to care.

Her eyes were so blue, even in the hazy streetlight. He'd never seen eyes like hers before. Georgia's were mesmerising too, but in a different way. There was an added intensity to Erica's. Did she wear contacts? They couldn't be natural.

She smiled and he was aware they were both standing there, his hand still holding her arm, refusing to move.

She kissed him. It could have been the drink but he didn't care, she was kissing him, her fingers finding their way into his belt loops, pulling him closer.

Her lips were soft, with a hint of salt from the food they'd just eaten and yet she tasted sweet. He backed her into the nearest wall. His hand found its way under her t-shirt, resting above her jeans.

She bit his bottom lip lightly before driving the kiss deeper. With his leg between her thighs, instinct was screaming at him to get her home, let his hand travel further up, get her top off.

A passerby wolf-whistled, breaking the moment.

'Shit, I'm so sorry,' she said, pushing him back. 'I shouldn't have done that. Fuck.'

For a second he was silent, catching up with the fact it was over.

'I have to go,' she declared and marched across Royal Exchange Square, cutting through the empty space. The large square was quiet, the various cafés were packed away with chairs and tables in stacked rows, and the sound of her footsteps echoed across the paving. Warning shots that with each step she took, Erica would be harder to get back.

'Erica, wait!' he called, but she was nearly at the arch to Buchanan Street and he could tell she wanted to be alone. She didn't even turn her head.

R obbie Nowak woke up on his living room floor with no memory of how he'd got there. *Must've had a seizure.*

He hauled himself up to a seated position against the couch and rubbed his eyes. God, did he feel groggy.

Two this week, that hasn't happened in a while.

He turned his attention to his neck, rolling his head from side to side. He was sore and stiff. He went to massage his neck but had second thoughts. Rubbing his eyes had used what little energy he had left. His arms weighed a ton.

Robbie leaned against the sofa, letting it take most of his weight. How long had he been out? At least he was at home this time. His body seldom warned him of an impending episode; he considered himself a ticking time bomb in public.

He could taste metal in his mouth. *Must've bitten my tongue.*

He sat like this for some time, struggling to keep his eyes open as sleep fought to take over his body. First the fit, then the sleep. *So much time stolen. Epilepsy was nothing but a fucking thief.*

He recalled his last memory. It was important to make sense of what he was doing when the seizure started.

He'd felt sick. Yes, that was it. He'd felt sick and come into the living room to crash out on the sofa, watch some TV. Then his brain was blank.

He felt incapable of going to the bedroom. It was only a short distance but he might as well have been contemplating a marathon. He would have pulled himself up to sit on the sofa had it not been for the fact he'd wet himself.

Robbie tried to raise himself. This time it wasn't tiredness stopping the manoeuvre, but a wave of nausea. He dropped back to the floor with a thud.

He groaned as his stomach cramped.

Was this food poisoning? Just his luck to get food poisoning and have a seizure on the same night. It was the beginning of the October holidays, he was meant to be enjoying himself.

He grabbed his phone off the coffee table and sent James a text. He'd be pissed off that Robbie had missed the pub tonight; James had been going on about it all week, he'd be in for a roasting.

He chucked the phone back on the table with more force than intended, but his arms were still coming back to life. They felt stiff.

The sofa wasn't such a bad option. Robbie decided to strip off to avoid messing it. He lived alone, no harm in sleeping naked for a bit. He eased off his piss-soaked trousers and boxers with a look of mild disgust on his face and piled them on the floor. He added his polo shirt and sunk back into the hollow of the sofa. His stomach was churning.

This had come on after he'd eaten that sweet. He'd had nothing else since a sausage roll at lunchtime. He shouldn't have had it, but it was the end of term. A primary four kid wouldn't miss one sweetie on their return. The packet had just been sitting there, in the middle of the table by the pencil tray, calling out to him. He'd wiped down the desks and vacuumed the floors before giving in and shoving the sweets in his pocket. Who leaves sweets out anyway? It would be rude to waste them.

They hadn't even been that nice. Maybe that's why they had been left. No flavour. He'd expected strawberry or raspberry but there was nothing. Nada. He would have snuck a second otherwise. Instead he dumped them at the bus stop – no point carrying that shite home.

He schlepped himself on to the sofa and rolled to his side. He let out another groan. His stomach was in agony, a sharp pain radiating out from below his ribs. He'd better not get the shits, he couldn't cope with that. Not when running to the bathroom was out of the question.

He let sleep take over. He could sleep for hours and hours after a seizure. He'd feel better when he woke up, and hopefully this stupid stomach cramp would be gone too. Sleep always made it better.

. . .

A WEEK LATER, Heather Moss would stand over Robbie Nowak's body, her face screwed up in confusion.

Puzzling indeed.

She walked to the other side of the stainless steel mortuary slab and inspected his left arm. She'd have to wait for the toxicology results, but initial tests had only shown a small elevation of silver in his blood. Curious. Apart from the expected blue tinge to the deceased's lips, there wasn't the slightest hint that silver had done this to him. Not even a bruise tarnished his porcelain skin.

Then there were his eyes. Severe xerophthalmia. Judging by his corneas, he hadn't blinked for days.

Never in her career as a forensic pathologist had she seen anything like it. Now she'd encountered two similar cases in one week. Epilepsy could be a factor, but it didn't account for the blinking. Nothing suggested foul play, so what was it?

God, she loved a challenge.

Saturday morning Erica woke up stiff from sleeping on a sofa and with serious *Fear*. Nothing was worse than waking up with your brain in immediate overdrive about what you might have done the night before.

She couldn't remember the last time she'd felt like this. After a manager's meeting in London? It was a long time ago, anyway.

Why the hell did I kiss him?

He was a good kisser, she couldn't deny that, but he was Georgia's uncle...She rubbed her temples, was she hungover? Maybe. Her stomach wasn't happy anyway.

Last night, Erica had been carried away in a fog of adrenaline, fatigue, and wine. The perfect storm for bad decisions.

The last time she'd drunkenly kissed a boy who she knew she'd have to see again was at school. That got complicated. *Ay, ay, ay. Why do I never learn?* It was a bit of a dick move to walk away from Pétur too. Where had he slept? She hoped he was ok. Should she text him? Later.

She checked her phone. Seven – might as well get up. She was desperate to see if Georgia was awake. There was a weird message from Quinn: 'Call me when you wake up'. Ominous. Quinn had never sent her a message like that before. Were the kids ok? Or, her wife, Holly? Worry grabbed at her stomach as she bolted upright, but last night's wine forced her to lie back down as her belly gurgled in protest.

She'd stayed in the 'family room' on the medical floor. Hospital jargon for the room they shunted you into while you waited for your relatives to die.

She could remember spending her eighth birthday sitting with Tobias in the family room at Glasgow Royal Infirmary. The young Erica had no clue what was going on. She'd been certain of her feelings that day though – a heavy sick sensation in the pit of her stomach telling her she'd never see her mum alive again and wondering where the hell her father had got to after sending her to fetch her uncle. Tobias not wanting to talk, wringing his hands, not wanting his wife to touch or comfort him, before taking off and not returning, intent on looking for his brother instead. *Why are we wasting our time here? We should be looking for Raf.* Erica had focused on the stiff NHS chair and stared at an arty photograph of George Square, the people walking through it a heady blur. All she'd wanted was a reassuring hug but it never came. Instead she was told off for crying.

Whoever designed the Chambers' attempt at unobtrusive décor had taken a simple approach to say the least. The room had a dark brown couch with two matching armchairs; in the middle was a cheap-looking coffee table – MDF top and black metal legs. Someone had made a feeble attempt at jazzing the place up with a single red carnation in a tall vase, confidently positioned in the middle of the table. On the wall behind the couch was an ageing fresco, an original feature dating back to when the building was first decorated, depicting a biblical scene. IN GOD WE TRUST was written over a gold banner in the centre. It was hard to trust anyone these days, never mind a faceless God. How many had sat here in the past few months and had to look at that as their relatives died? She didn't want to think about it; she'd been the lucky one this time.

A few more minutes lying down would do her good. She called Quinn from the safety of the sofa. It rang out. Erica huffed and considered texting Pétur. Her finger hovered over his name but she was saved the exertion of composing a message as her phone burst into life.

'Hey Quinn, what's up?' She cleared her throat. She was rarely thrilled with the sound of her own voice, but this morning it could have passed for a bloke's with no bother.

'Erica, it's Sam,' explained Quinn. Her voice quivered, tears threatening. 'She's not well.'

Fear knotted in Erica's stomach. 'What's wrong?'

Quinn sniffed, composing herself. 'She woke up in the night

screaming, saying her tummy was sore. We, we – ' she sniffed again. 'We took her to A&E and she started having seizures.'

Erica sat up, her heart racing. Sam was like a niece to her. 'Is she going to be ok?'

'I don't know. They've got no idea what's wrong.' Quinn's voice cracked. It was awful doing this over the phone, unable to comfort her closest friend.

'God. I'm so sorry.' Erica tipped her head back to dam the tears that were threatening. 'Can I do anything? Can I come see her? Who has Callum?'

'It's ok, don't worry, we've got everything sorted for now. Jesus, Erica. This is horrible.'

'Can I visit?' she asked again.

'No. Not yet. Not until we know what it is. I couldn't risk you getting it.'

Erica sighed in frustration. 'They've really got no idea?'

'Nope. It's weird: sore stomach, seizures, headache. She was complaining of pins and needles earlier, now she can barely move her legs. They thought it was viral but now they're thinking infection...' Quinn trailed off. 'They've just no clue.' Her breath faltered.

Jesus. Sam's symptoms were worryingly familiar. There was no way a Seelie could catch it though. That was absurd. Wasn't it?

'Will you let me know when I can visit?' Erica asked.

'Yeah, sure of course. I'd better go, Holly wants to talk to me.'

'If you need me to look after Callum, just shout.'

'Thanks, I will do.'

Erica said her goodbyes and let the phone drop to the sofa with a gentle bounce. First Georgia gets sick, now Sam? It was too similar to be a coincidence. Who could she ask about Seelies? Tobias would be no use. He took no interest in them. Bill maybe? He'd saved Georgia. Perhaps he knew what kind of virus it was.

She rubbed her eyes to dry the dampness of her tears. It was a stupid idea to think they were related – Seelies and werewolves were two different species. It was like worrying your cat would catch your cold.

Erica needed to see Georgia. More than ever before, she wanted to give her daughter a hug. Poor Quinn. If only there was a magic potion than could treat Seelie illness. No such luck.

She pulled her jeans on. They were dry and brittle from the mud, making them uncomfortable to wear. They'd have to do.

God, she needed water. Where did Tobias keep his stash? She'd seen some in Georgia's room, she'd pilfer that.

The medical bay at the Chambers was basic to say the least. They didn't need much – an examination room, a small ward, three private rooms and the infamous family room. A small office at the end of the corridor doubled as a staff room. Usually there wasn't much need for the medical bay so it had a skeleton team of staff, seldom more than one doctor and one nurse on at a time. Erica felt sorry for them – before this they'd probably only treated silver burns, broken bones, and not much else.

She checked the private rooms and ward on the way to Georgia's room. Empty. *Good, hopefully they'll stay that way.*

Georgia woke up not long after Erica had shuffled to her room at the other end of the corridor. G was groggy from sedatives but otherwise doing great. Sleep and recovery were top of the agenda. Erica didn't tell her about Sam – the kid had enough to worry about as it was.

After an hour or so of dozing, Erica was woken by one of the security guards, a staunch little bull-necked man with no manners.

'That guy who was here yesterday, who is he?' he questioned, his thick Glasgow accent making each word run into the next.

'Georgia's uncle. Why?'

'Well, he snuck in yesterday. I saw him and he's not one of us.'

The penny dropped. 'Look, I know he's Icelandic but G's Dad is too. He wanted to support his niece.'

'Naw, it's not that.' He was towering over her. 'I've done a check you see. Your little dog's Dad doesn't even have a brother.'

'What?'

'And,' he said with excitement in his eyes, 'he touched the sensor trying to get in. He's not even a wolf.'

'No, you must be wrong. We're talking about Pétur, yeah? Who was here yesterday?'

'That's what I said. Listen, it's not up for discussion. He's not allowed back in the building. End of.' He went to leave the room but turned on his heel as he reached the door. 'And listen, you can't be staying overnight either.'

'What? My daughter needed me, I had to.'

'Well, once is all you get. We need to use that room.'

'Can I stay in here then?' Desperation crept into her voice. She couldn't leave Georgia alone overnight in a strange place.

'No way.' She went to protest but he cut her off. 'Look, I know your dad used to be Leader but you can't go taking liberties. Tobias is in charge. What he says goes.'

Bullneck was one of Tobias's loyal ensemble. Great. Erica stood up, attempting to level the balance of power. 'She's eight. Do you really expect me to leave her alone overnight?'

He came closer and lowered his voice to a menacing growl. 'Like I said, what Tobias says goes. Fair is fair.'

Fair didn't sound very fair to Erica. Bullneck left before she could challenge him any further.

She slumped into the plastic chair beside Georgia's bed, making sense of what had just happened. Pétur couldn't be lying, could he?

Her mind went to Georgia's drawing, the three of them together, her mum's premonition of 'Uncle Fuzz'. If Jóhann didn't have a brother, was she losing her touch? Erica was an only child, so an uncle had to be paternal. Did she mean he was *like* an uncle?

Her head was hazy from last night's wine and wasn't doing a good job of keeping up with new information.

'He's *not* Uncle Fuzz,' Georgia said, her weak voice croaking, interrupting her mother's train of thought.

'Oh honey, I'm sorry. We didn't mean to wake you,' she said as she

brushed the hair from Georgia's face before planting a kiss on her
forehead.

'He's not... hairy enough. He's not black enough,' she continued.
'He's not right.' Her brow creased, she was agitated that the right
words weren't coming to her.

'So you heard that.' Erica sighed. 'I don't understand.'

'Uncle Fuzz is a wolf. Gran definitely said that. She wouldn't lie.'

'I know, but we're out of uncles. Do you think she got the uncle bit
wrong? Or maybe the security guy got it wrong – maybe Pétur is a
wolf?'

'His face is wrong. Something's missing.'

'Something is missing from his face?' Erica wondered if Georgia
was still high from the meds.

'I dunno. Gran just described him to me; I've never seen him. She
wouldn't let me see him.' She was getting frustrated.

'Look, it's ok. I'll sort this out.' Erica got up and grabbed another
bottle of water from beside the sink. She had an unquenchable thirst.

A swathe of navy was poking out from under one of the seats.
Pétur's duffel bag. He must have brought it with him yesterday,
expecting to be there a while. She'd been so focused on Georgia that
she hadn't noticed him carry it in.

Should I open it? It might put a quick end to the mystery.

'What is it?' Georgia asked, aware her Mum was looking at
something under the seat.

'It's Pétur's bag,' she said as she lifted it up to G's bed. It was heavy.
Surely this wasn't everything he had with him for travelling around
Scotland? Erica would need suitcases of clothes just for a week.

'Are you going to open it?'

'That would be wrong.' She paused and weighed the moral
responsibility to her daughter against her own curiosity. 'But one
quick peek won't hurt.' She unzipped the bag, stopping half way to
add, 'This is very bad by the way. You're not to do anything as rude as
this.'

Inside was a disappointment. No skeletons, figurative or literal.
Normal clothes, a pair of dress shoes, a thin windbreaker, and a

phone charger. She fished her hand deeper to find the same wireless headphones she had; he had good taste anyway. The most exciting thing was an old Gameboy. Erica hadn't realised you could still buy them.

She pulled out two jumpers and a pair of jeans, placing them on the bed in a heap to ease further investigations. They weren't folded, they'd simply been stuffed into the bag – how did he manage to look semi-presentable when he kept his clothes like this? She pushed a few t-shirts out of the way, attempting to see what she was touching. *Please don't be dirty pants.* But instead her hand found something passport-shaped at the bottom of the bag. She pulled it out, building the suspense for Georgia.

'Let's see who he is then,' Erica declared as she opened it.

Gallison, Pétur Ágúst was printed beside a mugshot of him: short black hair, trimmed beard and dark eyes.

Interesting, considering Jóhann's last name was Ottisson.

ERICA HEADED to her flat in Partick to collect a few supplies – new jeans, toiletries, pyjamas – everything she needed in case she managed to sneak in and stay overnight. Her girl needed her; she wasn't going to give up without a fight.

She didn't want to leave Georgia today, but she'd made a promise to Bill and had to honour that. He did save her daughter's life.

All the while she was going over what the security guard had said and the passport. Could it be true? But why would anyone lie?

The more she thought about it, the more it wound her up. She sent Pétur a text. *Meet me at the Chambers in 30 minutes. We need to talk.* It sounded ambiguous after what had happened last night, but she didn't care.

ERICA WAITED, leaning on her Jeep door. He was late and she was impatient.

Ten minutes and I'm leaving without him.

Pétur's bag was on the back seat. It would be a bit shit to go off with his passport and belongings. He was the one being dishonest though. She was saved the issue of dumping his stuff when he arrived five minutes later, two coffees in hand and a stupid grin on his face.

She glowered at him, her face not hiding the fact she was raging.

'What's up?' he asked, sensing the tension.

'You've got some explaining to do. Get in the car,' she said, turning to open her door. You're going to start with who the hell you are and what the fuck you want with my daughter.' She opened the passenger door with a flick of her wrist; displaying a hint of her magic ability. This was no joke.

They were on the motorway before she spoke again.

'Go on, I'm waiting.'

'I don't know what you mean.' He'd expected her text to be about what happened yesterday, maybe even an apology for storming off, not an inquisition about his identity. The unexpected interrogation was throwing him off kilter.

'Security saw you sneaking in yesterday. They've checked; you're not a wolf and Jóhann doesn't even have a brother – never mind one called Pétur.'

'Shit.'

'Shit indeed. I saw your passport, I know it's true. So why not cut the crap and tell me who you are?'

'You went through my stuff?'

'It was there – what else was I meant to do?' she snapped. 'I needed to know who'd been hanging around my daughter.'

'So because I don't have the right name, you think I'm a fraud? If you had a different name to Georgia you'd still be related. It doesn't prove anything.'

'Yeah, well, fair point, but that doesn't explain anything.'

'We have the same parents, he's my brother but we have different names, that's all.'

'But you can't be. I'm no expert but I know for a fact that two purebred wolves can't produce a Seelie. It's physically impossible.'

'That's where you're wrong, Erica. They can if you're cursed.'

22ND OF AUGUST 1988. Otti Jóhannsson wasn't in the room when his second son was born because he'd assumed he'd have time to take an important call in his study. The elves were threatening an uprising – not what he needed today.

Otti was so engrossed in the call, he barely heard the midwife shouting. It wasn't until she was right next to him that he registered what she was saying: 'Something is wrong with your baby. You need to come quickly.'

Was the cord around his neck? Was he breech? Was something wrong with his breathing? Was Otti's wife ok? He quizzed her on the way to the bedroom, every possible complication he could think of, but she wouldn't confirm what was wrong. Why had they opted for a home birth? Tradition, that's why. It seemed so stupid now.

'You should brace yourself,' she said before letting him enter. It didn't help calm his nerves.

The smell hit him like a punch in the face.

Warm and putrid, it stung his nostrils. He gagged.

'What is that?' His wife was crying and the second midwife remained silent. 'I said, what is that smell?'

Imagine leaving a pile of meat in the sun for months and holding it to your face. It was intoxicating. He retched and pulled his jumper over his mouth. His eyes were watering. He could taste the stench.

'It's your baby, sir.' The midwife was having a hard time remaining professional; he could hear the rising bile in her voice.

'My baby? Is he...?' He couldn't bring himself to say the word.

'No, he's fine. But the smell... We don't know what's causing it. We're going to take him away for tests,' the midwife replied. Otti got a first look at his son as he was whisked past. A fresh waft of the smell gave him a wet mouth.

The baby had a head of thick dark hair, which surprised him, as both he and his wife were blonde. Generation after generation had been fair-haired and blue-eyed in both families. It didn't make sense.

He opened a window before going to his wife's bedside.

'What's happening, Otti?' she whimpered. He took his wife's hand, struggling to find any words. 'As soon as he was born... That smell,' she trailed off, failing as much as he was to understand what was going on.

'I...' he began, but didn't know where the sentence was heading. He wanted to ask if the child was his, but this wasn't the time or the place.

'At least he was healthy,' she said.

'If you can call that healthy.' His wife looked at him, tears welling. 'Sorry, this is a lot to take in,' admitted Otti. 'I'm sure there'll be a logical explanation for it.'

OUT OF SIGHT, a black mass no bigger than your average man's fist bobbed under the bed. Some would describe it as a mist or smoke but it was neither. It had no density, it wasn't a thing, but it was here and visible to the naked eye. As Pétur was taken from the room it followed, weaving between legs and furniture. Today was the black mass's first day of existence and it wasn't as quick and limber as it would later become. Most would mistake it for a shadow or trick of the eye if they'd been paying attention. Lucky for the mass, no one was – they had plenty of other things to worry about.

The mass didn't have ears or eyes but it could sense the world around it and absorb what was going on. Being this far away from Pétur made the mass frustrated and scared. It would have to learn to keep closer.

The mass found Pétur being poked and prodded at and wasn't happy that its human was being treated so badly. The big human's faces were screwed up in disgust. They weren't showing him much respect. To the mass Pétur was the most important human in the world – it was because of him that the mass existed in the first place. Without him, the mass wouldn't be here. The mass had to become as intimate with Pétur as his shadow. Wherever Pétur went, the mass would follow. One could never be without the other.

AND SO BEGAN THE TESTS. Otti would never admit it, but he had a paternity test thrown in for good measure. The boy was his.

A month went by and they were no closer to finding a reason for the smell. It was unbearable and Otti did everything he could to avoid his son. He was glad there'd been a viral outbreak so he had an excuse to be at the Chambers all day.

.   .   .

THE MASS soon became a master at knowing when people were coming. It could feel the energy of a person or thing. It didn't worry much about things; it could pass through a cat's paw or a dog's jaw. But it knew humans were much more dangerous.

Pétur was different though. He wasn't dangerous; he was the mass's friend. At night the mass would stay under Pétur's bed, out of sight until necessary. When Pétur was sleeping, the mass would think about the wonderful days they'd had together. Pétur would often play with the mass. His parents said it was Pétur's imaginary friend. They didn't like Pétur or the mass. They would often complain about how Pétur smelled bad or made his mum's flowers die. As the mass grew stronger it learnt new tricks. It was early days but the world was a fun place to be. It had even figured out how to start small fires and make things move. If only things could have stayed that way.

'CURSED?' Erica exclaimed, not believing her ears.

Pétur drank his near-cold coffee, deciding where to begin. 'Yep, cursed. Before I was even born. It's why I'm not an Ottesen. My dad would say he tried, and I mean, I don't blame him, but he could have done more,' Pétur said, indifferent.

'What happened?' Erica asked, transfixed. 'I don't understand.'

'When I was one they sent me to live with my Great Grandmother, or Langamma as I call her, on the other side of Iceland. A place called Hólmavík. They used to visit occasionally but stopped when I was six. The smell was too much, but mainly it was because dad's convinced I'm bad luck. He thinks it's part of the curse. Iceland's outbreak was the start of it.' Pétur didn't want to list the lengthy catalogue of offences he'd been blamed for. It would scare Erica off.

'He can't blame you for the outbreak. That's coincidence. Surely?'

'It's what they believed. Bad luck or bad timing, it was easier to point the finger at me than admit the pack had a weakness.'

'So, this curse, what is it? It's not real. Surely?'

He laughed under his breath, nerves kicking in. It had been a long time since he'd had such a candid conversation about his little problem. 'It's real alright. When I was born there was this smell, like rotten meat. I don't know much else about it. Langamma only told me what I needed to know.'

'Which was..? Or is that it?'

'She said the curse was nothing more than a bad smell. Bad luck doesn't come into it unless you believe in superstitious mumbo-jumbo. It was just a smell. She fixed that so...' He shrugged before continuing. 'She said Mum and dad left me not because they didn't love me, but because they weren't equipped to cope. I was too special for them.' He shook his head, a stupid grin plastered across his face. Oh, the lies Langamma had told to protect him.

'So, why did they only visit now and again? I mean, if your great gran fixed the smell, what was the problem? If it was Georgia I'd bring her home.'

'They didn't want me home; like I say, they believed I was bad luck. The damage was done. As for visiting, well, I was too far away I guess. Dad was always busy with work, he couldn't leave to come see me.'

'And your mum?'

'She had Jóhann, then my sisters, and couldn't drive that far on her own. It was easier for her to fit into dad's plans,' he shrugged. 'I dunno, to be honest, I don't think she ever felt like I was hers. The curse stopped us from bonding perhaps... Who knows?'

'Did you get on with your great gran?'

He smiled, recalling fond memories of his Langamma. 'Yeah, she was amazing.'

'So, they suddenly stopped visiting?' she asked.

'When I was six something happened. They didn't speak to me after that.' He paused, preparing to reveal his final encounter with Jóhann, figuring out how much to share. 'They used to come visit me and Langamma to give us Christmas presents before the bad weather hit, usually in October. Langamma lived in the middle of nowhere, which was good for exploring and stuff – I used to make my own fun. Anyway, Jóhann and I were out playing and I was showing him a frozen lake I'd found.' He looked at Erica to make sure she was listening.

'Uhuh?'

'So, Jóhann is being a dick and one thing leads to another, he hits me, I'm out cold, and the bastard leaves me saying that something scared him.' He was glossing over details, not wanting to share the whole story.

'The more I hear about your brother, the more I like him,' she joked.

'The best part is he left me for dead in the middle of nowhere and I was the one who got in trouble.'

'So what did he say happened?'

'All I know is Jóhann was freaking out big time, shaking and hardly able to put a sentence together. He broke his arm running to Langamma's. Mum and dad took him home straight away and didn't return.'

'Jesus. Did Jóhann ever tell you what he saw?'

'He won't talk about it. Well, that's what my sister told me. He won't even speak to me.'

'Weird. How many sisters have you got?'

'Three.'

'Do you talk?'

'Just Ada and me, she's the youngest'

'What about your mum and dad, now you're older?'

'My mum gets in touch occasionally but I'm not bothered anymore. They don't feel like family. Sorry if that sounds harsh.'

'No, I get it,' she reassured.

'Langamma was my family. And Ada of course, but she's different.' He fished his necklace out. 'Langamma got me this.'

'Aha. And does it work? Does it bring you good luck?'

'Kind of. It's actually the reason you're not repulsed by me. It's enchanted, I think – I don't know how it works to be honest, but it stops the smell.'

He dropped the necklace under his t-shirt, the metal hoop hot against his skin. It often heated up when it was being talked about.

Just another one of its quirks, Langamma would say. He could do without them, especially when it became burning hot around religious artefacts – it was like having a searing hot branding iron on your chest. No thank you.

'So, what's this got to do with being a wolf? How come you're Seelie?' Erica asked.

'The smell, it's my wolf soul. It's dead. So I'm not an *Aumingi* or Seelie like you say. Langamma just made me like one.'

'Ah. And, your gran, is she...?' She trailed off – not wanting to finish, but hoping the intention was obvious.

'She died when was eighteen. Right before I went to uni.'

'I'm sorry.'

'It's ok, she was old.' He fiddled with the necklace before speaking again. 'I thought if I could show them after all this time I was alright and that nothing bad had happened, then mum and dad might at least talk to me. After Langamma I didn't have anyone else, you know?'

'But they didn't?'

'I went to uni in Reykjavík, where they lived, so I tried not long after I moved. Dad wouldn't even let me in the house, never mind talk to me.'

'Wow, so you lived in the same city and he wouldn't even acknowledge you?' she asked, aghast.

'He passed me on the street once. You'd think we were strangers.'

Erica was quiet, gauging how to react. Her relationship with Tobias was rocky to say the least but it was an entirely different thing to be snubbed by your own parents. 'But still, you've turned out ok. Who knows, you could've been like Jóhann if you'd been raised by them,' she winked, lightening the mood.

He laughed. 'God, imagine. The world doesn't need anyone else like him.'

E rica's phone buzzed in her pocket for the third time in ten minutes. She pulled it out and passed it to Pétur, not taking her eyes off the road.

'Can you tell me who that is? They keep calling.'

He turned the phone between his fingers and checked the caller ID. 'Someone called Quinn.' The caller hung up, taking him to the home screen. Three missed calls and one text. 'She says, "No change. Forgot to ask is Georgia ok?"'

Pétur's face creased with concern.

'You'd better text her. Tell her I'm driving but I'll call soon. I think there's a layby coming up.'

ERICA GOT BACK in the car after a long conversation pacing an unknown riverbank. Laybys are as common as hen's teeth en route to Callander, so they pulled off after fifteen frustrated minutes and ended up in an insurance company's car park. The view could have been idyllic under different circumstances.

'Everything alright?' Pétur asked. Erica's face was white.

'No, not really. Sam – a friend's kid – is sick.'

'What's wrong?'

'They don't know.' She recited Sam's symptoms to Pétur. Saying them out loud cemented her fears. 'Sounds familiar, huh?'

'It does. Weird.' He paused, taking the news in. 'God, that's not good.'

'Nope.' She bit her lip and looked towards the river.

'So, why was Quinn calling you? Does she think you can help?'

'Quinn's like a sister to me. Sam's like my niece. She'd called me this morning so was giving me an update.' She rubbed her temples, stress manifesting as a dull ache behind her eyes. 'They're thinking it might be bacterial meningitis.'

'You don't look convinced.'

'I know it's stupid but I keep thinking it's connected to our virus. I dunno.' She laughed nervously. 'I just can't shake this feeling in my gut.'

'Whatever it is, she's going to be fine,' he said, placing a reassuring hand on her shoulder. It was the first time they'd touched since last night and embarrassment washed over Erica before she was overpowered by the sense of dread flowing through her veins. Poor little Sammy.

'Do you think it has anything do with Georgia? They were playing together on Thursday,' she pondered, thinking out loud.

'Did you tell Quinn that Georgia had been ill?'

'I could hardly tell the truth. I said G had a bit of a cold today but nothing serious.'

'I've never heard of a human getting ill from a wolf.'

'Me neither.' Erica sighed, knowing she was clutching at straws. Still, she couldn't dismiss the notion. She'd have to ask Bill.

'WHAT DO you think he's got for you?' Pétur asked as they entered Bill Hammond's garden. The metal gate was old and peeling, hanging squint on its hinges so it was wedged into the paving stones, forcing you to side step in.

'No idea, but knowing my mum it won't be straight forward.' She knocked on the front door and took a step back to Pétur's side.

The house was different in daylight. The front garden was overgrown with tufts of brittle yellow grass rising as high as Pétur's waist. Taller leafy plants towered in sporadic clumps, most were brown but a few had pink flowers at the top; it must have looked like a meadow over summer.

The front door opened to reveal a smiling Bill.

'Erica! I'm guessing you have good news for me.'

SHE HANDED Bill a cup of tea, his gnarled hands struggling to grip the mug. They looked painful.

'You look a lot better today,' Bill said and took a sip.

'It's amazing what a difference a day makes.' She smiled, disguising a grimace, ashamed at the first impression she made last night. Thankfully her face was healed, a little bruised on the cheekbone but you'd hardly have known anything had happened. She took a seat next to Pétur on the couch. She misjudged and ended up very close to him, conscious of the heat radiating from his leg. Normal adults who hadn't kissed the night before wouldn't sit so close together worrying about leg heat – not through choice. She didn't want Pétur to get the wrong impression, so scooted over a few inches, hoping that no one had noticed.

'I can see your Mum in you,' observed Bill. 'You look just like her.'

'Thanks.' She didn't know what else to say, her mind was still slow from the wine and conversation wasn't flowing.

Awkward silence was avoided by the unexpected arrival of a ginger cat on the back of the couch. It took one look at Pétur, hissed, and left the room.

'Don't worry, all animals hate me,' Pétur said, pre-empting an apology from Bill.

'I don't remember seeing a cat last night. Was she hiding?' Erica asked.

'He, and probably not. More likely he was out causing trouble. Fetching me some mice.' Bill studied Erica's face for a moment, as if looking for more similarities. 'You'll be wondering what your mother left you.'

'It had crossed my mind.'

'Don't worry, it's nothing bad.' He laughed and rose from his chair, gripping his cane for leverage. 'At least I don't think so.' He picked up a folded piece of paper from the mantelpiece and handed it to Erica. 'This is the address she told me to give you. The actual gift is in the back room.'

Erica studied the paper; it wasn't an address she recognised. This was already looking like of one of her mother's signature goose chases. *Great.* Still, they almost always lead to something wonderful.

'Do what your mother wants and I'll give you old Misty's address.'

Bill continued, 'You said last night this virus is spread through the water supply. If anyone is up to something, Old Misty will know. That's if he's not involved himself.'

'And, who is Old Misty?' she asked.

'He's a warlock and a miserable old bastard,' he laughed. 'Misty likes to cause trouble, it's how he passes the time.'

'But why would he want to kill us?'

'He won't care who he's hurting. Misty will do anything if the price is right.'

'The price?' Pétur asked.

'He likes to barter; if you've got anything worth swapping he'll cut you a deal. But be warned, he likes to fiddle you if he can.'

'I won't be doing any deals,' Erica said.

'You think that now, but if you're going to find anything out then Misty won't give it away for free.'

'And what makes you think I want to find out who's behind it anyway? Surely that's a job for my uncle?'

'Because Erica, if you're anything like your mother you'll be hell bent on doing the right thing. Which reminds me, let me get your mum's box.' He walked to his back room. They could hear him rummaging.

'Do we want to get involved in this?' she asked Pétur in a hushed tone.

'We kind of already are. It won't hurt to see the guy. You know how bad the outbreak is; if it's not stopped soon more kids will die. And what about Sam? Maybe he can help her.'

'But I cured Georgia, why can't I give Tobias the incantation, let him figure it out?'

'It won't work!' Bill called through from the other room. Erica hadn't been talking as quietly as she'd thought.

She followed the clatter of things being moved and found Bill half-perched on a stool, reaching for a box at the top of the corner bookcase.

'Here, let me help,' she said, reaching up on her tiptoes. It was an old tin container not much bigger than a shoebox, battered, rusty, and dented. It had been decorated with an intricate gold border that was now long faded and flaking off. She tucked it under her arm, forgetting about it. 'Why won't the spell work?'

'It was a Mother's Love incantation. One of the most powerful kinds, as you well know.'

'There's no other way?' Bill gripped her arm as he got off the stool. She felt his bones creak as he manoeuvred himself.

'The virus is too strong. Nothing else would even touch it,' he said.

'And you think this Misty guy is capable of creating a spell so powerful?'

'Probably not, but that's why you need to find out who is.' He walked over to his desk and produced a key from the top drawer. 'For your box.'

She put the key in her pocket for safekeeping and checked her phone as she followed Bill back to the living room. Another text. Bad news – Sam's test results were negative and she couldn't move her arms or legs any more. Erica was forbidden from visiting until they knew it wasn't contagious. Surely they should know what was wrong by now? Viral, bacterial, hell even cancer. Something should be jumping out at them. A kid can't get that sick without an obvious cause.

'Do you think whatever this is could affect Seelie children too?' she asked, keen to dismiss the notion.

'Perhaps, though I didn't hear of it happening in ninety-one. What about in Iceland's '88 outbreak, Pétur?'

Pétur shook his head, shrugged his shoulders.

'But there's a chance, yeah?' She settled herself back on the sofa.

'There's always a chance, Erica.' With a shaky arm he positioned himself in his armchair. It seemed to require a lot of effort – Bill's face wincing in pain as he dropped on to the cushion. At last he continued: 'You need to talk to Misty if you want answers.'

'But, it could happen, yeah?'

He shook his head, not wanting to commit. 'I can't lie and say no. We are able to affect Seelies with magic.' he admitted. 'Misty interferes with the human race in ways beyond what most are capable of. I can't say anymore apart from he's the man you need to see.'

That was that then.

'What is this?' she asked, holding the box up to inspect it more closely. It was light but she could hear its contents sliding around inside.

'It was your mother's. She gave it to me with strict instructions to hand it over when you visited.'

'Do you know what's in it?' Erica asked Bill.

'No idea. You'll have to open it and see.'

She placed the box on her lap and studied it. How did her mum know she'd visit Bill? And what the heck was the address for? She shook it once more for good measure.

'Maybe it's a treasure map and some gold,' she joked. Her mum was the furthest thing from a pirate. It was more likely to be a donation to the local orphanage than stolen doubloons. A little imagination went a long way though – stranger things had happened.

'Come on then, open it,' Pétur said.

She took the rusted key and pushed into the lock. It was gritty, rusted inside as well, and she couldn't turn it. Two attempts and a sore hand later she passed the box to Pétur who was able to unlock it first time.

'I loosened it,' she said as she took it back.

She was hesitant to open it. She placed her hands on either side, thumbs ready to push the lid up, but she couldn't bring herself to do it. It wasn't that the contents would be bad; more that this was a final gift from her mum. Once opened, there wouldn't be any other gifts, and Erica was surprised to feel sentimental.

Pétur, unable to take the suspense anymore, placed a hand on her back and said: 'It won't be anything bad, go on.'

Getting a bit touchy feely there pal. She arched her back, pulling away a tiny bit, and he removed the offending hand. Was he blushing?

She sighed and took the plunge, lifting the lid with her thumbs.

Inside was an envelope addressed to her, a box of Cook's matches, and a photograph of Erica with her parents.

It was her eighth birthday and they'd had a picnic in the park after school. Her mum had asked a stranger to take the picture, much to the worry of her dad. He didn't trust others with the camera; it had been Erica's main gift that year, a Polaroid. She'd been begging for one for ages. Did she still have it? After using it all day on her birthday, she'd banished it to a cupboard because it felt unlucky, a jinx after what had happened that evening.

They looked so happy – the of three of them grinning, her dad holding Erica on his lap and her mum kneeling at his side with an arm draped over his shoulders. *They were happy*. She missed them.

How had her mum got it in here and out to Bill before –

'Is that you?' Pétur asked, interrupting her train of thought. 'It could be Georgia.'

She nodded and put the picture in her jacket pocket. She didn't want to look at it anymore.

She opened the letter.

Her mother's handwriting instructed her to find a hut and included a very detailed map and instructions in case the address wasn't enough. Perhaps this *was* a treasure hunt? But she wasn't to go in, just torch the place.

'She wants us to burn down a hut. Any idea what this is about Bill?' Erica asked.

He looked confused. 'Not a scooby. It's the first I've heard of the place. I know she used to visit me on the way to somewhere, but I never questioned what she was doing.'

Arson didn't fit the mother she knew. 'Is this really from my mum?'

'Positive. She gave it to me before she died and said to keep it safe until you visited. To be honest, I didn't realise it would be so long.'

'I guess we should at least check it out,' she concluded.

The request didn't sit right; there was more to this than her mum was letting on. Only one way to find out.

She got up to leave and thanked Bill again for his help.

'If you need anything, just shout,' she said.

'Don't worry, I won't forget to call in a favour if I need it.' He winked.

Erica was at the door when she remembered she needed to ask him an important question.

'Bill, before I forget again, who lives in your old cabin?'

'My cabin? It's been empty for years. I can't do the climb anymore so I guess it will be in ruin. What makes you think somebody lives there?'

'When I went there last night someone answered the door and they knew my name.'

He looked perplexed. 'Sorry, I have no idea.' He shook his head. 'Perhaps it was a ghost.'

'This should be it,' Erica said as she hopped down to the narrow grassy path, which curved off to God only knew where.

Across the water he could see the island they were crossing to. It wasn't big by any means but it towered out of the water – a thick cluster of trees and no sign of other life. *Great.*

Pétur was standing by the Jeep on a cobbled section by Balmaha's pier. 'You're sure about this?' he asked, watching the loch as it licked the grassy bank. The path couldn't have been more than a foot wide and didn't look like a road well travelled. His palms were already sweating.

'One hundred percent!' she called, already some distance ahead. He didn't have a choice, did he? He jumped down and jogged over to Erica. The small rickety pier came into view. He had a bad feeling before he even saw the boat.

Tied up and bobbing away was a small rowing boat, just big enough for two people. It looked like it was ready for the scrap heap, not for taking them over the loch. The wood looked rotten – split and greyed in parts, its green paint long gone apart from a few mottled sections, exposing it to the elements.

'Can't we just say we did it? Who would ever know?' An idea struck, a compromise. 'Or rent a bigger boat? One with a motor?'

'Pétur, once again, no. The letter said we have to. And we can't rent a boat, it would take too long. We don't have the time.'

A day wouldn't hurt if it meant they didn't sink. What use were they both dead?

'I'll do it on my own if you're scared,' she continued. He shook his head. 'Right, ok. Come here.' Pétur came forward and she gripped his arm before stepping on to the pier, tapping a few beams with her foot. 'I thought it looked dodgy but it's alright.' She let go and made her way to the boat.

Erica lowered herself down to the edge of the pier until she was sitting, legs dangling over to reach the boat, and guided it closer with an outstretched foot. When it was underneath her, she slid in.

Surprisingly, it held. He had visions of her going straight through the bottom. Of course, it might be a different scenario when he was in it too.

She looked at him, becoming impatient.

'Come on Pétur. It's fine.' He stepped on to the pier. The base of his neck was sweating. 'Oh shit, I forgot the petrol,' she blurted. 'Can you run back and get it for me?'

Any excuse to delay getting in the boat. He returned to the car and got the can they'd picked up en route. Erica wasn't convinced that matches would do the job on their own; she was probably right.

'I'm just going to get my hat!' he shouted to her. He made a show of rummaging in his bag despite knowing fine well where it was.

He pulled the hat on, taking a few attempts to get it sitting right, and zipped his jacket up, smoothing it out once, twice, three times.

He couldn't put it off any longer and again found himself on the pier.

'Are you quite ready?' she asked, smiling.

'I don't want to get all the way over there and find I'm not prepared.'

'Come on you dork. Just get in already.' She stood up to help him in, and the boat rocked. 'Ok, not a good idea,' she said, holding her arms out at either side to aid her balance. She sat back down with purpose, reached for the petrol can and placed it between her feet. 'Dangle your legs over and come in. It's easy.'

He sat as suggested and took a deep breath, hands gripping the edge of the pier.

'Can you swim?' she asked.

'Of course. I'm just... It looks rotten.'

'It's fine,' she said and gave it a stomp with her foot. 'Nothing to worry about.'

He realised he wasn't going to get out of this, so took one last lungful of air and pushed himself off the pier, his heart racing as he landed and took a seat opposite Erica.

'You can row, you're stronger than me,' she said, passing him the oars which had been nestled inside the boat. He positioned them in the water as she untied the boat from the pier. This was it.

She swivelled on her seat and pushed them away from the pier. No going back.

Rowing was easy, and Pétur concentrated on the rhythmic motion, controlling his breathing so Erica wouldn't know he was freaking out. He could feel the sweat on his brow – *why did I put on this stupid hat?*

It wasn't long before they were in the middle of the loch. She sat with her hood up, looking past him to the other bank. 'I think I can see it,' Erica announced. Pétur didn't want to turn round, so instead he continued to focus on the rowing and looked at his feet. *It must be deep here.* He caught a glimpse of the loch in his peripheral vision. *Dark. Who knows how far down it goes?*

He took another deep breath and gritted his teeth. His muscles burned as he rowed harder. He didn't want Erica to see him like this. He'd never stand a chance if she knew he was a wimp.

It would be so easy to fall in.

His mouth was dry, while a cold sweat bloomed on his palms and forehead. He fought to focus on the mechanical action of rowing. Anything to keep his mind from wandering to the sensation of water up his nose, a hand around his neck, *from the snares of the devil, deliver us O Lord* and –

A hand on his knee startled him.

'Pétur, are you ok? You don't look good.'

He looked at her, his head bowed down. 'Yeah, I'm fine, tired from rowing,' he mumbled.

She narrowed her eyes, not convinced by the lie. 'We're nearly there.' She squeezed his knee before returning her hand to under her thigh. It was chilly out here. The cool breeze prickled at his damp skin.

A few more strokes and they reached the island's small pier. He couldn't get out quick enough; he didn't even help Erica on to shore.

Pétur took off his hat and rubbed a hand through his hair. It was soaking. He couldn't look at her but knew she was watching.

'Hey, look at me.' She was in front of him, her hands on his biceps. 'Pétur, it's ok.' He raised his gaze to meet hers. 'What's going on?' He couldn't say. 'Come on, let's sit down,' she said as she led him over to an outcrop of rocks. They sat in silence, her head on his shoulder and a reassuring hand on his back. His breath stuttered as he fought to fill his lungs with air.

Five minutes later they were still sitting side by side. Pétur's breathing was nearly back to normal, but he wasn't right. He'd barely spoken a word since the boat started out over the loch and was wringing his hat between white-knuckled hands.

Erica sat with her knees pulled to her chest, arms hugging them. Even with her hood up, the wind nipped at her. It was too cold to sit around outdoors and Pétur didn't look like he'd be opening up any time soon. She was going to have to explore the place on her own.

Her mother instructed they'd find wooden steps near the pier, but the surrounding forest was so thick it was hard to see anything apart from the tiny pebble beach beside them. Smooth round stones crunched underfoot as she walked to the edge of the woods. She took one last look at Pétur (still staring into the distance, no change) and made her way into the trees. A well-worn path hinted at the direction she should go and, sure enough, about ten paces in she could make out the vague shape of steps moulded into the hillside, tatty logs containing each muddy step.

The island was small but of considerable height, forcing the steps to twist and turn up the hillside, following the natural flow of the land, finding the easiest route. They were large steps; the kind that make you wonder if you should take them one by one or bring your feet together on each step. Awkward. She lumbered on, giant strides stretching out her limbs.

Now and again the steps would flatten out to a landing providing a welcome pit stop. On the second landing she looked downhill but could no longer see the start – the trees were too thick. It wasn't so cold here and she was enjoying the shelter from the wind. Unlike the woods last night, Erica could hear birds and wildlife around her, with the occasional chirp or squawk reminding her she wasn't alone.

With sweat beading on her brow, she reached the top.

Through the trees she could see the wooden hut, perched at the summit of the island's biggest hill in a clearing, standing proud like an explorer's flag. It looked no larger than a generous-sized cupboard – more like an outhouse than a dwelling. Facing her, a battered and neglected door and window were squeezed on to the side of the building. Eighteen years of exposure to the elements with no TLC had taken their toll.

The circular clearing was a good fifty feet at its widest, dropping down to a steep hill with dense woods. The hut was bang in the centre, as if its creator had got bored of walking and erected it where they stood. It was so out of place.

Had her mother built it? She couldn't imagine Lucy wielding a hammer and saw. Its position was so random that it must have been built with a purpose, but why not hide it in the forest? Curiosity was getting the better of her.

The window was covered in a thick layer of dirt making it impossible to see in. She pulled the sleeve of her hoodie out from under her leather jacket and attempted to wipe some away. A little peek inside wouldn't hurt anyone.

Cleaning a palm-sized area of glass didn't reveal any instant clues, so Erica put an eye up to the pane, scared at what might be staring back, but it was useless. It was too dark inside. She moved over to let in a little light and looked again. There was something inside. Pictures on the wall? It was hard to tell.

A hand on her back made her jump.

'Sorry, I didn't mean to scare you,' Pétur said, laughing. She hit him on the arm and scowled. 'See anything inside?'

'Not much.' She stood back, hands on hips, and surveyed it. 'I just – I think if we're going to burn it down we should check we've got the right place.'

'She said not to go inside,' he said, cupping a hand to the window and looking in.

'But – '

'What if there's a body or something.'

'A body? My mum wasn't a murderer.'

'Stranger things have happened, Erica. You never know.' It sounded like he was only half joking.

She shifted her weight between her feet. She was thinking.

'If we're torching it, what harm will it do?' she reasoned as she bent down to grab a nearby rock. She didn't give Pétur time to protest before she smashed the padlock off the door. The wood was rotten so it came off with ease, taking a big chunk of door with it.

The hinges were rusted and needed a good jiggle to get going. Erica opened the door from arm's reach, scared at what it might be keeping in. Hovering in the doorway, she could just make out the corner of a desk beside a wire bin overflowing with paper.

'Go in then,' Pétur prompted. He was standing behind her, peering over her shoulder to get a better look.

'Just taking it all in. Gimme a sec.'

She grasped the doorframe with one hand and poked her head in. It was dark and a cloud of dust floated in the single shaft of sunlight created when Erica had wiped the window with her sleeve. It looked pretty.

She inhaled, stalling entry, getting a feel for the place. The air was musty, like the smell that hits you when you open a long-forgotten shed. Satisfied there was no body to be discovered, Erica crossed the threshold. The interior was as tiny as it looked from the outside, but they would both fit in standing.

In the far corner was an old table. It had a wooden chair tucked beneath it and a bin alongside. That was it for furniture. What surprised Erica were the hundreds of notes, photos and diagrams covering the wall. There wasn't a bare inch visible, and some sections were a few layers thick. She flicked through a nearby stack pinned to the wall – incantations, drawings, and detailed notes in an unknown language. Her mum was trying to make sense of something, but what?

She stepped further in and moved her focus to the desk. Pétur followed, his mouth agape as he took in the obsessive décor. The room seemed small with the two of them in it. She'd never been more aware of the negative space between two people as she was now. She moved away, hoping to break the tension – not a sexual tension, but the constriction of words unspoken. An act unrecognised. It would vanish if she mentioned what happened last night, but she couldn't muster the courage to bring it up – not out of the blue anyway. Timing was everything. It would have to wait.

Erica traced a finger over her mum's belongings. An open notebook lay on the table, a pencil resting on the page. It was like she'd popped out just moments ago, mid-sentence.

A candle stood half-burnt on a small copper plate, a thin layer of dust shrouding it. Erica took out her box of matches and was surprised to find the wick light first time. With the added light she could make out more of her mother's collection. Above the desk were two photos: Erica aged seven with her dad, and beside it a wolf that couldn't have been more than a toddler. It was hard to tell who it was in the dim light. It could be Erica, or perhaps her dad at that age? On closer inspection, two brown eyes peered out from behind the mass of black fur, so it must have been her father.

On the corner of the desk was a pile of books. It took a moment for Erica to register what was propped up against them – an envelope addressed to her.

Hesitating, she opened it.

You never did do what I asked, did you?

'How did she know?' Pétur asked. Erica smiled, shook her head and said she'd explain later. Typical Mum.

She slipped the note into her pocket and continued investigating.

'What do you think it all means?' she asked, as she unpinned a small piece of paper that was covered in rushed-looking writing. She recognised a few words from her own incantation book – it looked like a transformation spell.

'Do you think she was trying to become a wolf?' Pétur mused, looking at an anatomical study of a wolf's head.

'Or stop me being one? Or my dad? I dunno. Whatever it was, she was obsessed," thought Erica aloud. "Look at all this stuff.'

She hovered the candle over the notebook, wanting to inspect what was written, but it was no use. Her mother had developed a secret script; the pages were filled with glyphs and symbols she'd never seen before. Annotations were squeezed into the margins along with yet more drawings. Despite her lack of understanding, Erica felt this was something important – especially since each page was dated and seemed to go back a good six years. She couldn't burn what had clearly been a labour of love for her mother.

She unpinned the two photos from above the desk, popped them inside the notebook and closed it. She'd take it home and study it later. Erica then turned her attention to the stack of books on the right of the desk. Moving the candle towards them, a few titles caught her eye:

Mythical Beasts of Europe
Folklore of Scotland
Mythology and Lore: Isle of Skye

She slid the pile over and popped the notebook on top.

'I can't burn any of this. It seems important,' she said, sensing Pétur's disapproval.

'But it's what she wanted Erica. There's more to this than we know,' he pressed. 'She asked for a reason.'

'No, I can't,' she admitted as she pushed past him, carrying the hijacked pile of books. It was a tight squeeze but he didn't try to stop her.

She carried them a safe distance from the hut and placed them on a large rock at the edge of the clearing. She stayed crouched beside them, her muscles refusing to turn and face the hut, to acknowledge what she was about to do.

'Are we ready for this?' Pétur asked as he placed a hand on Erica's shoulder.

She rose but still couldn't turn, emotion getting the better of her. She needed a second to compose herself. His arms wrapped around her from behind and in one seamless motion her body moved of its own accord, burrowing into his chest. She wasn't much of a 'hugger' (bar Georgia, of course); her school friends had all been keen cuddlers and, as such, she'd developed a strong duck-and-swerve technique that would rival the most competent boxer. Anything closer than a foot was invitation only. And yet, here she was.

She wiped away a tear which was threatening to fall, pretending to scratch her face. This was the second time Pétur had pulled this move – her cheeks reddened at the thought of yesterday's emotional outpouring. *Sneaky empathetic git.*

'It's like she's just left,' Erica ventured, feeling the need to justify her mood.

'I know.' Pétur brought a hand to the back of her neck and rested his chin on her head. 'She wanted us to do this though.'

'But it's like I'm getting rid of the last piece of her.'

They stood in silence while he held her, stroking the back of her neck with his thumb. It was a move designed to comfort, not seduce. She was stupid for overthinking everything between them today, second-guessing her actions and feeling guilty, embarrassed to have been such a drunken mess last night. She relaxed; content in the hope that Pétur wasn't giving what had happened a second thought. He'd have mentioned it if it were an issue. She'd rather forget about it too – it was only a kiss after all. There were much bigger problems to worry about this weekend.

She closed her eyes and let out a defeated sigh, her thoughts returning to the task in hand. *Eighteen years.* How had it been so long? Erica thought about her mum everyday, the strangest things evoking memories; a customer's tread resembling her mother's bouncy walk, the smell of a wet wax jacket bringing back their woodland walks or the recollection of a joke they'd shared, out of nowhere thrown to the front of her mind for no good reason other than to upset her.

And there were Georgia's eyes. It was like looking into her mum's.

Tears were welling again. She pulled away from Pétur's embrace, feeling embarrassed that she was making a scene. She'd spent most of her life looking out for herself. Growing up she'd been alone; the odd telephone call with her grandparents in Australia had been the closest she'd got to comfort. If Erica had a problem, it was her who had to sort it out.

Motherhood had softened her. Or rather forced her to be honest and to talk about her feelings. *Jesus, what a foreign concept.*

Talk, it will make you feel better. Years of Quinn's constant nagging were wearing her down. She could already imagine the ribbing she'd get if she ever admitted that.

Erica was glad Pétur was with her, if he hadn't been there she'd have

struggled to carry out her mother's wishes. Final goodbyes were easier when you didn't see them coming.

'Why don't you go back, see if there's anything else you'd like to keep?' Pétur suggested. 'I'll stay here.'

She nodded and let out a huffy sigh. This was happening whether she wanted it to or not.

Erica pulled the chair out and sat down. Leaning back, she crossed her arms, stretched her legs beneath the desk, and closed her eyes. She wanted to feel her mother's presence, something, anything, she could hold on to. Nothing came; it was only a chair and a desk.

She exhaled and relaxed a little, taking her surroundings in for a final time. A quick skim of the wall for anything else important. Nothing jumped out at her.

'How many hours did you sit here? Is this where you were when you said you had *fairy business*?' She asked the hut for answers, but it kept quiet.

Her mother was often away, sometimes for days at a time. It came with being the most powerful witch in Scotland. That was another reason Erica kept quiet about her own abilities, as it meant that no one would ask for her help, develop expectations.

She clicked her fingers, sparking a small flame in the palm of her hand. Waving her palm back and forth, she passed the light between her fingers as if she was a distracted office worker twirling a pen.

Erica smiled. It wouldn't hurt to get her books out when she got home and start practising again. Maybe Bill would be able to jog her memory? It would be fun to practice with someone else.

Her mother made her spend hours working away until incantations and hand gestures were exactly right. Practice time never felt like a chore though, as magic came naturally – it was learning how to control it which was tough. *The devil's in the detail*, as her mum used to say.

After Erica's mother died, she'd shied away from practicing. It hurt too much; it was their special thing. Over time it became a distant memory – she had no reason to use her skills and no one to encourage her to practice. Life in the 'normal' world didn't call for it, aside from conjuring the night sky on Georgia's ceiling to help her sleep, the occasional retrieval of a book or coffee from across the room after she'd sat down, or – a personal favourite – tripping up the odd arsehole customer as they left the shop. That never got old.

She closed her fingers and extinguished the flame.

Spotting a mug filled with pencils, Erica pulled one out and held it as though poised to start writing. It was chewed at the end. She popped it back. Although her head was telling her to keep it, what use did she have for an old bitten pencil? As she put it back into the mug, a triangle of brown caught her eye. Now that the stack of books was gone, she could see the corner of a notebook wedged between the desk and wall.

Erica pushed the chair back. Poking her head under the desk, she pulled out her phone for light in order to combat the pitch black. What's more, she didn't want to touch any unsuspecting spiders by attempting to feel blindly for the book.

She fished it out carefully. It looked a lot older than the notebook that had been on the desk.

It was about A6 size, the kind you might keep in your handbag if you were so inclined, and had been well-loved over the years. The leather cover was worn and tatty at the corners, the spine exposed in places. In the top corner she could see a faint date... It looked like nineteen-seventy-something.

Erica opened it with caution, scared it might fall apart after lying untouched for years, and called for Pétur to come quickly.

Secured to the inside cover with yellowing tape was a note:

Hello Erica, have you found Pétur yet?

'What the hell? How did she know about me?' Pétur asked, gawping at the diary. He was standing over Erica, his hand on the back of the chair.

Like an afterthought, written in a different pen were the words: *hopefully this helps you understand him a bit better.*

Why would Erica need to understand him better? And more to the point, what did her mum know about him?

'I have no idea,' Erica said while she flipped through the pages. It had been a diary, but most of it had been ripped out. Only jagged, tatty frills remained between its pages. Flicking through, she could see the occasional block of writing, while the remaining pages were crammed with drawings, notes and scribbles. This was a much-loved journal; Erica's mum had treasured it over a long length of time. Well, until she'd ripped it to pieces.

Erica got up and pushed past Pétur, hoping to get a better look outside where the light was better.

She opened it to a random page:

10/01/1986

Only a quick one tonight, but it was vivid.

Erica lying on a bed, about 10 years old I think. She was crying (I HATE these ones, so hard when you can't comfort anyone). The room looked bare and dark. None of the telltale signs you'd expect to see in a child's room – pictures, toys, etc. There wasn't much in it apart from a few books. She was hugging her toy rabbit, Mr Hoppity. I'm glad she still has him.

She seemed so sad and lonely. My poor baby.

'This doesn't make any sense. I wasn't even born then, never mind being ten years old.'

It did sound like her bedroom at Tobias's though. A room whose walls she knew intimately; every nook and cranny, every imperfection and nuance, all were ingrained into her memory. She'd spent so many mind-numbing hours staring at them.

And Mr Hoppity! How could her mum already know how important he was? Gifted to Erica the day she was born, Mr Hoppity was an old-fashioned toy rabbit with stiff little limbs. He was just bigger than her hand, long floppy ears included. The toy had provided more emotional support than most people ever did – she wouldn't admit it, but sometimes Erica wished she still had him. He was Georgia's now; a present she hoped would bring her daughter good fortune, an opportunity to hit the reset button on her family's run of bad luck. In hindsight he'd brought as much luck to G as to Erica. Four rabbit's feet aren't better than one.

'What does it say?' Pétur asked, even more eager to hear about the contents of the diary now that Erica's face was screwed up with confusion.

'It's just stories.' That word didn't fit. They were too true. She needed to investigate more. A spot of rain on the page stopped her from going further. 'We'd better read this later, the sky's turning and we can't do this if it's raining.'

She slotted the diary between two of the heavier books and turned her attention to the petrol can, handing it to Pétur.

'Could you do this part?' she asked. 'I don't think I can.' She needed to get over her pointless sentimentality and just bloody burn the thing so she could get back to Georgia. Easier said than done. If she'd been on her own, the task could have taken all day – her mind felt it necessary to overthink and debate each step. *What if it was hiding more secrets?*

Pétur obliged and headed inside.

Erica could hear the sloshing of petrol as he set to work dousing the room. She closed her eyes and sighed, knowing her mum's possessions were already ruined. *Stay strong, keep it together.* Pétur reversed out, making sure everything was covered. There was no going back.

A few splashes round the outside for good measure and he was done.

'You ready?' he asked.

'As I'll ever be.' She paused, a thought occurring. 'Do you think we could get in trouble? I don't want anyone to worry.'

'Not much we can do about it.'

'Not necessarily,' she said and stepped forward.

With a quick wave of her hands, as if she was wafting smoke away, it was done. Not that she could tell, aside from a subtle shimmer around the building's edges, like a halo of diamond dust. Pétur's reaction told her it had worked.

'Where did it go?'

'Fairy magic. Oldest trick in the book.' He narrowed his eyes; looking confused. All he saw was an empty clearing. 'Fairies are masters at hiding,' explained Erica. 'That's why most people can't see them – only those with a touch of fairy magic can.'

'But –' he pondered his question for a second, 'what would happen if I touched it when it's on fire? Would I get burnt?'

'You know, I have no idea.' That was a good question; she'd never attempted arson before, never mind concealed it.

He shrugged his shoulders, content he wouldn't get a straight answer. ' I guess it's now or never.'

She put her hands on her hips and sighed. This couldn't be put off any longer. She took a few tentative steps towards the hut. She wished the rain had come to something but, despite the grey sky, it had failed to materialise.

As a final homage to her mother, she flicked another flame into her hand. This time however, she pulled at it with her fingers, extending it higher until it glowed a good ten inches high in her palm.

Standing a safe distance she threw it into the doorway, igniting the petrol with a hearty *whooooosh*.

She stepped to Pétur's side and he hugged her with one arm. She watched as the flames engulfed the hut – erupting from the bottom, licking the edges and catching the roof. A plume of grey smoke rose to the sky.

It wasn't long before the window blew out with a loud crack, making Erica flinch. Inside was a roaring inferno, fuelled by the masses of paper in such a tiny space.

'It sounds like it's really taking now,' he said and squeezed her shoulder.

'I know.' She watched in awe as the flames danced around the wooden structure, bright orange waves whipping at the dark box. It was mesmerising.

When part of the roof suddenly caved in, it was Pétur's turn to jump. With it came an eruption of dark black smoke which forced her back a few steps.

She stood in silence, watching the hut fold in on itself.

'And wit do ye think yer dain'?' a shrill female voice rang in Erica's ears.

Erica spun around to find thin air, but the annoying fly-like buzzing behind her told her that she hadn't imagined the voice. She turned towards the sound only to be greeted with empty air again.

'What's going on? You ok?' Pétur asked, panicked.

She flung a hand out towards him, a fountain of blue iridescent fairy dust washing over him and gifting temporary magical-sight.

'Can you see it?'

'It dearie? IT?!' the creature shrieked.

Pétur stood motionless, struggling to catch up with the sudden change of pace, before suddenly kicking into life with a yelp.

'To your left, your left!' he shouted, pointing at Erica's shoulder. 'What *is* that?'

She could hear the buzzing but wasn't quick enough to catch the culprit.

'Damn it,' she snapped, annoyed that she was being made a fool of.

'Yiv git nae right bein' here,' the voice chided.

'Hold still – let me talk to you,' Erica pleaded. It was impossible to have a conversation when the other participant wouldn't stay put.

The thing shot to her pocket, grabbed the matches, and flung them into the nearby trees. *Adios.*

'Now, sling yer hook.' It jabbed at Erica's ear lobe – *damn, that nipped.*

Pétur signalled with his eyes where to aim; a quick glance to the right was all it took. The buzzing swayed left to right, trying to cause confusion. Not this time buddy. She listened for a couple of beats before spinning, hands out and ready like she was swatting a fly.

Caught.

'Oi, oi, oi! Let me go ya big malinky,' the tiny thing squealed, surprised to be captured.

'What is it?' Pétur asked, in awe of the creature writhing between Erica's fingers. It seemed to glow and had a sparkling haze around it.

'Stay still, will you? You're going to hurt yourself,' she said to the creature.

'I willnae be dain' anything a malinky asks. Even if yer nae a Seelie cause ye can dust. Doesnae change awthin.'

The thing squirmed, its tiny hands pushing with all its might, struggling to free itself from Erica's grasp.

'Well then, just listen to me. This is my mum's hut and she's asked us to burn it so you've got no right to be interfering,' she informed with authority.

The creature became stationary.

'Yer mam?'

'Yeah, Lucy Hutchinson. She owned it, so it's her choice what happens.'

'Yer Erica!' A grin appeared. 'A cannae believe it's really you.' It couldn't hide the glee in its voice.

Pétur was staring at the joyful fairy. He had no idea how special this moment was. Fairies are naturally crabbit creatures and to see one exhibit any sign of joy is rare.

Erica considered the creature for a moment; she wasn't sure she'd ever seen one so close before. In fact, the only time she'd seen a real life fairy had been so fleeting that she often doubted if they were real at all.

This particular fairy looked like a six-inch-tall, sixty-year-old woman (but was closer to a more realistic fairy age of two-hundred-and-ten) and was wearing a tatty earthen-coloured dress and brown apron. Her top wings continued to flap at a slow speed which wasn't unusual; the gentle beat of a fairy's wings was as natural as breathing or blinking. It happened, consciously or not.

Her long dark hair, dappled with flecks of grey, stuck out at all angles. Had it ever seen a brush, or at least been within a few feet of one?

She stared at Erica, waiting for a reaction. Pétur (the gawping fish) didn't interest her.

'How do you know who I am?' Erica enquired.

'Yer mam talked aboot ye aw the time.'

'She did?' A swell of pride radiated from her belly.

'Aye, a bit much sometimes. Yer mam kid talk the hin' legs aff a donkey.' She pushed down on Erica's hands again. 'I'm sorry dear, but kid ye let me go? Yer squishin' ma bottom wings.'

'Oh right, yeah, sorry.'

She opened her hands, releasing the creature like you might a baby bird. The fairy dipped before coming to hover in front of Erica's face.

'I'm Margaret by the way.' She paused. 'But a guess you could call me Maggie, aw my friends do.'

'Pleased to meet you Maggie,' Erica said, bowing her head a little to show some respect.

Pétur remained quiet.

'Does that malinky work or is he a bit coo-coo?' Maggie said, twirling a finger by her temple.

'He's just not used to any of this.' Erica nudged Pétur in the ribs, knocking him out of his trance.

'Sorry. It's just...' He trailed off. The fairy didn't seem to care and turned to leave.

'Come and hae a cup a tea wi us. Ma husband will be dyin' tae meet ye Erica!' Maggie called.

They followed her into the forest, well off the track that had led them to the clearing. Despite the island's tiny size, they seemed to walk for an impossible amount of time, the forest getting denser with each step.

They turned at a large tree, which was so wide it would take three people to hug it, and Erica got the first glimpse of the fairy village. Her breath caught in her throat and Pétur let out a little squeak. It was like something out of a book.

A tiny stone windmill spun on the outskirts of the clearing and various little buildings, no bigger than doll's houses, protruded from the undergrowth.

In the centre there were rows and rows of plants. To a person it would be little more than an allotment, but to a fairy it was of gigantic proportions – an industrial operation.

'They're ma husband Brian's crops. Biggest fairy farm in all o' Scotland,' she informed them triumphantly. 'Watch yer big malinky feet on 'em mind.'

Erica's eyes were wide, taking the fruitful farmland in. Fairies are experts in growing enchanted produce – a skill made obvious by the thriving plant life before them. There were huge bushels of berries, sprouts standing to attention, a row of bright purple lettuce and a plethora of other nearly unimaginable vegetation. She'd never seen anything like it.

'What are these?' Pétur asked, bending to inspect a row.

'Snupberries,' said Maggie. Unripe strawberries, Erica thought. Maggie was having him on.

'And these?'

'Mucklepine grapes.'

'Wow,' Pétur said in awe.

'Only kidding ya big galoot, those are raspberries. Never seen 'em before?' she chuckled.

Pétur went as red as the berries. 'Erm, yeah, I just thought they'd be something magic, y'know.'

'Best raspberries in the world come fae Scotland. Try wan if ye want.'

He picked one off the bush and fell in line behind Erica as they made their way to a tree. He smiled as the sweet berry burst in his mouth.

Maggie knocked once on the trunk. 'Brian, oy, we've got visitors – oot ye come.'

'Visitors?' came a gruff voice from within.

'Aye, now get yer arse oot here.'

A door appeared at the bottom of the tree and out popped a male fairy, about the same age as Maggie. He was taller and had tatty brown dungarees on. His wild white hair made him look like a hillbilly mad scientist.

'Maggie, wit in God's name are ye doin' bringin malinkies here?'

'This is Erica,' she said, flying to Erica's shoulder.

Brian buzzed to eye level and studied her. 'Erica? As in *the* Erica?'

'The one and only,' Erica confirmed with a smile.

'Well I never.' He smiled and flew over to Maggie, enveloping her in a hug, bouncing with excitement. 'It's really her! And who's this?' he asked, turning his attention to Pétur.

'That's Pétur.'

'Ah, the ither – ' Maggie elbowed him the ribs before he could finish. 'Nice tae meet ye Pétur.' He flew over to Pétur's head and fluttered around him, poking and pulling at various parts. 'And wit are ye?' he asked, not expecting a reply. He hovered, having a good smell of Pétur's hair. 'Maggie come 'ere. Tell me what you think.'

She obliged and joined her husband. 'Oo, now I dinnae ken. Wit is that?'

'Nae a Seelie,' Brian concluded.

'But nae a wolf,' Maggie added.

Brian took another sniff. 'Are ye a zombie?' He didn't look bothered if he turned out to be right.

Pétur laughed. 'Not quite, but I guess somewhere in that realm.' He raised an eyebrow, unsure.

'Well wit ever ye are come an hae a cuppa wi us.' He waved a hand over to some nearby rocks. 'We'd invite ye in but, y'know, yer disgustingly large.'

Erica and Pétur made themselves comfy and waited for their

hosts to return. Clanging, banging and the occasional whelp came from inside the tree.

After a few minutes, the fairy duo emerged holding a human-sized mug between them. It was battered and chipped; its good days were long gone. They dipped and dropped, swayed and tilted as they flew it over; the large object was causing them trouble with balance, and it didn't help that it was full to the brim with liquid. Erica wasn't sure she wanted to know how they'd brewed such a large quantity of tea, but accepted the mangy cup with a smile. It wasn't often that a fairy entertained anyone of her size.

After a second performance of the bizarre balancing act, they each had a mug in hand. It wasn't a bad brew, all things considered.

Maggie and Brian returned with teas of their own and a plate of biscuits – biscuits no bigger than breadcrumbs.

'Sorry about these,' Maggie said, placing the plate on the grass. 'Dinnae hae an oven big enough for the likes of you lot.'

'It's ok, don't worry about it,' Erica said and took another sip of tea. 'So what did my mother do out here?'

'Oh this and that,' Maggie said.

'This and that?' Erica said, wanting her to expand on it.

'Aye, that and this. So wit brings you oot here?'

'Aye, we seldom get visitors these days. Thank God. Well, apart from – ' Brian started to say, before finding an elbow between his ribs again.

'Yes, yes, very unusual we get a visitor,' said Maggie.

'Well, it's a long story,' started Erica. 'It all began with a virus affecting us wolves.' Brian and Maggie didn't look concerned, but she carried on anyway. 'We're trying to find a cure for it. I'm not sure – and I know it's a stupid idea – but I think it's affecting Seelie children too. A friend of mine, her daughter is sick. It might not be the same virus but she's got the same symptoms. Like I said, silly but I think it's connected.' She stopped, she was rambling.

At the mention of a Seelie child being sick the trees and bushes around them shook. In the blink of an eye they were surrounded by a swarm of fairies.

'Tell us mare aboot the sick bairns,' one begged.

'Will they die?' another questioned.

'Will the Seelies be wiped oot?' an older fairy asked, wringing his hands.

They were being bombarded with questions left, right and centre.

'Shh, shhh, quiet,' Erica commanded, raising a hand to emphasis her need to calm the excitement levels. 'One at a time.'

'Tell us aw aboot the suffering,' a middle-aged fellow with a beard down to his ankles suggested.

Erica hadn't expected the fairies' hatred to be so blatant. She knew fairies didn't hide their malice towards Seelies, but not to this extent. Her mother often told her that nothing annoyed fairies more than discovering they'd been depicted as Seelie-loving cheery sidekicks over the centuries. The grudge went back so far that no one remembered how it began, but Seelie moves like that only made it worse. Not to mention how unnaturally large Seelies were. The slur *malinky* was a common jibe at this pet peeve. According to them, even human infants were monstrous in size. *Nothing but greed that*, the fairy elders would say.

Erica felt like she was in the middle of a campfire circle, telling ghost stories in the dark. The fairies were settled around her, cross-legged and eager to hear what was happening on the mainland.

'Please tell us!' a child fairy pleaded.

'Well, like I said, it all started with us wolves. If we catch the virus we'll be dead within days.'

Ooooooo went the crowd.

'But what about the Seelies?' came a voice from the rear.

Was it bad to be indulging the fairies like this? It felt bad.

'I'm not sure I want to talk about this too much,' she confessed.

'Oh no, please!' chimed a chorus of pleading voices.

They'd been more than hospitable; it would be rude not to keep them informed. Just the necessities. Plus, the more they knew, the more likely they were to help.

She took a second to brace herself. The fairies waited with bated breath.

'We're still trying to figure out if it's the same virus,' she continued, her voice serious. 'But first they get a pain like no other in the belly, then a headache like God himself is crushing their skull,' she clutched her stomach then her forehead – she was improvising the symptoms based on the wolves' and Quinn's updates, giving the crowd what they wanted. 'The lucky ones will go into a coma. The rest go stiff and die with their eyes open.' Erica's eyes widened dramatically as she stared into the crowd.

Recounting the symptoms, although embellished, brought home how serious Sam's condition was. Erica's stomach was churning but she didn't let it show. Thank God Georgia was ok.

'So why's that brought ye here then?' the bearded fairy asked, looking truly perplexed.

'We want to save them.'

Pfffft, what?!, why the devil wid ye dae that? yer aff yer heid and other absurdities came from the crowd.

'Why do you hate them so much?' Pétur asked.

'Ach dinnae even get us started,' Brian said, exasperated. He really didn't want to get started on that, he didn't know where to begin and didn't want to look silly in front of a zombie malinky.

Pétur looked down guiltily and returned to drinking his tea.

'I think I know what the answer's going to be, but would any of you happen to know about any enchanted plants that might help?' Erica asked, optimistic but unhopeful.

'Ha!' Brian let out a belly laugh. Other fairies were rolling with laughter. 'Yer hae'in a giraffe. But really dear, impossible to prescribe without kenning wit spell's affecting em.' Brian rose, holding on to his knees as they protested with a loud creak. 'But, figurin' oot if it's related? We might be able to help wi that.'

Erica's eyes widened, excited at the prospect of progress and being able to help Sam. 'Really? How?'

'We keep a record o' enchanted Seelie deaths, hae to after the infamous Seelie-r Killer of 1857. Passed that aff as arsenic poisonings but it wid be a hell o' a lot harder to disguise sumthin like that now,' he said, weaving through the seated fairies, 'Hae to keep an eye on things; prevention is better than cure.' A murmur ran through the crowd, it sounded more like agitated frustration than agreement. 'Just gimme a moment.'

Brian cleared the throng of watchful listeners and marched to a nearby tree. Why hadn't he flown? Too much effort for a short journey? Or, more likely, he was taking his time to make a point. They were malinkies worth giving time to.

He knocked on a door not much taller than Erica's ankle. No answer.

'Doctor Piobar, a moment o' yer time if ye will,' Bill said, knocking again.

The door creaked open.

'Wit is it?' the doctor snapped, not happy to be disturbed. 'A wis sleepin' Brian. It's ma day aff.'

'A ken Arlen but a moment please.'

'Wit's it worth?' he stepped into the forest clearing, giving Erica a better view of the disinterested doctor. He was younger than expected, with the looks of a malinky thirty-year-old and a thick head of dark hair that was messy from sleeping. His long, crumpled nightgown further confirmed that they had indeed woken him up. No wonder he was miffed.

'Al owe ye a dram, how aboot that?'

The doctor thought. 'Tae,' he bargained.

Brain thought. And thought. 'Aye, awright. Tae drams.'

'Gid man. Wit is it then?'

'Erica,' Brian said, signalling over to her and Pétur. 'Eri – '

'Erica? As in Lucy's daughter?' the doctor asked, his mood improving.

'Aye, wan and the same.'

Arlen gathered his nightgown to knee height and ambled over. He studied her before letting a smile take over his lips. His eyes twinkled as he flew level with her face.

'Erica! It's really yersel,' he beamed, flying into her neck and squeezing tightly. She'd never been hugged by a fairy; it was gentle and rough at the same time. His wings tickled her chin. 'I wis there when ye were born. Such a shame,' he cleared his throat, his eyes losing their sparkle, 'such a shame aboot yer mam.'

'Thanks,' she said, unsure what the normal response to that was. Eighteen years of practice don't make perfect.

'Ma God, ye've grown,' he said flying back to beside Brian. 'A bit much,' he added under his breath.

'So, can you help?' she asked, hoping to steer the conversation back on track.

'Aye probably. Fir three drams. Wit dae ye want me tae dae?'

'Yer a cheeky beggar Arlen Piobar.' Brian placed a hand on the doctor's shoulder like a proud father. 'Erica's wantin tae ken if there's been a spike o' Seelie deaths. Enchanted like.'

'Ah noo. I ken that aff the tap o' me heid,' he said, tapping his temple, 'there is. Has been for the last seven or so months. Nuthin tae dae wit us though.'

'I didn't think it was,' Erica interjected, afraid Arlen would take offence.

'A' ken. Dinnae worry. Dae ye need to see the books?'

'No, no. I don't think so,' she paused, thinking. 'Unless you can tell us what's causing it..?'

"Fraid not. If it's nae us we dinnae go any further, just the basics and that's it.'

'How do you know about the spike?' she asked, finishing her tea and setting the empty mug on the grass.

'We've got a mannie on the inside. Keeps us in the loop. If it's tae dae with magic we ken.' He shot the other fairies a warning glare, in case they had any ideas.

'Have you told anyone about the spike?' Pétur asked.

'Na,' Brian said. 'Not oor job tae hae the Seelie's backs. Like Arlen said, if it's nae us we dinnae get involved.'

Erica ignored the connotations of that. 'And what about in '91, was there a similar spike then?'

'Oh Jeez. Yer gain' back. Lemme check,' Arlen said and flew to his tree. He disappeared through the door.

'Does anyone else monitor Seelie deaths from magic or is it just you?' Erica asked, the idea of Tobias knowing about the spike but keeping quiet occurring to her.

'A dinnae see why not. The point is though, Seelies shouldnae make 'emselves so darn easy to kill. Wouldne hae this problem then.'

'Are they easy to kill?' Pétur asked, sipping his tea.

A chorus of *oh yes, of course* and a few too many pre-planned killing methods erupted from the crowd. Pétur nodded, not wanting to hear more.

Arlen returned, a leather book in his hands. Half-moon glasses were pushed to the edge of his nose, making him look quite the part.

'''91 wis it?' he asked.

'Yep, that's it,' Erica confirmed.

'Aye, similar spike.' He turned the book towards her to show the data. The writing was miniscule and far too small to read but she nodded anyway. 'Nae as lang but similar.'

'You've really no idea what it is?' she asked, hopeful that their 'inside man' had provided more info. 'Or if it's even the same virus as '91?'

'That's a hard one lass, but ye see this?' He pointed to symbols no bigger than full stops. She nodded regardless. 'Well, that means it's magic. Orally ingested, undetectable spell. So same method with baith spikes,' he said, flipping between dates, attempting to show her. 'Could well be the same in '91 as it is noo. It's no often we cannae detect at least the nature o' the spell. Lumio, telica, venpotio, et cetera.'

'So, you still can't help?'

'I'm sorry lass. I ken this means a lot to ye but it's oot o' oor hands.'

Erica smiled, understanding. 'Don't ask, don't get.'

'Nae a truer word spoken,' Maggie agreed.

THEY TRUDGED through the forest and back to the clearing after staying another half an hour. Erica smiled to herself. Say all you want about fairies, they can be lovely hosts when they want to be.

Brian and Maggie had insisted they take some cuttings. 'Yer mam wid want ye to ave these,' he'd said, thrusting a load of clippings at her. Pétur was acting as packhorse.

She turned round in time to see him picking at an enchanted marrow, a long yellow thing bigger than his forearm.

'Don't you dare eat that Pétur. It'll make your eyebrows fall out.'

He drew his hand back.

Brian had promised to get in touch the next time he was on the mainland, delivering his goods. She'd have a full witching pantry in no time – if Pétur didn't scoff it all first.

Back at the hut clearing, Pétur placed their bounty by the stack of pilfered books and stood by Erica's side, awaiting further instruction.

'Help me put this stuff in the boat.' Erica sighed, she didn't want to be here any longer. The hut was now a smouldering heap; it wouldn't survive much longer before burning itself out. She could feel the beginnings of a bad mood. 'Sorry for snapping, that was just a bit intense,' she admitted as they turned to leave the hut's remains. This wasn't his fault.

He half-smiled, showing he understood.

They walked down the muddy steps without talking, Pétur carrying the books, Erica the plants.

He loaded the boat first, settling in at the far bench.

'Oh, so I'm pushing us off, am I?' she said with a grin. She was only half-joking – the journey across had told her that Pétur wasn't a fan of getting his feet wet.

A phone call to Bill and her mobile's GPS told them that Misty's was over an hour away. Erica's flat was much the same distance thanks to the twisting roads of the National Park, so they found a local hotel to eat in before heading to Georgia's bedside. Plus, they wanted to read more of the diary out of the sight of an inquisitive child. Given what Erica had read who knew what its remaining pages hid?

They settled on a village called Drymen, the only place of any notable size they'd passed through, and wandered into the first eatery they saw. Erica didn't have any patience left to be picky.

Pétur stood at the bar and watched Erica as she relaxed into the armchair beside an open fire. She pulled out her phone and tucked a loose piece of hair behind her ear before making a call. She traced shapes on the diary cover, biting her bottom lip while she waited for an answer.

She looked gorgeous, despite only being in a simple grey hoodie, worn jeans and mud-stained trainers from the night before.

Should he bring up last night? Something had to be said. Tension had hung between them all day, with each waiting for the other to address what had happened. Yes, they were drunk, but he wasn't the type to let these things go. You didn't kiss people and forget about it. Did he want anything to happen again? He didn't know, he was Georgia's uncle (did that make it odd?) but he couldn't deny that he was attracted to her.

He'd been looking at her for a while. *Verging on creepy, Pétur.* He realised he should be making more of an effort to get drinks, so turned his attention to the bar. It was busy, a mix of locals and tourists. The foreigners (himself included) far outweighed the Scots, with accents from around the globe cutting through the noise.

Pétur rested his arms on the bar and tried to make eye contact with the barmaid. She was distracted by another patron but was clearly trying to get out of the conversation to serve others; every time she went to move away – body language already signalling her mind was at the other end of the bar – the man would start up again and ask another question.

'I'm going to have to serve other customers now, Connor,' she said and turned before he could protest. 'Now, what can I get you gents? Who's first?' she asked looking at Pétur and the man beside him.

'I think this young lad was here before me.' The man answered with an American drawl, throwing a thumb in Pétur's direction. He said 'lad' like it was an exotic word he'd just picked up today.

'No, no. After you, I'm fine to wait.'

'Why thank you. One double Glenmorangie and a white wine.' He pronounced the whisky as if attempting to hold marbles in his mouth. At least he was trying; some of the linguistic butcherings in Iceland were far worse. Pétur's surname name proved difficult for English speakers – the double 'l' being their downfall, the breathy 'tst' noise causing trouble – if they even realised they were saying it wrong to begin with. On that note, did he pronounce Glenmorangie right, or did he just think he could? He'd ask Erica later.

'That's not an accent from around here.' The American said, interrupting his train of thought.

'Correct. Iceland to be exact.'

'Oh awesome! We had a layover there on the way here. Lovely country.'

'Thank you, we do our best.' Pétur smiled, not wanting to encourage small talk. The last two days had sapped him of energy.

'What brings you here then? Holiday?'

'Kind of. That and family.' He cocked his head in Erica's direction.

'Ah, your wife?'

Pétur laughed under his breath. 'No, she's just a friend.'

'But you have Scottish relatives?' He handed over a ten pound note for his drinks.

'A niece.'

'Aw man, that's so cool. I've got to say this is one of the most beautiful countries we've been to. We'd love to have relatives here.'

The barmaid passed the man his change and turned her attention to Pétur. 'And for you?'

'A can of Irn Bru and a pint of the IPA here,' he said patting the tap badge nearest him before he turning to his new friend. 'Have an awesome trip here anyway, I'll talk to you later.'

Returning the sentiment, the guy took his cue to leave.

'OK, DARLING. I LOVE YOU, BYE,' Erica said as Pétur placed her drink down. 'Georgia, on the ward's phone – she sends her love,' she offered as an explanation.

He sat opposite and got comfy. 'She's doing ok?'

'Yeah, I feel bad for leaving her though. I got her loads of books and stuff this morning, but she sounds bored out her mind. I hate leaving her on her own.'

'I'm sure she'll be ok for another hour, plus she's been through a lot – she'll have slept for most of the day.'

'It's almost hard to believe it happened.'

'It's like a dream isn't it?'

'Speaking of which,' she said, her eyes growing wide as she sandwiched the diary between flat palms, 'shall we read some more of this?'

'Oh, go on then,' he said, pretending not to care.

'I guess we should start from the beginning. Yeah?' She opened it to the first page and read.

Pétur took in his surroundings, waiting for her to give him the gist. The pub had quintessential Scottish décor – stone walls decorated with stags' heads, spears and shields, with tartan carpet and upholstery to match. It was tasteful though, and very, very cosy. He imagined that the occasional lock-in happened from time to time.

Erica remained silent; he decided to take matters into his own hands and moved his chair alongside hers. 'If you're not going to tell me what it says, I want to read it too,' he said, smiling.

'Sorry, I'm just trying to take it all in.' Erica turned the book so it was angled between them. 'So, it begins in nineteen-seventy-six going by the dates.' She pointed to the top right of the page where the date was. 'Which would make her fourteen. But I think this is the start.'

'What do you mean?'

'Well, it sounds like she's always had these dreams,' explained Erica, 'but this is the first time she realised one's come true, so she's going to write them down after this.'

'Come true?'

'Yeah, kinda like a premonition, I guess.'

'Like a psychic?' he said furrowing his brow, sceptical.

When it came to Georgia's power, Erica was learning as they went along. Erica's mother seldom spoke about her own Gift. What Erica knew came from secondhand information, hearsay and general chit chat in the years after losing her parents.

It wasn't uncommon for witches to have some divination power, but it was usually conjured by means of crystals, scrying mirrors, potions and even the clichéd crystal ball.But Lucy had something special. She didn't need anything to see picture perfect visions of the future.

It was news to Erica when Georgia was old enough to explain about her visions and how clear they were, telling her that Gran was helping her tame her skills. According to the diary this wasn't a phenomenon you could turn on and off. Visions would come, wanted or not.

Soon after Georgia was born, Lucy told Erica she mustn't worry about her daughter's gift, it had been a fleeting conversation and with so much going on she hadn't given it a second thought. She'd taken her mother's word and put it down as another part of their lives they could box up and forget about. But it would seem this was a lot more serious than she'd been led to believe.

'She's seeing the future. This explains so much.' She placed a hand over her mouth and leaned in, analysing page two.

'What do you mean?'

'You're going to think I'm crazy, and believe me, I used to think the same thing, but Georgia talks to her too.' She took a sip of drink. 'Ever since mum died, we've spoken to her through our dreams.'

'Ok...' Pétur was looking cynical again.

'Honestly, full-on conversations – that's how I found Bill Hammond. She told me to go. I wondered how she knew so much.'

'So you think she's seen into the future through her dreams? But how is she still talking to you?' he asked. 'She's dead,' he added in a hushed tone, like it might have been a secret.

'I mean, this isn't a shock,' she revealed, motioning to the diary. 'I knew Georgia had the same divination powers, and she's told me she sees things that happen, it's the after-death part that confuses me. It made perfect sense that she could see the future when she was alive, but I've never heard of being able to communicate through other people's dreams. The answer must be in here. Hopefully.'

'Have you asked her how she does it?'

'I did, years ago. She won't tell me. She says not to worry about it.'

She flicked forward a few pages while Pétur craned his neck to read. She was going too fast so he gave up and enjoyed his beer.

His pint finished, Pétur asked if the diary included anything about him.

'Maybe. Your name's mentioned on a few pages – nothing interesting though.' She flipped back a few pages. 'Like here, she says "I'm worried about Pétur. Does he remember what happened? Does it affect him later on?"' She returned to where her fingers were keeping place. 'Here she's worried about a boy. Do you think it could be you?'

This caught his attention and he sat up, pulling the book towards him. The beginning was missing, the previous page only hinted at by a tatty edge in the centre of the book.

Perhaps it's happened?

Today he sat in the woods and cried. He cried in silence on a rock, his tiny shoulders heaving as he sobbed.

He cried so much he was sick – on all fours, vomiting into a bush.

Such a sensitive little boy, he needs his family, he's only little.

He returned to the rock and pulled something out of his pocket. He inspected the bounty in his hand. Enchanted forest mushrooms. Enough to kill.

God, please don't do anything silly.

He was poised to bring his hand to his mouth when: 'Psstt, over here,' came a whisper so soft it may have been spoken by the wind itself.

He shoved the mushrooms back in his pocket, eyes wide at being caught. He looked around, unsure if he'd imagined it.

'Over here,' came the voice again.

His ears pricked up, trying to pinpoint the source. He looked around in vain. There was no one.

'Follow my voice,' it said. It had a silky tone and lengthened its syllables in a way that made the sound flow through him; around him.

His eyes narrowed, unsure if he should venture after the voice. He was considering it.

'Come on, it's fine. Come find me.'

'I'm not allowed to talk to strangers,' he blurted.

'It's ok. I'm a friend' (I wonder who it was?).

'You are?'

'Yes, now come.'

He thought for a second. 'No. Leave me alone.'

The sound of snapping twigs signalled that something was coming towards him. He hid behind the large craggy rock he'd been sitting on and peeped over the top.

A man emerged from the trees. He didn't look much older than thirty and was wearing a t-shirt emblazoned with the word 'Nirvana', baggy jeans, and those monochrome trainers all the skaters wear. He looked a bit old for skateboards, but each to their own. I'd never seen him before.

He'd better not be here to harm my boy.

'I know you're hurting,' the man said, the same soft voice as before. He

was met with silence so continued: 'I also know what really ails you.' He
paused, hopeful that the conversation could carry on face-to-face. No luck.

Fuzz's eyes were as wide as saucers. He turned to duck further behind
the rock, his back to it and his knees to his chest. The man would have
surely known he was there, but he maintained his distance.

The man spoke again. 'What is scaring you is the fear of being alone.
You think you're an outcast, a freak with no family. Well, I just wanted to
tell you not to be afraid. Everything will be ok. I promise. Now, come to me.
You don't have to be alone when I'm around.'

How did he know? Was he like me? Could he see the future? How odd to
have a stranger know so much. Thank God he'd got there before Fuzz had
done anything silly.

He looked genuine enough, but there was an uneasy quality to him –
something didn't add up. Maybe it was his lopsided smile or the way he held
himself, he looked uncomfortable. I was frightened for Fuzz, regardless of
the well-timed intervention.

Fuzz let out a sob and the man moved towards the rock. I woke up.

'DID THAT HAPPEN?'

'Not that I can remember, but they sound young. Although it sounds like something I wouldn't forget. Why is she calling him Fuzz?'

'Apparently it's a nickname for you. I've not really figured that out yet, Georgia just told me it's what her uncle's called in the future. She says it's not right… But you're the only uncle so it has to be you.' She shrugged and Pétur responded with a look of indifference, so she changed the subject. 'What do you think she means by *Perhaps it's happened*?'

'That thing with Jóhann I guess? I don't remember crying after though. And I definitely didn't try to kill myself.' He pointed to the drawing of a wolf's head underneath. 'And I don't know what a wolf has to do with that.'

'Hmm, well the bits with me in have been right so far. It's so odd she knew this before she died, so much mucked up stuff. Every detail of it – makes me feel a bit sick that she saw it all.'

'Like what?'

She flicked through, looking for something she was willing to share that would illustrate her point. Passing the book to Pétur, she said: 'I can't watch you read that. I'm off to the toilet.' Erica upped and left.

05/11/94

Erica was lying on a sofa in a room I didn't recognise. She was restless, tossing and turning. She's much the same now, thinking too much before she goes to sleep. It keeps her up.

It's dark but a thin chink of light is shining on to her, illuminating her silhouette. She has a blanket and a proper pillow. She must be staying here.

She turned and rubbed her eyes, before covering her face with her hands and letting out a heavy sigh.

Erica: Shit, this is hard.

She looks young – 16 or 17?

She flipped the blanket down and pulled up her t-shirt to reveal a noticeable bump.

A baby? This young? It's so hard to imagine. She's only little now, asleep in the bed beside me after a bad dream.

She tried a smile but failed, then bit the corner of her bottom lip; she does that when she's stressed. She looked at her belly, running a hand over it.

Erica, whispering: Baby, are you awake? Give me a kick if you are.

I could make out movement at the top of her bump as the baby kicked.

She smiled.

Can't sleep either, huh?

It was only then that I noticed her eyes were puffy, like she'd been crying a while.

I wished I could go over to comfort her but as usual I couldn't move from my viewpoint. I willed myself to wake up. It was too painful. She was so sad, I could feel it.

She sniffed and looked at her stomach once more, a hand resting at the side, her thumb stroking it.

You'll be a week overdue tomorrow. Is that why you can't sleep? Are you worried about meeting everyone?

She shut her eyes, a tear rolling down her cheek. She composed herself before talking again.

Me? I can't sleep because I'm thinking about you. I know I've told you about what's going to happen, but now I'm...

She stopped, her breath stalling as she fought tears.

...give me another kick if you want to play a game.

She paused, watched her belly. Another kick came.

Good girl. I need you to think about what you want. Do you want to stay with me, or do you want a new family – the one I told you about? Close your eyes and think really hard. Have you got that? Good. I need you to make a wish. I'll do it too.

She closed her eyes.

Wish for who you want to be with and then, with all your might, ask the universe to send us a sign if you want to be with me. A nice clear sign, something obvious.

She smiled before opening her eyes and letting out a quiet laugh.

You're right, I should tell you more. It's only fair, I've told you so much about who your new family might be, I need to give myself some airtime.

She pushed herself up, repositioned the pillow then got comfy again.

Well, I know I told Quinn earlier that I didn't have a name for you, but that was a little white lie. You're allowed to tell them sometimes, don't worry. So, I'd call you Georgia and we'd stay here for a while I guess. Quinn says that's ok because I'll get my inheritance money soon... I'll explain about that later... Anyway, hopefully, it will be enough to put a deposit on a flat, a place of our own. Holly – Quinn's girlfriend – she's going to give me a job in her shop when I'm ready. Making coffee. Could be fun. You'll like Holly and Quinn. They're amazing.

She cocked her head and studied her bump again. Her hands ran over it in slow circles, feeling her baby move. When she spoke again there was a new, deeper sadness to her voice.

You know, I don't have much but I think we could make it work. I might never be the best mummy in the world but I'll always try my hardest for you. That must count for something.

She turned to her side; pulling her t-shirt down and the blanket over her.

Keep wishing until you go to sleep. Think nice happy thoughts about where you want to be, and the universe will listen.

She lay for a few minutes, staring into the darkness and wiping away the occasional tear.

At last she closed her eyes and relaxed.

Night Georgia. I love you.

AFTER FEW MINUTES ERICA RETURNED. He didn't know what to say so avoided the content of what he'd read. He was dying to know what the sign had been but resisted asking; no doubt it was a touchy subject.

'Do you think she knew they were – what's the word again?'

'Real? The future? Premonitions?'

'Premonitions, yeah.'

'I think so; she seems very matter of fact. After one came true, I think she wanted to keep a record of them.'

'Why didn't she try and stop any of it though? She keeps saying how sad we are.'

'That's a good question.'

'And why do you think she kept these specific ones? Most of them are short and pointless, then there are ones with the corners turned down. Why those?'

'Your guess is as good as mine.' She laughed. 'I know just as much as you.'

Very little stood out; innocent looking doodles, nothing significant. He flicked to the next dog-eared page. A cold chill ran down his spine.

'How far have you read?' he asked, panicked.

'Not that far, why?'

'I don't want you reading this.'

'After what I let you read, I think it's only fair.' She smiled and went to take the book from him; he slid it out of her reach. She didn't know how serious he was.

'I mean it Erica,' he snapped.

She looked at him, to establish if he was playing or not. He read the first few lines again, gauging if he even wanted to risk her looking later. No. He ripped the page out.

'Pétur!' she shouted and made a grab for the book, but he was too quick. The couple at the table opposite looked at them.

'I'm sorry but I can't...' He stuffed the page into his pocket. She was outraged but there was concern in her eyes too. 'There's some stuff about me I don't want you to know yet.'

'So it's definitely you?'

'It looks like it.'

SHE RETURNED WITH MORE DRINKS, a second round after their food, and a dram of whisky. Was she trying to get him drunk? Take advantage of him? He was happy to play along.

'Now what do you call this?' She slid the dram towards him.

'Glenmorangie,' he replied in a favourable attempt.

'Not bad. And you're Gallison?'

'Nearly. Still needs work.' He smiled and inspected the whisky, giving it a sniff. 'I think we should half this.'

'No way, I can't stand it.'

'This one or all whisky?'

'All whisky, it's vile.'

'Call yourself Scottish,' he scoffed. 'Oh, go on. For old time's sake.'

'You've had too much. I've only known you a day.'

'We all have to start somewhere.'

He took a gulp of the brown liquid, his top lip curling in. How could people drink so much of this stuff? And for fun no less! He passed the glass over to Erica.

'I've had a thought. I'm driving, can't do it.' She slid the glass back to him. His features flinched as he finished the dram. He stuck out his tongue in disgust, grabbing her hand on the edge of the chair and making a mock-gagging noise. 'Happy?'

He'd grabbed her hand as a joke, to exaggerate his disgust, but now they were skin to skin he was hyper-aware of their unspoken issue. He froze, working up the courage to look her in the eye and bring up the subject of last night, when a familiar voice piped up.

'You look like you're having a good time.' The American.

Pétur turned to face him; a tall man in a checked shirt tucked into his belted jeans, with a lady who Pétur presumed was his wife.

'You inspired me to get a whisky.'

'And the lady's not too keen I see,' he chuckled.

'It's horrible,' Erica confirmed.

'Now there's a good Scottish accent, are you from round here?' His voice rose at the end of each sentence, making him sound excited about everything.

Erica's accent wasn't what Pétur would call a strong Scottish lilt. It was gentle, and he wouldn't have thought she was from Glasgow, expecting that to be a harsher sound – *Weegie*, was that the right word? Hers was nice; he could listen to her talk all night.

'Bearsden, Glasgow, so not far I guess.'

'Glasgow? We went there. Didn't like it as much as Edinburgh.' His wife patted his arm, scolding him for being so honest.

'I think you're either one or the other. Few people love both,' Erica conceded.

Pétur was still holding her hand so loosened his grasp. She didn't acknowledge the move. The chance to mention last night had passed – he'd have to wait until later.

'Now, are you married?' asked the woman. 'I can spot a happy couple when I see one. I have to admit, I've been watching you from across the bar and you folks look so elated,' the wife ventured. Pétur's cheeks reddened. *Embarrassing.*

Erica laughed. 'No, not at all. I have a daughter, Georgia. He's her uncle.'

'Georgia? Oh my goodness! Jack, would you hear that?' She tapped her husband on the arm again; ignoring the fact she was wrong about them being a couple. She had the same upbeat accent. 'We're from Georgia.'

'As in the state not the country, I'm guessing,' Erica confirmed with a smirk.

'Of course,' she said, laughing. Pétur was losing interest in the conversation so began to flip through the diary. He wouldn't usually be so rude, but the whisky was already having an effect.

'What a coincidence. I've never been.' He could tell by Erica's tone that she too was wishing the couple would leave. Did she want to talk about last night?

'Oh my, you should go one day. It's beautiful. Not as beautiful as here, but still gorgeous.'

'Maybe, one day.'

'Georgia is a wonderful name as well. Here, you could call the next one Savannah, that's where we're from.'

Erica chuckled. 'No more kids for me, I'm done.' She raised her hands in mock surrender.

The guy picked up the end-of-conversation-vibes and turned to his wife, linking an arm with hers. 'Come on Emily, let's leave these two alone. They've got more whisky to enjoy. Y'all have a good night.' He winked and guided his wife away.

'Of course, we'll catch y'all at breakfast,' his wife chimed in with a small wave goodbye, assuming they were staying in the hotel. Wrong again.

Assuming makes an ass out of you and me. Pétur continued to skim read the diary, hoping Erica would be the one to bring up last night. He'd lost his courage. A page near the end caught his attention and he opened the book wider, holding it in one hand while the other hand found his pint of beer.

'There's no bloody way I'm calling my kid Savannah,' Erica said when the couple were a safe distance away. She laughed, expecting a reaction from Pétur, but he was too engrossed in reading, his lips moving with each word.

He had heard her though. 'Maybe not, but you'll call your son Trevor.' He looked her dead in the eye before continuing, a smile on his lips. 'And you're going to marry my brother.'

❀

10/04/1998

Another long one tonight, and one of the most vivid yet.

I was sitting at the bottom of a king size bed, Erica was in front of me. Propped up with pillows, knees bent, she was focused on something in front of her but I'm not sure what.

It was a nice room – big and tastefully decorated. There was a monochrome floral design on the wall behind her; I noticed it straight away because when the light caught certain bits it reflected like metal. Very fancy. The light was dim, only two side lamps lit the room.

There were white sheets on the bed and I could make out a bathroom to my right. At first I thought it might be a hotel room but then I spotted a picture on the bedside table next to Erica, a photo of her and Georgia (I presume).

Erica had her hair down, swept to one side. It was so odd to see her with it down! She looks beautiful; I can see Raf in her. The smooth jawline and charming smile. She has my blonde hair but that's it.

I'd say she was about 30. She had on a maroon zipped hoodie and loose black joggers, she looked tired. There was an air of stress about her but I couldn't put my finger on it. She was smiling but I feel she was worried – she kept biting her bottom lip for a start.

She picked up a glass of water from her bedside and took a sip. She had a white hospital band on her wrist. I hope she's ok.

Her attention moved back to whatever was on her lap.

She was smiling, in awe. Her hands playing with whatever was there.

I saw a tiny fist poke above her knee. She was playing with an infant.

A knock at the door made her look up.

'It's open.' She said, before the door swung open behind me. 'Hey G.'

A young girl climbed on to the bed and shimmied in beside Erica.

The girl looked so like Erica! It's Georgia for sure. About 11 years old? It's scary how much they look alike; she looks like the Erica I know today.

Erica looped an arm around her and she cuddled into her mum.

'Uncle Fuzz is coming up the drive. Diane looks well pregnant.' She said and stroked the baby.

Erica laughed. 'I wouldn't say that to her face.'

'What? It's true. She looks more pregnant than you now.'

'Yeah, but, everyone's different. Just... Urgh, I'm too tired for explanations.' She crossed her eyes, pulling a silly face, and made Georgia laugh.

'Do you think you and Dad will have as many kids as Uncle Fuzz and Diane?'

'Let me get over this one first, G. Way too soon for that question.' She smiled and planted a kiss on her daughter's head.

'Oh, I found this on the bathroom floor.' Georgia passed her a small object. A ring, I think.

Erica took it, examined it.

'That's your dad's, you'd better give it to him.' She passed it back. 'Hey, can you do me a favour and see what he's up to? He's been in there ages.'

'Yep, sure,' Georgia said and scooted down the bed. She was so close to me.

'Oh, and one more thing, can you pass me a hairband? Mine broke.'

Georgia headed to my left and lobbed a band at her mum who caught it mid-air. Erica brushed her fingers through her hair, scraping it back before tying it in a messy bun.

Behind me I heard a faint conversation.

'Can't lose that, my wife would kill me.' A man with an accent, Swedish maybe?

Erica didn't have a wedding band on. She probably took it off when she was pregnant. I know I had to.

I sensed someone behind me, I heard the door opening.

'What's up?' The bouncy accent again.

'And what have you been up to?' Her eyes lit up at the sight of her husband.

'What do you mean?' he laughed.

'I can hear you boshing about in there. You're up to something. Why aren't you coming in?'

'Because then you'll know what I've been up to.'

'Hmm. Now I'm even more worried.'

'All with be revealed, don't worry. How's Trevor?'

'Babe, be careful. It'll stick.' She smiled, shaking her head.

'It's what the universe wanted. We can't change that.' I can hear the grin in his voice; he's enjoying winding her up. She laughed,telling him to get lost.

For what it's worth, I like the name. Trevor has a nice ring to it.

Footsteps grew closer, someone is coming upstairs. I hoped it was Fuzz; I couldn't wait to see him, see how he is. But I didn't get the chance because I woke up.

'THERE'S no hope in hell I'm calling my son Trevor!' Erica called to Pétur. He was getting changed in the bathroom, while she was propped up in bed, on top of the sheets, and reading the diary. Her sofa wasn't made for sleeping on, so they'd agreed to be civilised adults and share, no mention of last night, thank God. Case closed. With only a t-shirt and shorts on she was getting cold, so Erica hopped up to move her 'decorative' cushions so she could climb in. She kept one for propping her head up; the headboard was at an awkward height for leaning on. It was all the extra cushions were good for. At least they looked good for her non-existent guests.

'And what about marrying my brother?' Pétur asked, emerging from the en suite.

He was wearing a pair of checked pyjama bottoms and little else. Erica couldn't help but check out his exposed upper half. Baggy sweatshirts were wasted on him. He wasn't going to be winning the Mr Universe competition any time soon, but there was some pleasing definition going on.

It was a popular misconception that werewolves were *ripped*. Look at any book cover or movie franchise and you'd see they were blessed with chiseled abs, perfect pecs and bulging biceps. Models straight off the Abercrombie catwalk. This wasn't the case in real life, much to Erica's annoyance.

Yes, most Purebreds had good metabolism but werewolves came

in as many shapes and sizes as the average human. Erica had once been described as the 'girl next door', which she took to mean sweet, wholesome and forgettable. A bad comparison. Well, apart from the last part. Short and a size ten, she wasn't the Amazonian beauty from the books, more like a pint-sized plain Jane.

Erica had been looking at him for a second too long, her gaze lingering as she folded the sheets down. Even worse, she failed to answer Pétur's question.

'Sorry, I was looking at your necklace' she lied, and he knew. 'I don't think we even need to discuss your brother.' She climbed under the sheets and rearranged the pillows behind herself.

He joined her, firstly removing the decorative-slash-useless cushions on his side of the bed, and turned inward, resting on one arm. She reached for the necklace dangling from his neck. She was pleased to see an acceptable amount of hair on his chest. Not too much, just the right amount. She hated it when guys shaved their chests, it looked odd. Another tick in Pétur's boxes. *Am I really going down this route after last night? Stop thinking about him like that.*

'So what happens if you don't wear this?' she asked, distracting herself.

'Wait up, I want to talk about this more,' he said and picked the book up.

She let go of the necklace and mirrored his seating position.

'What else is there to talk about?'

'Well if it's not my brother who is it? And why is your mum so obsessed with me?'

'Can you honestly see me marrying Jóhann? How would that ever happen?'

Pétur skimmed the story, looking for clues he might have missed. 'Georgia calls him Dad.'

'As if that's proof. She could call anyone that.'

'Ok, true. But still.'

'Can you really see him leaving his wife and Purebred children to be with me?'

'Who do you think it is then?'

'I dunno, we're talking four or five years if Mum guessed my age right. Anything could happen in that time. I'm crossing my fingers for a rich, handsome Swede. We can have lots of blonde, blue-eyed children. We'll be like the von Trapps.'

'I feel like you're not taking this seriously.'

'It's hard to. It doesn't seem real,' she sighed. 'The thing is, I've never wanted to get married – I've never even had a proper boyfriend. It's too much of a one-eighty for me to accept.'

Relationships were messy. Why complicate a good thing?

'You've never had a boyfriend?' He sounded sceptical.

'Nope.'

'I don't believe you.'

'Honestly.' He eyed her with suspicion and she just smiled back at him. 'I mean, maybe at the start of secondary school, but they don't count, and I've had guys I've slept with regularly, but I wouldn't call them boyfriends. I don't believe in love and all that stuff.'

'You don't believe in love?' He looked shocked, hurt even.

'Don't get me wrong – I'm sure other people fall in love, just not me.' She got up and put her hoodie on, still feeling the cold. How Pétur was coping with so little on, she didn't know. Not that she'd be encouraging him to cover up any time soon.

'Why not you?'

'It's just, I'm – ' She played with the toggles of her hoodie and leaned against her vanity table, searching for the right words. 'I'm cynical. I don't think it's worth it.'

'Worth what?'

'The time, the hassle... There are better things I could be doing.' She turned to face the mirror and undid her hair, letting it fall to above her shoulders before running her fingers through to reveal loose waves.

'That makes me sad for you. You're shutting yourself off from something wonderful. Love isn't meant to be happy all the time. You have to have the bad to appreciate the good; it wouldn't be worth it if it was easy.'

'It's not that. Georgia is my priority. I love her, that's all that matters.' She could hear the sharpness in her voice. She stared at her own reflection, faffing with her hair. She didn't want to fight, so eye contact wasn't an option until the subject was dropped.

He returned to reading with a sigh. She'd sounded a little snappy but it was a lot to handle. She'd just been told how the next five years of her life would go and it was the opposite of what she wanted. Bang, all choice was gone.

She regretted being testy, but she and Pétur were just too different. There was no point in arguing over a matter they both believed in, but being the petulant moody cow she was, it was tough to bite her tongue. Still, she was doing better than usual.

THEY WERE QUIET FOR A WHILE, before she got into bed. Again tension hung in the air – thankfully a different kind this time – but Pétur seemed too engrossed in the diary to notice. Or he didn't care. She was the only one who was wound up and to be honest it wasn't his fault, it was the damn diary's. And Tobias's. Ok, mainly Tobias and his stupid curfews.

'Sorry,' she said, feeling the need to clear the air and rid herself of guilt before sleeping beside Pétur. 'I'm just stressed. I hate leaving Georgia on her own. If she's not with me, she's with Quinn. She's never been on her own overnight before.'

'She'll be fine. The doctors and nurses won't be far away. She was happy when we left her.'

'I know but it must be scary for her. I should be with her.' She'd been fine when they left a few hours ago but she was still a little dopey from the sedatives. Erica was worried. What if G woke in the night and needed her? Hospitals could be full of scary sights and sounds.

'We'll go as early as possible tomorrow. I promise.' Pétur turned to Erica, gesturing to the diary in a bid to change the conversation. 'Why do you think your mum was seeing visions about me?'

She exhaled audibly; this diary was bringing up more questions than answers. 'I honestly have no idea,' she replied.

'It's like – and I know you're going to laugh at me – it's like we were meant to meet. But the problem is, I don't know why.' He'd been right; she did laugh.

'What makes you say that?'

'We've overlapped so much, and the way she writes about me, it's like she really cares. She's watching out for me.'

A connection occurred. 'Does this have something do with the page you tore out?'

'I still don't want to talk about that,' he shot back.

It was her turn to take the hint and go quiet.

He was on his back, two pillows behind his head, reading the diary with a look of concentration. His left hand reached up and twirled his necklace between finger and thumb.

She moved closer and took the pendant from him, studying the rustic hoop and strange black symbols carved into it. It was less than two inches wide; hard to believe it could make any difference.

'If I took this off you, what would happen?'

'You don't want to know.'

'I do, that's why I asked,' she smiled.

'You really want to find out?'

'Uh-huh,' she nodded.

'You sure?'

'Yes,' she said, laughing.

'Right, move back a bit. You don't want to be too close.'

'This sounds intriguing. Do you turn into a zombie or something?' She put her hands out in front of her, doing her best impression of the undead, crossing her eyes. *Urrrr.*

'Not quite.' He laughed and slid the cord over his head, placing it on the bedside table.

Under the bed the mass spread out, free of its confines. It was good to be out in the open again. It had been such a long time. It turned and twisted to fill the space under the king size bed, stretching itself out to make full use of its hiding spot.

'So, nothing happens?' she said, disappointed there wasn't more of an immediate show.

'Wait for it.'

So she did, for what seemed like ages, but was only about ten seconds. Patience wasn't her strong suit.

It hit. The pungent aroma of rotten flesh nipped at her nostrils. She could taste it.

Once, Erica's mum had left a packet of pork chops in the car after they'd fallen out of her grocery bag. They'd endured two weeks of hot summer sun before she'd discovered what was causing the smell. The car was never the same again, no matter how many air fresheners they hung. It had lingered – acidic and putrid.

This was a hundred times worse. She covered her face with a pillow (*not* a decorative one, they'd missed their time to shine), sure she was about to gag. 'Put it back on,' she mumbled.

The mass could feel Pétur's presence above but also another human. It wasn't safe to come out. The mass throbbed – a force was trying to pull it back into Pétur. No! Not yet, this wasn't fair.

'You sure?' he mocked, his hand lingering over the necklace.

'Yes.' She nodded; her eyes were welling up. The smell was getting stronger.

He slowly (a little *too* slowly) slipped the cord over his head and clasped his hands over his stomach, waiting. 'Won't be long.'

The mass's throbbing centre soon rivalled a quickening pulse. In a matter of seconds it was a terrifying crescendo, so strong it made the mass tremble before oscillating for a few beats. In an instant the mass was back in the talisman. Stuck.

'Don't you smell it?' she asked, covering her mouth.

'Not a thing.'

'Oh God, that's awful.' She could still taste it.

'Well, you asked for it.'

She uncovered her face, doing a few test sniffs to be sure. It was still there, but not as bad. She stuck her tongue out, pulling a disgusted face.

'Why can't you smell it?'

'It's the wolf thing. Only werewolves can smell it and since it's that half of me which is causing the problem, I can't pick it up.'

'Wow. That was something else.' She got out of bed and headed for the bathroom. 'I need to get rid of this taste.' She grabbed her toothbrush and brushed her tongue, the fresh minty taste cooling her mouth and dulling her taste buds. At the side of the sink was a small vase filled with roses. They were withered, black and drooping like the life had been sucked out of them. *I only just bought them.* So much had happened this week, she must be mistaken. Using her spare hand she chucked them in the bathroom bin with a loud clang.

'Hey, there's one more thing I want to ask you!' he called.

'Oh God, sounds ominous,' she said after spitting into the sink.

'Are we ever going to talk about the fact that you kissed me?'

She cringed, shutting her eyes tight; glad she was alone so he couldn't see how red she'd gone. 'Nope, never. In fact, we're going to pretend it didn't happen.' Not as forgotten as she'd hoped then. 'Doesn't matter anyway, does it?' she said, masking her embarrassment. 'My heart belongs to your brother.'

D ennis Reid lay stiff in his hospital bed in Glasgow Royal, on the other side of the Clyde to little Sam.

He'd felt unwell on Friday night but had put it down to being a bit of a glutton. He couldn't say no to his wife's steak pie, especially when she'd made an extra large portion on account of their son Joe being home for the weekend. It was a shame Joe hadn't brought the grandkids but, bearing in mind Dennis's current predicament, that must've been an intervention form the good Lord above. He didn't want the boys seeing him like this.

Dennis had woken at 2am with God-awful stomach pain. He'd suspected food poisoning. It wouldn't be his wife's pie, no; Sheena had never poisoned him once in fifty years of marriage. He'd had porridge for breakfast, a ham roll and crisps at the bowling green, a bit of chocolate when he was on guard as the lollipop man, then tea. No likely candidates there. He'd had that sweetie off young Robbie – disgusting thing – but surely no one in their life had got sick off a sweetie, foul taste or not.

When sickness failed to come he'd lain on the bathroom floor and decided it was the worst heartburn and indigestion he'd ever experienced.

'It's his appendix,' Joe determined.

'Or a heart attack,' Sheena fretted.

'For God's sake just get me some Andrews Livers and leave me be,' Dennis had snapped.

The powder did nothing and Dennis deteriorated further, his hands and feet beginning to tingle.

Now, here he was. His arms stuck to his sides, wires hanging off him connecting him to God only knew what. Sheena and Joe were by the bed. He could hear them. They thought he was sleeping but the reality was he couldn't open his eyes – they'd locked shut.

E rica couldn't sleep. She looked at the clock: one-thirty. She'd been awake for hours.

She'd fallen into a dangerous spiral of thought as soon as she'd closed her eyes – progressing from worrying about Georgia and Sam to wondering why she'd kissed Pétur to every other worldly problem. Her mind was in overdrive.

Quinn had sent her a text before tea. Sam's illness wasn't viral or bacterial, meaning it couldn't spread. Erica would need to visit tomorrow. The idea that it was connected to Georgia's virus buzzed around her brain, an idea she couldn't shake. The symptoms were just too similar and the fact Sam had been with Georgia was too much of a coincidence.

She lay on her side, facing away from Pétur, trying not to fidget too much and wake him. It had been more than two years since she'd shared a bed with anyone other than Georgia for a full night. That had been after a manager's meeting in London, and even then it wasn't an entire night.

But this was different. This was her own bed, in her own house. How long had it been since a guy had stayed over here? An easy one to answer: never. It was a golden rule, it didn't feel right to have Georgia involved in her private life. This was their sanctuary, men didn't need to infringe on it.

Which was precisely the point. How could she get married when she'd purposely never had a relationship? Who could be so wonderful they could change her mind?

Nick? A turbulent on-off relationship over the last three-and-a-bit years. Turbulent was the wrong word. They were both on the same page; it was never exclusive between them. She would never use the term *friends with benefits*. It made her sick – what a horrible phrase. They worked together, which made it complicated. Work was a small world and you had to be careful.

Things started innocently enough; Nick was moved to her shop to cover a member of staff leaving suddenly. There was an instant connection and it didn't take long for things to cross the line. She was an assistant manager at the time and could have got in serious trouble – you weren't meant to fraternise with colleagues.

It was amazing how you could learn to lie. Closing up together? Easy to fool about downstairs. Drinks after your shift or going to his? The lies came too easily sometimes.

It continued after Nick returned to his own shop and was even worse now that they were both managers. Nights away on courses or at meetings in hotel rooms... Well, it was practically a given that some employees would end up in sordid affairs. All the better when no one else knew what was going on.

He was adventurous and risqué, traits that appealed. Sex was fun, a distraction to be enjoyed; it should never be boring.

He'd been quiet recently. There were rumours he had a girlfriend but he'd denied it when they'd met this week. Did that bother her? Perhaps. Ok, yes it did. But only because it meant her fun was over. It had to end sometime. He wasn't the type to take home. Aside from the fact that Nick was furthest you could get from family-man-slash-boyfriend material, there was also a feeling that didn't sit right. He was holding something back. She had an instinct for these things, a *'dar*. If you keep enough secrets yourself, you soon learn to notice the signs in other people.

The most blatant secret was a locked cupboard in his bedroom. No matter what she tried, Seelie methods or otherwise, it wouldn't open. Nick joked it was the entrance to his sex dungeon. Unlikely – he wouldn't keep that locked.

To be fair, it was part of the appeal. Who doesn't love a mystery?

Nick was the opposite of Pétur – tall and slim, chiseled good looks, and wavy shoulder-length honey-blonde hair he wore swept to the side but tied in a man-bun at work (she wasn't keen on the 'mun', but learned to overlook it). He had a light blonde streak at the front, a popular topic to tease him about, but he denied dyeing it. His thick, scruffy, gingery brown beard confirmed this – a small blonde patch fixed under his bottom lip. She should be more sympathetic; she often got accused of similar because of her dark eyebrows but Georgia's were the same. Sometimes genetics made their own rules.

Given the choice, Nick would spend his days drinking, playing computer games, and smoking weed (Erica suspected the latter was to blame for the skeletons in his closet). On paper they were incompatible... And yet she kept going back for more.

A disgusting amount of fellow baristas fancied him. He was known as 'Sexy Nick'. Not the most original name, but hey, it stuck, what can you do? Of course, he knew this, like his ego needed inflating any further. It wasn't hard to see why girls fawned over him. The gorgeous smile and way he played with his hair, pushing the Jesus-esque mane out of his face with a move practiced a thousand times. It was like watching an expensive perfume ad.

Then there was his accent. He was from Orkney and had the voice to match, although he was often mistaken for a Welshman, which wound him up something rotten. His voice was calming, the way he rolled over the 'r's and bounced from word to word.

She'd expected things to fizzle out when he went back to his own shop – never in a million years did she think they could keep their secret rendezvous going this long.

Having Georgia changed everything; every relationship is serious when you throw a kid into the mix. How soon should you mention her? How soon should you let her meet someone? Erica couldn't be bothered with it, never mind the droll pressure of keeping a boyfriend interested. She was a single mum and didn't have time to juggle boyfriends with the rest of her life. And let's not even get started on the effort of hiding magic, wolves, and God-knows-what from potential Seelie mates. The arrangement with Nick was perfect; their trysts never lasted long enough for that to be an issue.

Erica rolled on to her back and rubbed her eyes, pulling her fingers down her cheeks. Pétur was making funny noises in his sleep, the occasional low whimper.

She cringed recalling her last encounter with Nick, but it was so typical of her – why was she even embarrassed? She should be used to letting people down.

He'd been sitting up in bed, sprawled out and relaxed, crumpled sheets covering his crotch and nothing else. They were in his poky bedroom, it was a mess. Clothes, pizza boxes and half-finished rotas strewn on the floor. A typical boy's room with the smell to match. It didn't help that he was smoking a roll-up at the time – she wouldn't miss that if the girlfriend rumours turned out to be true.

He took a long draw before talking. 'So, do you fancy doing something Saturday? And don't say you're working. Hazel told me you're off.'

She was sitting on the edge of the bed, the opposite side to him and the one nearest the door, getting dressed. She pulled her t-shirt on, stood up and looked for her trainers. It was impossible to find anything in this pigsty.

'Erica? You hear me?'

'Yeah, it's just, where are my shoes?'

He pointed to the floor behind her and his signature shearling jacket (another thing she hated, it made him look like even more of a hipster, but he wore it every damn day). Sure enough they were under it.

She slipped them on without undoing the laces, the backs were ruined anyway. Work shoes never lasted long.

He was looking at her for an answer.

'I can't do tomorrow,' she said, undoing her ponytail before putting her hair back up.

'The next day then?'

'Nope. Nor the next.'

'When then?'

She made sure she had her belongings before answering. Grabbing her jacket off the chair in the corner (also laden with dirty clothes) and patting it down – keys, purse, phone, all there.

'I think this might be the last time I see you for a while.'

'What? Why?'

'It's the school holidays, I'll be spending my spare time with Georgia.'

'So? Can't we do something together?'

'All three of us? What? No, never.'

'Ah, you're ashamed of me,' he said, smiling, hiding a half-truth to wind her up.

'Don't make me feel bad.'

He got up and came towards her, the cover falling to the floor, and tossed his roll-up into a nearby ashtray.

'We both know that's impossible.' He put his arms around her from behind, pulling her into a hug before kissing her neck.

'And you know I can't stay. It's nearly three.'

'I think you'd be surprised what we can do in fifteen minutes.'

'Get off!' She laughed and pushed him, but he was having none of it.

'I'll let you go if you promise to do something with me this weekend.'

'Right, ok. I promise.'

'Really?' He sounded more surprised than her.

'Yes. I promise to think about it.'

'That's not good enough,' he said, laughing. He tightened his grip and swung her on to the bed. He pinned her down and she pretended to put up a fight. He kissed Erica's neck again, pecking and biting in a bid to wind her up.

'What did you have in mind?' she asked between giggles.

'Cinema, three o'clock. Me, you, and Georgia.'

'Why the sudden urge to meet my kid?' Ever since they'd run into him mid-Tesco shop three weeks ago he'd been on a mission.

'I'm getting older. I think my biological clock is waking up.'

'Ha bloody ha. You hate kids, you told me.'

'Ok, you got me.' He let his grip go and slid on to his side, a leg straddling hers. 'We've been doing this for years. I just think it's time I met the family, you know. It might give us more than an hour before you dash off on the school run.'

'We're just having fun. I'm not sure I want Georgia in on this too.' She prized his leg off and got up. He didn't protest. 'I need to go Nick. I can't be late.'

'Let's just try it, yeah?'

'Fine. Whatever shuts you up,' she said, grabbing a balled-up piece of paper off the floor and taking aim at his chest. She opened his bedroom door. 'See you later buddy.'

"Till next time pal.'

The cinema was meant to be today and she'd only remembered at the last minute. He was already there, waiting, and didn't buy her reasons for bailing even though she'd told him the truth. Well, as much of the truth as you could tell a Seelie.

He'd sounded nonchalant but she could tell he was mad. Hurt, even. Really hurt.

He was making a big gesture by reaching out to Georgia; he knew how important she was in Erica's life. Granted it wasn't the gesture she wanted, but it was appreciated anyway. She should have cancelled sooner. Now he wouldn't return her texts.

If only she'd known earlier. Why hadn't her mum warned her that Georgia would get ill? She would have seen it.

These days Lucy rarely appeared in Erica's dreams. In fact, there had been years between visits, but Erica presumed her mum was angry and disappointed in her. Everyone else was. She'd been upset at first but learned to live with it. Her mother talked to Georgia most nights. No doubt she preferred her. Erica didn't blame her.

How much did Lucy know about Erica's life? The idea worried her. She wasn't ashamed of her lifestyle, but it wasn't one she wanted her mother watching – Erica's life couldn't have been further from what her mum expected of her.

Pétur's breathing was quicker; he was almost panting. She turned on her side to check that he was ok. In the dim light of the room she could see his eyes darting about beneath their closed lids. She rolled on to her back and stared at the ceiling.

Erica sighed. Thinking about her mum depressed her. As if she needed to add to her burdens this weekend. *Yeesh.*

What happened was hard to grasp. Once she started thinking about that night, it was impossible to stop dissecting and over-analysing – not that it ever got her anywhere. Erica doubted she would ever know the full story of her mother's death. In truth, she didn't want to. The pieces she had were more than enough.

Did she blame her Dad? Yes, of course. What annoyed her most was that he'd not only ruined the rest of her childhood but also the precious eight years they'd had together. He overshadowed every happy recollection – the searing heat of resentment burned through her memories like a flame to a photograph. Still, she clung on to fond memories of him, remembering he didn't mean it and that wasn't him. They'd been happy. He was a good dad. He made one mistake and paid for it. She understood better than anyone how easily accidents could happen when bad luck seemed to follow you around. She got that from him, which explained a lot.

Her train of thought was interrupted by Pétur letting out a loud moan, like he was trying to shout. Should she wake him? He was still deeply asleep, his eyes continuing to move from side to side. His face looked pained.

Why the hell had she kissed him? He was Georgia's uncle... Out of everyone to kiss, why him? She was a constant fuck-up, that's why.

Before she could delve any deeper into her own self-loathing Pétur sat up, eyes wide, and took a sharp intake of breath like he'd been starved of air.

The ice-cold wind tore at Pétur's skin. Despite pulling his scarf and hat tighter it still found a way to nip at him.

He squinted, the gale making his eyes water and sting. He wasn't sure where he was. He continued to study the landscape but nothing distinct stood out.

He was at home, but the harsh covering of snow had ruined any chance of seeing anything familiar. He looked at his feet. It wasn't snowing yet there were no footprints around him. How had he got here?

The wind continued to howl.

There was no sign of civilisation, not even the wire fence of a local farm to guide him or hint at the presence of a road.

Pétur took a hand out his pocket and tried to shield his eyes. Without gloves, the cold soon made his fingers sore and stiff. It was futile anyway. The land around him remained barren.

Movement to his left startled him and he shoved his hand back into the pocket's protective warmth. He had no idea what he was looking at – a white shape shifting over the blinding snow, almost fully camouflaged. Pétur caught sight of a snout. A bushy tail. Big ears and limber legs. It was a small arctic fox – he'd never seen a wild one before.

The fox darted over the snowy field and occasional hillock, sniffing as it passed, paying him no attention. Pétur watched it for a minute, trying to figure out what it was searching for. Snout to the ground, it would run a few feet, head twisting and sniffing before something would catch its attention, leading it to bury its nose into the powdery snow. Seconds later it would move on, empty-pawed.

The fox had come from somewhere less exposed; there was no way it could survive in a place as desolate as this. Even the most skilled predator would need a den. Following the fox offered his best chance of finding shelter. His only chance. Let's face it, he could toss a coin for which direction to go and the odds would be the same.

He walked in the fox's direction, holding back so as not to scare it, tracing its paw prints through the glaring white expanse.

It was only then that he clocked his snow boots. Ankle high, laced up the front with a cosy wool lining and rubber outer shell. Navy blue, like the ones he owned when he was a kid. He didn't think he'd owned a pair since, being a city boy he had no use for heavy-duty snow boots.

The snow was deep and – although the fox had gracefully trotted through – Pétur was struggling, the snow rising almost to the top of his boots. He pushed his hands deeper into his pockets and carried on. The wind was cold against his cheeks, making them sore and tight. He couldn't stay exposed much longer.

The fox continued its hunt for food, darting around and ignoring its stalker. It was becoming more frantic and there was an urgency to its movements; Pétur had to work hard to keep up. Perhaps it was closer to finding its loot.

He'd not had to walk through snow like this since living with Langamma. He'd forgotten how hard it was, like wading through water. Not that he did that often either.

The fox stopped, motionless apart from its twitching flattened ears. Its eyes widened in terror, fixed ahead. Pétur stopped too, twenty feet away. He followed the direction of the animal's gaze but couldn't see anything. Straining his ears to listen, he heard nothing apart from the howling wind.

The fox turned quickly and ran towards Pétur as an almighty crack filled the air. The sound enveloped him, freezing him to the spot as it echoed.

The first crack was followed by hundreds of smaller ones, like the snapping of dry twigs, followed by a wet *zing* like a shotgun reverberating. The fox was heading straight for him when reality hit.

They were standing on ice and it was shattering like a broken mirror, a fork of icy cold water rushing towards Pétur as the ground opened beneath his feet.

Helvítis!!

Even with a head start the fox wasn't quick enough and soon

plunged into the water, scrabbling at the sides to make a break. Each time it lunged towards the edge another large section of ice would break off, dunking the animal underwater again and again.

Pétur didn't wait to see if the fox made it out, the crack was nearly under his own feet. His heart was thumping at what felt like a thousand miles an hour, his muscles already burning as he pushed them to their limit, the deep snow slowing him down.

Despite Pétur's best efforts, the ground disappeared from beneath his left foot as he pushed off. For a brief moment he was safe, his right foot finding purchase as he charged forward, but he soon found himself doing the splits between two shards of floating ice, with no solid ground to push on.

He grabbed at the nearest edge and only found a handful of snow before it too broke away. His left leg sunk into the cold water, followed by his right. It took a split second for the rest of his body to follow. It wasn't until the ice-cold water reached his crotch that he let out a pained gasp pursued by a quick succession of breathless *fucks*.

The freezing water hurt like hell; his head was submerged as it pulled him under, hands still clawing at the slippery ledge.

He surfaced, large painful gasps filling his lungs as he fought to stay afloat. The edge became further away as more shards continued to break off.

He treaded water for a short time, taking in what was happening – a desperate attempt to remain calm. *Panic was the biggest killer.* The crack had lost its momentum and was no longer cutting the ground in half. There was no sign of the fox.

The eerie laser-like noise continued to cut the air while Pétur turned in the water, great splashes erupting from his arms as he thrashed. His limbs already felt disembodied and heavy. He had to do something. How had he got into this situation? He had no memory of venturing out here.

Gasping, his lungs hitched, once, twice, three times as he fought to regulate his breathing. But it was no use. The sudden shock had winded him.

'Help!' he called out, knowing full well there was no one to hear him. He shouted once more for good measure.

Nothing.

Hot tears burned his cheeks as fear possessed him. *Not now, Pétur. You've survived this once, you can do it again.*

He'd hated water since he could remember. His childhood memories were interspersed with a mishmash of night terrors. Even before Jóhann had subjected him to his closest brush with drowning, he'd wake up drenched in sweat, the feeling of a hand lingering on his neck. The sensation of being held underwater was so real he could feel it clawing and burning at his windpipe. He used to wonder if it was a past life playing tricks with his brain until he'd finally confided in Langamma and discovered his parents' attempts at 'exorcism' were to blame. There were days when his phobia was so bad that even a bathtub made his anxiety skyrocket.

This was different though. No hands held him under. He had to react fast if he was going to stand a chance. Time wasn't on his side. In these conditions, hypothermia would soon kick in and he'd have no hope of hauling himself out. The ledge nearest him would be best; where the crack stopped.

He swiped at the loose fragments of ice with a limp hand to make a clear path before testing the edge with a fist. It felt solid enough. He rested his arms on it, giving his legs some downtime. It took his weight with little protest.

Stopping was a bad idea as his muscles quickly seized. He kicked his legs, each stride harder than the last. He willed himself to be propelled out of the water, he'd settle for even an inch.

Edging his elbows further forward, Pétur continued to kick so that he lifted his abdomen out above the surface. He held his position for a few seconds, allowing his jacket to drain, relieving the weight a little.

Again he hauled himself forward, his crotch making contact with the ice. It was the final push he needed and before long he was lying on his back, panting.

I'm out. And on my own this time.

He smiled before letting out a relieved laugh.

The reprieve was short-lived as a familiar cracking noise returned. The clear blue sky above disappeared as Pétur went under, his body submerged in seconds.

THIS TIME he didn't surface.

D arkness.
Even with wide eyes searching for a hole in the ice, there was nothing. His hands made contact with the solid sheet above him and he slammed two fists against it.

He screamed. A bubbling foreign noise made mainly of wasted air.

Pétur continued to push his fists against the thick ice, limbs flailing, before he grabbed at the zipper on his jacket to wrestle it off. He didn't need the added weight of a fleece-lined parka holding him back.

It floated away from him, brushing against his arm, startling him, as he tried in vain to break the ice.

He struggled to hold his breath. A thick, heavy weight expanded in his chest, gripping at his windpipe as he ran out of air. He had twenty seconds if he was lucky.

Soon his body would win. He would breathe in and water would flood his lungs. *Just like before.* It would stop the transfer of oxygen to his blood and he would black out. Game over.

Pétur stopped banging the canopy of ice as his eyes adjusted to the dark. It was still black around him but he was seeing the darkness instead of being submerged in it. A strange peace came over him.

Something touched his arm from behind, like the fingers of a lover stroking him from wrist to elbow – gentle, reassuring.

He twisted around to see what or who was there.

Nothing.

A light touch caressed his back and this time he felt four fingertips on his right shoulder.

Again he turned to be greeted with an empty expanse of water.

It wouldn't be long now. He readied himself, braced for the final breath, floating in the black expanse, one hand steadying himself against the icy roof. He'd given up.

Out of the corner of his eye, a shape caught his attention and he turned clockwise without thinking. A black mass floated through the water before darting out of sight like it was playing a game. The water was dark, but this was darker. Blacker than black.

This was it. He was going to die. You couldn't cheat death twice.

He continued to float, suspended like an abandoned puppet, but death remained a stranger. In fact, the feeling of peace was getting stronger. The heavy pain in his chest and unrelenting urge to breathe were gone. Air was the last thing on his mind. He wanted to find the black mass.

A hand on his lower back invited him to turn round. The shadowy mass was there. It wanted to be seen.

It moved through the water like milk through a fresh cup of tea, smoky tentacles bleeding into the liquid around it.

This time it didn't dart away but instead came closer. It spun around him like it was checking out its new playmate, sizing him up. Looping around Pétur's torso and flowing over his limbs like an agile octopus, the black mass then stopped in front of his face. It hovered but Pétur could see no defining features, only a black, inky, mist-like mass.

He wasn't scared. Instead he stared into it, wondering how it was moving of its own free will. He felt safe.

It gave up inspecting him and whipped around his back with the sensation of a hand gliding from belly button to shoulder. Pétur turned, wanting to see more of this mysterious creature. His gut told him it was the thing keeping him alive. He should be long gone by now. Two to three minutes underwater and your blood vessels burst, causing organ failure. Yet here he was, fine.

The mass was gone so he pivoted against the icy roof on his extended arm, turning a full circle, his eyes squinting into the darkness, hoping to catch a glimpse of the mysterious creature.

Below him, the water stretched into deeper blackness, it could be ten feet deep or a thousand – it was impossible to guess with no light. That was the scary thing about water – you never knew what secrets it hid. Well, that and the ever-present threat of drowning.

The ice above showed no signs of breaking so Pétur had to take his chances. He pushed off with his hand, tumbling forward until his feet made contact with the frozen ceiling and propelled off, diving into the unknown.

Swimming wasn't his forte; water was to be avoided at all costs so practising was never an option. Even seeing an expanse of water made Pétur's palms clammy.

And yet, here he was diving into the black abyss. He could feel how clumsy he was, there was no rhythm to his stroke, his legs moving out at odd angles, but he was moving forward so he didn't care.

With caution he continued on, aware he couldn't see so could hit something at any moment. It was dark at the surface but down here was something else. Fingers wrapped around his wrist for a fleeting moment, stopping him. Pétur righted himself and floated, hoping his eyes would adjust.

He flapped his arms back and forth, a mediocre attempt at treading water as he studied the darkness around him. Had he imagined the mass's touch? His eyes were struggling to focus and he couldn't make out his own hand in front of his face.

Had he seen any sort of mass the last time? It felt familiar. Was this part of the act? He'd spent most of his life wishing the memory of that day to disappear but it remained crystal clear. He'd read about people blocking horrific events from their mind, a kind of coping amnesia, so why couldn't that have happened to him? As far as he could recall there was no mass, he was out so quick there wasn't time. And yet, the notion that he hadn't been alone in the water that day had often niggled at him.

He was ready to continue diving deeper when two hands gripped his shoulders. Whatever this was, it was in front of him.

He moved his face forward and widened his eyes, attempting to let in more light.

A few seconds passed with no change.

Pétur convinced himself it was a hallucination when the mass came into sight again, floating as before, just inches from his face. He smiled, *hello old friend*.

They stayed face to face for what could have been seconds or might have been minutes – it was impossible to tell. The world was fuzzy at the edges and tranquillity washed over him. Pétur didn't know where he ended and the rest of the world began.

It was nice.

He leaned closer to the black inky mass, smiling as if blissfully drunk. He wanted to talk, ask what it was, but it would be a waste of time and energy. Instead he watched it swish in the water, a motion as relaxing as watching waves crash at a beach.

The atmosphere changed in a heartbeat as icy cold hands closed around his neck. He grabbed at his throat, pushing them away in vain. The centre of the mass lightened before a terrifying face rushed at his own, a priest's collar around its bodiless neck. Its mouth widened as if planning to swallow him whole. He shut his eyes, bracing for pain.

It shrieked, a high-pitched wail that Pétur was sure was in his head rather than being heard by his own ears. A flashback of his previous experience hit him, as vivid as a movie playing in his head – Jóhann's hand on his head, the other on Pétur's shoulder holding him under. *Dad says we'd be better off if you were dead...* Grasping for purchase on the edge, his own hands splashing, feeling for ice. *This is all your fault... You're evil and deserve what's coming to you... Drown the demon! Drown the demon!*

Jóhann's voice deepened, becoming a man's voice – *Be gone Satan, inventor and master of all deceit!* running through Pétur's six-year-old mind like a roaring chant, repeating over and over until it became too noisy to understand. That had caused him to black out, not the blow to the head or Jóhann's sloppy attempt at drowning him.

It was as if his memory was travelling backwards. Images were running through his head at breakneck speed. With a jarring halt they settled on the vision of a priest, his pure black eyes bored into Pétur's soul as he held him underwater. He was only a baby and unable to fight back, water stinging like hell as it went up Pétur's nose. He couldn't breathe and panic set in as he desperately attempted to struggle free. The priest was too strong and his face contorted into that of a determined lunatic with each twist Pétur made. This man was not going to let go. *'BE GONE SATAN!'* the priest roared in a frightening voice.

Pétur recoiled, eyes tight shut, trapped by the invisible hands. He thrashed, trying to wrestle himself loose. It was no use. They were getting tighter.

Was this what it was really like to drown? Last time had been a dress rehearsal, this was the real deal and it was worse than anything he could ever imagine

He kicked out his feet to hit the mass despite not knowing where to aim. He was getting desperate.

A shriek echoed in his ears and he chanced opening his eyes, hoping to see where to direct his flailing limbs. The mass was gone and he was now surrounded by hundreds of children's faces. White as ghosts and without bodies, they bobbed in the darkness, scowling at him. Some had their eyes rolled back like broken dolls, but continued to sneer, others glared at him like they wanted to rip him limb from limb.

They chanted indistinguishable words, becoming louder and louder.

He squeezed his eyes shut, ignoring the heads around him. Why was this thing attacking him? Was this because he didn't save the fox?

'What can I do? How can I help you?' he pleaded, surprised to hear his voice. The chanting was deafening. 'Please, what can I do?'

His mind flashed to Lucy's premonition. Surely it couldn't be true – it was a cruel trick his subconscious had invented, he was certain of it. But still, the page had been burning a hole in his pocket all day. He felt guilty for ripping it out of the diary but Erica couldn't know the truth about who had saved him. Not yet. Not ever. To be given life by something so wretched, it was no wonder his family disowned him.

The chanting faded to silence.

He opened his eyes, scared at what he might see but was greeted with darkness. The hands around his neck were loosening – had it given up?

He turned in the water, wanting to see his attacker and gauge his chances if he tried to escape. Nothing until the mass flashed in front of him. He could have sworn he saw his own death-white face contorted in agony, like it was wearing an obscure mask to mock him.

He twisted, trying to keep his guard up but it was gone again. He swung his arms and kicked, wanting to reach the surface. It was safer there.

A hand grabbed at the bottom of Pétur's jeans, pulling him back. There was nothing solid to aim for, so Pétur continued to thrash his legs. On flipping round he could see a thin chink of light above him. It was tiny but it was what he needed to muster the energy to break free.

He was deeper down than he'd thought, the light only getting larger by a tiny fraction with every few feet he swam. He was really pushing himself, his muscles burning with each stroke. There was a hole in the ice and he was going to make it, even if it killed him.

Two hands grabbed his boots and jerked him back. The movement broke his momentum and a searing pain ripped through his muscles as they relaxed. Pétur kicked a foot free before wrestling the other boot off and propelling himself forward. The light above was getting larger, he was getting closer.

His shoulders ached as he widened his span, propelling himself a little further. He shouted as he forced himself upwards for the last few feet. An almighty roar, his face in a grimace, but no bubbles came out. Curious.

He shot an arm upwards and out, the cold air above feeling amazing against his skin as he broke through the surface. But his hand failed to make contact with the ice sheet and he bobbed back under.

Pétur was gathering what remained of his strength, getting ready to swim to the top when a familiar hand grabbed his trouser leg. He jerked his leg with little effect and extended his arm for a second attempt. With each inch he travelled forward, it pulled him back two. Once or twice the tips of his fingers made it through the surface but it was no good, he was nowhere near the edge.

'This time you're staying with us!' a child's voice screamed, the shriek echoing in his ears.

He was ready to give up and admit defeat when a hand plunged through the water and grabbed his wrist. The children pulled him but his rescuer was strong. The grip tightened, a second hand soon cupping the first, and he became the rope in an absurd game of tug of war.

He continued to kick his legs, hoping he'd land a lucky strike and give his rescuer a much-needed extra second.

A LOUD *POP* WOKE HIM.

Had his arm dislocated? No, his surroundings were different. Everything was white.

His vision cleared, as if looking through parting fog, and he could see himself on the ground a few feet below. The world was silent.

Someone was hunched over him, rotating between doing mouth to mouth and hitting his chest. They were much smaller than he was and wore a furry deerstalker hat. Was this who had really saved him before? Please God say yes. Not that *thing*.

The popping noise hit again and the world was black once more.

He coughed, tipping on to his side as he vomited water on to the ground.

'Oh, Pétur. Thank God,' a female said, hugging him before leaning back and landing a hard smack on his left arm. 'Don't you ever do that to me again, you bastard,' she scolded.

It was Erica.

She took off her hat and put it on him, followed by her coat, which she draped over his shoulders. 'We need to go, you'll freeze to death out here.' She helped him up. 'Come on, I know the way home.' She walked away but he didn't follow. When she was a few feet away she turned to ask: 'What's wrong? Why aren't you coming?'

'I can't.' He didn't know why he said it. The words came by themselves. 'I'm not meant to.'

She stepped towards him and began to speak but he didn't hear a word as the ice below him opened, swallowing him whole.

'PÉTUR, PÉTUR. SHHH, IT'S OK.' Erica was kneeling at his side, her thighs straddling his hip as she rubbed his back. He could feel the sweat pouring off his brow, dripping down the side of his face. 'It was just a bad dream, it's over now,' she continued to soothe.

He was gasping, unable to calm his breathing. Hot tears threatened his eyes.

'Deep breaths. It's going to be ok.' Her voice was calm; a mother's voice. Erica got up, filled a glass of water at the bathroom sink and sat on the edge of the bed by his side. 'Have this, slowly, and focus on your breathing. You're fine, I've got you.'

He took the cup with a shaking hand.

'I'm sorry. This is embarrassing.' He mumbled, unable to make eye contact.

'Don't worry about it.' She smiled and took his free hand, stroking his thumb with hers. 'It happens to the best of us.'

He looked at the clock – two in the morning. He was never having whisky again, that was some nightmare.

'You ok now?' she said, standing up and cupping his cheek.

'I think so.'

'Good. Let's try and get some more sleep. We've got another long day ahead of us.' She slid into bed on her own side and shimmied over. 'Come on, lie down. I'll be big spoon.'

He lay on his side and she aligned her body with the shape of his back, looping her arm under his and making herself comfy.

'Think happy thoughts and happy dreams will follow.'

This must be what she does with Georgia. It wasn't patronising. He was safe. A strange familiar feeling even though they'd just met, but maybe that was why they'd met? Somewhere in the back of his mind, through the hazy fog of his nightmare, dots were beginning to connect.

Erica leaned on the kitchen counter, waiting for the kettle to boil. She looked at her phone; it was just shy of 6am. She'd had a shite night's sleep, worrying about Sam mainly. She'd given up and snuck out of bed ten minutes ago.

She messaged Quinn to see if she was awake.

The kettle clicked off and she filled her mug, the tea bag floating to the top as the steaming water cascaded into the cup with a satisfying trill.

Her phone vibrated against the counter, echoing in the quiet room. She grabbed it, worrying the outburst would wake Pétur.

'Morning,' she said, her voice sounding more stable than the morning before.

'Hey, what're you doing up?' Quinn asked.

'Same as you probably. Worrying.'

Quinn sighed. 'There's no change. I slept at the hospital, Holly went home to Callum.'

'How's he coping with it all?'

'I don't think he knows what's going on to be honest. We've not really told him. Is that bad?'

'Nah, he's only two. Ignorance is bliss at that age.'

'Have you told Georgia?'

Erica inhaled sharply, feeling guilty for keeping Georgia in the dark. 'Actually, no. I wasn't going to until we knew what was wrong. She'd freak out. You know what she's like.' Quinn was so quiet that Erica could hear the machines beeping in the background. 'How're you holding up?' she asked, breaking the silence.

Quinn let out a deflated chuckle. 'As well as can be expected. I just wish it was me that was poorly.'

'I know.'

'You'll visit today, yeah?'

'Of course. I need to do some stuff this morning then I'll be over. I promise.' *Like visit a potential psychopathic mass-murderer and see my daughter in werewolf hospital... Some stuff my arse.* 'Can I bring you anything?'

'No, we're good. Your charm and sunshiney cheer will be more than enough.'

'That's the Quinn I'm used to,' Erica sniggered. 'Well, text me if you think of anything. I'm at your service. Just this once. Don't get used to it.'

'What would I do without you?'

'You'll never know. I'm the pest you just can't get rid of.'

Quinn laughed. It was nice to cheer her up, even if it was only for a moment. 'I'd better go. I need a coffee or something. See you later.'

Erica hung up and fished the tea bag out of the mug; thankful she didn't have to add it to a growing mountain like Bill. She grabbed the milk from the fridge and thought about the day ahead. Her mother often warned her not to make promises she couldn't keep but it had been easy for Lucy, she could see the future. Erica on the other hand had no clue what was coming. If only she'd known what the rest of the day would bring, hospital visits would be the last thing on her mind.

Erica looked at her phone. No news from Quinn. No news was good news. Hopefully. She felt terrible for not visiting yesterday, even though it wasn't her fault – by the time Quinn had given her the ok to go, it was well past visiting hours on the children's ward. She'd go this afternoon, after this flying visit.

Georgia had been in good spirits today; they'd snuck in a McDonalds breakfast for her. Who wouldn't be pleased after that? Fingers (and everything else) crossed that Misty would give them the answers they so hoped for, then they could get back to G and keep her company. Pétur could stay with her when she went to see Sam. A perfect plan.

They were sitting outside Misty's house in Clarkston. Erica had been annoyed to find he wasn't home, but Pétur pointed out it was half past ten on a Sunday morning and she couldn't expect anyone to miraculously be where she wanted them to be without any warning.

There was nothing to do but wait in the car. She turned to Pétur. Feeling in a better mood after last night, she was ready to tackle a big question.

'Right then, Ewan McGregor. I think it's time to address the elephant in the room,' she said, taking a sip of her petrol station coffee. It wasn't as bad as expected. Verging on dishwater but drinkable.

'Ewan McGregor? I don't get it.'

'It was pretty niche to be fair. Ewan McGregor in that film, Moulin Rouge, he's always going on about how wonderful love is.'

'I don't think I've ever seen it.'

'What? Really?

'It's a bit of a girl's film though isn't it? I doubt I'd like it.'

'Oh my God, no way. It's right up your street. Listen,' she drank her coffee again, 'stop avoiding my question.'

'I don't think you've asked me one...?' He grinned, narrowing his eyes at her.

'Ah, correct. Fair enough.' She paused for maximum impact. 'I want to talk about my mum's premonition of Diane.'

'Diane? Why?' He sounded taken aback.

'Are you kidding? I thought you'd be all over this. You've been super keen about me marrying Jóhann.'

'Oh, that.'

'Yes, that. What did you think I meant?'

'Nothing. Let's not talk about that,' said Pétur.

'This wasn't the reaction I was expecting. I thought you'd be over the moon. You're the only one who got a clean-cut answer.'

'Yeah well I've been avoiding thinking about that.'

'Ah, not so happy-go-lucky when it's *your* destiny being scrutinised..?'

'It's complicated.'

'Not really. So, we're talking four years, maybe. You must have more than two kids or why would Georgia ask? So three or more kids in four years, you must meet her soon. Like, really soon. If you don't already know her.' He shot her a look as if to say *shut up*. 'Oh, wait! Is that it? That's the problem, you already know her?'

He sighed.

'Not going to venture any more info?' She smiled, giving his thigh a gentle hit, keeping it light-hearted.

He took a sip of his coffee and glared at her. *If looks could kill.* 'She was my ex. Well, is my ex. We dated when I was in Australia. She cheated on me. Multiple times. Broke my heart into a million pieces. I took her back. She cheated again. She could be fucking dead now for all I care.'

'Ok...' She could take a hint.

She tapped the steering wheel, becoming impatient. They'd been here half an hour; she was getting bored. As far as suburban Glasgow went, Clarkston was hardly a hive of activity.

'I'm going to try again. Maybe he was ignoring us before.' She hopped out of the car and was halfway up Misty's garden path before Pétur joined her.

A complete contrast to Bill's bungalow, Misty's was pristine. There wasn't a leaf out of place in his perfectly pruned bushes.

She made her way to the teal front door, rang the bell and gave three hard knocks for good measure.

Nothing.

Looking at the quiet street of fancy houses with manicured gardens, you'd never expect a warlock to live here. His house could even be described as quaint. Erica imagined this mystery man tending to his hydrangeas, waving a cheery hello to his neighbours. If only they knew.

'What do you want to do now?' Pétur asked.

She clicked her tongue, thinking of a plan. 'I don't know.' She knocked again.

'He's not in.'

'I know, genius.'

'Then why are you knocking?'

'Shhh – '

'Are you looking for Harry?' a lady's voice ventured.

They turned to find a smiling face appearing from the house behind them – a lady in her sixties wearing a glorious floral chiffon blouse. She closed her front door and made her way towards them with the excited bounce of a nosy neighbour who at long last has something to be nosy about.

'He won't be in now,' she confirmed.

'Any idea where we might find him?' Erica asked, coming down the steps to meet the woman. Harry must be Misty's name with the hoi polloi. 'I'm his niece, just visiting the area, thought I'd pop in on my way home,' she added to give a logical reason for snooping.

'Let's see.' The neighbour thought for a second, wanting to prolong the suspense and enjoy her moment. 'Sunday morning, if he's not in he's usually in his shop. Up to something.' She tagged on the final sentence with narrowed eyes.

'And where might that be?' Erica made her best attempt at a trustworthy smile.

'His shop? Oh, not far. It's an odd little shop, I don't know if you'll want to go. It's a lot of hokum if you ask me.'

'Hokum?'

'Yes. Pure hokum. The things he says he can do. Scams I say.'

Erica opened her mouth but wasn't sure what to say. She didn't have a clue where this conversation was going.

'Sorry, I know he's your uncle. I just don't believe in it myself.'

'That's ok. I feel the same way to be honest,' Erica said, no idea what she was agreeing to. 'I'd just like to see him before I go. Let Mum know we popped in.'

'Where have you come from?'

Oh my God.

'Perth,' she lied. Why Perth? What an odd place to pop into her head.

'Lovely place Perth. We like to visit when we can.'

'Yes, it's beautiful. I'm sorry but we're kind of in a rush.' She trailed off, hoping the lady would get the hint, but directions weren't forthcoming. She gave in and prompted: 'Could you tell us where the shop is?'

'Oh the shop, yes.' She had her thinking face on again.

Was this woman barmy? Erica half-smiled, attempting to coax the next sentence out.

'If you go back the way you came and out on to the main road, turn left.'

'Uhuh.'

'And then straight to the roundabout. You can't miss it.'

'And what's it called?' Pétur asked. The lady turned on her heel to face him like she'd forgotten he was even there.

'Oh it doesn't have a name, dear. It is what it is.'

A shop without a name. Was that even legal? How did he file his taxes?

Misty's neighbour had informed them that parking was impossible near the shop but, as it was only a five minute walk away, they'd be best to leave the car. They took her advice and made their way up the busy main road running through the centre of the town.

The shop had many nicknames with the locals. The more affectionate referred to it as *Harry's*, others the *Potion Shop*, and many just as *the shop they wouldn't dare set foot in*. There was one common opinion of Misty's shop – you didn't go in unless you absolutely had to...And even then you thought twice about it.

It wasn't long until they reached the roundabout and sure enough, Pétur and Erica saw a row of four shops under a humble canopy.

A chip shop, photography studio, and corner shop displayed their bright facades with pride, leaving no doubt what lay inside. Sandwiched in the middle was what they were looking for.

The shop looked very different to what you'd find on your average local high street. A glass door and large window were topped by dark green signage, upon which were the words *Curiosities, Oddities and More* in white and gold hand-painted script. Beneath this, the sign read *No problem too big, we have the answer!*

This place was getting more intriguing by the minute.

The shop's window display was sombre and didn't give much away. Dark green velvet curtains hung either side of the window, making it appear almost like a theatrical stage rather than a store. Three dark wood plinths of different heights sat against a black backdrop. On each plinth was a single item, much smaller than its podium, giving a look of great importance. There were no labels; the viewer was left to guess each object's use.

Glass bottles sat on two of the pedestals; one tall and conical, the other stout, flat-bottomed and spherical. Both were sealed with a cork, and Erica recognised the smaller as a bog-standard love potion – a deep red, viscous liquid with a thin line of dittany oil settled on the top. Pointless in her opinion, since they rarely worked (or so she'd heard). In the other was a deep black liquid; she was clueless about that one.

'What do you think that is?' Pétur asked, pointing to the tallest plinth at the back. On it sat an animal's skull, with two large white crystals sitting in the eye sockets. It looked almost human but the teeth suggested it was a monkey. Eerie.

'No idea. Creepy though.' She could see why the locals had reservations about the place.

'You sure you want to go in?'

'Scared, Pétur?' teased Erica.

'No. Of course not. But, erm, ladies first,' he said and stepped aside, giving her a clear path to the door.

She laughed, but only to mask the fact she was feeling the same way. Even though Erica knew the shop's window display was complete crap, she was spooked.

The frosted glass door hid any further clues to the shop's contents, so there was nothing left to do but enter.

'Here goes nothing,' she said, pushing it open.

A jingling bell above the door announced their arrival.

'I'll be with you in one minute!' a jovial Glaswegian voice called from the back. 'Feel free to browse in the meantime.'

Pétur closed the door behind him and smiled, raising one eyebrow as if to say *what the hell*. Inside was as strange as the window suggested. Shelves lined the walls with two sets jutting out a metre or so, dividing the left-hand side into three areas. At the far end was a very old-fashioned counter, complete with antique cash register. On the opposite side, tucked in the corner, an area was sectioned off by floor to ceiling velvet curtains.

It was dark inside – give it a candelabra and sawdust on the floor, and it would rival the décor of a medieval castle.

Erica took the lead and stepped further into the shop, heading for a cabinet in the middle. When she sensed Pétur was lingering in the entrance, she reached for his hand, pulling him towards her.

'Come on, no harm in looking.'

He cocked his head with a look of indifference and allowed himself to be coaxed forward.

Enticing done, she dropped his hand and returned her attention to the display cabinet. It reminded her of furniture you'd find in a museum or posh jewellers – dark wood with intricately carved legs; it spanned a good eight feet and dominated the shop floor. The top was glass, surrounded by a thin frame of matching carved wood, which rose to a slight peak in the middle like the roof of a house.

She ran a finger along its edge as she wandered its length, tracing the rivets and dips of the ornate design as she went. *This must be a bugger to dust.* The case was lined with velvet and had the same sparse product offering as the window; more potions she didn't recognise, crystals, and a tatty leather book.

A noise from behind made her jump. Pétur was inspecting a small copper cauldron and not being quiet about it. She went over to join him to see what was making the racket.

'What is all this?' Pétur asked, holding a long copper utensil with a small ball at the bottom, moving it this way and that to see what it did. He was in the section nearest the door, which was filled with cauldrons of various sizes and colours, along with mixing devices, storage containers, and utensils. Lakeland for witches.

'It's for making potions.' She took the item from him, turning it round the other way. 'And you're holding it wrong. Think of it like a tea strainer.' She squeezed the bottom and the seamless ball at the top opened. He took it back and copied what she'd done, but nothing happened.

Erica left Pétur and made her way to the next section – candles. Every size, shape, and colour you could imagine. On the bottom shelf was a box labelled *Starter Kit,* it wasn't too bad in terms of contents. Four pillar candles; white, black, gold, and silver. Ready to be charged with any energy you required. She'd have to pick one up; Bill had made her realise how much her supplies were lacking.

'Remember Miss Adams, you need to repeat what we've done for at least a week before you'll see any results,' the man's voice commanded as he let a young woman out from behind the curtain. 'Love takes time to bloom. Especially one that lasts a lifetime.' His voice had a beautiful drawl, like a Shakespearean actor.

Erica stood up and looked at Pétur from between the shelves, raising her eyebrows to say *Did I hear that right? What the fuck?* He widened his eyes in agreement.

'Of course Harry, I understand,' the lady assured him before heading for the door.

'Well I'll be damned,' exclaimed Misty, blinking. 'Wait a minute Miss Adams; I want you to meet Erica – my greatest creation to date,' he boomed.

She had her back to him, how did he know who she was?

She turned to find a grinning, grey-haired man who appeared to be barely in his fifties. Not what she imagined *Old* Misty would look like. He was shorter than Pétur, which was saying something, as P couldn't be more than five-seven on a good day. He was dapper in dark grey trousers with a matching waistcoat and polished black boots. A green pocket square completed the look. The real focus was his styled moustache that was expertly twirled at the ends and only rivalled by his coiffured grey beard.

He moved towards her, bringing her into a hug before she could protest. She stood frozen, awkwardly holding the box of candles and unsure if she should return the gesture.

She wasn't surprised to see that he had a small silver hoop in his right ear and his long grey hair was fastened in a bun. It seemed to fit with the clothes.

He released her and stood back, admiring her like a work of art.

Misty laughed, unable to hide an ever-widening smile. Miss Adams stood, awaiting further explanation.

He clapped his hands together abruptly. His three guests jumped, causing him to laugh more. He was giddy.

'I'm sorry, it's just been so long. How old are you now? No – don't tell me,' he said raising a hand to silence her. To be honest, Erica wasn't sure she could even remember right now anyway. He scratched his chin, muttering dates under his breath. 'Twenty-six' he ventured, pointing a finger at her. Another grin took over his face as he spun to Miss Adams. 'Erica's mum couldn't have children. Full stop. No ifs or buts. Couldn't have them.' *Excuse me, what?* He placed a hand on Miss Adams's shoulder and walked towards the door. 'Goes to show that nothing is impossible, not with Harry anyway.' He winked.

Miss Adams seemed as bewildered as Erica. She nodded, a smile forming, and said her goodbyes before leaving the shop.

'And who is this?' asked Misty, focusing his attention on Pétur.

'Pétur,' he replied. Erica was sure his voice had wavered.

'Boyfriend I presume? Come, come.' Pétur didn't get a chance to correct him as he was hooked by the arm and led towards the back of the shop. Erica was given the same treatment on the way past. You didn't get a choice with Misty.

He was a force of nature, the most exuberant man Erica had ever met; he had more energy than a cocker spaniel after a hundred shots of espresso.

Misty drew back the dividing curtains with gusto to reveal a small round dining table with three candles in the centre. Their flames danced in the draught before settling straight again.

'Sit, sit,' he commanded. So they did.

Erica placed her box of candles on the table with an unsure hand. The sudden rush of activity had thrown her off kilter.

'So what brings you here? No, don't tell me.' It was all games with this guy. 'You have a daughter, so I know it's not for treatment like your mother.'

'I'm sorry, can we slow this down?' Erica asked, finding her voice.

He looked at her, bemused. 'I apologise, I'm getting carried away. I'm just so excited to see you again. I suppose we'd better start at the beginning.'

MISTY POPPED into a back room for a few minutes, leaving Erica and Pétur to entertain themselves.

'This is weird,' Pétur mouthed to her.

She shrugged, raising an eyebrow. She couldn't make sense of it either. Given the last few days, anything was possible. *Expect the unexpected.*

'Ah, here it is,' Misty proclaimed as he appeared by Erica's side with a worn box file like you'd find in an office. It wasn't what she expected him to be looking for. 'I keep files on all my patrons, though I haven't had to get your mum's out in a while.'

'Was she here often?'

'Not much, I don't think she agreed with my way of doing things.'

'And what would that be?'

He twisted the end of his moustache between finger and thumb. 'See, your mum got the good stuff because she could give me a good price.'

'And women like Miss Adams?' Erica asked.

'Women like Miss Adams can only pay me money, it's not so useful to me but it's better than nothing. I have to pay the bills somehow.'

'Does that not seem a little harsh to you? Giving people false hope doesn't seem fair,' she said.

'Hey, I didn't say the other stuff never worked.'

Weren't real love potions, the ones that actually worked, illegal? She kept her mouth shut.

'So, what price did my mum pay?' she enquired instead.

'I never discuss prices outside of the deal. She paid what she thought was fair.'

'You could be a millionaire if you gave everyone the same treatment,' Pétur ventured.

'True but people would soon get suspicious – I for one don't want to be on the wrong end of a witch hunt.' He got up and went over to an apothecary cabinet, squatting down to reach the bottom drawer from which he produced three glasses. They were perfectly round apart from the bottoms, which were levelled flat. Misty placed them in a triangle on the table in front of his empty chair. He returned to the drawer and pulled out a carafe of dark purple liquid before pouring a small amount into each, no more than a two-finger shot.

Erica placed a hand over the third glass before he could pour. 'I shouldn't, I'm driving.'

'No, I insist, we need to talk. Plus this isn't alcoholic. It's much better than that.' He winked.

She removed her hand and allowed him to pour. Misty placed one glass in front of Pétur before offering the last to her. She obliged. What could go wrong?

Pétur studied the thick fluid. It looked like syrup. He swirled it in the glass, a film oozing down the sides where it touched. 'What is this?'

'Homebrew. My own recipe. Sláinte.' Misty bellowed, raising his glass to toast.

Erica sniffed, cautious of what it might contain. It was sweet. She tipped the glass back; the liquid slowly making its way down the glass before reaching her lips. She took a small sip. It was ok. It reminded her of strong blackcurrant squash, like the attempts Georgia used to serve before she'd explained that you're meant to add water.

'How did you know my mum?' Erica asked, watching the contents of her glass settle again. Misty poured himself another.

'We met not long after she came to Scotland, through a local coven. We were close for a while.' She wasn't sure if she liked the connotations of that last sentence, so she ignored it.

'Did you know my dad?'

'Yes, eventually. He was a good man.'

'And they couldn't have children?' She'd often wondered why she was an only child. Her parents had seemed the type to want a large family, but she'd assumed they'd settled for one after finding out how much of a bossy terror the first was.

'Nope, they tried for years but your mother couldn't have any.' He opened the folder after blowing a little dust off.

'So is that what you do in this shop? Treat infidelity and broken hearts?' Pétur joked. His eyes looked glazed but he *had* finished off the drink in one gulp. Alcoholic or not, this was no fruit juice.

'That's two things, yes. There isn't much I don't do to be honest.' Misty reached round the candle centrepiece and poured Pétur another.

'Isn't Clarkston a weird place to open a shop like this?' Erica mused.

'Not really. It's the perfect mix of city and suburbia. Plus the people round here have money to spare, they can afford to indulge in what might seem a crazy final option.' He laughed, pre-empting what he was going to say. 'And if I was in the city centre it would be too busy, I'd have all kinds of nut jobs in.' *I'll drink to that,* she thought.

'Is most of it crap, or do you keep any good stuff on the shop floor?' she asked. No point mincing words. Misty didn't seem fazed.

He inspected the candles Erica had been looking at. 'These are ok but then they're only candles – it's what you do with them that counts.' He studied her, his eyes narrowing as he made contact with hers. 'Tell me, what can you do?'

A tough question, she didn't know her own limits. She'd only touched the tip of the iceberg. 'A bit of everything. I'm not sure to be honest.'

'I can tell. You're wasting your talents, Erica.' She'd heard that line a thousand times.

'I don't have the time.'

'Everyone has the time. You just have to make it.'

'Try making time with an eight-year-old.'

'What's your speciality? You must know that.' he said, ignoring her excuses.

She mulled it over. 'I guess I prefer the light-based stuff?'

'Ah we've got a Lumio fan on our hands,' he said, smiling. 'Your mum was good at that too. Anything else?'

'I know it sounds stupid, but I like playing with locks too. Figuring out how to unlock them.' She was playing with her thumbnails, flicking one edge with the other. She didn't like talking about her magic skills. She didn't like talking about personal stuff full stop.

Misty nodded, his smile widening. He was enjoying making her open up, pushing limits. This was how he got his kicks.

'Why didn't you do that at Bill's? With your mum's box?' Pétur asked.

'I was embarrassed to do it in front of him.'

'Bill?' Misty enquired.

'Bill Hammond. He was the one that sent us here'

'Don't be embarrassed in front of Bill,' said Misty. 'He's got nothing on you. You just need to read the books, you're a bit rusty that's all.'

Erica kept quiet, managing a half-smile. Her witching prowess had been under too much scrutiny the last few days. She was fed up of having to justify herself.

'So, what's in the box file?' Pétur asked. Erica liked homebrew Pétur – he was so much more forward.

'Oh, this?' Misty asked, grabbing the open file with two hands. A look of excitement appeared on his face as though he'd forgotten he'd even brought it out. 'I thought Erica might like to know a bit more about everything.'

He rummaged in the box. His hand stopped, and Erica could make out the back of a photograph before he returned it to the pile.

'Actually, I need to ask,' said Misty, 'why did Bill send you to see me?'

'Long story, but there's been another outbreak in our Pack. Bill thought you might know about it.' She wanted to sound casual, catch him off-guard and make him spill.

Misty rubbed his chin and laughed, although he didn't look amused. 'He did, did he? That old bastard, can't let it go.'

Erica went to have another sip of brew but had second thoughts; she could already feel it going to her head. It didn't feel like being drunk, instead it was like a beautiful tranquillity washing over her. Every suspicion, doubt, and worry was melting away. She felt safe. This was stuff designed to make you talk, and Erica didn't like that one bit.

Before she could ask Misty what he meant, he continued, 'I take it Bill told you the whole story?'

'He didn't tell us anything,' Pétur said.

'He wouldn't. Always half a job with that bloke.'

'Best pals then?' Erica joked, injecting a little humour.

'Bill's had a problem with me for thirty-odd years. He needs to get over it. There's far worse out there than me…The Underground Occult. The Warlock in Edinburgh who practises voodoo. There's even talk of a rogue fairy in the Highlands. He's out of touch that man, thinks I'm the source of all evil in the whole of bloody Scotland.' He downed his shot, calming himself. 'Anyway, whatever you hear, it's nothing to do with me. Your mother could see I'd changed. She forgave me, he needs to do the same.'

Erica had touched a nerve. She weighed up whether to pursue what the hell he was talking about or not. Time to change tack.

'Does Bill not approve of you – of this?' she asked, waving a hand about to illustrate she was meaning the shop.

'Bill just doesn't approve, full stop. Although he was happy I helped your mother. I think he had quite the soft spot for her.' *Ignoring that too...*Erica didn't need the mental image.

'So what can you tell us about the outbreak? Bill must have some reason to think you'd know about it.' She paused, deciding how to play this. 'You're obviously very powerful, maybe you can help us stop it?'

'Impossible unless I knew what was actually causing it.' He stroked his moustache. 'Tell me more about the symptoms.'

She did her best to fill him in with confirmed details from Sam and Georgia's experiences. 'Any ideas? Does it sound similar to any incantations you know?'

He sighed, annoyed it was outfoxing him. 'The Seelie doctors – what do they diagnose it as?'

'Nothing, that's the thing, so they can't treat it.'

'Interesting,' he said with a quiet voice, 'that's the problem you see. Most spells will be untraceable to Seelies. Tests will comeback like they're perfectly healthy. The poor things will be confused as hell!' His voice crescendoed to a roar.

'So absolutely no clue?' she said, defeat ringing heavy in her voice.

'I'm sorry dear. I'll do some research if you like.'

'I'd appreciate it.' Erica sighed, deflated.

There was an uncomfortable silence as the mood in the shop plummeted.

'So, you're to blame for Erica?' Pétur shot her a smile, lightening the atmosphere. She punched him in the thigh, *cheeky bastard*.

'Your mother was my greatest challenge. I thought I'd perfected everything; I wouldn't have risked it otherwise. Not on her.' Misty looked at the photograph he'd fished out. 'I didn't know until it was too late.'

'Know what?'

'About Lewis. About your brother.' He placed a photograph in front of her. A brown-eyed wolf stared back.

Pétur was watching Erica drive with a smile on his face. That brew was strong stuff.

'What do you think Misty's homebrew is made of?' he asked, realising he had no idea what he'd just drunk three glasses of.

'Probably enchanted brambles if I was to hazard a guess. Maybe blueberries, I dunno.'

'What are brambles?'

'They're little purple berries, a bit like raspberries but smaller. Fairies grow them, the enchanted ones anyway.'

Like hrútaber maybe? Things were getting lost in translation. It didn't matter. Berries were berries, it was what they did that interested him. 'So, they're magic?'

She scrunched her face up, moving her head from side to side. 'Hmm, not so much magic, just different. Like how alcohol makes you feel a certain way, enchanted fruit has its own thing too.'

Satisfied with that answer, Pétur looked out of the window and admired the view. They were leaving the village of Balloch, having travelled north for the last forty minutes. The scenery was opening out, green fields tumbling towards mountains on the horizon. Erica hadn't been happy at the idea of heading back to Balmaha, but Pétur didn't mind. He was enjoying the excuse to see more of the National Park, but then, it wasn't his car and he wasn't driving.

He glanced at her again, her eyes fixed on the road. She was biting her bottom lip – the diary said that meant she was thinking, she was stressed.

So Erica had a brother. Not just a brother but a twin. A twin who lived in Bill's old cabin. She was certain she'd talked to him the other night but she hadn't said much more. Pétur was learning his limit with questions, you could get away with a few before being snapped at. Fair enough, they hardly knew each other.

That explained the diary; apart from the entry he'd torn out, which was still in his pocket. The connections he'd made last night were pulled thin now, the reason for her mum's vision was back to being a mystery.

His head was fuzzy. He closed his eyes and rested his temple against the window.

Of course, Pétur knew all too well what it was like to be erased from a family.

His own sister had also found him by accident. She was looking for documents before going to uni, needing them to apply for funding, and stumbled across his birth certificate. He was surprised his father had even kept it. Ada, the baby of the family, had not rested until the truth was out.

His two other sisters, Anna and Kristín, had also got in contact, but when they all met, he sensed the connection wasn't the same. The older girls were sterner, more serious than Ada. Sometimes people just aren't on your wavelength, despite having the same blood. Still, he was grateful they'd at least tried.

Erica on the other hand, was on his wavelength. In fact, last night had been good fun. Which was something given the circumstances.

He snuck another look through a half-shut eye. Today she had on a baggy jumper and tight skinny jeans. She looked good; he could tell she had a good body. She'd looked amazing in pyjama shorts last night. Her legs were shapely and taut with the hint of a tan. She must be sporty.

Last night was different. After reading the diary, it was odd looking at her like that – she was his niece's mum and would never be anything more. She might even marry his brother.

They'd sat on her sofa and drank wine, with the Clyde and lights of Govan providing a nice ice breaker. She had an amazing view from her flat, ten storeys up in Glasgow Harbour.

After his earlier beers and whisky it hadn't taken much to feel the effects of the wine, despite the hours they'd spent with Georgia between. He'd thought of the evening before, of kissing her. She was a good kisser. The idea of making a move crossed his mind, only to be beaten down by a new feeling: an incestuous uneasiness. She was off limits.

The evening's drink had given him the courage to ask about the kiss. Dutch courage. *No – Icelandic courage.* It had been a weight bearing down on him the whole evening. Despite thinking nothing could ever happen between them, it hung over their conversation on the couch. He had to ask or it would drive him crazy. She'd been joking when she said her heart belonged to Jóhann, but maybe she'd been thinking the same as him. There was a chance again.

He smiled at the memory of her lips, the bad feeling from last night gone. She was available again. He might even be the man in the diary, you never know. Should that scare him? The idea that he might end up with Diane had turned his stomach. Thank God that was quashed now.

Erica was right not to have had a boyfriend. Although, did he believe that? No. How could you be twenty-six and not want a relationship? Wasn't it human nature to pair up? The urge to merge.

His mind wandered to visions of merging with Erica –

'You know it's super creepy to smile like that with your eyes shut. What are you thinking about sailor?'

He jolted awake and sat upright. 'Nothing. It's just the homebrew.'

She narrowed her eyes, suspicious, but accepted his answer before starting a rant: 'Misty's really annoyed me.'

'I can tell.'

'All that way and he won't tell us anything about the outbreak. Not one thing.' She raised her index finger, shaking it over the dashboard. '*I can tell you what I find, but what will you give me in return?*' he'd said as they left the shop. What an arsehole. Although he'd relented and admitted Lewis – who, it turned out, was a wizard-wolf – might know more.

'We can always go back.'

She laughed. 'I'm sick of driving. I don't think my poor car knows what's going on.'

'You don't leave Glasgow often then?'

'Only when I need to. The occasional trip to the beach or woods with G.'

'And yet you've got the fancy car. I told you it was an unusual choice for a city girl like you.'

'You're just saying it to wind me up now, aren't you?' She shot him a smile and playfully thumped his thigh.

He was going to end up black and blue with this girl, but he liked it.

'SO WE HAVE to go up there?' Pétur asked, eyeing the steep hillside. He was thankful he had his boots on but was more used to designated routes than clambering up random slopes.

'Yep, all the way to the top.' She was already off the path, positioning herself beside the small stream, ready to jump.

Better than a boat I suppose.

She hopped over the stream with ease and waited for him, hands on hips. He sized up the gap; it couldn't have been more than two feet. An easy jump. He bent his knees, ready to make the leap, thought better of it and straightened again.

'What if someone sees us? I don't think you're meant to go off the path in National Parks.'

'We'll deal with that if it happens. Which is more likely the longer you piss about.'

She motioned him over with a tilt of her head, eyebrows raised. She would go alone if he didn't cross, and he'd be in the bad books for sure.

He bent his knees again and, with clenched fists, he swayed back and forth three times, readying himself for the leap.

'This isn't the Olympics P.'

'Alright, alright. Give me a second.' He psyched himself up again.

She was struggling not to laugh. Despite attempting to mask her grin behind a hand, her shuddering shoulders were giving it away.

Here goes.

After the build-up he ballsed it, his left foot missing the bank by a fraction. The mud gave way, sliding him backwards into an awkward semi-splits position, the betraying foot landing in the stream.

'Fuck!' he cried out as the ice-cold water soaked him to the ankle. He brought his leg up to the bank, lost his balance, and ended up with both feet in the water.

She was still laughing, which only made the situation worse. He shot her a death stare.

'Here, let me help you,' she said, extending a hand, shoulders shaking with barely-hidden laughter. Pétur grabbed her by the wrist for better purchase and she mirrored his hold. She pulled to lift him but instead he brought her towards him.

He'd only meant to scare her a little, make a joke of it, a spot of light flirting, but the bank was too muddy and she skidded into the stream beside him.

'You dick!' she screamed.

'Honestly, I didn't mean to pull you in,' he panicked, shocked at himself.

She stood stiff, open-mouthed, chest heaving – the water had taken her breath away.

'I can't believe you just did that.'

He braced himself for a playful punch but it didn't come. She was livid.

She climbed up the bank and, not looking back, strode into the forest.

PÉTUR WIPED his muddy hands on his jeans, he'd had to grab hold of a nearby plant to haul himself out. How she managed with no effort he had no idea.

Erica was a good fifty yards in front, already at the edge of the flat woodland. He made up ground with a slow jog but it was difficult to get decent speed. The ground was spongy in parts, the moss providing an unexpected cushion every dozen or so steps, making it easy to lose your footing.

He made it alongside her.

'Hey, listen. I didn't mean to do that.' He was a little out of breath.

She didn't even turn to face him. 'Erica?' He moved in front, wanting her attention.

'That was a real dick move, Pétur,' she huffed.

'I know, but it was an accident. I meant to scare you, not pull you in.' She glowered at him before pushing past and continuing up the hill. 'So it's funny when my feet are wet, but not yours?'

She stopped and turned to him. 'Yeah, but that was an accident. If you hadn't been such an arse I'd be dry.'

'But I didn't do it on purpose, I swear!' he shouted.

'Just shut up will you,' she snapped and carried on climbing.

He sighed and followed her through the bracken. They walked in silence for a good five minutes before she spoke again.

'I'll get you back. I hope you know that.'

'I don't doubt it.' He pulled himself up to an outcrop of rock, and extended a hand to her. 'So am I forgiven?'

Erica took his hand and narrowed her eyes at him. 'Try anything and you're dead.' He helped her up, with no funny business. 'I will consider forgiving you.' She poked a finger at his chest – 'Consider.'

'I'll take what I can get,' he grinned.

She returned the smile but it was obvious she was still mad. His socks were squelching so no doubt hers were the same – he'd be mad too. Time to change the subject.

'So what are you going to say when we get there? Surprise, I'm your twin?!' he said, jazz hands outstretched.

She looked at him, unamused. 'I have no idea. Do you think he even knows about me?'

'Probably not, or wouldn't he have come looking for you?'

'It depends. Remember what Misty said.'

Misty had warned them that Erica's twin wasn't normal. Was that the right word? There'd been complications anyway.

'I guess it comes down to why your mum told him he was out here.'

'Considering she told me nothing, I can't see why he'd be any different.'

They continued up the hill, making a slow ascent. As the crow flies it wasn't a great distance but the difficult terrain and rough foliage made it tough, forcing them to zigzag their way up.

To make things worse, time wasn't on their side and it was nearing sunset. At this time of year, once the light began to fade it was gone in thirty minutes. It would be impossible to see after that.

'Do you think there are adders here?' he asked, pushing his way through heavy bracken. Some of the ferns rose well above his crotch.

'Adders, like the snake?'

'Yeah, the snake.'

'I dunno – I mean, maybe?' She stopped, turning to him. 'You've freaked me out now. Do you really think there are snakes here?'

'I have no idea but I hate snakes.'

'Why would you say that if you don't know?' she fretted.

'Because I hate snakes. I wanted you to say NO.'

She grunted, exasperated.

'Do they not scare you?' he asked.

'Of course they bloody scare me, so I don't want to be reminded of them when I'm tit-deep in ferns,' she said, frozen to the spot.

He laughed and snuck up behind her, careful of his footing. Who knew what he was standing on.

'Ssssss,' he did his best snake impression, and grabbed her from behind, lifting her from under the arms, his own enveloped around her in a bear hug. She kicked her legs out as he spun her ninety degrees.

'Get off!' she cried through bouts of laughter.

'I'm ssssaving you from the ssssnakesss.' He hooked an arm under her legs and carried her to the edge of the bracken as if carrying his new wife over the threshold of their marital home. 'That'sss you sssaved, my lady.'

'You're a fool P, do you know that?' She laughed, straightening her jacket.

'Only around you.'

'And a smooth one at that.'

He smiled, making his way after her. He was in her good books again.

. . .

NEAR THE SUMMIT, the bracken and long grass levelled out to a covering of copper-brown pine needles. The ground was even softer, almost bouncy in parts. He'd seen a video of trees swaying in the wind, their roots moving the soft ground beneath, making it look as if the land was breathing. Did the same happen here? That would be cool to see.

'Are we nearly there?' He asked, pestering her.

'It's in the clearing up ahead. Can't you see it?'

'See what?'

'The cabin.' She paused for a second, a look of realisation coming over her. 'Of course, it's dusted. You can't see it.'

'Bloody fairy dust. Can you do that thing again? I want to see it.'

She turned and motioned her hands towards him. A tingling sensation passed over him and a dazzling glow appeared around his limbs. He held out a hand and stared in awe at the sparkles around his fingers.

Ahead, Pétur could make out a small cabin. It was of habitable size, much bigger than her mother's hut, but not much larger than a decent sized living room. It was picturesque, like the chalets of the French Alps, except rising only one storey – the classic wooden cladding, gentle sloping roof with a shuttered window and door. All it needed was a dusting of snow.

'Are you nervous?' he asked.

'Shitting myself.'

'You'll be fine,' he soothed, placing a hand on her shoulder.

They were at the top, a mere thirty feet from the cabin. She pulled at her jumper, adjusted her jacket and ran a hand over her hair.

'Do I look ok?'

'Better than ok,' he said, hoping he sounded reassuring rather than creepy.

She smiled. 'I guess it's now or never then.'

Erica linked arms with Pétur and led them towards the cabin.

'Shhh. Wait,' he whispered, placing a hand on hers and bringing them to a halt.

'What?'

'I'm sure I heard something.' He brought a finger to his lips. They listened but could only hear the low rustle of the wind through the trees. 'Must be my imagination.'

They were about to start off again when a faint growl caught her attention.

'No, I heard it too,' she whispered.

They stood motionless, holding their breath in the hope of hearing a sound they could make sense of.

He couldn't see anything, but the thick undergrowth to their backs could have hidden a thousand sins. The snap of a twig made Pétur turn, and he gently pushed Erica behind him – a move that surprised him on reflection, as he didn't know he could be so chivalrous in dangerous situations.

Out of the forest three werewolves emerged, each one baring its teeth and growling: a low, threatening rumble that shook Pétur to the bone.

The largest was easily four-feet tall on all fours. It had been years since Erica had seen anyone but herself and Georgia in wolf form, and the sudden appearance of these beasts had taken her breath away, even more so than the ice-cold stream had earlier.

Her heart was racing; she could feel it going a mile a minute, each beat banging on her ribs with a hefty, reverberating thump. Pétur was doing his best to shield her, but it would do little against the brute force of an attack, especially given the fact they were outnumbered.

Like her own wolf form they were jet black, their thick fur puffed up to make them look larger and more threatening. Their long limbs were stretched out, backs arched to show they meant business. She looked at their paws; they were as big as dinner plates, complete with huge dirty white claws gripping at the turf.

Pétur edged back, his hand clutching her side to keep her close.

'Got any ideas?' he whispered, not taking his eyes off the creatures.

She shook her head. *Not yet.*

They continued to back away, but it wasn't long until they had edged up to the cabin. Erica jumped as her elbow made contact with the wall. The three wolves moved in. They were surrounded.

'Please, we're like you,' she said, putting her hands up to surrender. She'd wanted to sound strong but the fear in her voice was obvious. There was no pretending anyway – they'd smell it.

They approached, each one continuing to growl. Spit foamed at their bloodthirsty mouths, and their large white teeth – with the canines as long as Erica's index finger – were bared in a permanent snarl. Erica and Pétur were screwed.

'I'm here to see my brother, Lewis,' she said, reasoning with them.

They didn't listen or didn't care. She could feel their hot breath getting closer. There was only one thing for it – she was going to have to Turn and fight. She didn't want to but could see no other option. The pair were going to be ripped to shreds at any moment; so she could at least go with some dignity. Others could explain to Georgia that her mum had died trying; tell everyone that Erica wanted to live, she still had spirit in her, and she didn't give up easily. A heroic death.

Erica was thankful she'd written a will years ago. Quinn would look after Georgia – anyone but Tobias. Her child couldn't suffer the same fate she had. Georgia was only eight; the same age Erica had been when she was shipped off to her uncle. History wasn't meant to repeat itself. Everything would be fine – better even?

In fact, no. No way. She'd fought too hard for the life they had. She wasn't going to leave her baby. She could do this. For Georgia.

Erica slid her jacket off, dropping it to the floor. At the same time, she quickly removed her shoes by standing on the heels to free her feet.

'What are you doing?' Pétur whispered in a panic.

'I'm going to have to Turn,' she shot back, unzipping her jeans. 'I don't want to rip anything.'

She had to think positively to give them a chance. She'd keep her underwear on, to save a little self respect in front of Pétur, but the rest of her clothing she'd need to keep in one piece so she could wear it back to the car. Then again, this was a good bra, they didn't come cheap and she'd bought this one at full price. *Really, Erica? That's a priority right now? Get on with it.*

'Do you mind?' she said, aware Pétur was watching as she edged her jeans down. When did she become so shy?

'What?'

'Can you not watch me undress?'

'Oh God, yeah, sorry,' he apologised and shut his eyes. He was backed against the cabin wall, palms flat against it. She could see beads of sweat on his brow. The largest wolf was so close it was terrifying. It must be the Pack Leader, looking so confident as it scoped her out. It watched her every move with great interest, its snout mere inches away from Erica's belly.

They locked eyes. It was hard to believe there was a person behind those animalistic features.

'I don't want to have to do this. I just want to see my brother.'

No reaction, apart from a deep growl from one of the smaller wolves. Where was Lewis? None of them looked like the picture Misty had shown them.

When had her body last forced her to Turn? Two months ago, in quiet upland wilderness, north of Glasgow. Jesus, it hurt like hell – it was no wonder that so few did it anymore. Erica had got it down to a fine art, only having to Turn every six months or so.

She checked to make sure Pétur's eyes were closed and carried on edging her jeans down. She focused on her breathing, readying herself for what was to come. She kept eye contact with the Alpha as she bent to ease her trousers over her knees before using her feet to take them off and push them to one side: a move she'd done a hundred times before, but usually with a much happier outcome.

Turning hurt more than childbirth but, thank God, it didn't last as long. It was swings and roundabouts but she knew which she'd rather be doing – at least you got a baby at the end of the other. This finalé was a lot less appealing.

The process of Turning was similar to those scream-inducing contractions near the end of labour. After Georgia's birth, Quinn asked Erica what it had been like. Her comparison was having someone break every bone in your body while swirling a chainsaw inside you, over and over again. Of course, that's pretty much what Turning was – minus the chainsaw, obviously. Thank God it was over in less than a minute.

She hated the noise of it. Every bone in your body changing, lengthening, and reshaping. *Crunch. Snap. Crack.* The awful cold but burning rush as your organs were pushed and shoved into new positions. The breaking of your jaw and nose as it morphed into a canine snout. Then there was the fur. It appeared in an instant with a sickeningly hot itch.

Only her jumper to come off, then it was showtime. A lump had formed in her throat, heavy and rotten. She was going to have to do this. Then there was the prospect of fighting. She'd never fought another wolf in her life.

I'm going to fucking die.

Of all the ways to go, this wasn't what Erica had envisioned. Most people hope for the clichéd old age in your sleep scenario. She was bad at crossing the road, so she'd accepted that might be an option. But this? No way.

With shaking hands, she grabbed the bottom of her jumper, psyching herself up to pull it off and remove the final hurdle. The hem of Erica's top reached her midriff when suddenly a fourth wolf appeared from nowhere, crashing into the large Pack Leader's body. Its muzzle smashed into her, smearing spit over her stomach, its big teeth dragging across her exposed skin.

Pétur grasped Erica's arm as they watched in awe. The smaller wolves retreated a good six feet back and stood with bowed heads, tails between legs.

The large wolf whined like a scolded puppy as the newcomer pinned it to the ground, its legs flailing. The fourth wolf wasn't as big, but it was dominant. The larger animal could have taken this new arrival with ease, but instead it became passive, allowing itself to be held and sat upon by the smaller werewolf, which had its back legs straddling its opponent.

In an instant, the creatures began to transfigure. The sound of their bones cracking into the upright, human form set Erica's teeth on edge.

They were as naked as the day they were born.

'For fuck's sake Archie, that's my sister. Didn't you hear her?' Lewis rose from the ground, releasing Archie – but not before giving him a hard shove on the shoulder.

Erica wasn't listening to the argument that followed. She was too transfixed by her brother's tail.

MISTY HAD HINTED at her brother's appearance but said you had to see it to believe it. Not half.

It was hard not to stare and even harder to make sense of – Erica's brain struggled to keep up. She watched Lewis shouting at Archie but it was as if the whole world had fallen silent; her brain only wanting to focus on one sense: vision.

His whole body was covered in dark fur. It was thickest on his legs and torso. The only bare parts were the palms of his hands and upper face. The strange thing was that, despite his outward appearance, when Lewis smiled Erica could see the image of her Father – they had the same brown eyes and charismatic smile.

She didn't know what was more of a trip – looking into her father's eyes or Lewis's other anomalies. The tail was unmissable. The large black bushy appendage remained unchanged after he Turned. However, Archie's body had blocked her brother's left foot and that too stayed in wolf form to just above the knee, giving him a slight limp and faun-like look.

Lewis made his way towards Erica as she finished buttoning her jeans. Pétur was still frozen by her side, eyes wide. It was good to know she wasn't the only one struggling to comprehend the situation.

Her brother pulled her into a tight embrace, his head nuzzling in beside hers. He was much taller than her and had to stoop down. He smelled musty – *boy sweat*.

'So it *was* you,' he exclaimed.

She brought her arms up and returned the hug, the fur on his back feeling alien to the touch. It was coarse, like brush bristles. This didn't feel real; she didn't know what to say.

He stepped back, his hands holding her upper arms, and looked her up and down. When he smiled, his canines were longer than the rest of his teeth, which gave him a vampire-like grin. In return she studied his face, looking past the mass of black fur. His nose looked like it had been broken a few times and sat at odd angles in two distinct places. It was such a peculiar feeling to be face-to-face with a stranger but feel the hint of a connection. A sort dynastic déjà vu.

'You're just how I imagined.' He laughed, her dad's laugh. 'By the look on your face I'd say I don't live up to your expectations.'

'No,' she said, shaking her head, 'I mean, yes, but this is just so much... I mean, I didn't even know I had a brother until a few hours ago.'

'Really?' He looked hurt. 'Mum told me all about you.' His accent
had a surprising Highland twang. It was so different to hers.

'What? Really?'

'No, I'm kidding.' He hit her lightly on the arm, biting his bottom
lip to suppress a grin. 'Come inside, let's talk. It's bloody freezing out
here.'

THE CABIN'S quaint après-ski theme continued inside: bare wooden
boards for walls, ceiling and floor. The kitchen, if you could even call
it that, was a DIY table positioned by a stone fireplace. It looked like it
had seen better days, its two-by-four legs splayed apart like the legs of
a deer on ice. Lewis pushed the door closed to silence the howling
wind outside; the only sound now was the fire which popped and
crackled in the warm hearth. The heady smell of smoke hit Erica's
nostrils on entry. She liked it; she'd always loved open fires but had
never had one. There was a romance to them; the idea of sitting
round it with loved ones toasting marshmallows or bread... Like
anyone ever did that. Her notion of family life was skewed. Erica
picked up another comforting smell – possibly a stew or soup, which
bubbled away in a cast iron pot hanging above the flames.

The size of the room was unexpected. The interior was a lot larger
than the outside of the building suggested, but knowing that four
adults lived here brought a new meaning to the phrase 'living in each
other's pockets'. There was no way Erica could live here. Sometimes
her two-bedroom flat was too small for her and Georgia.

'Please, sit,' Lewis said, motioning to the tatty sofas arranged
around the hearth. Erica opted for the one nearest the fire. As she sat
down, a spring poked into her bum cheek but she could cope with it.
P joined her, the look on his face suggesting that he was also
negotiating lumpy upholstery.

'I need to grab my shorts, I'll be right back,' explained Erica's
brother. 'Make yourselves at home.' He left the room through a door
behind them and his fellow wolves followed, leaving Erica and Pétur
alone. She was relieved she wasn't going to have to spend the next

hour or so avoiding eye contact with her brother's willy or his friend's boobs. Once aware, it's impossible not to look – our minds are designed to make life as awkward as possible for us.

Erica's heart was working overtime after their close encounter; she turned to Pétur who looked equally dumbfounded. Lost for words, she returned to taking in her brother's home.

Above the fireplace hung an array of dark metal pots and pans along with various sizes of knives. Crockery was stacked in neat piles along the mantelpiece. Everything looked like it had seen better days, but it was looked after. There was a definite feeling of pride in the house, each item had its place and was used to its full potential.

She was happy to see most of the remaining wall space was lined with shelving and guessed they were once used for Bill's books. Most of the shelves were now empty. She'd have to see if Bill wanted some new bookcases organising next time she visited him.

As the light was fading, Lewis returned to the room to light the many candles which were dotted about. He took a match from a box on the mantel before crouching down to the fire. Erica couldn't help but stare at his tail. It poked out from a hole cut in the seat of his shorts and swayed back and forth like a content dog's.

It wasn't long before the other wolves joined them, parking themselves on the remaining sofa. Archie continued to eye Erica and Pétur with suspicion. He was the largest of the three with a shaved head, muscular build, and sharp features. He had a large tribal tattoo flowing from his right elbow, up over his shoulder and down to his back. Erica recognised him as the arsehole who had ran at her car on Friday. Today he'd goaded her to fight. What had she done to warrant this hostility? Dick. She didn't like him and knew the feeling was mutual. She chose to keep quiet about their previous encounter for the time being, not wanting to ruin her brother's first impression of her.

The other two were more reserved. One was a small man who didn't look much older than twenty, dark haired with a mousey face – he came across as the timid one as he stared at his feet, avoiding eye contact. Maybe he thought they were getting enough from Archie.

The other could have been a character lifted straight from the pages of an adrenaline-filled werewolf comic. The only female of the small Pack, this girl was stunning – nothing short of a Wolf Goddess. She had the kind of looks that intimidated Erica, despite the fact she'd been the only one bar Lewis to display any warmth. She shot them a welcoming smile before sitting opposite, her perfect white teeth adding to her beauty. She must have been six feet tall, a good head above Erica, with gorgeous clear skin and a halo of black hair. Erica had always wanted perfect curls like that, her own wavy hair often looking like a half-arsed, straw-like mess.

Lewis blew out the match and flung it into the fire before perching on the arm of the sofa beside The Goddess.

'Anyone want a cup of tea? Or something stronger?' her brother asked.

A chorus of acceptance rang out. Archie rarely looked away from Erica, never mind blinked. She stared back, fighting the urge to tilt her head and stiffen her jaw in obvious defiance.

'Shall I introduce everyone?' the Goddess asked, interrupting Erica's silent standoff. She sounded East Coast. Edinburgh perhaps.

'Yeah, sure. Go for it,' her brother agreed, filling a metal kettle from a questionable-looking tap above the table. Where did the water come from? Surely they weren't able to get plumbing here.

'This is Dean,' she said, pointing to the mousey boy. 'Archie. And I'm Diane.'

Erica raised her hand, attempting a weak wave and half smile. 'Well, I'm Erica, which you already know, and this is Pétur.' She pointed a finger at him.

'So, we finally meet,' said her brother with a smile, as he placed the filled kettle on to a stand in the hearth. 'You'll know why everyone calls me Fuzz now, yeah?' He let out a hearty chuckle.

'I'm guessing that's down to the fur..?' she quizzed with a nervous smile. Was it ok to mention these things? She didn't feel right calling him Fuzz, not yet.

He laughed. 'It's ok to talk about it,' he reassured, as if he was capable of reading minds. *Please God; don't let him be able to do that.* 'It's what mum called me when I was a baby, something to do with an ultrasound. It stuck.'

'We couldn't figure out how Uncle Fuzz could've been Pétur,' she said, placing a hand on Pétur's knee before quickly pulling it away. The gesture felt far too intimate. 'It all makes sense now.'

'I'm definitely fuzzier,' he smiled, his eyes twinkling. He was holding back on emotion, she could tell. They were peas in a pod. 'Erica, Pétur – tea?' Lewis asked and took six cups from the mantelpiece, laying them out on the coffee table. They were old and worn, chipped in places with the telltale brown stains of heavy use. Still, she'd seen worse. He produced a similarly fatigued-looking teapot and filled it with boiling water from a kettle over the fire.

He tucked a strand of loose hair behind a pointed ear as he poured the water, keeping his long wavy locks out of his face. Teamed with his unkempt beard, Lewis could pass for a castaway, stranded on a deserted island for years.

'So, you all live here?' Erica asked, feeling the need to fill the silence while her brother played house.

'Yep, full-time,' Diane answered. 'Have done for the last four years. We're starting our own Pack off the grid.'

'Does Tobias know?'

Lewis laughed. 'Tobias doesn't even know I'm alive, Erica. As far as he knows, this little problem was fixed before I even took my first breath.' He perched on the sofa arm, waiting for the tea to brew.

'What do you mean?'

'You really don't know anything about me, do you?'

'Honestly, I didn't know you existed until this morning. I'm sorry.'

'No need to apologise, it's not your fault. It's mum's. She had trouble with honesty.'

She could feel the malice in his final sentence so, for the second time today, she asked if they could start at the beginning.

'So why didn't mum tell me about you?'

Lewis sighed. 'It would be part of her big plan no doubt. She was obsessed with allowing fate to run its course. If you'd known, you might have tried to find me before today.'

'And why does it matter that I waited until today?' Erica asked.

'The repercussions, the timeline, the journey – I don't know what you want to call it, but mum was adamant that whatever she saw had to happen, no matter what. Personally I think it's a load of shit. If it's meant to be it'll happen, no matter what you do.'

'Why do I feel like you know something I don't?' There was an underlying tone, a key fact that he was missing out on purpose. She could hear it in his voice.

He turned to Diane. 'It's getting late. Could you and the others go find us some food?' She complied, kissing Lewis on the cheek before leaving with Archie and Dean. He returned his focus to Erica and Pétur. 'Mum knew how bad things would be for me, how depressed I was, but she still let it happen. She could have stopped it but it was more important to let her visions happen. I was so lonely Erica – I needed you. Can you imagine how different our lives would be if we'd at least had each other?'

Her hands balled into fists at the thought.

L ewis sat himself on the coffee table, taking one of Erica's hands in his own. His palms were rough like sandpaper.

It was funny, the biggest thing, even above the tail, was that her brother was right-handed. Twenty-six years of being a lefty, subjected to unoriginal 'you know that means you had a twin that died' comments, and here she was. The beggars had been right. Almost.

Her brother spoke, lifting her out of her thoughts.

'How's Georgia? You said she was sick. You found Bill?'

'She's fine. Nearly better,' she paused. 'How do know she's called Georgia?' Erica hadn't gone into detail on Friday.

He laughed, pulling his hands from hers and slapping his thighs like a pantomime actor. 'You've caught me out. I do know a little bit about you, thanks to our pal Misty.'

'And Misty knows so much about me how..?' She crossed her arms, uneasy that a stranger was sharing personal details behind her back. Why was she always the subject of gossip? At least she was able to provide some entertainment.

'I suppose he hears stuff from his son.'

'His son? And who would that be?' she snapped. She wasn't thrilled to feel like the unwilling centre of attention.

Lewis sprang up, reacting to the change of tone. 'Let me pour us some more tea.'

'I think I have a right to know if someone is spying on me.'

'Nick,' he said, pausing mid-pour. 'Nick is Misty's son.'

That sneaky bastard. Her gut feeling had been right all along, he was hiding something. *How much does he know about me? Was he only with me so he could spy?* A chill ran down her spine and a rock tumbled into her belly. It wasn't that the relationship was meaningless – it was the deceit that hurt. He could have said or asked, where was the harm in being honest?

'Nick?' Pétur enquired.

'A friend,' she shot back before returning her attention to Lewis. 'Nick is Misty's son?'

'Mum didn't tell you?'

'You're more clued up than I am.' She got up and leaned an arm on the mantel, resting her head against the wall. 'Is there anything else I need to know?' she asked, dejected. 'Seriously, I can't take any more surprises.'

'Nothing. Well – Nick, Misty and I play cards together once a month. We're good friends. I don't know if that qualifies as a secret though.'

There was silence as Erica let her brain catch up. The fire crackled, causing a spark to fly out on to the hearth.

'Do you and mum still talk?' she asked, her voice calm as she stared into the flames.

'No. Haven't done for years. My choice.'

'How come? Her visions?'

'And those bloody books, you've maybe not – '

She cut him off. 'No, actually don't tell me. We've already gone way off topic.' She took a deep breath. Time to get back on course. The more she heard about her mother the more agitated and distracted she got. She was here for a reason, anything else could wait. 'You'll know there's been another Outbreak, yeah?'

'Of course.'

'Well, my friend's daughter is sick. I don't think it's a coincidence.'

'And she's not...? She's human – a proper Seelie?'

'Yes but there's a connection and I think you all know more than you're letting on.'

'I don't know much, all second-hand information. Diane goes to the meetings.'

'Well, tell me what you do know,' Erica said, putting on her most reassuring, calm voice.

'I reckon you'll know as much as me, but I have theories.'

'Theories?' Pétur piped up, intrigued.

Lewis took a deep breath, deciding to where to start. 'Ok, so,' he said, exhaling through pursed lips. 'They keep telling us it's infecting wolves through the water supply. So it has to be coming in at the purification stage or later. It's not organic.'

'What makes you say that?'

'We purify our own water here. Straight from the sky. Never had any issues.'

'So that's proof that someone is intentionally poisoning wolves?' Erica queried, wanting to make sure she understood.

'It would certainly look that way. I'd expect to have experienced at least one problem over the past twenty-six years otherwise.'

'Hmm.' She'd long suspected that was the case, but Tobias hadn't confirmed anything. It was only ever referred to as a 'virus', which you caught if you were unlucky, not because you'd been poisoned on purpose.

'And these Seelie kids, you definitely think they're suffering from the same poison?'

'I'm sure of it. The fairies have proof that Seelie magic deaths spike when we have outbreaks.'

It was his turn to hum and haw. 'Well, I've never heard of any Seelies getting ill from it. Kinda shits all over the water thing too doesn't it? Or they'd all be sick.'

That hadn't occurred to her. She took a long sip of tea, weighing the idea up. 'You think it's more targeted than we suspect?'

'I'd say, if your Seelie theory is right, you're looking for a wolf with magic ability. An inside job. Know anyone that fits the bill?'

Just herself. Or the man sitting opposite her. But best not to accuse your twin brother of murder on the first day you meet.

She shook her head.

'And this kid, have you tested her?'

'For what?' she wondered.

'To see if an enchantment is definitely making her ill?'

'I didn't even know that was something we could do.' Why hadn't Misty mentioned it? *Arsehole.*

'Follow me!' Lewis called, heading to his bedroom.

. . .

THE BEDROOM FLOOR was monopolised by four mattresses. No bed frames or bases, just beat-up mattresses on the bare wooden floor. It was like a squat.

She stepped over piles of clothes and God knows what else, following her brother to the far wall and his potion kit.

'Excuse the mess,' Lewis blustered. 'Archie does my nut in with his clothes.'

'It's ok, I've seen worse.' Nick's was definitely worse. If this was a squat, Nick's rivalled a crack den.

A ragged curtain hung from the ceiling to divide the middle of the room. 'Just in case the others come back,' said Lewis as he pulled it closed behind them. 'Avoid the nosy questions.' He winked. If that curtain was all the privacy he got with Diane then heaven help him. She didn't envy his lifestyle. 'Let me just move some stuff,' Lewis said, putting a stack of books on the floor to clear space.

His kit was rudimental but it more than covered the basics. He opened a tatty cupboard which sat on the desk. It looked like it had once belonged in a bathroom. He was mumbling under his breath, pulling out potion bottles and ingredients before changing his mind and popping them back.

'How do you know all this?' Erica asked. Her mother hadn't taught her any of this stuff – why just Lewis?

'I was raised by fairies; I know enchanted produce like the back of my hand. With that comes the responsibility of knowing what to do when things go wrong.'

'Ah, I didn't think the fairies cared.'

He grinned. 'What? No way, fairies are responsible creatures. Well, that and they want to cover their backs. Prove their innocence.'

She laughed. 'Now, that makes sense.'

He settled on a selection of leaves and herbs and added them to a mortar. 'Here, grind these to a pulp.' He shoved it along the table, thrusting the pestle at her before he got to work mixing oils.

'What is this? It smells amazing.' It looked like pesto.

'I can write all this down for you, if you want.' He dipped his finger into the mixture before sucking it clean. 'Tastes great on chicken too,'chuckled Lewis.

'You sure you're meant to do that?'

'It's all natural! Bill would laugh at me and call me a hippy, but it works. I believe in working with what the land gives you. Be careful though, it's enchanted. Get the quantities wrong and – ' He drew a line across his neck before inspecting Erica's handiwork. 'Right, that looks awesome.'

'What now?'

'Now, we mix this in.' With great care he poured the oil mixture into the herbs while stirring. He looked at her, his eyes wistful. 'This is nice, the two of us together at last.'

'I'm still processing to be honest,' admitted Erica. 'Have you always known you had a sister?'

'Pretty much, yeah.'

'I wish mum had at least told me about you. We could have promised not to meet.'

'Mum didn't like taking chances.' He stopped stirring and pulled a glass beaker towards them with such force it made Erica jump. 'Sorry, don't want to get too melancholy. Let's change the subject,' he suggested. 'Can you pour? Hold on, one sec.' He placed an offcut of fabric over the glass, securing it with a rubber band. 'Don't worry, it's not Archie's pants. Go on, pour it over.'

The weight of the pulp sagged the fabric into the beaker and clear liquid trickled through.

'How long 'til it's ready?'

'Twenty minutes. Come through and sit by the fire. I want to know more about my niece.' He smiled, his eyes lighting up.

'WE NEED to go back to Misty,' Pétur said for the hundredth time. They'd spoken in circles all the way to Glasgow. Erica was on the edge, about to snap, frustration getting the better of her.

'No. This is getting us nowhere Pétur. We need to be in the

Chambers doing actual research. We've wasted too much time already.'

The weekend had become a wild goose chase. The last few days had been a convoluted journey from one person to the next with no answers. She was sick of it. Everyone giving them tiny titbits of useless information and sending them off to God knows where. Either they were fobbing her off, or this knot was too far gone to be untangled.

She needed to stop spending so much time chasing pointless leads and be with Georgia and Sam. She'd abandoned them for the sake of a futile mission.

It's all connected, just listen to me. Her brother's theories had sparked her own ideas, but the specific link eluded her. It was there though – she could feel it. A bit of research and a visit to the hospital to test Sam should be their next step.

'And what are you going to research exactly?' Pétur quizzed. He didn't look convinced.

'I dunno. Something, anything, everything. Nearly a hundred Pack members have died, and there'll be more... Not to mention all the Seelies we don't know about.'

'So you still think Sam's illness is connected?'

She hit the steering wheel in frustration, a little too hard. 'Yes, Pétur. It is.'

They were parked in Wellington Street, not far from the Chambers. She started to get out of the car but was stopped by Pétur talking again.

'I think you're wasting your time Erica. Give Misty what he wants and we can get a straight answer. You know fine well he knows more than he's letting on.'

She breathed out with a sharp huff, before getting out of the car and ducking back in to tell him, eye to eye: 'Do what you want Pétur. It's your money. The number forty-four or sixty-six buses go to Misty's. Now, get out of my car.'

She slammed the door and walked away. Hearing Pétur close his, she turned and locked the car to find him trotting up behind her.

'So you're mad at me for suggesting a different plan?'

'No, I'm mad because no one ever fucking listens to me. When it comes to this Pack they talk down to me, I'm the little orphan girl who has nothing to offer. Well fuck that. I'm sick of it,' she said, jabbing the car keys at his face. That was a step too far, so she put them in her pocket, taking a deep breath. 'Listen, either help me or do what you think is right. Don't waste time arguing about it though.'

PÉTUR CHOSE to follow her lead, joining her in the Chambers. They took the elevator in silence, tension hanging in the air. Pétur was very into studying his fingernails. She shoved her hands in her pockets and stared at the ceiling. *Great.*

She was surprised to find Tobias sitting by Georgia's bedside. He sprang to his feet when they entered the room, like a child caught with his hand in the cookie jar.

'Tobias,' Erica said, eyes narrowing.

'Erica.'

'What are you doing here?'

'Just checking my great niece is ok.'

'Since when did you develop a conscience?'

He ignored her jibe and went to leave the room.

'Wait,' Erica said quickly, stopping Tobias in his tracks by putting her hand on his chest. 'What's that on my daughter's arm?' she asked, going to G's bedside and inspecting a plaster on her child's inner elbow. A blue bruise poked out from underneath.

'Just a few blood tests. Georgia is the only one to survive this; we need it for research.'

'And what gives you the right to do that without asking me?'

'I didn't think it was necessary – I'm her relation too. Plus you've been gone for the best part of the weekend. You were hardly here long enough to ask. Surprising, to be honest.'

'And what's that supposed to mean?'

'If it was *my* child I wouldn't have left her bedside. Instead you've been out gallivanting and drinking with that.' He eyed Pétur like he was dirt. God, she would love to hit the twat square in the face.

Instead of resorting to unbridled violence – after all, her daughter was watching – Erica counted to five before answering: 'I'll remind you that it was you who stopped me from staying. I would've been here twenty-four-seven if you'd have let me.' Tobias smirked, as if to conclude it was a poor excuse, forcing her to justify her absence further. 'And, for your information, we've been working on finding a cure for this.'

'And?'

'And what?'

'How's that coming on?'

'We're getting there.'

'Oh, come on Erica. Even your degenerate mother would have the answer worked out. You should know your worth by now. Don't push too far, it only leads to disappointment,' he said, each word dripping with condescension.

Remember you're setting an example Erica. Violence is not the answer. Unless the question is Tobias and it's justified? Could she make a new rule please? She'd held back for eighteen years, he was trying his luck and her moral fibres were wearing thin. She balled her fists before taking a deep breath and rising above his remarks.

'You do not touch my child without me here, ok?' She poked at his chest with her index finger. A few sharp jabs would have to satisfy her need for bloodshed. She could settle for a bruise at least.

He lowered himself to her eye level, his dark brown eyes staring into hers, his nose an inch from her face. He spoke in a near whisper, puffing stale whisky breath at her, but the menace wasn't lost. 'Watch yourself Erica. I got rid of your mother and I can get rid of you... And your little ice dogs. It's only a matter of time.' He pushed his way past before she had the chance to retaliate.

THEY STAYED with Georgia for the best part of an hour, but Erica was wound up, the anger coiling tighter and tighter inside her like a loaded spring. It was hard to read The Puffin Book of Stories and sound cheery when all you wanted to do was smash your uncle's head off a wall.

'We need to go do some work upstairs darling,' Erica said, hopping off the bed. 'We won't be long. Do you need anything?'

Georgia shook her head. 'Can I go home soon, Mum? It's boring here.'

Erica hated to admit it but Tobias was right about one thing – she had left G alone more than she would have liked. Despite leaving her with stacks of books, plenty of drawing materials and the iPad, she'd been neglecting her maternal duties. Striking the right balance was always tough, but the Pack and Sam needed Erica to find answers. Should she be honest with G about Sam being sick and what she'd been doing this weekend? Not now – maybe later. She didn't want to cause G more worry then disappear off again.

'I know. I'd be bored too,' she said as she stroked a few stray hairs away from her daughter's face. 'Maybe home tomorrow. Perhaps Uncle Pétur will stay with us too?' She looked at him, forcing a smile. She wasn't mad at him, just the situation. She didn't want him to think she was an asshole.

'I'd like that,' he said, a smile creeping across his lips. He looked surprised.

'Ok. Back soon, I promise.' She eyed her socks and shoes on the radiator – still drying from P's earlier act of dickishness. *Wait, should I still be mad about that?* – but sometimes it was nice to be barefoot. P obviously thought the same, as he followed her to the elevator, cold laminate underfoot.

'You're still angry, aren't you?' he asked after the doors closed.

The rickety lift rose two storeys before she answered, body language speaking for itself, her arms crossed tight against her chest. 'Yes I fucking am.'

'You know, you swear a lot.'

'It helps me release tension. You have a problem with that?' Pétur sniggered, his shoulders shaking. 'What?'

'You're so angry all the time, swearing like a sailor.'

'And why's that funny?'

'You're this petite, pretty blonde girl and then you open your mouth and it's like *Ahhhh*,' he said, putting his hands up like a pouncing lion and shaking about. 'You're not how I expected you to be.'

'So someone can't look like me and swear?' The word 'pretty' was filed for later. That was a welcome compliment.

The elevator doors pinged open and he followed her out. 'No. It's just funny.'

'You're an odd little man, P.'

'Less of the *little* please.'

Erica was about to reply when she found the library doors locked. Odd, she didn't even know they could be. No bother though as she placed her hand on the doorknob, feeling its inner workings with her mind's eye. It was satisfying to feel the levers click up one by one before flicking the bolt inward.

She opened the oak double doors with a deep breath. 'Here we go then.'

The library was rarely used. Not a new issue, it was reserved for the more research-inclined wolves and they were few and far between at the best of times. However, like the libraries of the Seelie world, the majority of the occult was online these days, rendering this room and its contents somewhat obsolete.

A dark wooden table, easily fifteen feet long and surrounded by matching chairs, took pride of place in the middle of the room. Each chair was upholstered in red leather with the gold Scottish Pack crest in the centre. If she hadn't lived with Tobias for ten years, she would have guessed his dining room looked much the same – instead he'd opted for John Lewis' finest. Even he was capable of surprises.

The surrounding walls were lined with shelves, plus there were four freestanding cases spanning the length of floor, along with a small mezzanine level which looked packed with literature. There were a lot of books – she'd be damned if she knew where to start.

'So, where do we start?' Pétur asked, right on cue.

Erica sighed and made her way towards the table. It was covered in a thick layer of dust. She ran a finger over it. *God, that was satisfying.*

She eyed her father's thinking chair in the corner. She didn't have the heart to look at it today. Instead she focused on the crisp line carved into the dust.

Inspiration struck. 'We need to find a record of the deaths from Scotland's ninety-one outbreak. Start building a picture.' Like the game murder-in-the-dark, victim location might be what they needed to narrow their leads.

He looked about. 'Any idea where they might be?'

'Not a scoobie. Let's split up and start searching.'

FORTY MINUTES LATER, they didn't seem to be any closer to finding what they were looking for. She was still seething over her run-in with Tobias. What had his threat meant? *He was such a pompous prick.*

'Any luck?' she asked, trudging up to Pétur on the mezzanine.

He was sitting on the floor surrounded by stacks of books. As he turned to answer he knocked a large pile over, causing the heavy hardbacks to cascade across the floor with a loud thud. He looked at them, made a face, and chose to ignore the mess. 'No. It's all biblical or scripture. There's a whole section about vampires over there.' He waved a hand towards the bookcase on his left.

She leaned against a wooden desk and rubbed her temples, defeated. 'Maybe Tobias is right. I might as well give up.'

Pétur rose, his knees cracking. He gave his right one a rub before settling alongside Erica. 'I didn't think you gave up that easily.'

'It's been a tiring weekend.'

'So? You can't let your uncle get in there,' he said, pointing at her forehead.

'Even you think this is the wrong way to go about things.'

'No I don't. I trust you.' He rose and positioned himself in front of her, taking hold of her upper arms. 'And I believe in you. We're going to figure this out.' She forced a weak smile and looked at him, unsure what to say. She was no good at face-to-face gratitude.

He smiled back, holding her gaze. His hands remained on her arms. The electricity between them grew; that tantalisingly magic moment before something happens. Will they? Won't they? That's the thrill.

His gaze flicked between her eyes and her lips. She wasn't going to be the one to make the first move this time; it was up to him if this was going to go further.

He's Georgia's uncle hung at the back of Erica's mind before disappearing. It's not like they were related, he was no different than any other man in that respect. It would seem she'd slept with the wrong brother to begin with. If you could even use that phrase – there had been no sleeping involved. In fact, had it not been for Georgia's arrival, Erica would argue nothing had been involved. It was that quick, and it had been awful. What if crap sex ran in families? Surely life wouldn't be so cruel?

However, copping off with your kid's uncle was a bad idea. Things could get messy. But he *was* from Iceland – when would she ever see him again? Something about Pétur said he wasn't one to find family and forget about them though.

And then there was that bastard diary. Would it be that bad if –

He kissed her. Her mind emptied, all she could think of was the gentle scratching sensation of his beard, the heady juxtaposition of it and his soft lips. The memory of the other night flooded back, causing an immediate rush of feelings for him. She wanted more.

She slid her hands under his sweatshirt and grabbed at his hips. He moved to between her thighs, pulling her closer as her legs closed around him. She squeezed tighter as his mouth moved to her neck, kissing under her ear. *Fuck*, she loved the rough tickle of his beard on that spot. A moan escaped before she could help herself. He drove the kiss deeper, biting and sucking at her skin. That was going to leave a mark but she didn't care.

She could feel him getting hard and didn't hesitate to start undoing his belt, only stopping the motion of unzipping his jeans when he lifted her, hands under her bum. He spun one-eighty to the couch behind them, laying her down before sliding in between her legs. *A smooth move... Sexual incompetence doesn't run in families after all.*

He was back to kissing her mouth, tongues finding their way between heavy breaths. They both fumbled to pull their jeans off, not wanting to break contact despite the awkward positions it was forcing them into.

Seconds later he was back between her legs, one foot on the ground to steady himself.

'Wow,' she said, her breath slowly returning to normal. 'I was not expecting that.'

He smiled before kissing her neck. 'Me neither.'

They lay in silence for a while, collecting their thoughts, him behind her on the small couch and both naked from the waist down. Erica loved the feeling of being 'little spoon' after sex. Skin to skin was comforting, the perfect ending as her body recuperated.

The serenity wasn't to last though.

They both tensed as the library door opened, like a frightened animal in headlights might do, as if being motionless made them invisible. Pétur's hand gripped her hip.

Footsteps made their way into the room, stopping a few strides in. She held her breath.

Their unexpected visitor didn't move.

Pétur was sure that anyone else in the library would've been able to hear his heart beating, it was going that fast. The blood in his ears drummed so loudly – too loudly. He breathed through his nose, keeping quiet, but all he wanted to do was pant, get oxygen to his muscles as he panicked.

What the hell was this person doing? Why had they stopped in the middle of the library?

He eyed his jeans a few feet away, alongside Erica's under the desk. There was no way they could get them on without being discovered. All they could do was wait and hope that whoever it was disappeared as suddenly as they'd arrived.

Erica turned towards him. He widened his eyes, hoping the question of what on earth she was up to translated. She raised her eyebrows in a show of cocky bravado before using his shoulder for leverage. Was she really going to sneak a look at this person?

Pétur grabbed her arm, pulling her back down and tilting his head to show he wasn't up for these games.

'Erica?' Tobias's voice. *Shit.*

His heavy footsteps echoed throughout the room. An eternity seemed to pass between each one. He stopped at the bottom of the stairs to the mezzanine.

'Erica?' Tobias sang.

A loud creak told them her uncle was coming up. Pétur's stomach was in knots. He'd never been caught in a position like this. Tobias would see them – any minute now. The two of them huddled together on this tiny sofa, his cock out for all to see. Erica no better. He could grab his jeans now, pull them on before Tobias saw. Save a little dignity. They were going to be discovered regardless. He could at least do it with clothes on.

Tobias was halfway up the steps; he'd be high enough to see them soon.

A cold rush ran over Pétur as Erica dusted him. She grabbed their discarded clothes and threw his jeans at him. He balled them over his crotch to protect his modesty.

He froze, the blood in his ears a deafening crescendo, underscored by a rhythmic *thump thump thump*. His heart was going to burst out of his chest soon.

Tobias crested the stairs and was only feet away. Erica held a finger to her lips, her other hand slicing the air telling Pétur to be quiet and stay still.

Tobias spotted the books on the floor. He didn't look happy – his eyes reduced to slits and his lips puckered. He walked over and bent down to inspect them. He turned a few over to read the spines before throwing them back to the floor and chuckling to himself.

He walked to the bannister. Erica took the opportunity to flick 'V's at him as he passed, her face scrunched in exaggerated anger.

Tobias walked and talked like an absolute prick. Even at his current snail's pace, he had the swagger of a man who thought the world owed him everything. He was terrifying.

Keep it together. Don't let your breathing get the better of you.

Tobias paused for a few minutes, surveying the floor below. It felt like hours passed.

'That stupid little bitch,' Tobias said to no one. Pétur jumped, checking to see if Erica spotted the embarrassing slip. No reaction, good. Tobias turned to the bookcase that Pétur had been emptying. Halfway across the mezzanine, Tobias turned, looking straight at them. This was the end. He could see them – why else would he turn?

He looked to Erica, whose face was also creased with confusion. Was Tobias looking at them or behind them? Had he heard something? *Am I breathing too loudly? Have I given us away?*

Erica looked her uncle in the eye with sheer defiance. There was no fear with this girl. Pétur's mouth was hanging open like a fish as he looked between the two of them. Neither of them were blinking. It reminded him of staring competitions at school; he was no good at them and never won.

Tobias lost interest in whatever had caught his attention and carried on making his way towards the bookcase. Erica continued to stare. Her jaw was tensed; he could practically feel the anger throbbing from her. God, she hated that man. He didn't blame her.

Erica had only hinted at her life with Tobias. Tiny puzzle pieces which had been dropped into conversation painted an upsetting picture. She'd been left on her own a lot, told she wasn't to be seen or heard and was forgotten about. Pétur hadn't asked Erica if she'd done anything about it – unlikely since she left when she was eighteen. In fact, it was none of his business what had gone on in her past. Hopefully she was happier now. She seemed happier.

Tobias skimmed the books left in the half-empty bookcase. Unable to find what he was looking for he moved to the next, stooping down while holding a finger to his lips, mind deep in thought. Unsatisfied again, he straightened up, letting out a deep breath. His attention turned to the bookcase containing witchcraft and, like a man on a mission, he marched over. This time he was successful and pulled out a book. It didn't look like much – a dark cover with gold writing on the front – but the look on Tobias's face showed he'd found what he was looking for.

He smiled. It was strange, his smile had a wickedness to it, real malice, but Pétur could see a resemblance to Erica's own grin. The difference was that she did it when she was being playful, but there was genuine hostility in her uncle's expression. How odd it must be to have the image of her dead father confront her daily. No wonder she avoided him.

Pétur looked back at Erica. Her muscles were less tense but the anger remained. Her eyes narrowed. He scooted over and placed a hand on her knee. He looked her in the eye and hoped she could tell what he was thinking. *It's going to be ok.* She continued to watch her uncle. She probably wasn't having the same internal dialogue and still wanted to bash Tobias's face in. Fair enough.

Pleased with his find, Tobias left; book in hand, locking the door behind him.

The couple sat in silence for a minute or so, making sure he was gone. They exchanged smiles. They'd got away with it.

It was Erica who made the first move, allowing herself to laugh as she pulled her jeans on.

'Look at your face, P!' she laughed. 'You were bricking it. Did you forget I could do that?'

'Yes,' he said, accidentally shouting. He cleared his throat, bringing his voice down to normal volume. 'I thought that was the end. Why didn't you do it sooner?'

She undid her hair and scraped it back, tidying it before retying her ponytail. 'Kinda forgot I could do it, if I'm honest.' She bit her bottom lip; that playful grin was back. Pétur didn't find it funny. He gave her a death stare and pulled his boxers on.

'What do you suppose he was looking for?' she wondered, inspecting the witchcraft bookcase. She ran a finger over the shelves, stopping at the vacant space left by Tobias.

'No idea, bit odd really.' He was attempting to put his jeans on but misjudged his footing and stumbled. Thankfully his second attempt was successful.

'Hmmm,' she breathed with a huff, perplexed.

'Can you imagine if he'd caught us?'

'He would've been raging.' She turned on her heel and wrung her hands together. Her eyes were wide with excitement. 'So, up here isn't proving fruitful. I have an idea – follow me.'

THE BASEMENT. Damper than an otter's pocket. It smelled like one too – musty, old and stale. Or at least what he expected one would smell like. He'd never sniffed an otter. In fact, wait, what pocket was that phrase referring to? Scratch that.

Erica flicked the six light switches by the elevator door. *Click, click, click, click, click,* and *click.* Strip lights buzzed into action at sporadic intervals, not all of them wanting to work. The pair waited, hoping some were slow to fire up but only a handful of the lights came on.

It was dark. The few lights which worked gave out a dirty, dusty light, akin to meagre candlelight. Still, it was enough to see. Just. The floor was simple concrete, the kind you'd find in a garage. It was thick with dirt, the occasional elastic band or paper clip hidden in the fuzzy grey muck.

Pétur wished he had shoes on. Not only were his feet already foul with dust but they were freezing too. He looked at the sole of his right foot – black. No point going back for shoes now, he'd need a wash first.

Erica didn't show any fear when it came to going deeper into the room. Pétur followed, not wanting to look like a coward. The basement wasn't as grand as the flamboyant floors above. Despite the dim light, he could see a haze of dust floating in the air like a gentle but intense snowstorm. The air became more dense as they moved; even the smallest of movements caused the space around them to be consumed by the grey flecks.

There was an odd atmosphere here. Maybe it was the pockets of darkness, the many hiding places between the racking, or the standard feeling of basements the world over, but Pétur was certain he was being watched. The hairs on the back of his neck stood on end.

He'd watched a programme about how fluorescent lighting could make you see ghosts. A local library's basement was reportedly haunted, but it was later found to have a high electromagnetic field, or EMF, and humans didn't respond well to that. It made you go a bit mad, especially if exposed for a long time. Maybe the broken lights were still emitting a current, the EMF causing the hair on his neck to stand up.

'Split up again?' Erica asked, standing in the corridor between two racks. 'I'll take this one, you can look there.' She pointed to her right.

'What are we looking for again?'

'A file, a book, I dunno. Something that documents Pack deaths.'

'Ok, cool,' he said and disappeared into his own corridor. What he really wanted to say was *I'll stick with you, thanks.*

The basement was divided by eight rows of industrial racking, the kind you might find in a well-organised garage or shed. The metal units were tall, a good head and shoulders above him. The top one nearly touched the roof – all available space had been put to good use. The row nearest Pétur was full of old cardboard document boxes, tatty and torn, a layer of dust settled on each one.

He could see Erica moving through her shelves, even climbing up to reach higher boxes. Her jumper and jeans were covered in dirt but she didn't seem to care.

'Found anything?' Her face appeared through a gap in the boxes.

'Nothing. This is all crap.'

'I'm sure they're here. I've seen enough detective shows to know the best files are kept in the basement.' She disappeared and a gentle thud told him she'd jumped down. 'So?'

'So what?' He took a box from the top shelf and placed it on the floor, ready to empty its contents. The box was damp – not wet, but cold and flimsy.

'So, it's been at least an half an hour and you've not mentioned that we had sex.'

He wasn't expecting that. 'And you want to talk about it?' He slid a box over and found her on the other side. She scrunched her face up before answering.

'Not really, but you seem the type to want to. I'm avoiding an awkward conversation later.'

'What is there to say?'

She laughed.

They were interrupted by the buzzing of Erica's phone. Pétur was surprised she had a signal here.

'It's Quinn,' she said, answering the call. 'I'd better take this.'

Had he wanted to talk about it? He hadn't had a chance to think. The whole weekend had been a whirlwind of activity; it was taking a while for anything to sink in. They'd slept together – what did that mean? Were things going to be awkward when he was next with Georgia and Erica? Had he made a huge mistake? Maybe she regretted it. No, she wouldn't have mentioned it so casually if she did.

He could hear her wandering the rows of racking, *uhuhs* and *oks* keeping the conversation going with her best friend.

A feeling in the pit of his stomach niggled. The last one-night stand he'd had (*his last*, ha – his only!) was at uni. Her name was Sabína and he'd been very drunk. Did he regret it? No, but it had made him realise that single encounters weren't for him. So why had he chosen to sleep with his niece's mother? Talk about making things more complicated than they already were. Erica had been clear about where she stood with relationships, but something had taken over in the moment and he'd acted on impulse. He wouldn't apologise for what had felt right.

Maybe it was the diary. He was certain it was him in the vision. Who else could it be? It made the most sense – perfect sense in fact.

He wouldn't call his son Trevor though. Óskar, Rúben, or Stefán perhaps... Not that he'd been thinking about it or anything.

'Yeah, ok. Well, keep in touch Quinn.' She finished the call from the furthest wall of the basement. Without saying a word she returned to her row and went back to looking in boxes.

'Everything ok?' he asked, putting his box back. It had only been invoices for medical supplies.

She remained quiet and he was about to ask her again in case she hadn't heard him, but at last she spoke.

'Not really.'

'Is Sam ok? Want to talk about it?'

He was sure he heard a sniff.

'Not really.' Silence again. 'Sam had another seizure,' she paused again. 'It's not looking good.'

'Oh God.' He pushed his box aside to check she was ok, but she pushed it back.

'No, look, I'm fine. Let's keep searching. We have to stop this thing.'

THEY'D CHECKED every box and folder. Nothing.

All that remained was a dark and desolate corner at the back of the room. The four nearest lights were out, so it was pitch black. Both had avoided it, and Pétur couldn't even look at it. Anything could be lurking there.

'We'll look together,' she said, hands on hips as they stood side by side, sizing it up.

'How are we going to see anything?'

'Don't you worry about that.' They remained rooted to the spot. 'Well, on you go. You first.' She stepped aside, ushering him onward.

He exhaled and made towards the pitch black. *Time to be brave.*

The corner was extra musty, the pungent aroma of dampness caught in his throat, making him swallow hard. He was right by the racking and could see only darkness in front of him. Erica bumped into him when he stopped.

'Sorry,' she muttered, hand on his arm. 'Right, you ready?'

'Ready for what?'

'Watch.' She let go of his arm with a gentle caress that sent a tingle down his spine. *What was she going to do?*

One by one, golf ball-sized orbs of blue-white light floated into the air, hovering above them in a straight line. After the first, he watched in awe as she shaped another three with her palms, like Langamma used to roll chocolate truffles, and send them into the air. It was mesmerising.

The racking was now lit.

The corner above them looked wet – no wonder it smelled so bad. It might have been leaking and festering for decades. Hopefully what they needed wasn't on the top rack or it would be ruined.

They set to work looking through the files and document boxes. Erica found an old leather-bound book stuffed at the back of one shelf. It dated from 1776. Someone needed to get in here and clean it, get the right storage sorted, or all of it would be lost.

Three shelves examined and little found. Only the top one to go.

Erica started to climb, a method that had become second nature after investigating the other sixteen or so top shelves. This one, however, wasn't cooperating. The shelf split and buckled as she put her full weight on it, making her jump to the floor.

'You'll need to give me a lift,' she said turning to Pétur. He went to lift her under the arms but she stopped him. 'No, not like that. We're not dancing.' She smiled and pointed between her legs. 'Shoulders. I'll be able to get higher.'

'Alright, I'll try my best,' he said and ducked level with her thighs. It wasn't the most graceful lift but he managed, his knees shaking as they rose. Once he straightened himself up, she wasn't difficult to hold – she wasn't big, but the added height was weird and sent him off balance. 'See anything?'

'Not yet. Move forward will you?' She was holding on to his head and giggled as she covered his eyes when he went to step forward.

'Ay, be careful or I'll drop you!'

'Accidentally or on purpose?' she chuckled.

'I'm not sure yet.' He stepped forward, chest against the racking, and she moved her hands to the top shelf. Above his head he heard the scraping of boxes across the gritty shelf.

He assumed her search was as unproductive as the rest when she said, 'Can you move forward any further?'

'Not really.'

'Hmm. Put your hands under my feet.'

'Under your feet?'

'Under my feet.'

He did so and she pushed forward. *Jesus.* His forearms shook as her full weight bore down.

'Got it,' she said, falling back on to his shoulders.

He felt breathless – that had been a hard position to hold. 'What is it?'

'Exactly what we came for.'

The book lay open on the library table. A simple leather ledger, its contents looked like it could belong to a bookkeeper or accountant. Pages of meticulous columns detailing name, date of birth, date of death, registration district and – most importantly – cause of death.

The most interesting fact was found on the book's spine. 1990-1999. It was alone, with no other records kept before or after. Why had this decade been banished to the darkness of the basement? The damp hadn't got to it, meaning it couldn't have been there long. Something was off. But wasn't something always off where Tobias was concerned?

She read names out to Pétur who in turn listed every 1991 outbreak death on a piece of paper. It was slow going, but they were getting somewhere.

'Joseph Conway, September twenty-second, 1991, Dundee. And I think that's the last one.'

He looked at the two sides of A4 he'd scribbled down. 'Is that it? I thought there'd be more.'

'This outbreak wasn't as bad as what we're dealing with now.' She looked at his paper. Forty-one names. Thirty-two of them under sixteen years of age. Horrible. It hurt to think it was worse this time.

'So what next?' he asked.

Why did she have to lead the way? This was her plan though; he'd wanted to go straight to Misty.

'Erm, order them by location I suppose.'

'This is going to take ages,' he huffed. Erica was exhausted too. It would be a tedious task.

'I know. Why don't I read out the location and you tally them up?'

She'd heard about an E. Coli outbreak when she was little. Was it pinpointed to a butcher or a dairy farm? She couldn't recall, but she did remember feeling scared. The news was full of reports of children dying not far away from Erica's safe little home in Bearsden.

There's always a pattern with these things, you just need to spot it. Every outbreak needed an epicentre.

THEIR OPTIMISM DIDN'T last long. This was impossible.

Tallying up numbers had got them nowhere. Locations were sporadically spread, with neither rhyme nor reason for the outbreak's distribution. There were more deaths in Glasgow and Edinburgh, but that was a false lead. Of course the big cities would be affected more. Whoever was responsible was doing a good job of keeping things widespread.

Frustrated wasn't even the word.

'Rughhhh!' she said, the noise turning into a half-growl, half-scream. 'This is getting us nowhere.'

She screwed up her notes and flung them across the library. Much to her annoyance, they didn't go far and landed with a defeated plop.

Pétur reclined in his chair and stretched out his muscles, the old chair creaking in protest. He fished for his necklace and brought it to his mouth, massaging the hoop between finger and thumb. He was thinking.

Erica sighed and laid her head on the table, her arms a makeshift pillow.

This was what defeat looked like.

Pétur's chair scraped as he got up, his feet padding around behind her. His hands spread over her shoulders. He rubbed them, rolling the muscle and creating pressure with his thumbs.

She sighed again but this time with pleasure, she couldn't stop herself as his hands worked their magic. She smiled and peeked a look over her shoulder. He smiled back. Caught.

'Let's go over things again. Look at the information we do have, instead of what we're missing.' She sat up and wiggled her shoulders, loosening them. He carried on massaging her, his torso pressed against her back.

'Ok.' She closed her eyes, enjoying the feeling of his touch; she could entertain his affection for a while. 'We know the names of the children who died in ninety-one.'

'And?'

'We know where they died.'

'Uhuh.'

Was that not it?

'What else?' Pétur asked, moving both hands to focus on one shoulder.

'Erm...'

'Well, we know its not contagious or everyone would have it.'

'Right.'

'So it's just children and the occasional adult affected,' he said as he switched to work on the other shoulder.

'Ok. And where's this train of thought going?'

'Bear with me. I'm thinking out loud,' he sighed. Neither knew what to do. She could feel the knot of frustration twisting her stomach. She had to get up and do something or it would explode.

Erica's phone buzzed. A message from Quinn flashed on the screen. *Just wanting to check how Georgia is. No cha –* She didn't want to unlock it and read the rest.

Pétur pressed deeper into her shoulder. She could feel his thumb moving over the knots in her muscles, working them out with a satisfying *ping*. He stopped and kissed the top of her head. Her muscles tensed, a reflex so mechanical it was as natural as pulling her hand away from a flame.

It starts with an unimportant kiss, then next thing you know it's been ten years and you're arguing in Tesco about who last bought the loo roll and the act of holding hands seems passionate.

Cut it off now or forever hold your peace.

'Don't.' She shook her head. 'Don't ruin it.'

'Don't ruin what?' He removed his hands and stepped back.

She turned to face him. 'This is what I wanted to talk about earlier. We're so different P. We shouldn't have done... what we did.' She looked up towards the mezzanine. Her usual brashness was gone; she needed to be more sensitive, he deserved that much at least.

He looked hurt and narrowed his eyes with suspicion, certain he'd got the wrong end of the stick. 'So you want me to forget about it? Pretend it never happened?'

She got up and walked to the other edge of the table, a literal barrier between her and this awkward conversation. She hated confrontation.

'I don't think that would be a healthy thing to do.'

'Right, so...?' He sounded confused.

She sighed. 'Earlier on, I wanted you to know I don't want anything else to happen. Y'know, make it clear. I don't want to lead you on.'

'Isn't it a bit late for that? Or is sleeping with someone the norm for you, another part of conversation?' There was venom in his voice. She was sure he didn't mean it. At least she hoped he didn't.

She studied the fingerprints on the dusty desk and pondered her reply, making sure it was correct. No room for error.

'It's not.' It came out quieter than expected. She felt like a little girl being told off by a big bad adult. Her heart was racing, threatening to make her voice shake. That was new; she'd never been like this with a guy. She swallowed the lump in her throat and carried on. 'You deserve to know how I feel. I don't want a relationship. It's not that it didn't mean anything, but this is the end of it.'

Pétur looked at her, hands on the back of the chair, his arms tensed. He moved his gaze to the floor.

The silence hung in the air like a balloon waiting to burst until Erica spoke. The conversation could've ended there, but she couldn't hold it any longer. 'You're as much to blame as I am.' Her voice was quiet again.

'What?' he said, snapping his head up to make eye contact.

'You're as much to blame as I am. You made the first move, I didn't force you to have sex.'

'No, but don't you realise that most people aren't like you? Sex actually means something.'

'It did mean something.'

'No, not like that,' he fired back. 'It's a commitment, it means you like a person. This wasn't some drunken fumble after a night out; forget about it in the morning. There's a connection between us.'

A connection? What the hell did that even mean? Physical attraction didn't equate to anything more than simple lust.

'A connection?' she laughed. She wanted to call him out for sounding like a fifteen-year-old girl but thought better of it. 'This is what I mean P. We're chalk and cheese.' She ran a hand over her hair, smoothing it. 'I know the diary – '

'This has nothing to do with that book,' he snapped, cutting her off.

'It does. How can it not?'

'I could say the same for you,' he sneered.

'And what is that supposed to mean?'

'You're going to fight against this no matter what. Even if it means throwing your own happiness away.'

She flung her arms up in frustration. 'That's the point Pétur. It wouldn't make me happy.'

'How will you ever know if you don't even try?' He pushed the chair in with a squeak, frustration getting the better of him too. 'What's happened to you that you have this crazy overreaction to a simple kiss on the head?'

She looked at him, unable to answer. There wasn't a simple response; a relationship just wasn't on her agenda.

'I'm going,' she spat out in anger. 'Before we both say something we'll regret.' She turned on her heel, grabbing her phone from the table and heading for the door.

SHE HAD ISSUES. She knew. It wasn't normal for a twenty-six-year-old to have such an aversion to dating.

Erica was lying on a metal desk in the basement, staring at the concrete ceiling. Her arms were crossed, nostrils flaring while she silently raged inside, still furious.

Had she overreacted? Ok, yes. It was a simple kiss on the head – it wasn't like he'd got down on one knee and proposed. She didn't want to hurt him though, and wouldn't it be worse to ignore the little things and lead him on?

The contents of the diary did have a bearing. The bastard was right. Erica could come round to the idea of another child – Georgia was desperate for a sibling after all. But married? No, no, no.

There were nights she'd lain awake for hours wondering what was wrong with her. A lot of her friends were settling down, and a surge of marriages after they left uni had made her question herself more than ever.

Wasn't marriage the logical next step at her age? *Like she'd made any of the previous steps to get there.* That was it – her life was out of sync. She was doing everything in the wrong order.

She'd ticked all the right boxes while at school, only for them to be tipped upside down when Georgia arrived. Go to uni, get a job, forge a career... Then who knows? More boxes would surely come. Had G not been forced into the equation, children wouldn't have been on the radar either. Erica had surprised herself with how rewarding she found motherhood. *Maybe I like company after all?*

P might be right; she was stopping herself from trying anything. Surprise yourself once, and you might do it again. Maybe. There was that knot in her stomach.

A dull ache throbbed in her lower back. She hadn't wanted to go to Georgia; she needed peace and time to think. Here was the perfect place – it wasn't the comfiest though. Realising she should have sent Quinn a text by now, Erica shifted her weight to her elbow and propped herself up. She should have visited by now but wasn't in the right headspace for hospitals. *Definitely need to calm down first.*

She sent a quick reply to Quinn and sat up. She let her legs dangle over the desk for a while, swaying them back and forth. *What to do next?* She couldn't give up. How to find the right information though?

Erica bit her bottom lip. It was getting late; it had been a long-ass day. Nothing would be better right now than taking Georgia home and having their sofa night. But it wouldn't be fair when Quinn couldn't do the same.

Pushing herself off the desk and dusting her bum down, Erica saw plumes of dust shoot out around her, making the air hazy. She twisted round to see the damage – her jeans was black. Her elbows weren't much better so she could only assume her back was the same. Everything needed a wash anyway, herself included.

She surveyed the room, hands on hips. She was here, so she may as well check they hadn't missed anything. Her mind had been focused on talking to Pétur and worrying about Sam.

She made her way back to the dark corner. They'd found the ledger here, so maybe there was more to be discovered. It had been put it there on purpose – what other secrets was someone trying to conceal? Again she cupped her hands, creating orbs to provide some much-needed light.

Getting up the shelving would be harder without P there to give her a boost, but she had to try. She put a foot on the bottom shelf, gently shifting her weight to find its weak spots. Satisfied she'd found an area strong enough, she moved her full weight to the foot. It held – so far so good.

Doing the same on the second shelf proved harder as the gap between shelves was wider. She needed to reconsider her penchant for skinny jeans if this kind of behaviour was going to become a habit. After a few failed attempts she succeeded. She was more limber than she gave herself credit for.

She pulled herself up. Again it held.

Twisting to manoeuvre to the third shelf, shelf number two creaked under her left foot. What followed had to have happened in slow motion, there was no other explanation for it.

Her stomach sank, like when your car descends into a hidden dip. The shelf lurched, and there was nothing she could do but give in to gravity. The sudden jolt made her lose balance and, despite a flailing attempt to grab the shelf, there was nothing to stop her tumbling backwards. The surreal yet familiar feeling of free-falling took over. Only for a second, but enough for your brain to think *OH FUCK*.

E rica was sitting in the window seat of her shop.
      It took her a few seconds to realise she shouldn't be here.
Something was off. Her head was fuzzy.

She looked at the pastry fridge to see Sasha serving customers while Hazel manned the till. Nothing unusual there.

It wasn't busy, so it could have been a Wednesday or Thursday afternoon. It was usually dead then. The shop still buzzed. Hers was one of the smallest coffee shops in Glasgow and only had seven tables – it didn't take a lot for it to look rammed. Luckily most of their customers preferred to take away, most of them calling in from Queen Street Station opposite.

She checked out the station entrance. This was her favourite seat but it was often taken. From here you could people-watch. There was nothing more fascinating than people, especially travelling people. Each person had a story – from the commuters trapped in trivial daily repetition to the lovers saying goodbye; the students going home with laundry bag in tow to the guys coming back from the rigs past Aberdeen. Everyone had a mission when they visited Queen Street.

She was so engrossed in watching the to and fro that she didn't notice the person standing beside her.

'Aren't you going to give me a hug? Or even a hello?' a familiar Australian accent asked.

'Oh my God, Mum. I'm so sorry,' she chimed and sprang up to embrace her.

Lucy kissed the top of her daughter's head as she held her. 'You ok?'

'Not really,' Erica replied and sat down.

Her mother pulled the other leather armchair closer and took a seat. 'Want to talk about it over a coffee?'

·   ·   ·

TWO ESPRESSOS LATER, Erica had filled her mother in on the weekend's misadventures. She hadn't realised how much they'd crammed into seventy-two hours. No wonder she was tired.

'So you're still wanting to help Sam?' her mother asked.

'Any ideas? You managed to save G.'

'That's a bit different though.'

'How so?'

'Well, she's my granddaughter. I know her.'

Erica narrowed her eyes. 'So you know how to help, but you don't want to because you don't know her?'

'No, I'm not saying that.'

'Then what are you saying?'

Her mother paused, looking for the right words. 'I think, sometimes, you're best to stay out of other people's problems.'

'But she'll die Mum. I can't forget about her if there's a cure. How would I sleep at night?'

Lucy took her daughter's hands in her own. 'There are enough problems in our own world without interfering with Seelies too. There are repercussions when you meddle with them. I guess it's life's way of keeping us from crossing over too much.'

'She's not just a Seelie though mum. She's like a niece to me.'

'I know. But she's not your niece,' she corrected, matter-of-fact.

'I wouldn't be here without Quinn. I owe her this.'

'I know you think you owe everything to Quinn, but it's not worth it Erica.'

'Not worth it? Saving a child's life isn't worth it? What do you mean?'

Lucy was silent and turned to face the window, avoiding eye contact with Erica. There was more to this than Lucy was letting on. Erica pulled her hand away and sat back.

'Is that really why Lewis doesn't talk to you? What happened?'

'That has nothing to do with a Seelie.'

Erica raised her eyebrows, urging her mum to carry on. She was met with silence. 'I deserve to know. You kept my twin brother hidden from me. At least be honest now.'

Another stretch of silence as her mother thought. The sounds of the coffee grinder and milk steamer filled the dead air as Sasha worked hard to keep up with the queue. At last, Lucy spoke: 'You've read the diaries, yes?'

'I've read a diary. I didn't know there were more. One was bad enough.'

Lucy nodded. 'Well, Fuzz doesn't agree with the fact I knew what was going to happen and didn't stop it. He doesn't understand that's not how the world works.'

'Did you even try to change things?'

'What would be the point? A vision is a vision.'

'But you knew how bad it would be, and you still let us suffer.'

'You wouldn't have had Georgia.'

'You don't know that.'

'You would have moved to Australia with your grandparents and none of this would be happening.'

'Don't you believe in fate though? Wouldn't it find its own way – minus the pain?'

'I had to be sure. I couldn't take any chances.'

Erica analysed the comment. 'Wait, you're the one that made that stupid will and shipped me off to Tobias, aren't you?'

'That was a precaution. I had to make sure you stayed after what happened. I didn't know your dad would blame himself for my aneurysm – ' she was on the verge of rambling.

'Aneurysm?'

Her mother looked at her, confused. 'A brain aneurysm.' She continued to study Erica's face, watching as the penny dropped. 'Did no one ever tell you the truth?'

'Dad left me a letter. Told me he hit you. I didn't question it. Not that Tobias and I would talk anyway.'

'We were fighting, I'd told him about Lewis, I wanted your brother to come live with us. He was mad I'd lied. Things were said that shouldn't have been. He slapped me. Bad timing.'

'That's all you have to say, bad timing? Bad fucking timing?' Erica said, her voice a growl.

Lucy's gaze fell to her lap as she played with her wedding ring.

Erica's anger rose but she pushed it down. She needed answers.

She took a deep breath before asking, 'Did you know what would happen before you met Dad?'

'Of course.'

'So you knew how you were going to die when you met him?!' The anger was rising again, her voice getting louder; she could no longer suppress it. 'You recognised him when you met and you stayed? You fucking stayed? That's so messed up. Did you even love him? Actually no, don't answer that.' She stood up and paced. Customers were staring. Thank god this wasn't real. 'All this pain and heartache and you knew it would happen.'

'But so much good as well,' her mother countered, reaching for Erica's hand.

Erica laughed. 'No, you don't get to play that card. You didn't go through what we did.' She stormed off but the shop door jammed as she tried to leave.

'Alright Erica?' Sasha asked from behind the bar.

'Peachy,' she snapped and made her way to the rear office. She needed to be alone, to cool off.

Her passcode wouldn't work. She was trapped on the shop floor.

Why am I not waking up?

Erica sat back down with her mother, shoulders hunched. 'You obviously know how this whole sordid tale turns out. Tell me how to help Sam. You owe me that,' she said.

'No. There'll be consequences. Think of Georgia, it's for the greater good if you let fate take its course.'

Erica smiled but was not amused – you couldn't argue with stupidity. 'Tell me who's causing it then.' Lucy shook her head. 'Why won't you help? What caused this...?' Lucy waved a hand in the air, shaking her head as she breathed out. How could her mother willingly allow this to happen?

Lucy was quiet as she debated telling the truth. Erica looked at her, a woman she'd idolised for years but now she didn't know her at all. All those lies and twisted truths. How could she let this happen to her own children? If it were her choice she'd have done everything in her power to prevent it. There were no hard and fast rules with magic, maybe visions were sent as a warning to take another path. *How could you never try?*

'You interfered when it came to Georgia. You wrote on that window, caused the diversions. How is this any different?' Erica pleaded.

'What window?' Lucy's face was creased in confusion, her brow heavy.

'The message you sent me the day Georgia was born. I suspected it was you, that you'd paid someone to do it or whatever, but when I read your diary entry about asking for a sign that confirmed it. I would have given her up if you hadn't done that. You changed things then, so why not now?'

Lucy smiled, a quiet laugh escaping before she spoke. 'That wasn't me. Those entries are a warning.' She clasped her hands together, bringing them to her mouth, thinking of the best way to explain. 'You were always good at maths and science,' she said. 'So try to determine the common denominator between the longest visions.'

The common denominator? She went over the visions, ignoring the shorter, less interesting entries; her brother in the woods, contemplating suicide; being on the couch, bargaining with her unborn child; her future self with a newborn baby. She stared at the sandwich fridge beside them, as if a brie panini would provide an answer. 'Decisions? Like, life-changing decisions? Crossroads? Moments when we took a specific path?'

Lucy shook her head and raised a hand to stop Erica blurting out more words. 'No, well, I suppose yes, but it's more specific than that. Think about Lewis and Pétur. It's more obvious between them.'

Erica sighed. 'I don't know what your vision of Pétur was. He tore it out.'

'He did? He's so embarrassed of his past... He shouldn't be though. It's not his fault.'

'Listen, as much as I'm enjoying this masterclass in clairvoyance, can we get back to Sam and the virus? We can talk about who sent me the message another time. Just tell me how to stop this.'

'Take my hands,' Lucy said, offering them. 'I need to show you something.'

Erica slid her hands into her mother's, unsure where this was going.

In a blink she was standing by a frozen lake, Lucy by her side.

'Why have you brought me here?' Erica shivered.

'You'll see.' Lucy cradled Erica's hands and stared into the distance. A smile teased at the corners of her mouth.

Erica followed her gaze but could see only snow. At the horizon's edge, mountains rose to pierce the sky with nothing between them but the two out-of-place onlookers. The land was desolate.

Lucy's long skirt flapped in the wind. Erica hugged herself, hands in her armpits; this was no place to be wearing her work t-shirt.

Two boys crested a ridge on the other side of the lake. The youngest looked about six and the other not much older. They were wrapped up with thick puffy jackets, mittens, and woolly hats. Erica was jealous; she could do with her furry deerstalker hat. That thing was bloody cosy.

The boys were marching along, idly taking in their surroundings, stopping on occasion to investigate the odd rock or tuft of grass. There wasn't much here to entertain them.

The eldest gathered a handful of snow, turning the powder between his hands until it became a ball. He took aim at the unsuspecting junior who was busy kicking snow on to the lake's icy surface.

Bam, it hit him on the back of the head, the icy flakes trickling down his back. He snapped upright, his face pulled into a shocked grimace. The older boy laughed.

Erica watched as the boys took turns pelting each other with fistfuls of snow. They were having a great time.

Or, they were until the older boy bent over in pain, clutching at his face. He brought his hand down to reveal a bloody cheek. It was only a small graze, but the shock caused tears to prick at his eyes.

He shouted at the younger boy as he thundered over to him.

'What's he saying? I don't understand. What happened?' Erica quizzed her mum, the foreign tongue a mystery.

'He says there was a stone in it. He's accusing the boy of doing it on purpose.'

The younger boy protested, edging backwards. He shuffled towards the lake as carefully as someone on a high-rise ledge, stopping abruptly when his foot hit ice.

'Fyrirgefðu, fyrirgefðu, fyrirgefðu,' the little one whimpered. It sounded like a plea, an apology. The other was having none of it. He leaned over him, willing the boy to make a move. They locked eyes. The smaller one sobbed, his words unintelligible; the big one lost his temper and sent a fist flying into his opponent's face.

The boy had done so well at avoiding the ice, but the blow forced him to stagger back. He didn't have time to react before the ice split below him, plunging him into the dark water below.

The older one dropped to his knees, to help Erica thought, but it soon became apparent he had other ideas. He held the boy under as small hands flailed across the water's surface.

'Can't we do anything?' Erica panicked. She couldn't move, her feet felt as though they were cemented to the ground.

'Don't worry,' Lucy said, 'this is why I've brought you here.'

'To watch a kid die?'

'Shhh, have patience.' She returned her focus to the lake.

The older one was maniacal; a terrifying grin spread over his face as he shouted into the water. Erica wished she could understand what he was saying. It sounded like he was reciting lines, the way he was enunciating and pausing between sentences; it was like he was working from a script.

Erica's heart was racing, she felt sick. Did her mother really want her to watch a child die?

As the younger boy's hands went limp and disappeared into the water, a dark figure appeared on the horizon. In the blink of an eye it was beside the kneeling boy who was now on his knees, breathing hard at the side of the lake. His eyes stared into the water, unaware of the new presence.

It didn't take a genius to work out who it was. The long black shroud with skeletal hands poking out of the sleeves and hood pulled up were a dead giveaway. It was Death.

A bony digit summoned the boy's full attention. 'Jóhann Ottesen?'

'Já,' the boy stammered. Erica gasped.

'Do you know who I am?'

'Já,' he repeated.

'Good. Then you'll know how serious your actions are.'

The boy nodded, frozen in fear.

'You've interrupted a little game I was playing. Ruined it in fact. You've made me very mad,' Death said, keeping its voice calm. 'What do you think your punishment should be?'

Jóhann remained silent and shook his head, unsure what the answer should be. Why had Death switched to English? Did it know Erica and Lucy were watching and wanted them to understand too?

'Stay there,' Death commanded.

Death reached into the icy hole and swirled its arm. The move reminded Erica of someone looking for a rogue spoon in a soapy washing-up bowl. Seconds later, Death pulled Pétur from the water, laying him down with care. Pétur's small body was limp, his lips blue and his face ghost-white.

'Not yet my boy,' Death reassured, the voice a whisper. The figure stroked Pétur's face before yanking Jóhann over. There was a loud snap.

'My arm!' Jóhann cried.

'Never mind your arm. Help your brother. Breathe into him.'

'He's dead!' Jóhann wailed, inspecting the arm he was now cradling.

'Breathe,' Death commanded.

Jóhann dropped to his knees and looked to Death once more before pinching Pétur's nose with his good hand and blowing into his mouth.

Once, twice, three times he exhaled between sobs. Pétur came to life with a weak splutter before vomiting water on to the snow.

Death was gone.

Jóhann ran.

ERICA AND LUCY were back in the shop.

Erica pulled her hands from her mother's like she was touching a flame.

'What was that?'

'Like I said: a warning. This was important enough for Death to intervene. There's a path we have to stick to, and God help us if we try to deviate from it.' She paused, before adding, 'and I thought it would benefit you to understand Pétur a little better. What's wrong with him isn't his fault.'

Erica's muscles felt tight and her stomach churned. 'What? So you can time travel now?'

'No, it was a vision I had when I was fourteen. I was shown it for a reason.'

'So what does that have to do with anything?'

'That was the vision Pétur tore from the book, Erica. The connection is Death. You have to protect yourself. Let fate run its course; it's not your job to save the Pack and it's certainly not your job to save Sam.'

Erica wasn't sure how to respond. Her head was worse. It was like being drunk, the world was fuzzy at the edges and her thoughts wouldn't string together. She struggled to form a sentence. 'Did you deviate? Is that why...' She rubbed her forehead to shift the feeling. Why the hell wasn't she waking up? Usually she could will her way out of meetings with her mum, switch it off. Not today though. Something was wrong.

'I've already told you too much. Focus your efforts on Georgia. Everything else will work out as intended.'

'I'm willing to take the chance. Tell me what you know and let me decide what I want to do.' It took more effort than usual to form a sentence.

Her mother sighed for the umpteenth time. She looked as fed up as Erica. 'Are you feeling ok? You don't look right.'

'I'm fine, stop avoiding my question.'

Lucy looked at her, studying her eyes, gauging if she was indeed fine. Remembering how stubborn her daughter could be, she gave in. 'Do you remember your dad's safe?'

'Vaguely. What about it?'

'You'll know when you find it. That's the final piece, you've already got all the information you need.'

'I do?' She looked her mother straight in the eye. Was she bluffing?

'You do.' She cleared her throat. 'You've been looking at it the wrong way. Remember what I said: Answers come when you're ready to hear them.'

'No specifics for me?'

'That's enough for now. Are you sure you're ok? Your pupils are odd.'

'If you know more, you need to tell me.' Erica heard her voice slur.

'Erica? Honey, you're going to hate me for this but trust me.'

'Huh?'

She didn't get an answer; instead Lucy slapped her hard across the face with an almighty crack.

ERICA WOKE up on the basement floor; flat on her back with no idea how long she'd been there. The back of her head throbbed with pain. She brought a hand up and found a sizeable lump. *No blood though – that was a good sign, yeah?*

She pushed herself up on her elbows. Her stomach was a little ropey but her vision was ok. That horrible fuzzy drunk feeling was gone.

Erica checked the time stamp on her message to Quinn. It hadn't even been five minutes; she can't have been out for long.

Time to put her mother's instructions into action.

E rica had lost her vigour upon standing and had serious second thoughts. Going from horizontal to vertical had caused a headrush like no other and she'd had to grab hold of what was left of the offending racking to steady herself. Instead of jumping feet first into her crusade, she eventually ended up draped over the edge of Georgia's bed. This was the fastest pace she could muster. The best laid plans et cetera, et cetera.

She'd been here nearly an hour and it was getting late. It seemed cruel to enforce a bedtime on G though, especially given her current bedbound status. Instead they'd made friendship bracelets and Erica read a story Georgia had written – another to add to the collection she was amassing at home.

Quinn had sent two texts asking where she was. Erica wasn't proud to admit she'd ignored them. The ache in her head derailed any plans to visit the hospital, and it was well past visiting hours now anyway. Guilt hadn't yet kicked in, but she was braced for it. However, her mother's cryptic message had given new hope to helping Sam, so all wasn't lost.

She sat up and looped the thin orange and pink bracelet around her wrist, but the thread kept slipping, making it impossible to knot. 'You're going to have to help me, G.' She held her arm out, bracelet dangled over it.

Georgia tied it with ease and pushed it down to join the other six of various colours that were looking tatty after months of wear. 'Are you sure you're ok Mum?'

'Of course. Just a bump on the head.' She prodded the egg-shaped lump to prove she was ok. It hurt like hell, but G didn't need to know. She did, however, feel fine so it was time to get going.

Satisfied that her mum was telling the truth, Georgia returned to working on another bracelet, this time blue, red, and white. 'When do you think Pétur will be back?'

'I don't know darling. He's not replied to my message.' Erica rose and undid her ponytail, letting her hair fall to her shoulders. The tightness over the bump on her head was nipping. 'He'll be back soon though, promise.' She kissed G on the forehead before making for the door.

'Where you off to?'

'Just need to check something. Back in a mo.'

BRACELET-MAKING PROVIDED great thinking time and, thanks to it, Erica concluded that current Pack member information would be kept in the safe. Surely that must be what her mother was alluding to? It would make sense that recent deaths would provide further answers. Who knew what else Tobias kept in there? *The final piece*, she couldn't wait for this to be over. During her father's time as Pack Leader she'd seen a safe in his office. It seemed logical they would protect wolf names under lock and key.

Standing in the lethargic lift as it climbed floors, she worried about Pétur. Where had he stormed off to? And, more to the point, was he ever coming back? The dick hadn't replied to her two texts. Ok, she was the dick for starting the argument but did he know how often she double-texted? Never. She'd broken a rule for him, the least he could do was reply.

With a shrill *ping,* the lift deposited her on Tobias's floor, portraits of previous Pack Leaders leading the way to his office. They all looked miserable dressed in their red and gold regalia. For the first time in years she stopped to look at her father's portrait.

He was a handsome brute with swept back hair and dark eyes that – even in a forced neutral gaze – looked kind. His beard was trimmed and preened but Erica remembered him being scruffy. Appearance wasn't at the top of his agenda. That was Tobias's thing. Her mum often had to force her dad to get his haircut. He'd be proud of Lewis's wavy locks, that's for sure.

She studied him, comparing his likeness to Tobias. Time hadn't been kind to her uncle: crow's feet ran deep at the corners of his eyes, great ravines creased his brow. Tobias was looking old. She imagined her father, how he would look if he'd kept his position. It could never have happened, regardless – Raf was only Pack Leader through circumstance, born fourteen minutes before his twin. They may have looked almost identical but they were chalk and cheese. Raf wasn't cut out for Pack Leader. He was a dreamer, a people lover, a romantic. Tobias was a sadistic arsehole and destined to take control.

A pang of guilt washed over her. Only, it wasn't her guilt was it? She had believed what she'd been told, so how could she be blamed for that? Still, eighteen years of hatred is hard to box up. She moved on, remembering why she was here. She could deal with her dad later.

Tobias's door was easy to unlock. Unsurprising, she was yet to encounter a lock she couldn't open... Apart from Nick's. That made sense now; it must be protected with magic. As long as a lock was mechanical, Erica was only ever seconds away from entry. Very handy if you ever happened to forget your shop keys.

Tobias's office was the best room in the Chambers – naturally, since it was historically the Pack Leader's. The room's stand-out feature was a hexagonal area, home to a large mahogany desk with a red leather top and gold fittings. This section of the room formed part of the building's tower, in the far corner of the office. With arched windows on each face, the tower gave unrivalled views of Hope Street – you could see the West End on a good day, with Glasgow School of Art peeking out over the rooftops too.

A plush swivel chair was tucked under the imposing desk, meaning that the Pack Leader sat with his back to the city vistas. Two matching mahogany chairs with red velvet upholstery were placed in front, waiting for you to occupy them. Only if told to, *obviously*.

When she was a child, Erica would sit in the swivel chair while waiting for her dad to finish work. Staring out at the people below, imagining where they were going, what their lives were like. Of course it wasn't her uncle's chair then. Now even passing to his side of the desk would be a cardinal sin, a direct attack on the respect of the Pack Leader in Tobias's eyes.

The room was heavy and tense despite her uncle not being there.

He had an aura which lingered. Most morons did – they had a way of conducting themselves that made even the air around them repulse. She sat in his chair and swivelled, right to left and back again. He would hit the roof if he caught her, and she liked that idea very much. In fact, she wished that she and Pétur had got together here instead of the library. The ultimate screw you.

Tobias made her blood boil. If she allowed herself, she could remember the Christmases she'd spent alone in her room. The birthdays she'd been forced to forget (what was the point after a while?), the times they'd gone on holiday and left her behind. Perhaps she'd recall when she was twelve and he hit her (sadly not the first nor last time), splitting the side of her forehead open. She was a wolf – it would heal quick enough, why bother seeing a doctor, just go to your room. A scar through her eyebrow reminded her of that day. It was small and barely noticeable but annoyed her every time she put makeup on.

She pushed her anger down and scanned the room for the safe. Nothing obvious stood out. A search of the desk returned nothing – each drawer opened with little protest, apart from a deeper one on the bottom. A simple flick of the wrist revealed a whisky stash and some dubious-looking books.

The cupboards around the office were equally disappointing. Erica had often wondered what was hidden behind those cabinet doors but only found more unloved books and secret whisky.

Where else could it be?

She remembered her father opening a safe in front of her. Given the twenty years that had passed and the little attention she was paying at the time, it wasn't a surprise that the exact location was baffling her.

She reclined in a chair and sighed. Another dead end.

Her phone buzzed. It was P – he needed in.

PÉTUR WOULDN'T SAY where he'd been, but something was wrong. Aside from the fact he was in a mood, he was also a terrible liar – he couldn't make eye contact when he said he'd been 'in the pub thinking'. She didn't tell him about the bump on her head. That was embarrassing.

'It has to be here somewhere,' he said, leaning cross-legged against Tobias's desk. 'A safe can't just disappear.'

'I know, it's so frustrating, but where else can it be?'

'There's no secret panel in the wall?'

'Hmm, I'm sure I'd remember that.'

'But maybe not.' He knocked on the wooden panelling either side of the door. 'You're sure Tobias isn't going to walk in?'

'No, but I'm past caring to be honest. What exactly are you looking for?'

'I'm trying to see if any of them sound hollow.'

'And?'

'Nothing.' He straightened himself up.

She joined him and gave the wall a tap, copying his technique. She had no idea what she was listening for, but was buying time before deciding their next move.

'Just checking for yourself?' he asked with a wry grin.

'Of course. Nothing there.'

'You don't know what do next, do you?'

'No idea,' she said, sighing.

'No spells you can do to reveal a hidden object?'

'Probably, but my knowledge isn't that great. I'd need my book.'

Books. The bookcases were the only areas they hadn't checked. The shelves were too narrow for a safe, but Erica and Pétur had run out of options. It was worth a go.

She studied the titles, pulling the odd book out to inspect the wall behind. There wasn't much of interest; most were werewolf history with a smattering of ancient Glaswegian records, and a large section that appeared to be in Latin. None would help solve their current predicament, but browsing the books was giving Erica's mind time to rest, and calculate their next move on the sly. She was a subconscious problem solver; she just needed to engage the right parts of her brain.

P looked on, watching Erica's fingers trace over the shelves, taking their contents in.

'Looking for anything in particular?' he asked.

'Not really. Just browsing.'

He picked up the book Tobias had taken from the library. It had been left on top of the bookcase, hanging over the edge of the top shelves. The cover had a copper pentagram embossed in the centre. Its dust jacket was nowhere to be seen. 'What a strange choice. Why do you think he's reading this?'

'God knows with Tobias. He's a mystery unto himself.' Erica found it quite relaxing flitting around the shelves; she doubted anyone had taken the time to enjoy these books for years – dust was threatening to bury most of them.

Dust.

She walked to the furthest shelf, closer to the desk. Two shelves up there was a gap where the dust was gone. A book had been removed.

'Give me that a second,' she commanded, holding a hand out to P.

He passed her the book and she slid it into the empty slot. Perfect fit. Pushing the book in slightly further, she heard a *click* followed by a *clunk*. Something had happened – but where?

'Did you hear that?' she asked Pétur, wanting to make sure she wasn't hearing what she wanted to.

'I think so. Do it again.'

She withdrew the book with a *clunk click* then slid it back in. *Click clunk.*

Both looked around the room desperate to see where it was coming from.

'It must be mechanical, so it can't be opening anything too far away.' Pétur ducked to the cabinet beneath her and looked in. There was nothing out of the ordinary – certainly no safe. 'Do it again.'

She did as asked. *Clunk click. Click clunk.*

'It's definitely in here.' He emptied the contents of the cabinet on to the floor, pulling out lever arch files and notebooks. 'Have you got your phone? Give me some light,' he said when it was empty.

She shone the light, but there was nothing to see apart from an empty wooden cabinet.

'I don't see anything,' she said.

'No, there's something there, move it over a bit. Let me see the edge again.'

They were bent over each other as if in a bizarre game of Twister. He put his upper body into the cabinet.

'I need light Erica.'

'I'm doing my best P.' She slid her hand under his armpit and he directed it to a better position.

She could hear him picking at something. The noise reminded her of Georgia's sticker sheets. Sometimes the edge was so thin you'd be picking at it for ages before freeing the bugger, nails scraping at the paper as your frustration grew.

There was a machine-like *pop* and P extracted himself from the tiny space. 'There's your safe.' He looked as smug as smug could be. *Clever git.* She ducked in, wanting to see it for herself. Sure enough, he'd swung open a wooden panel to reveal a galvanised safe. *Jackpot.*

Erica shuffled closer, positioning herself between P's legs and placing a hand on the combination lock. The numbers zero to ninety were emblazoned on the front, with tiny lines indicating divisions between digits. Safes were tricky but she'd conquered them before. The training from forgetting her shop keys was coming into action. That was a key though. This was different.

She closed her eyes and turned the dial, her mind's eye taking on the task. Her senses were engaged as she felt for a subtle click with each correct number. A trial and error process of going clockwise and anticlockwise finally got her somewhere. A dozen tries in she had: Two-three divisions over-one-nine divisions over-eight *click click click* – she mucked up, wrong direction.

It happens. She took a deep breath and started again. She could feel P's breathing behind her; he was just as tense. Two-three divisions over-one-nine divisions over-eight-seven divisions over. Her middle cousin's birthday. Interesting.

The door popped open with a satisfying clunk.

Erica hadn't expected to find what she did. At the front was a leather-bound journal, a USB stick and a plastic document wallet filled with various slips of paper. It was the other stuff that was odd: two bags of red sweets and six bottles of water. The lid of each bottle had been subtly marked with red pen.

She emptied the contents on to the floor to inspect them further.

'Why would you keep sweets and water in a safe?' P asked.

She frowned; there was no simple answer. 'Come on, help me gather these things up and put everything else back in the cabinet. We can look at this later; the longer we stay here the higher the chance Tobias will catch us.'

'Maybe he just really likes red wine gums but people keep stealing them,' Pétur ventured. The two cellophane bags and six water bottles sat in the middle of Erica's dining table like an obscure work of art.

'Plausible, but these aren't wine gums. They smell funny.' She was right; he'd been hit with the odour when she opened the bag. It had taken him a while to place it, but the aroma was unmistakable – they smelled like the multivitamins he took as a child. Herbal and earthy, he was sure grass would taste similar. Despite their fragrance, the childhood supplements had been strawberry flavour. Maybe these were the same?

'Go on, let me try one,' he said and grabbed at the bag. She snatched it out of reach.

'No, not until we know what they are. I'm forever telling Georgia not to take sweets off strangers – don't make me start on you too,' She pretended to tell him off, pulling a stern face.

Pétur made a show of pouting. He really wanted those sweets, even more so after being denied them. He'd steal one later when she wasn't looking.

'How are you getting on with that list?' he asked, eyeing the sheet of A4 in front of her. She'd printed a map of Scotland and was marking the location of each death in the current outbreak with a red dot, in the hope that the visual image might throw up more answers than the tally marks had.

'Ok. But I'm not seeing any patterns.'

'How many have you got left?'

'About half.' She looked at her empty wine glass. 'I might get a refill and phone Quinn. I really should have seen Sam today. I feel awful for not going.' She rubbed at her temples, stress getting the better of her.

'It's not your fault, a lot's happened today.'

'It doesn't change that I didn't go. Plus it's not like I can tell Quinn what's happened.' She rose and made her way towards the kitchen. 'You ok for a bit?'

'Yeah, fine. I'm going to grab my laptop and see what's on that USB.'

PÉTUR WAS nervous to click the folder icon. His cursor hovered over the foreign object on his desktop. Its title didn't help – 02201601 – it only deepened the mystery. Maybe Tobias had a repulsive kinky fetish or kept a catalogue of his toenail clippings. There was only one way to find out...

He clicked and the folder expanded to another window. Nine folders popped up, this time with less ominous names. He'd expected everything to be password protected but it wasn't; it couldn't be anything important. *What an anti-climax.*

The folders were titled after months, February to October. He clicked on October and a spreadsheet opened. Pétur squinted, making sense of what he was reading. It was a record of data, but that was all he could be certain of. Column titles included things like SUB, ACT, Y/N, OUTCOME. The latter's column was filled with Ds and As with various dates next to them. *What the hell..?*

'Can you make any sense of it?' he asked Erica, who was back after getting through to Quinn's voicemail.

'I dunno. He's obviously using a code of some sort.'

'Well done Sherlock.'

She elbowed him in the ribs. 'GQH – those are Georgia's initials. And look, that's yesterday's date.' She pulled the laptop closer, her interest piqued.

'Could be coincidence?'

'Or hospital records, like admissions maybe?' She sounded sceptical.

'Wouldn't they keep those in the medical bay?'

'Probably. I dunno, weird, eh?' Her phone vibrated on the table so she slid the laptop back in his direction. 'That's Quinn calling back – why don't you look through the file folder thingy?'

She headed to the bedroom, phone in hand, while Pétur set to work on the folder. It was white plastic and cracked at the edges. It didn't look like it would be of much interest, but it wouldn't do any harm to look. He'd used a similar folder for his course notes when writing his final dissertation at uni. *Urgh, never again* – he was having horrible flashbacks just thinking about it.

Tobias's folder was stuffed full of handwritten notes, diagrams, formulae and spreadsheets. It reminded him of the wall they'd found in the hut.

A wave of dizziness suddenly came over Pétur. Misty had said he might feel a bit off for a few days. Should he tell Erica what he'd done? He should have been honest when she'd asked where he'd gone earlier but couldn't be bothered with another fight. Erica would kill Pétur if she found out what he'd done. He'd expected a high price, but it wasn't money Misty was after. It was worth it though, the main focus had to be stopping further infection, figuring out where it was coming from. Anything was worth it for this to end.

He emptied each section of the folder out, creating neat piles which he arranged on the table. Most of it made no sense – it was clearly research, but the details remained a mystery to Pétur.

Frustration and defeat added to his light head. He sighed, rubbing his brow. Was he coming out in a cold sweat? *Please just be my imagination.*

He watched Erica pacing the hall outside, the *uh-uhs* and *oks* out in force. She was such a good listener on the phone, why couldn't she be like that with him? As he'd sat on the forty-four bus to Clarkston, he'd thought about their fight. He had come to a conclusion. Erica would always put herself first, so he either worked with it or quit while he was ahead. It wasn't that she was selfish (*ok, that too*) but more that she was so used to getting her own way. At least, that was his line of thinking – understanding women wasn't his forte.

Even if he was right, it didn't change the fact she'd been a bitch. Erica was right – they were consenting adults, but when it came down to it, a one-night-stand with your daughter's uncle isn't the smartest move. She no doubt expected he'd go back to Iceland and forget about them. Was she so stone cold that she didn't care who she slept with?

More to the point, it wasn't as if he was trying to tie her into a relationship this afternoon. *Who the hell did she think she was?* Did she think so highly of herself that she believed they'd sleep together once and ten minutes later he'd be begging her to go steady? Relationships took time – they didn't materialise in hours, binding you together forever more. In fact, the months of getting to know each other were the fun part, not knowing where it was going only added to the appeal.

I was only rubbing her fucking shoulders. He was getting worked up, time to change the subject.

Pétur picked up the notes nearest him and shuffled through them, scanning each page before placing them back in the folder. It was frustrating not knowing what they were. They could be the answer or they could be complete crap.

He could hear Erica's conversation loud and clear. He shouldn't have been eavesdropping, but was hard not to listen as she raised her voice in frustration. 'What? No. I've just been busy...No. Not like that. I'd never be too busy to see Sam...Uh-huh, yeah. Look, it's just complicated, ok?...Tomorrow morning, I'll be there...Fine, whatever.'

Silence. He carried on putting the papers away as he heard the fridge door being opened, followed by the slow glug of liquid being poured. Wine no doubt. The glass clinked as the bottle was replaced. Erica paused before shutting the door.

'Do you want a beer?' she called.

'That would be great, thanks.' Pétur made his way to the kitchen island that divided the room. 'Everything ok?'

She turned from the fridge, placing a bottle of beer in front of him. It was chilled to perfection; small droplets of condensation patterned the glass. Taking a corkscrew from the drawer, she used it to flick the bottle cap off with a satisfying *hiss*.

'Quinn's pissed off at me.' She sipped her wine. 'Not that I didn't see that coming.'

'She's just worried and taking it out on you.' He swigged his beer as he walked over to the couch, making himself comfy at the far end.

'I should be there for her. She was there for me. I guess I deserve the silent treatment.' She slumped down at the opposite end of the couch. 'Anything useful in the folder?'

'Nothing. Well, not that I can see. It's all jargon to me.' He stretched out his body, stifling a yawn. It had been a long day. 'Can we watch a film or something? I could do with some light relief.'

'Sure,' she said as she made her way towards the bedroom. 'I'm just going to get my hoodie.' She paused and turned back to him: 'Just don't make it a sappy love story.'

'I'M sorry if I came on strong earlier,' he said during a lull in the film. It was best to be the bigger person and apologise, start fresh – even though he wasn't the one in the wrong. It would make life easier. He had a game plan and needed her on side to test the theory out.

'And, I guess...' He could hear the reluctance in her voice. 'I'm sorry for acting like a crazy bitch.'

'I thought that was just your personality. Is there a specific occasion you're apologising for?'

The look in her eye said she was considering hitting him, but instead she ran her tongue along the edge of her upper teeth and sighed.

'I suppose I deserve to be wound up. You git.'

He smiled. He was learning that aggravation meant affection with Erica.

She looked at her phone, clicking the home button to illuminate the screen, which was blank save for a geometric wallpaper.

'Still no response?' he asked.

'No,' Erica replied, shifting on the sofa impatiently. 'She's never given me the cold shoulder before.'

'What did you text her?'

'Just that I was sorry, that I'd explain things when I saw her.' She drank some more wine. 'I've been thinking...' she began.

'That sounds dangerous.'

'Maybe we should see Misty tomorrow.'

His eyes widened and his muscles tensed. 'How so?'

'We need to find out who's behind this, so it doesn't happen again. Everything is pointing to him.'

'Everything?'

'Ok, every*one*.'

'Sounds like a plan.' He feigned an exaggerated yawn. 'Where am I sleeping tonight?'

'My bed again.' She narrowed her eyes, gauging his reaction. 'Or is that awkward? This sofa isn't made for sleepovers. And Georgia's bed...'

It was a couch created more for fashion than function – comfortable to sit on, but too narrow and boxy to sleep on. 'No, no,' said Pétur. 'You won't freak out if I accidentally touch you in the night though?'

'You'll have to wait and see.' She pursed her lips, studying his face. 'You feeling ok?'

'Yeah, of course. Why?'

'Dunno, you look a little off.'

'Nah, just tired. In fact I might go to bed.'

HE TURNED on to his back. He was definitely coming out in a cold sweat. The cotton sheets clung to his damp torso with a sickening stickiness, not the normal after-sex sweat he was used to. Erica hadn't mentioned anything, even if she had noticed. *Good*.

The door to the en suite creaked open, a halo of yellow light around Erica's nude silhouette. She slipped into bed beside him and reversed into his crotch, slotting them together like puzzle pieces, his own body turning to meet hers.

He ran a hand up her side, tracing the curve of her waist and resting it below her breast, his hand cupped over her ribs. She had the softest skin ever; each inch was like stroking velvet.

'Do your massages always end like that?' she asked into the darkness.

'Usually. Apart from once.'

'Oh.'

There was silence once more. He didn't want to push it; that was enough about today. They'd made up, it was time to forget their earlier fight and let sleeping dogs lie.

She twisted around and he repositioned his hand under her other breast. She scooted closer, slipping an ankle between his and resting a hand on his waist. The other was folded at her chest, sitting at an awkward angle.

'What's that one doing?' he said, directing his eyes to the spare hand.

She laughed. 'I don't know where to put it. Quick, sit up a bit.' He did as Erica asked and she slipped it under his neck. Her fingers played with the hair at the base of his skull. Was Erica always so relaxed after sex? The touching, the tenderness, even her muscles were less tense. He liked this Erica.

'Will you come with me to see Misty tomorrow?' she asked.

'Why do you need me? You're a big girl.'

She half-smiled. 'He kinda scares me if I'm honest. If he is behind all this, he's a nutcase. He does seem a bit... wacky.'

'And do you think he is?'

'What? Crazy?'

'No, behind it all.'

Her fingers paused their dance through his hair as she pondered. 'It seems the most feasible answer. And he was pretty shifty about giving us answers.'

'And if he isn't to blame? Who else then?'

She breathed out, exasperated and shaking her head. He could smell wine as her hot breath hit his neck. 'I can't see who else is capable.'

'But just say it wasn't him. There must be someone else,' he quizzed.

She pushed herself up on her elbow. 'Why do I get the feeling you know something I don't?'

He settled her down gently with his hand on her chest. She sunk into the mattress but he could feel her body had tensed.

'It's nothing.'

'It sounds like something.'

Pétur rolled on to his back, his hand stroking his beard once before finding his necklace and bringing it to his lips. Erica propped herself up on a pillow and he wrapped his free arm around her, bringing her closer. Her soft skin felt good next to his. He was still clammy.

'I went to see Misty.' His voice was quiet, like a child who'd been caught doing something naughty.

'I knew you'd been up to something. And?'

'It's definitely not him.'

'You believe him?'

'Honestly. I'm certain,' he said without a shadow of doubt.

'Did he tell you who it was?'

'Not really, no. He just confirmed everything we already know.'

'Hmm. What did you have to pay him?'

Pétur laughed under his breath. 'More than I could afford if I'm honest.'

She brought a hand up to his chest and rested it at the base of his ribs, letting her body sink into the crevice between his arm and torso. Her skin felt hot against his.

'I can pay half if it helps?'

He chuckled, if only it had been money. 'It was my choice. Let's forget about it.' He didn't want to tell Erica what he'd paid with. She would lose her shit.

She snuggled into his chest, thinking, letting the revelation sink in. 'It was nice of you to go to Misty's. You didn't have to.' Kissing his collarbone, she added: 'I'm sorry you wasted your money.'

'It wasn't a waste,' he told her, 'I just want to help you. Anything to help your Pack and Sam.' He could feel her smiling.

'Who does that leave us with then?' she mused.

'Well, I think it's safe to say Tobias is up to something.'

'Right,' Erica replied. 'I'm the last person you need to convince about that! But he couldn't do it alone – where's he getting the magic from?'

'When Misty asked what you liked, what did he mean? Are there lots of different kinds of magic?'

She breathed out with a sigh, thinking. 'It depends. Do you just mean magic like I can do, or any kind of supernatural stuff?'

'Is there a big difference?'

'Oh yeah. Magic is hard enough but I couldn't even list a fraction of the supernatural.'

'Ok. Well, tell me about magic.'

'Christ. You don't ask much do you?' She shifted, getting herself comfortable in readiness to deliver a big explanation. He stroked her arm with his thumb. 'Well, there are potions like Lewis can do, but I never learned any of that. Then you've got Lumio and Telica magic, my specialities. Mum only taught me those, but there are loads of forms of magic.' She scrunched up her face, figuring out what to discuss next.

'No hurry. I just want the basics,' he reassured her.

'I know, I just don't know where to begin. Erm...' She paused, thinking again. 'So, some witches can shapeshift. Like wolves do – but they can transform into all sorts of animals. Oh, and divination of course. Like mum, seeing the future. Now, let me think.'

The pause went on while Erica weighed up her options. Pétur could practically hear the cogs turning in her mind. She went to speak but had second thoughts, returning to pondering, so Pétur decided to make things easier for her.

'Lets narrow it down,' he suggested. 'The fairies said it was orally ingested. Misty said he spoke to Arlen and he'd cross-checked his books. It's a definite now. What would do that?'

'It'd have to be potions. I can't think of anything else that would work.'

'That's what I thought, but I wanted to make sure. So, who does that?'

'Well, a few folk. That we know of.'

'You said it yourself. Tobias needs the magic but who is he going to trust with the lives of his beloved Pack?'

'Not many people. If any.'

'Exactly,' said Pétur, determined. 'I was thinking about this earlier and I've come up with two names. I don't think you'll like either.'

'Ok. Go on,' she said, drawing out the vowels.

'The first is your brother.' He paused, giving her some time to process his idea. 'And the second is Nick.'

Colin Anderson was drunk. Completely blootered to put it lightly.

He'd promised his wife he wouldn't be out late. Only going for one, he'd assured. He knew it was a lie. The bitch wouldn't let him out otherwise.

It was now the wee small hours of Monday morning. Hopefully the moany cow had calmed down. *Dae this, dae that.* Fuck off and do it yourself.

He staggered a few feet to the left, nearly toppling off the pavement. *Time for a wee rest, close my eyes for a bit.*

Colin made his way to the closest bus stop with the straightened back and gurning face of a baby giraffe learning to walk. *Sober as a judge, honest guv.*

He slumped on to the cold metal bench and closed his eyes. The world spun around. *Bad idea.* He snapped his eyelids open; the merry-go-round came to a gradual halt. A woman walked past as he spat on the ground; she wrinkled her nose at him. He went to remark that she was a state too, but Colin found that he couldn't talk.

Michelle would kill him if he got back like this.

His eyes (well, one of them) focused on a packet of red sweets sitting on the bench. Food would settle his stomach and his dizzy head. He made a grab for them but depth perception wasn't on his side. The sweets fell to the ground, the bag falling open and scattering candies across the pavement. *Bugger.*

A seagull waddled over to the mess. He was a big bastard, nearly bigger than Colin's highland terrier, Lennon. Scrabbling about on the floor for something to eat was well beyond even Colin, so he left the bird to the sweets, watching it chomp down a few with gluttonous speed.

He lightly closed his eyes, forgetting about the stomach-churning spin that followed. Saliva flooded his mouth. *Nope, not going to be sick. Not today.* Colin tried to focus on his surroundings. There weren't many people out – the pubs had closed ages ago and Crow Road was mainly houses. Not much to distract his mind and stop his last pint making a reappearance.

Instead, he looked at the gull. It was still necking the sweets. *Greedy little bastard.*

Colin had no idea what the time was – he'd 'accidentally' left his phone at home to avoid a rollicking from Michelle. Hopefully the kebab shop was still open.

The gull was staring straight at him. It hadn't moved for a good while and if Colin had had the balance to do so, he would have got up and shooed the wee git away. It was creeping him out.

'Witdaeyewant?' he slurred.

The gull took two uneasy steps towards him and keeled over, stiff as a metal poker, dead as a dodo.

Definitely time for a kebab.

Pétur jolted awake, the sensation of ice cold sweat prickling his skin. Erica had moved to her own side – no surprise there, she didn't strike him as an all-night spooner. Thank God for that. He pawed at the sweat which had pooled on his chest. Disgusting.

He'd been slipping into another night terror when his brain dragged him back to reality. His terrors had been bad recently, but yesterday's was the worst he'd ever experienced. The memory of it propelled his brain into overdrive.

Pétur let out a fractured sigh. Panic threatened to set in – his stomach twisted and his chest tightened. He couldn't just lie here and let stupid thoughts take over. Erica would think he was crazy. Thinking that a glass of water might help, he slipped out of bed and tiptoed to the kitchen. He didn't care that he was naked; any perverts would need a telescope to see him. And who didn't love a nighttime stroll in the nude?

He located the glasses with minimal effort but failed on keeping noise to a minimum, chinking two together as he brought one out. The sound echoed into the dark. He froze, as if being motionless could mute the loud noise. The room returned to silence, no thanks to him.

He let the tap run at a trickle, afraid a noisy faucet would create more racket but the deafening tinkle as it filled the glass forced him to get it over with fast, notching the stream to full blast.

Pétur downed the water with a few swift gulps. His brain was returning to normal pace, having been distracted with the effort of keeping quiet, but his heart was still pounding. Sweat beaded on his forehead, and a large drop rolled down the side of his face on to the worktop. Gross.

This couldn't be a normal reaction. He'd have to phone Misty tomorrow.

For now though, he needed to be clean. Avoiding Erica's en suite in a bid to keep noise to a minimum, he headed to the flat's main bathroom. Pulling a cord to flood the room with light, Pétur checked himself in the mirror. His skin looked paler, his eyes darker. Apart from that you'd never know. If eyes truly were the window to the soul what the heck was he looking at now *his* soul was in Misty's possession?

When Misty had explained what he wanted in exchange for information it had come as a bit of a shock to say the least. But after careful consideration it felt like there was little to lose and much to gain. After all, Misty claimed to have done this a million times before, what could possibly go wrong? In hindsight it had been a total waste of time, although, credit where credit's due, Misty had gathered all the information they'd struggled to get in a few days in just a few hours. Shame there were no new leads and little indication at where to go next.

He turned the shower on, twisting the controls to the highest temperature. Waiting for the water to warm up, he held his hand under the flow, but he just couldn't get warm. The sweat though – it was getting beyond a joke.

Pétur lifted his necklace over his head and placed it beside the washbasin before standing under the shower jets. It felt heavenly, cleansing his skin and providing temporary heat. This was Georgia's domain, so Pétur had to use a shower gel which was pink and glittery, poured from a bottle adorned with princesses. But he didn't care – soap was soap at the end of the day.

He closed his eyes and massaged his face clean.

THE MASS STRETCHED out before slipping into the hall. Ah, it felt good to be free again. Yesterday's release had been an irritating taunt. Pétur hardly ever took the talisman off – if only there was a way to destroy it and remain free.

The mass would have some fun and enjoy the open space before returning to the necklace. There had to be a way to get rid of it. Fire. Fire would work. All it needed was a boost of energy.

It flitted into an empty bedroom and became bored, quickly

dashing out again to stop dead in its tracks upon entering the master bedroom. Fast asleep in the bed was another human.

The mass floated towards her, checking for signals that she was awake. No movement apart from shallow breathing. The mass crept under the bed before scaling the bedside cabinet and peeking over the edge of the mattress.

The human reminded the mass of Langamma. This one had a good soul and cared for Pétur. This was a human to trust.

Satisfied the human wouldn't hurt Pétur, it ventured back into the hall and through to the kitchen. This was a good room. So much energy to feed off!

With excited speed it zoomed on to the kitchen worktop and circled a few times like an enthusiastic puppy chasing its tail. The radio blasted into action for a fleeting moment, the kettle flicked on and off, and the cupboard doors opened and closed.

The mass had to calm down and behave.

PÉTUR FROZE IN THE SHOWER; sure he'd heard a strange noise. He strained to listen above the sound of running water. Nothing. He must be imagining things. He was already paranoid about his change in temperature; why not add strange noises to the mix?

He carried on washing his body, the hot soapy water doing a good job of warming him.

THE MASS REGAINED its composure and set to work on gathering energy. This room was wonderful, what with all its appliances, but it was the wrong type of energy. The best fuel for fires was hatred.

This wasn't a good house for hatred. Far too happy. Pétur's family home had been perfect, it had been full of it and gave the mass an endless supply of energy.

It made its way to the master bedroom. The other human was stirring now, but wasn't awake enough to pose a threat. The mass zipped under the bed.

The human turned, was it going to rise? She was still again. Now was the time to act.

With great care, the mass crept under the bedcovers into the space Pétur had occupied. It spread itself out, becoming paper-thin. It ventured closer to the other human. Still no hatred. It would have to touch her to know what secrets her heart was hiding.

It edged forward at a frustrating pace. Better to be slow than caught.

At last it reached her.

The mass enveloped her legs causing her skin to break out into goosebumps. She shivered.

Now, what are you hiding?

The mass quivered with joy. This was the perfect heart to leech energy from. Names filtered through the mass as it absorbed the associated power. Tobias. Jóhann. Lucy. Erica.

Yes! The energy buzzed through it like electricity.

With lightning speed, the human threw the sheets aside, causing the mass to retract. She grabbed pyjama bottoms from the floor and wiggled into them.

Feeling rejuvenated, the mass travelled down the bedside cabinet and on to the floor, seeking refuge under the bed. The human headed towards the kitchen; it was time to get back to Pétur.

He was still washing. Good. The necklace wasn't hard to find, discarded by the sink. What a horrible object it was – dirty, dirty thing.

There wasn't much time. Pétur would put it on soon.

The mass compacted itself to the size of a tennis ball, concentrating its energy, and launched at the talisman. Once, twice, three times it struck the metal. With the final strike a spark flew and the metal caught. Blue flames rose over the metal hoop.

Yes, yes! Be gone!

The mass hid behind the toilet and watched with glee.

The flames got bigger.

. . .

'OH JESUS!' Pétur cried, scooping the necklace into the sink and turning the tap on. The water hissed and fizzed over the red hot metal.

I hate when it does that.

'P, you ok?' came Erica's voice through the door.

'Yeah, yeah. Sorry, did I wake you?'

'No, I thought I heard weird noises in the kitchen.' She mumbled more but he didn't hear. She raised her voice, 'Are you sure you're alright? Funny time for a shower.'

'Honestly, I'm fine,' he reassured her. 'Get back to bed, I'll be with you soon.'

He picked up the wet pendant and looped it around his neck.

THE MASS RETURNED to its prison. Why didn't Pétur want it to be free? They could achieve so much together.

Erica stopped at the corner of Sauchiehall Street and looked into Nick's coffee shop. It was one of the retail units joined on to the main shopping centre in the middle of Glasgow. Buchanan Galleries had been the busiest mall in town until nearby St Enoch's had been renovated. As a consequence of its position, Nick's coffee shop was quieter than hers – commuters bring more money than shoppers.

The large glass windowed front provided a clear view inside. She'd sent P to see Georgia and made the five-minute walk from the Chambers, eager to visit before the lunchtime rush. Monday morning, nine o'clock, it would still be dead.

She studied the man behind the counter as he served. The trademark bun, cheery smile, *butter wouldn't melt*. Could he be capable of killing? Surely not. Although he'd kept so many secrets she wasn't sure she knew him at all.

Pétur had asked if she and Nick were sleeping together. Ok, not in so many words – he'd insinuated it. His macho pride needed to know who the competition was. She'd lied of course, saying they were just friends. She'd conceded some truth though, and admitted she was sleeping with someone – Pétur deserved to know he wasn't alone. *It's not going to stop anytime soon* she'd told him, surprised that Pétur didn't look hurt or taken aback. Perhaps she'd misread him.

Erica made her way into the shop, heat and the sound of classical music hitting her as she entered. She could feel her nerves rising and swallowed hard. Nick hadn't clocked her, his back was to the shop floor as he prepared a coffee, so she skipped the queue and made her way to the end of the bar to wait.

She leaned on the low marble shelf and the customer waiting at the till eyed her, wondering what this girl was doing, skipping the line. Erica forced a half smile.

Nick turned, placing a small Americano on the customer's tray. He couldn't contain a grin as he spotted her.

'Hey pal,' he smiled, patting his hands on his apron almost nervously. 'I thought you were off this week?'

'Nicoholas.'

'Uh-oh. That sounds like I'm in trouble.' He pulled an exaggerated worried face at his customer while he rung the order through. The man paid, wishing Nick good luck. 'What have I done?' he asked.

'That's what I want to find out.'

'Sounds ominous. Any clues for me? Just so I know where to begin.'

'I hear you've been playing cards with my brother.'

'Ah.'

'Uh-huh.'

Nick asked the next customer to wait a minute and scanned the shop for a colleague to help out. He spotted one clearing tables at the window and beckoned him over.

'Tom, can you cover the counter for a bit? I need to sort out shift cover with Erica.'

Tom obliged and a worried-looking Nick led them to the office-cum-prep room a few feet away. He didn't speak until he was out of earshot, away from everyone else.

'So you know about Lewis?'

'Why didn't you tell me?' she snapped, following him in.

She let the door close behind her with a thump, the security latch clicking into place.

'It wasn't my news to share.' He opened his mouth but had second thoughts, attempted the sentence again. 'He told me not to say.'

Erica pulled a chair out from the desk. The office reminded her of Nick's bedroom. It was chaotic to say the least. Piles of paperwork, sticky notes peppering the edge of the shelves, a picture of Tom from this year's Barista of The Year hung skewiff on the bulletin board complete with doodled eyepatch and knocked-out teeth. How could he find anything in these conditions?

He leaned against the large chest freezer which dominated the tiny room, crossed his arms and waited for her to speak.

She rubbed her forehead, wondering where to begin. There were so many questions buzzing around her head, her own thoughts were beginning to feel claustrophobic.

'How long have you known about me?' she asked, hoping he got the hint.

'What? Like, what you are?'

'Ye-ess,' she said, elongating the syllable. 'And how much do you know?'

Nick stretched his fingers out and pointed to a digit for each revelation, starting at his thumb. 'You're a werewolf. Most of your family are wolves. You're a witch like your mum. Your daughter has the gift of second sight. And... I think that's it.' Nick shook out his hands.

'And how long have you known all that?'

'A while.'

'How long Nick?' she asked, agitated.

'Most of it? Years. And about Georgia's gift? I guessed when I met you a few weeks ago.'

'Years? Did you not think to mention it?'

'Why? It doesn't change anything. Plus it's more fun to have secrets.'

'And what are yours?' she retorted.

He blew out a hearty chuckle. 'Magic ones? Or do you want the full list?'

'We'll start with magic.'

He stroked his beard and looked at the corner of the room, pretending he was deep in thought. 'Well, I'm like my dad. The usual sorcery stuff and a few quirks of my own.' His Orkney accent made her feel like she was listening to a bizarre fairytale, each word bouncing along with his jovial accent. He smiled, eyes twinkling, excited to see her reaction.

'Quirks?'

'I'll show you later.' He reached a hand out and held her cheek, stroking it with his thumb. 'Is this why you didn't meet up with me? You mad?' He sounded sorry.

'I am mad, yes, but that's not why I didn't meet you. Georgia really was sick. In fact, that's why I'm here.'

ERICA TOLD Nick the story in great detail, careful not to miss anything out. She was more honest than she had been with her mum. Swore a lot more. Got worked up a hell of a lot more.

'And do you think it's me?' He looked offended.

'No, no. Of course not. I mean you were only two in eighty-eight when the Iceland outbreak happened. And you were in Orkney. I want to know if you think your dad could have anything to do with it though. Like I said, Pétur is certain Misty is innocent.'

He sighed, mulling it over. At least he was giving it some serious thought; she'd expected him to jump to his dad's defence.

'My dad does some shady stuff and I can't say I agree with it all, but he wouldn't do this.'

'Positive? He's got the power, the motive, and the means.'

'He's a dodgy bastard but he wouldn't go on a killing spree. You might not think it, but he's got morals.'

'Most people have morals until they can justify not having them. That's human nature.'

'It sounds like you're the one I should be questioning Erica,' he jested.

She laughed, not sure he was joking. 'So if it's not your Dad, who else? You obviously have a better grasp of witching hierarchy here.'

'Honestly, in terms of power, it's my dad and Bill – '

'Bill's too frail, I doubt he moves from that house for weeks at a time.'

'Exactly, so if it's not my dad then we need to start looking at things differently.'

'Any ideas?'

'Yeah. You won't like it though.'

'I'm starting to forget what that sentence actually means,' Erica said, rolling her eyes. 'I've heard it so many times in the last few days.'

He reached over to the desk and pulled a few sheets of blank paper from the printer.

'Time to go old school.' He winked then drew a line down the first piece of A4, dividing it in half.

AN OLD-FASHIONED PRO and con list – sometimes the simplest ways were the best. Now it was written in black and white, it seemed so obvious.

She'd bagged herself the window seat in Nick's shop and was studying the six sheets they'd churned out. Misty, Tobias, Lewis, Pétur, Nick, and Erica. It was only fair to include themselves given that the finger of suspicion had been pointed. In the spirit of fairness, she was prepared to humour the last three on the list.

Or at least, she'd thought it would be merely a matter of entertaining Nick. She wasn't expecting the revelation it would bring.

Erica sipped her Americano before shuffling the wildcard to the front. She needed to read the list one more time before confronting the person. Confronting was the wrong word. The person was unaware of what they were doing, so it would be an epiphany to them too. The real problem was how to stop them.

She sighed. She didn't want to be right but there was no denying the facts: the dates added up, the means were there, ok, there was no motive...But then you don't need one when you're accidentally poisoning people.

Poor Pétur.

Whatever curse had been placed on him, killing his wolf soul and turning his family against him, it was wiping out the world's Packs. It was no coincidence that he was born on the same day the Reykjavik outbreak began. Pétur was carrying the virus. No, Pétur *was* the virus. Being an avid traveller, he was doing a great job of contaminating the globe's water supplies, spreading the virus wherever he went. He was an unintentional ticking time bomb, and the only thing stopping him going off was that cryptic necklace. Had his great grandmother known?

Nick had done most of the work filling in the gaps, surmising how the virus spread. Erica suspected he knew fine well it wasn't guesswork. No doubt his dad had told him. The answers were coming a little too conveniently to be a whimsical theory. Regardless, she was happy to have found answers.

Her phone buzzed, reminding her she should be with Quinn. *Shit*, once again time had run away from her.

'COME ON QUINN, PICK UP.' She was ringing for the third time in five minutes. The second time the call went to voicemail, Erica had gathered her stuff and was power-walking to her car.

Hello, you've reached Qui —

Voicemail again. Reaching the Jeep on Wellington Street she called once more, still no answer. She'd promised Quinn she'd be with her by ten thirty. No more chances, she couldn't be late. But she was late, and Quinn would be pissed off. She'd let her down again.

TRAFFIC WASN'T TOO bad and it only took her fifteen minutes to reach the children's hospital in Govan. There'd been a dicey moment on Waterloo Street when Erica had come to a standstill and second-guessed herself, but once she was out of the city centre, the choice to take the motorway paid off. Govan Road was always chocka at this time of day; if she'd chanced that she would still be sitting in traffic.

As usual, hospital parking was a nightmare but the large multi-storey by the entrance had spaces, meaning she could dump the car and dash towards the car park's pedestrian exit. An elderly couple wandered into an already-full lift, so Erica skipped the wait and took the stairs.

She hadn't been running for weeks, months even, and could feel the burn in her legs as she thundered down the car park stairs two at a time before darting over the grassy parkland towards the colourful entrance.

Not being a fan of hospitals, Erica was surprised to find herself admiring the large open-plan foyer as the automatic doors glided open. It was a new building and you could tell it had been decorated with children in mind. It didn't feel like the scary, sterile, doom and gloom hospital decor she was used to. It was nothing short of an explosion of colour; the expected white walls being overtaken by pops of vivid colour on the window frames, reception desk, and even the seating.

Not wanting to cause a scene, she slowed her pace from running to a determined walk and made her way to the lifts and floor directory. An interactive guide told Erica she was looking for Ward 1D, as Quinn had said they were in the paediatric ICU. Just one floor up. Nice and close – good.

The lift doors opened, spilling people out into the lobby. She dashed in, only to find there were no buttons. *How the hell do you select a floor?* She popped out, the doors closing behind her and the lift leaving. Erica studied the walls, before spotting a number pad between the doors. *What kind of lift makes you select the floor before you get in?!* She mashed the first floor button until another lift arrived.

THE LIFT OPENED to the first floor and once again she wasn't disappointed by the décor. This had to be the cheeriest hospital she'd ever been in. Whoever designed the medical bay at the Chambers could do with taking notes.

Now wasn't the time to admire the interior designer's handiwork though, and at first opportunity her brisk pace returned as she hunted for 1D. The guide said right and right again to reach ICU. She pushed the doorbell and squooshed a glob of antibacterial hand gel into her palm as she waited to be let in.

A nurse greeted her on the other side. 'Can I help you?' she asked, eying a sweaty Erica up and down.

'I'm here to see Samantha Hunter. They're expecting me.' She was surprised to realise she was out of breath.

The nurse inspected Erica again, making no effort to conceal her suspicion of the ward visitor. 'I'll take you to her.'

· · ·

ERICA OPENED the door and leaned against the doorframe of Sam's room. Both Quinn and Holly were dozing on the edge of the four-year-old's bed. In the centre, lost in NHS bedsheets was the tiny body of her pseudo-niece. She'd thought the sight of Georgia had been bad. Sam was worse; a breathing mask obscured most of her face – the child-size apparatus seemed far too big – and a tangle of wires snaked out from her little torso.

It was heartbreaking.

With bated breath she entered and placed a hand on Quinn's shoulder.

'Hey,' Erica whispered in a bid to wake her friend.

Quinn came to and wiped the side of her mouth before rotating her neck to loosen the muscles. Sleeping on the edge of a hospital bed was taking its toll. They can't have left the room much over the past two days. Exactly what Erica had failed to do for Georgia.

Quinn shook her wife's wrist.

'Holly, Erica's here. Wake up.'

Holly came round and blinked a few times to entice consciousness back. Her eyes were bright red and sore.

'Oh hey, you made it,' Holly said, her voice croaking. If it was meant to be malicious, the tone was lost.

'Sorry to wake you... I just... How is she?' Erica whispered while pulling a chair up alongside Quinn.

'No need to whisper,' Quinn said. 'She's sedated, you can't wake her.' Her eyes welled, the tears glistening under the harsh hospital lights.

'Still no idea what's caused this?'

'Nope. Nothing,' Holly said, dejected.

Quinn sniffed, composing herself. 'So,' another sniff, 'where have you been?'

Erica sighed, seeing the disappointment in Quinn's eyes. She could feel a death stare coming from Holly's direction. She owed them the truth, as much as possible.

'I don't even know where to begin,' she said, playing with her bottom lip between finger and thumb. 'It's been an odd weekend.'

'I'll say,' Quinn said, her eyes heavy.

It was time to be honest. 'So, erm.' Erica was stalling. 'I have a brother.'

'What?'

'Yeah, I know. I only found out about him this weekend. I met him yesterday.'

'A brother? What? Is he older?' Quinn blurted, shocked.

Erica let out a quiet laugh. 'It gets better. We're twins.'

'Twins? Wow,' Holly said, her eyes wide in amazement.

'How did you not know about him? Where's he been?' Quinn asked. She was sitting up straighter, the distraction of Erica's news doing a good job of bringing the light back to her eyes.

'He had a few problems before he was born,' she said, playing down his condition. *Just half-wolf, the usual.* 'Tobias wanted my parents to get rid of him. After all "they would still have one healthy baby".' Erica could imagine Tobias saying that, *idiot.*

'Jesus, I hate that man,' Quinn said, her jaw tensing.

Erica smiled; Quinn was the only one who knew the true extent of Tobias's wrath. She'd spilled the truth after Quinn found out that Erica had been sleeping in her car. At the time, her then-hockey coach had promptly gone round and broken Tobias's nose with a swift right hook. Heroes come in all shapes and sizes.

'So, Tobias knew about him all this time and never told you?' Holly asked, her Irish accent cutting through Erica's fond memories of Tobias's comeuppance.

'Not quite. Tobias was one hundred percent against keeping him. Cause you know, it's not like my brother's life would be my parents' choice,' Erica said sarcastically. Quinn let out a breathy laugh. 'My mum lied and said he was stillborn. She told my dad the same. That wasn't right, but I get it...I guess.'

'She was just protecting him. Mother's instinct isn't it?' Quinn defended and glanced at Sam.

'Exactly. So, he was sent to live with people who could take care of him.' The fairies would revolt at being called *people*. Fingers crossed their 'inside mannie' wasn't within earshot.

'What's wrong with him, if you don't mind me asking?' Quinn broached, looking sheepish. Erica didn't mind – it was a valid question.

Jesus, how to describe this. 'Not much really, I don't know a lot about it. He's got one leg shorter than the other so has a bit of a limp. I didn't want to ask him too many questions.' *And his tail gave me all the answers I needed.*

'Fair enough. What's his name?' Quinn fidgeted in the hard plastic seat, bringing a knee up to her chin. She looked young and vulnerable, but the creases around her eyes hinted that stress and worry were getting the better of her youth.

'Lewis.'

'Lewis. Lewis Hutchinson.' Quinn tried the name out, smiling. 'So Georgia has two uncles now? She's growing her collection.'

Erica couldn't hide a coy smile, so she rubbed her temple, hiding her face. None of this seemed real. So much had happened this weekend – her brain couldn't keep up. Her mind wandered to Pétur and the truth about him. Her smile faded.

'What's that look about?' Quinn quizzed, her eyes narrowing.

'Like I said, it's been a busy weekend.' Erica forced a happy smile.

'What else has happened?' Holly pestered her, picking up on the strange vibe she was giving off.

'Nothing,' she countered.

'That means something,' Quinn joked, shooting Holly a knowing look.

Time for another half-truth. 'Ok, ok. Only because I know you won't drop it unless I tell you.' She manoeuvred in her chair, buying herself a little time. 'I slept with Pétur.' She braced for their reaction, she'd only told Quinn about P via text on Saturday.

'Erica!' Quinn gasped.

'Bad move Hutch,' Holly jibed.

Erica rolled her eyes. 'I know. I know.' She did know, but she hadn't been able to stop herself. It was just too good. Although today's revelation would make a considerable difference.

'When did this happen? You've only just met him. Were you drunk?'

'Erm, yesterday. After I met my brother. And no booze. Not the first time, anyway.'

'The first time? What? How many times – no wait, I don't want to know,' Quinn said, waving a hand to stop Erica from talking.

Erica held up two fingers despite Quinn's comment. She followed them with a third and should have stopped there if she was being truthful. But she kept going, adding digits until she had seven. She liked winding Quinn up and was happy to provide a distraction today. 'Give or take,' she winked, making a show of the display.

'Erica!' Holly scolded, shaking her head.

'I hope to God you're joking.' Quinn laughed.

Thinking about P reminded her why she was there.

'Listen, why don't you two get some fresh air, stretch your legs?' Quinn was hesitant, so Erica persisted. 'Really, it's ok. I'll stay with Sam.'

'It might do us good,' Holly conceded.

'Five minutes,' Quinn bargained.

'She'll be fine,' Erica said.

'C'mon,' Holly said, extending a hand to Quinn as she headed to the door.

'Won't be long,' Quinn called over her shoulder. Erica wasn't sure if it was directed at her or Sam.

As Holly closed the door, Erica moved to the vacant seat nearest Sam.

She sighed, despair twisting in her stomach. Part of her wanted Sam's condition to be magical – it was better than being clueless, but a diagnosis wouldn't do any good. She was no nearer to knowing how to stop the virus.

She closed her eyes, holding back tears. It didn't matter what her mother said, Sam was family. Erica had driven Quinn and a tiny Sam home from hospital on the day Sam was born. Erica was invited to every birthday party, every Christmas. Sam even called her Auntie Erica.

Erica had saved Georgia. She'd find a way to save Sam too. Families look out for each other, no matter what.

She reached into her pocket for the tiny bottle. It couldn't have held more than 10 millilitres but her brother reassured her it was more than enough to test with.

She reached up to remove Sam's breathing mask; she'd have to do this quickly. The door opened, causing Erica to snap her hand back, awkwardly bringing it up to make it look like she'd been leaning on Sam's bed. She was no good at acting natural when she was up to something. Never had been.

'Forgot my hoodie,' Quinn said, removing it from the back of Erica's chair. 'You ok?'

'Yeah, just, you know.'

Quinn pulled Erica's head to her stomach and hugged her. She didn't need to speak.

She turned before opening the door again. 'Thanks for coming. Holly's parents are flying over today and...' she shrugged, knowing she didn't need to finish the sentence. Her own parents wouldn't bother to make the two-hour car journey. No surprise. 'Back soon.'

'Hey, Quinn,' Erica said, stopping her in the doorway, 'she'll be fine. I promise.'

'I wish I could believe you.' She closed the door.

Alone again, Erica retrieved the bottle from her pocket. Holding it up to the light she inspected it, swishing the contents from side to side. It didn't look like anything special, in fact it looked like ordinary water.

Not wanting to be disturbed again, she made her way to the door and rested her palm against it. With a click the lockless door was shut tight. She'd say it was jammed if anyone tried.

Erica made her way over to Sam, her footsteps sounding loud in the small room. She felt guilty, despite knowing she was doing this to help. Pulling the mask away from Sam's face, Erica tilted the girl's head back before tipping the clear liquid down her throat.

Lewis said it could take five seconds. She counted down. *Five, four, three, two, one –*

Sam's head jolted back, causing her chest to arch upwards and her arms to lie limp at her sides. Her muscles relaxed as a long breath left her body with a quiet growl.

Nothing yet. *Good.*

As Sam's body returned to its original position, a luminous purple haze came from her mouth like smoke from a dry ice machine. It cascaded down her chin, evaporating into the air. Erica thought that was it, but after a weak cough the torrent became darker and thicker, shrouding Sam's entire body in a dense fog the colour of an aubergine. It ran off her body, down the sides of the hospital bed and disappeared before it reached Erica's shoes.

Shit.

E rica checked herself in the elevator mirror as it climbed to the Chamber's medical bay. She hoped no one could tell she'd been crying. Sam's illness was magical. There was no doubt about it. The test had confirmed Erica's worst fears. So what now? She needed to find a cure more than ever, but was damned if she knew where to start.

Telling P her revelation over his involvement could wait, until she composed herself at least. Half an hour wasn't going to do anyone any harm. Besides, she still didn't know how to handle this. Quarantine until further notice? She wasn't worried about him spreading it further, not if he kept the necklace on. She was allowed a break.

She found Pétur sitting by Georgia's bedside. Both were in fits of laughter – Erica was reminded how nice it was to see her daughter so happy.

'Oh hey. Everything ok?' P asked.

She pulled a seat alongside G's bed and slumped into it. 'Yeah, just a bit full on.'

'What's wrong?' Georgia asked, her face scrunched up with concern.

'Nothing, nothing. Work stuff,' she lied and forced a smile. P looked at her, a face that said 'we'll talk later'. *Indeed they would.* 'What are you two up to?' she asked, attempting to sound cheery.

'I'm teaching Pétur how to make friendship bracelets but he's rubbish.'

'I'm trying my best.' They both giggled, thick as thieves. 'It's hard with big hands though. These are fiddly little things.'

The thin strands of cotton did look funny between his fingers as he looped them together. Years of braiding and styling her and Georgia's hair gave Erica an unfair advantage, but she didn't mention it.

'Mum will show you, she's the master.'

'I think he's too far gone,' smiled Erica. 'You either have it or you don't.'

'And you have it?'

'Of course. I'm a pro,' she boasted, full of playful bravado.

'Go on then. Show me how it's done,' he challenged, unpinning his mangled attempt from the bedsheet and passing it over.

'What exactly are you trying to do here?' she said, turning it round to inspect the tangled mess.

'It's a spiral knot,' Georgia confirmed.

'Really?' Erica was surprised.

'Right, it's not that bad,' Pétur said in defence.

'It really is. It looks like an old ship's rope.' It was a string of lumpy misplaced knots. She pinned it to the sheet and smoothed it out, pulling the eight strands of cotton towards her. 'Right, stand here and watch,' she directed and signalled to her left shoulder.

Pétur did as she asked and positioned himself, ready to learn.

'Bring one up, pull it like a number four, then loop it through.' She showed the move three times. 'Go on, you try.'

He bent over her, his arms enveloping her body and took the threads, his head on her shoulder. He was freezing cold; she could feel the iciness through her jumper. 'Ok, so like this?' he queried, bringing the cotton around his index finger and thumb to form the 'four'.

'Ah, no, that's where you've gone wrong.' She took his hand and repositioned the thread. It was cold to the touch too; funny, his body temperature hadn't been unusual this morning. 'You were going under. Go on top until the spiral reaches the right. Then bottom, then back to top.'

He blew out in mock exasperation, a dash of real frustration mixed in. 'This is too complicated for me.'

'You'll get used to it once you find your rhythm. Honestly, it's easy.' She looked at his fingers as he fumbled with the knot. He was struggling because he was freezing; his nails were tinged blue.

A cough at the door cut short their little tutorial. It was Tobias's aide, John Simmons, dressed to the nines as usual.

'Sorry to interrupt, but your uncle requests you see him right now.'

NO SURPRISE, the elevator ride to the top floor was silent. John avoided eye contact, choosing instead to focus on his clasped hands. Erica was relieved he stayed quiet – it gave her some much-needed time to think.

She felt it was too soon to shop P to Tobias. Doubt was niggling her. Part of her didn't want to believe the truth, but she knew she was delaying the inevitable. Erica had to be sure because once the words were out and Tobias was in on the theory, it would be game over for P. She'd never forgive herself if she was wrong. Any ounce of doubt was worth listening to and the voice in her head was shouting that Tobias was an equally guilty party. Erica knew he was up to something.

The elevator pinged open and once again she was on the eighth floor, the long-dead Pack Leaders judging her from the walls as she passed by, her dad the final critic before she entered Tobias's lair.

John kept his distance and stopped a few feet behind. Odd, he usually had a thing about controlling doors.

'Am I to go in?' she asked, John's new manner throwing her off.

'Of course.' He gestured a hand forward to usher her on.

She rested her hand on the gold handle. Her gut instinct told her that something was off – the door was ajar which was ringing alarm bells for a start. She looked at John once more. He was watching intently, but she sensed a flicker of nervousness wash over his face. A little twitch in his right eye gave the game away.

'Don't you want to go first John?' Erica asked, pretending to be polite.

'No, no. After you Erica. Ladies first.'

She wouldn't get away with stalling much longer. She gripped the handle and thrust the door open before taking a quick step back into the hall.

A torrent of water cascaded down the doorway, followed by the clang of a metal bucket. The splash soaked her shoes.

'What the fuck?!' came Tobias's cry from inside the office.

John's eyes were wider than a rabbit in headlights. He retreated a few steps and brought out a defensive hand, a feeble barrier between his body and Erica's.

'For God's sake John, help me get her in!' Tobias called, his voice thundering from the room.

He was too quick and strong and had her from behind, his vice-like grip around her upper waist, pinning her arms. Ignoring her kicking legs, he picked her up but she landed one foot on the doorframe, stopping them from entering like a cat refusing to go in its basket for a trip to the vet. Between Tobias's strength and John's efforts, the two men were able to push Erica through the door and into the office.

'Get the ties!' shouted Tobias. 'Get the tape!' He sounded panicked. She'd never heard him like this before.

John rushed to the desk and grabbed the items, dropping them in the process. He looked like an enthusiastic toddler, his limbs all over the place as he struggled to tape her kicking legs together.

Tobias was losing his grip; Erica could feel herself slipping as she squirmed.

'She's going to get away! Do something!' Tobias barked.

Had Erica not been the unwitting centre of attention in this bizarre carry on, it would have been amusing to watch. John snatched the closest object to him, a gold lamp with a green glass shade. Instead of doing the logical thing of hitting her with the heavy base, he dunted her with the shade. It did little to stop her wriggling, but it hurt like hell.

It bought them precious seconds though. For a brief moment, consumed by confusion, she stopped struggling and they flung her into the nearest chair. A *ziiiiiiiiip* echoed in the room as she was tethered to its wooden arms, cable ties cutting into her wrists.

The room was silent apart from the sounds of the breathless, exhausted trio and the ticking of the antique carriage clock on the desk.

'Get her legs, John,' demanded Tobias between gulps of air.

Trying to get his breath back, he was doubled over, hands on his knees like he was recovering from running a marathon.

Erica was too flummoxed to fight back as John repeated the cable tie treatment on her legs.

'Would anyone like to tell me what this is all about?' she piped up.

'Shh,' Tobias snapped and picked up the empty bucket, placing it to one side before closing the door. 'Not a word from you until I say.'

Erica watched as he made his way to the desk and produced a cross and a bottle of holy water. Both looked cheap and tacky, like the tat you'd pick up in a church charity shop. The water bottle was small and plastic, emblazoned with a gold cross and the words HOLY WATER on the front, in case there was any doubt over its contents.

She scanned the room – a pile of identical bottles lay in the corner. One guess what had been in that bucket...

Tobias was walking with a stiff ankle, recovering from the sudden exertion or (she hoped) perhaps she'd managed to land a good kick on his shin.

Clutching the shoddy cross in one hand and the bottle in the other, Tobias positioned himself in front of her. Holding both in line with her head he took aim. She realised his intentions a second too late and got the full force of the water in her face.

It went up her nose and in her mouth, taking her breath away. It tasted stale. She snorted, clearing some of the offending liquid from her nostrils. Erica felt an acidic nip in her throat as some of the water went down her airway. Over her spluttering, she heard Tobias and John chanting in Latin, while the latter shoved the cross in her face.

She did not need this shit today.

A few more gulps and the pain from her nose subsided; air was back in her lungs, she could talk again. 'Is this a fucking exorcism?'

The moronic duo continued to chant, ignoring her question. Silence eventually fell, so she tried for an answer again.

'Can someone please tell me what the hell is going on?!'

Tobias placed the cross on the desk and pulled the other chair in front of Erica. He took a seat, so close their knees were nearly touching. He had a definite limp; she must have landed a good blow to his leg.

He took a deep breath, brought his hands to his face and closed his eyes. Was he praying? At last, he spoke.

'I just want to know why you did it.'

Surely this can't be punishment for breaking into his office. *He's off his nut.*

Erica shook her head, played dumb. 'You're going to have to elaborate.'

He stared at her before turning his attention to the skivvy. 'John, can you leave us for a moment?'

'Are you sure? I mean – '

'It's ok, the bind should hold for a while, she's powerless. Go.'

So that's what the bizarre ritual had been about. Pity binding rituals didn't work.

John left, closing the door behind him. With just the two of them in the room, the air hang, heavy. His eyes pierced into her, the same as her dad's but with no sparkle. Funny how personality can affect the smallest things.

'I know you hate me; you've made that more than clear, but why attack the Pack? They had nothing to do with our grievance.'

'How about you untie me and we'll talk?'

'I think you're fine as you are,' he quipped.

She weighed up her options. She could undo the cable ties but it would create a commotion. Best to keep things quiet and calm. As for what he was accusing her of, she had no idea. He was going to have to spell it out for her.

Tick tock tick tock went the clock.

'Tell me why you did it, and we'll go from there,' Tobias said.

'I honestly have no idea what you're on about.'

He was getting restless; she could see the frustration in his eyes.

'Ok, if you're not going to tell me why, then at least tell me how to stop it.'

'Stop what?'

He laughed. 'Erica, this little act is wearing thin. Come on – it's over now. You've had your fun, now tell me how to fix it.'

The penny dropped. 'You think I'm behind the outbreak? Are you mad?'

'You can stop the charade. I know it's you.'

'And how did you come to that conclusion?'

'I've been monitoring the situation. I spotted the trend, but it was how you were doing it that had me stumped.'

She studied him with narrowed eyes. Did he really think she was behind it? Or was this a way for him to pin the blame on her?

He carried on: 'It's taken me a while, but I've realised how you've been able to target specific people. It was so obvious once I thought about it.' He laughed. *Pillock.* 'Then when you broke in here to steal the evidence, I knew I had the proof I needed.'

'I'm still not following you.'

He bared his teeth and leapt forward, landing a hefty slap on Erica's right cheek. The opposite side to her mother's assault – she was really getting worked over this weekend. The pain radiated a fiery heat. Erica composed herself, moving her jaw from side to side. Deep breaths, it will pass.

'If you're going to keep playing the dumb bitch, I do have other ways to make you talk. You've got one last chance to tell me how to stop the virus.'

She stared at him, saying nothing.

'Right, very well.' He hobbled over to the desk and fished through the contents of the locked bottom drawer.

'You're sick aren't you?' she questioned. 'You've got it. That's why there's a sudden urgency.' He paused and shot her a steely glare. He wouldn't give her the satisfaction of an answer but she knew...It all made sense.

Tobias returned to rummaging, eventually producing a small black box and a large glove. He pulled the glove on; it was one of those oven mitts you see on late night infomercials, super thick with silicone ridges. "Withstands heat up to so-and-so degrees, take anything straight out of the oven!" They could have a new tagline now – "Even protects werewolves from silver, you'll never believe it!"

Shit.

Tobias held the silver bar between gloved finger and thumb. It was only four inches long and a quarter of an inch wide, but it could do some serious damage. She didn't like where this was going.

Tobias trembled as he pulled it from the box. If it touched his skin, even slightly, he'd be burned like he'd stuck his hand on a grill.

This was not good.

He brought the bar to Erica's right side and rolled her sleeve up, exposing up to her elbow. He held it steady a good ten inches above her bare arm.

'One last chance, Erica.'

Slow down, we're in a hurry – advice she gave her staff when dealing with angry customers. Take a breath; give yourself a second to think before reacting. Make the right choice, not the classic knee-jerk comeback that starts a fight.

Deep breath. She could undo the ties and have Tobias against the wall in a second. She'd have to escape quickly, so depending on security's reaction time that could risk leaving Georgia on her own. Get caught and she'd end up subjected to worse than a silver bar on her arm. Nope, next plan.

Tell her uncle the truth about P and the same fate would befall him too. She didn't want that.

Final option: continue as she was, get more answers; find out what Tobias knew. Would he actually burn her? It seemed a step too far, even for him. *He was bluffing, surely?*

'Fine! he snapped. 'Have it your way.' He looked pleased with her choice.

Erica gritted her teeth and tensed her jaw. She was aiming for stoic but her reaction fell somewhere near an aloof whimper as the bar made contact with her arm. It was barely touching her but it sizzled her flesh like raw meat on a barbeque, the smell of burning skin and rotten eggs hitting her with lightning speed. She'd heard that werewolves had sulphur running through them; it seemed like some rumours were true.

Wow, that hurt like a motherfucker.

Tobias lifted the bar away from Erica's arm.

She looked down; an open wound two inches long stared back. Pink, fleshy, and black at the edges. Ok, so he was crazy enough to hurt her. *Noted.* Two deep breaths. Let's make sense of what he's discovered, get him to clarify his train of thought.

'Do the sweets and bottled water have something to do with this?' she asked.

He let out a frustrated roar and brought the bar down on the same spot. She hadn't prepared herself this time so her whole body tensed, straining against the cable ties as the metal touched layers of tissue and muscle.

'I wasn't even born in eighty-eight, you psycho!' she cried out. He pushed the bar harder into her arm. 'I was only one when it reached here.'

He pulled it back, panting. The smell of charred flesh and eggs was overpowering.

Erica was scared to look, but had to inspect the damage sooner rather than later. It was deep – a clear ravine across her arm.

'Tobias, please. I swear. This has nothing to do with me.'

'Bullshit!' he shouted. 'I know your mother started this. That's why there's such a gap, it's taken you this long to develop your powers, get your plan together. It's obvious why you want to carry on her attack, I get it, but it stops now. You've got me, so leave my Pack alone.'

'Are the sweets and water from the safe causing this?' she asked again, ignoring his ludicrous theory. If they were, then her doubts about P being the only source of the virus were right.

'For fuck's sake girl!' He held the bar close to her face. It was black and the acrid stench of her own burned skin nipped at Erica's nostrils. 'How far do you want this to go?'

She focused, engaging her mind's eye to undo the cable tie which held her right leg; she wasn't going to let Tobias touch her face with the silver. He didn't twig what the *ziiiping* noise was until she brought her foot to crotch height and shoved him backwards. His dodgy virus-riddled ankles couldn't support him as he staggered on to the floor and the silver bar went flying under the desk.

'John can't do anything right,' he mumbled as he picked himself up, pure anger filling his eyes.

'Neither can you,' she said, undoing the remaining three ties and standing up. 'Binding spells are a load of shit Tobias.'

THEY WERE AT STALEMATE.

She locked the office door so John couldn't come in. He'd rattled the handle a few times only for Tobias to call him off. He knew this would be a fairer match one on one. They stood in silence, facing each other like cowboys with no pistols. She would be the first to draw; he was out of ammo.

'Tell me what you know and I won't hurt you,' she said and raised her hand, palm out. It was a harmless move but Tobias's ignorance was her only defence.

'You're killing people with hexed water and sweets,' he quivered.

'How do you know that? How are they hexed?'

'Like I said, I've been monitoring things. I saw the trend and realised they were the cause.'

'And?'

'They've got silver in them. And,' he explained, glancing at her arm, 'you know what that does.'

'Silver? In the water?'

'I bet you were surprised when your little runt got sick, 'eh? Well I confirmed my theory when I gave her sweets the other week.'

'You did what?' she said, her voice lowering to a growl.

'You gave yourself away saving her. Silly move.' His pompous confidence was back.

'You gave my daughter something you knew would kill her?' She closed her fist, causing Tobias to grab at his neck as if he was being strangled.

The nutter smiled. 'I almost thought you weren't capable. Go on, kill me you bitch. Like you did my brother,' he gasped.

She let go, opening her fist which saw him stagger backwards against the bookcase.

'I had nothing to do with my dad's death.'

'No but your mother did. Only it wasn't enough to kill my brother – you had to take my Pack too.'

'You've had it in for me all this time,' Erica said, incredulous. 'I'm not my mother. You can't punish me for what you think she did.' She stood square with him, poking at his chest. He took it, flattening himself against the shelves, gauging what she was capable of. 'Dad killed himself of his own accord – why can't you admit that?'

'Because he wouldn't leave me!' he wailed. His emotions were all over the place, his trademark chilly disposition breaking. The virus was taking over him. 'She must have cast a spell on him or something. He wouldn't do that to me.'

'But he did. This isn't some form of twisted revenge, Tobias. I know you want it to be me. But it's not.' She was panting between sentences – adrenaline and anger had taken over. 'I've never been good enough for you. I've fallen short my whole life, constantly struggling to meet your expectations. The irony is,' she explained, chuckling, 'that I've even disappointed you now. I have nothing to do with this.'

He didn't look convinced but she took his silence as agreement. 'You're sick. Maybe if we work together we can find a cure. Isn't that worth a try?' she continued. Not a word from him, in fact he wasn't even looking at her anymore. 'Fine, have it your way,' she snapped, turning to find Pétur standing behind her. His face was ashen, his lips and skin blue, and his pupils fully dilated. He was shivering.

'What the – '

'J-J-John f-f-found a k...key.'

Erica grabbed Pétur's upper arms and rubbed, ignoring the searing pain from her burn as she tried to get some heat into him.

'What's wrong? What's going on?' she asked.

Tobias remained flattened against the bookcase, frozen in terror. He wasn't going to help. No surprise there.

'I neeeed to seeee M-M...Misty,' he stuttered before dropping to his knees. He looked like he'd drowned in the Clyde, a dead body washed ashore.

'P, what's going on?' she said, bending down to him.

'M...M...Misty.'

He passed out.

So cold.

Erica helped him walk to the car. Was he drunk? The last time he'd staggered like that was after Reynald's engagement party. *No more shots, please.*

The car journey was a hazy blur. Why was Erica asking him so many questions? *For God's sake, let me sleep.* Did she never shut up? She'd shaken him awake three or four times. She wasn't making any sense, asking him what was wrong again and again and again. Like she'd never been drunk!

He answered but it came out as slurred nonsense. Best to keep quiet, sleep it off.

Clarity returned for a fleeting moment with the memory of what he'd done. Boy had he fucked up.

'Misty,' he said. It didn't sound like his voice. Low, slow, miles away.

'I know P, we're nearly there.' Why was she shouting?

He kept nodding off. God he was so tired, he couldn't keep his eyes open. And the cold! Get the heaters on. He half-opened an eye to locate the button, but his hand wouldn't comply when his brain asked it to move. Never mind. Shivering was doing a good enough job at warming him.

Whose jacket was this? A thick green thing with a fluffy hood. This wasn't his. Did he steal it? It was draped over him like a blanket. It was cosy, not his though, better slide it off.

Time to sleep again.

Car door, gravel, time to sleep.

A hand on his arm. 'Wake up Pétur.' Misty's voice.

'Can he walk?'

'We can try.'

'He keeps blacking out.'

'What's wrong with him?'

Time to sleep.

He opened his eyes to see the ever-immaculate Misty, who today was sporting a navy waistcoat with matching trousers and a collarless shirt. He could have been going to a wedding. Pétur wanted to ask where he was heading to, but his mouth wouldn't work.

'We're going to help you into the shop,' he said, looping an arm around Pétur and taking his weight on his shoulder.

Darkness as his head rolled forward.

'Oh no you don't.'

Back to reality, each step was like running a marathon. He closed his eyes to concentrate better.

'No sleeping,' Erica said.

'No,' he slurred, the short word lasting an unusual two syllables too long.

Once inside, Pétur was placed on to a funny sofa. He'd seen one like this somewhere. It only had one arm. Where had he seen it? What were these called? Was it Italy or Austria? Venice or Vienna? What was he trying to remember again?

Two fingers on his neck. He moved his arm, wanting to shove them away, but it refused to lift. His arm weighed a tonne. Never mind, the fingers were gone.

'How long has he been like this?'

'Em, I dunno, maybe half an hour. He was cold all morning though.'

'It's very erratic. Hmm, curious.'

'What the hell is going on Misty?'

'Did he not tell you?'

'What have you done?'

'I can't discuss business transactions without permission Erica.'

Time to sleep again. He wished the two of them would shut up and give him some peace.

'Oh no you don't,' Erica said, shaking him. He opened his eyes to find her kneeling beside the ches– damn, the word was on the tip of his tongue.

'You,' he said, unsure of where the sentence was heading. Erica's brow was furrowed, concerned.

She cupped his cheek, her hand was warm. 'What have you done, P?'

Why won't my bloody mouth work? He knew what he wanted to say but his jaw refused to move. He'd never been this drunk before.

Reality hit again. *Shit shit shit.*

'Here, give him this,' Misty said, handing Erica a cup. She held it to Pétur's lips, pouring the sweet liquid into his mouth as he parted his lips a fraction. It was a struggle to swallow and his body forced him to cough. He could feel it travelling down his throat like hot syrup, and a feeling of warmth spread over his body.

'What's going on?' he asked, his voice nearly a whisper.

'I'm not sure, this has never happened before.' Misty looked concerned; his normal happy-clappy demeanour was reduced to pensive pacing around the shop floor.

'Tell me what's happened P,' Erica encouraged. She stroked Pétur's face, and he noticed the huge wound on her forearm.

'What's happened to you?'

'Never mind that. Tell me about you.'

He looked to Misty for support. Was he allowed to tell?

'You'd better fill her in.'

He took a deep breath. His lungs stung with the air he inhaled; it was like having pins and needles in his chest. This was a bizarre situation to explain. Pétur began, wincing: 'Yesterday, you know how I said I'd been to see Misty?'

'Uhuh.'

'Well I didn't pay with money.'

'Right.'

She already looked mad.

'It was kind of a pay-half-now, pay-the-rest-later deal.' Pétur didn't want to say any more. His head felt odd – not painful, but like his thoughts were outside his mind, and there was a dull ache coming from somewhere. He could feel sleep threatening again. She stared at him, waiting for more answers. 'I, I...'

'Yes?'

'I paid with half my soul.'

'Your what, sorry?' She looked at Misty who had stopped pacing and was watching over them, rubbing his chin thoughtfully. 'Did he say soul?'

Misty nodded.

'Are you mental? That's not a thing,' she scoffed. 'Tell me that's not a real thing?'

'Erica, I'm a four-hundred-year old warlock,' explained Misty. 'I didn't get to this age by eating porridge every morning.'

'Four hundred years old?' her voice quivered. It was her turn to pace as she rubbed her temples. 'This is a joke, yeah? Stuff like this doesn't happen in real life.'

'I think you've been living with Seelies too long, my dear,' Misty joked.

Pétur sat still, but his head spun. He slumped into the chair. Sleep was a better idea. Five minutes, that would do.

'No, no, no,' Erica said, scooting to his side. 'Stay with me P.'

'You're bad,' he whispered, his voice sounding gravelly.

'I'm bad? You're the one who's made a deal with the devil.'

'Hey, hey, hey – less of that! I'm not the devil. Just a guy trying to get by,' Misty said, defending himself.

'On other people's souls!' Erica shot back. 'That's some trademark psychopathic shit right there.'

Misty grabbed the nearest chair and swung it nearer to the couple, turning it so he could straddle the seat the wrong way round, his elbows and head resting on the back. He sucked his breath in through his teeth before making a squeaky duck-like noise as he thought.

'It's not as bad as it sounds Erica. Half now, half when they die. There's usually no problem and barely anyone notices. It's like donating a kidney. Harmless.'

She glared at him. 'This is hardly harmless.'

'This isn't a normal reaction.'

He quacked a little more – thinking, considering the options.

'Can't you just put back what you took?'

'It's not that easy. The transaction's been made. The deal done. What do I get in its place?'

'Are you being serious? He's going to die.'

Die? Not today, thanks.

'Hey, life's full of chances. Some you win, some you lose.'

'Fuck.' She was back to pacing. 'Money. I can give you money. How much do you want?'

'More than you can afford.'

'You'd be surprised.'

Pétur shut his eyes. More shivering.

'I'm still here,' he whispered, his eyes refusing to open. 'Just resting. Don't worry,' he sighed. Pétur suddenly realised how crazy it was listening to Erica negotiating for his life. What was he worth? Thousands? A million? A pound? Langamma would argue that he was priceless.

It would be nice to see her again. She'd be waiting at the gates for him. A nice hot chocolate in her hand like when he'd come in from playing in the snow. *Let's cosy up by the fire and have a chat.* They had a lot to catch up on. If Pétur could go to sleep, he'd be able to make sense of it all. He'd be fine, he'd be fine, he'd be fine. *Shhh.*

'Look, just put his soul back and then we'll figure out payment.'

'You're serious aren't you?' Misty asked.

'Deadly.'

Pétur's lips curled into a weak smile. If he could laugh he would have. *Interesting choice of words Erica.*

'Ok, right. We can try. I've never put a soul back before.'

'You do know how to, don't you?'

'I guess it's the same as taking one, but in reverse?'

He didn't sound convincing. *No biggie, this is just another adventure. No boarding pass needed. Let's go!*

Erica sighed. 'Look, whatever. Just try.'

Footsteps indicated that Misty had gone to the back room.

'It's going to be ok P. I promise.' She kissed his cheek, leading to another weak smile.

She likes me – but he couldn't make his mouth utter the jibe he wanted. *Kissing cheeks now, huh? It'll be marriage next.* He said the words to himself instead.

Pétur knew she was being dramatic. He wasn't going to die. He was the man in the book. The playful guy with an accent. Baby Trevor's dad. Erica wanted *him*. He wasn't sure of her reasons, but he wasn't going to question the universe. She wanted him and that was that. Pétur wished he could go back and tell his seventeen-year-old self to cut his floppy hair, grow a beard and bin that ridiculous lip piercing – there's a hot girl waiting for you in Scotland. She's the real deal! Yes! Don't waste any more time!

He felt cold again and his thoughts seemed distant, like whispers in an empty room. The pins and needles in his lungs were gone, but now they were full of something other than air. That couldn't be a good thing.

'Misty, hurry. Put it back in!' Erica called.

'I'm trying, I'm trying. I can't get this blasted lid off.' His voice was close by again. 'Here, you try. I struggle with these potion lids. Old fingers you see.'

Pétur sensed Erica getting up. Misty moved to the apothecary cabinet. He heard the rough scratch of a match being struck, followed by a hint of smoke. Candles were being lit.

'One more thing...' Misty's voice disappeared again.

'What's that?'

'His soul.'

'It's an empty jar.'

'Can't see auras like your mother then? Did you get that bottle? Fantastic, I hate those things. Don't get me started on potion set-ups. Tricky wee buggers. If I'd thought ahead I would have stayed ten years younger... Or at least kept a set of working hands,' he chuckled.

'Holy shit.'

'What is it?'

'I've realised something,' exclaimed Erica. 'Oh my God, it all makes sense.'

'What does? You've lost me,' said Misty, shaking his head.

'It doesn't matter. Look, is he going to be ok?'

'Twenty minutes and everything will be where it's meant to be.'

'I can't believe I'm going to say this, but I have to go. There's something

urgent I need to do.'

She's leaving? What? No.

Erica was back at Pétur's side. 'P, I know who's behind everything. I need to go see them. I'll be back.' Another kiss on the cheek. 'Be safe, yeah? I'll see you soon.'

'Listen,' Misty said, 'you'd better be back soon to sort payment.'

'Yes, yes, I know. Trust me – I'll be back ASAP.'

Footsteps followed by a door slamming shut. She was gone.

Even with his eyes shut, the room was spinning. This was worse than whisky, or tequila, or sambuca, or... what were other drinks? Who knew? Who even cared?!

Pétur wanted to clear his throat, dislodge whatever was filling his lungs but, when he tried to cough, nothing happened. His muscles weren't up for active duty.

'Give me two minutes and we'll begin.' Misty sounded a thousand miles away.

Sleep was coming – he could feel it.

'Pétur?'

Was that the sound of ice cracking?

'Pétur?'

A chill ran from Pétur's toes to his head, snatching the breath from his chest... Or it would have, if he'd had any breath to be taken. As the shiver raced to the crown of his head, Pétur's eyes flickered open and there was nothing. Not even darkness.

A DEEP INHALATION of breath and Pétur was awake again. His eyesight was hazy, like looking through frosted glass. A few blinks later his vision improved and he could make out shapes dotted around the room. Despite the haze, he could tell this wasn't a room he'd been in before.

From his vantage point lying down, the walls around him were so white they seemed to glow. They were bare and, although the room seemed light, he couldn't make out where the source of it was. There wasn't even a light in the middle of the ceiling.

His head tingled. If this was a hangover it wasn't like any hangover he'd experienced before. In fact, he was enjoying the sensation. He shut his eyes and took a few deep breaths.

The silence in the room felt unbearable. It wasn't a ringing sound as such, but seemed closer to the annoying background hum of a machine – true silence, as it happens, is one of the most deafening noises imaginable. Quiet yet ever-present; once you hear it, you can't ignore it.

Pétur held his nose and blew, hoping to make his ears pop. He'd had a brief spell of tinnitus after a Fall Out Boy gig in Amsterdam, but this was something else. His ears popped, but there was no change.

He turned around to see if he had company in the bed – why else would he be in a stranger's room, feeling like he had the hangover of the century? Nope, no one else there. He was utterly alone. *Where the hell am I?* He sat up and ran a hand through his hair while he took in his surroundings. Whoever decorated this room had been going for the minimal look – everything was white. Nor had they gone crazy with the furniture. There was the bed, bedside table, desk and chair. All white. Even the carpet was white. Heaven help anyone who enjoyed a glass of red wine in here.

Lifting the covers, a little scared at what he might find, Pétur discovered he was wearing black joggers and a black t-shirt. They weren't his clothes. With no memory of the night before, he had no option but to get his detective's hat on.

Not being able to remember whose house you were in was bad – sexual encounters or not – so, first things first, he had to find some clues. The bedside drawers seemed a good place to start, plus searching them would require minimum effort. Reaching over, he was surprised to find they were empty. Not a thing in them.

Sensing this was going to be harder than he'd first thought, Pétur got out of bed and set to work on the desk. It had three small drawers, which he discovered were all empty too. Standing with his hands on his hips, he surveyed the rest of the room. It was like being in a showhome – not one ounce of character or indication that anyone lived here.

What now? Wait in the room until the mystery homeowner returned? Or be gallus and see what – or who – waited on the other side of the bedroom door?

He didn't get a chance to decide as the door opened and in walked a hooded figure. Silhouetted by the light, the shape appeared to shine. 'Who's there?' Pétur asked, sounding like he'd spent the night propping up a bar.

'Don't worry,' came the reply. 'You're safe now.'

'D o you want a cup of tea?' the hooded figure asked. Pétur's mouth hung open, the words caught in his throat. 'I'll take that as a yes,' the person said before leaving.

A hooded figure wearing trainers was getting him a cup of tea. No face, only darkness in the hood, a kind of black shroud with tatty edges. A hooded figure with what Pétur was sure had mere bones for hands. And, yet, it sounded like a girl. Well, a lady. A normal, ordinary, female adult.

Where the hell am I?

Pétur's mouth was still hanging open. He snapped it shut.

'Milk, no sugar,' the figure said, placing a white mug on the bedside table.

Silence hung in the air, getting louder until it spoke again.

'Come on, drink up Pétur. It'll get cold.' Pétur sensed a smile in its tone as it spoke.

It was speaking Pétur's native tongue. Unusual.

Pétur brought the mug to his lips with caution. It smelled ok. It looked ok. His throat was so dry and scratchy; it was worth taking a chance so he gulped the liquid down. It was the best cup of tea he'd had in his life.

His throat felt easier, so he chanced talking. 'Who are you? How do you know my name? Where am I?'

'So many questions Pétur. Please enjoy your tea before you start the inquisition. We have plenty of time.'

He took another gulp, he'd had half the cup now. His mysterious host watched as he drank. Pétur eyed the figure; making sense of the situation, guessing where he was. Despite the distracting glow of the room, Pétur was certain that the hood was hiding a skull. Those hands were indeed skeletal and the crossed leg, although hinting at some sort of physical mass, was nowhere to be seen – where you'd expect to see a hint of fleshy ankle, the classic black and white Vans were filled only by a sliver of white bone.

'Enjoying your tea?'

'Yes thanks,' he took another gulp, nearly finishing the contents off. 'But please, where am I? And what...?' Pétur couldn't bring himself to finish his question, but was relieved he could at least find the words.

'What am I?'

Pétur looked, doe-eyed at where the face should be. The figure rose and made the few short steps towards him.

He blinked and the room was gone. Now he was in a red stone cave – dusty, dry, and cavernous – sitting on the floor. Impressive stalagmites and stalactites surrounded them like prison bars, and he could see corridors hollowed into the rock; they disappeared into pitch darkness and looked like they could go on forever. The deafening silence intensified.

Pétur's breath quickened, yet there was no air. His lungs didn't protest.

'I'm a little disappointed you don't know, but we'll overlook that for now.'

'I think I know who you are if that helps,' offered Pétur.

'Want to hazard a guess?'

He wavered, not wanting to offend. He could feel its icy glare. 'I think... I think you're Death.'

'Heyyy-oo bingooo!' the tall figure hollered.

Further silence.

It circled him, like a lion sizing up its kill.

'I can't lie,' revealed Death. 'I'm surprised to see you so soon.'

Pétur didn't know what to make of that, so kept quiet. Didn't Death know everything, all comings and goings?

It stopped circling.

'You're a girl. I didn't expect that,' Pétur ventured, desperate to fill the silence so it didn't deafen him again.

It laughed. 'Every time. I'm Death, yes – the voice fits. But do you see any other gender-defining qualities? No. I'm a skeletal being translated into human form. I have no gender, no sex. Non-binary please. This voice is just left over from my last incarnation, changes every time. I expected more of you.'

Why was Death talking like the two of them had a history?

'Sorry. I didn't know,' Pétur said, ashamed. He realised he was on his knees. When did that happen?

'Don't worry, it happens to the best of us.'

'I... I like your shoes?'

'Oh, Jesus. I didn't realise I still had them on. Been Up Top, mingling,' it said, gesturing flamboyantly, but entirely serious. 'Best take them off, they'll get dirty down here.'

The trainers disappeared and were replaced with skeletal feet.

'Any idea why you're here Pétur?'

'Well, I'm guessing I'm dead?'

'Sharp. But any ideas on the cause?' Death sat and held a hand out, scanning an invisible list, its finger tracing the details. 'You're not due for a while, and yet you're here. You don't get to Hades by mistake on the way to work. I mean, it's not even Purgatory.'

'Hades?'

'Yes. Hades.'

'You're going to have to elaborate,' said Pétur.

'Think of this as a waiting room, except – unlike Purgatory – I can't place you anywhere.'

'Why not?'

'No soul. I can't pass you on if you don't have a soul. It would be like passing on an empty bottle and expecting the person to drink.'

'Ah.'

'Ah?'

'Ah, I might know where I've gone wrong.'

'And where might that be?'

'I went to visit Misty and – '

'Misty? Say no more!' Death laughed.

Pétur was quiet. If Death told you to do something, you did it. He looked around the vast cavern and took in his surroundings. It was a dull place, apart from him and Death it was empty. Was he meant to spend the rest of eternity here?

'Where are we with the narrative?' Death asked, springing to life and on to its feet.

'Excuse me?'

'I lose track of you lot; tell me where we are with you. Why did you go to Misty?'

He took a deep breath, contemplating where to start. 'There's an outbreak, with the wolves, Erica and I were trying to find out who started it.'

'Erica, huh? Lucy's daughter?'

'I think so.' Had Erica said her mother was called Lucy? Pétur was struggling to remember.

'Come with me Pétur, let's talk somewhere a little more... exciting.' Death circled its hand in a whimsical gesture.

Pétur blinked and found himself in the middle of a fairground. People mingled all around, a throng of folk heading to rides, amusements, and food wagons. To his right he could see a huge ferris wheel illuminated against the dark evening sky, reaching as high as heaven itself (wherever that was from here). Opposite him on a grassy strip were rows of candy floss stands, arcade games, and the more tame rides.

'Come on, get up. People will start looking soon.' Death ushered him with a flourish of its hand. Pétur rose to his feet and walked beside the figure like an obedient dog. Perusing the stalls, Death asked: 'Do you like games Pétur?'

'It depends what you mean. I like playing computer games.'

'Toe-mato, to-mayto. Games are games. You like to amuse yourself, that's what I'm getting at.'

Pétur looked at Death with blank eyes. A young couple nearby were trying their luck at the strength machine by taking a hammer to a huge button. Their efforts didn't go very far, but they were happy with themselves nonetheless; fawning over each other, hugging and kissing like nobody's business. The man picked the woman up by the waist and spun her around.

'What I'm saying is, you understand that I need to keep myself busy.'

'You're Death,' said Pétur. 'Aren't you busy enough?'

'I have Reapers, and you know, after all this time it gets a bit samey. Ugh.' They made their way to a shooting galley, metal ducks whizzing by in a row. 'Want a go?'

'No thanks.'

'Really? It's super fun.' Death raised the plastic rifle and shot six times, the ducks tipping over with a tinny ping. It offered Pétur the gun again. 'You sure?'

'Ok, one shot.' He raised the gun, and with shaking hands took aim and pulled the trigger. Miss.

'That's not like you.'

Pétur didn't know what to make of that. They walked away from the range, deeper into the fair. Taking an unexpected turn, the pair arrived at the rear of some rides and the worker's caravans that lined the perimeter of the park.

'We won't be long,' Death said, leaning against the back of a burger van. 'Any questions for me? You've been very quiet. Usually people are on their knees begging for answers by now.'

Pétur thought for a moment – or at least what felt like a moment; time wasn't particularly tangible here. The meaning of life? No, that question was too big to begin with. Was there really a God? Nope, too vague for a straight answer. He settled on a good opener, an easy one to get Death started. 'Why do bad things happen to good people?'

Again, Pétur sensed Death was smiling. 'That's a great question. One of my favourites.' It cleared its throat. 'Imagine a world where only good things happen. Got it? I bet it looks like a wonderful place, yes? But that's your utopia. You've put everything into 'good' and 'bad' columns. Who's to say your columns are the correct ones? You know, when I'm Up Top that's the thing I hear asked the most – why do bad things happen to good people? Meh meh meh... And my answer? *Because it's all relative.* When the same thing happens to a 'bad' person, you think 'Oh, they deserved it.' It's not a bad thing happening anymore, it's justice. So, you see, it's relative to your outlook. People seldom think they're a bad person. You get that label from other people when they make their own columns. Does that make sense?'

'It does, but I don't think it answers my question.'

'No?'

'No. Not at all.'

'Oh,' Death said, sounding disappointed. 'Ok, think of it this way.' They were now in an endless meadow: a carpet of flowers met a perfect blue sky at the horizon. Pétur ran a hand over a sheaf of grass that rose to his knees – it was rough and brittle as it touched his palm. This place was beautiful. Death continued: 'Have you ever walked through a meadow after a downpour? Did you notice that the flowers seem a little brighter, the grass stands a little taller, or that leaves become a little more radiant? Even the most resilient plant needs a bit of rain now and again. Without it, the meadow would reduce itself to husk – barren and lifeless. Only with a little rain can it reach its full potential.' Death turned to Pétur. 'Does that answer your question?'

'So, what you're saying is, it's character building?'

Death hummed and hawed. 'I guess that's a factor, yes.'

'Well, when you put it like that...' Pétur blinked and they were back at the fair.

Two men appeared from behind a nearby caravan. Their voices were raised, angry words were exchanged.

'So you're just going to accept this?' Death asked. 'Stay in Hades for eternity?'

'I didn't know I had a choice.'

'Everyone has a choice Pétur.'

'You said I couldn't go anywhere without my soul.'

'Ok, fair point, your choice was a few steps back.'

The two men were now really going at it, fists flying and collars being pulled.

'Are you hinting that there's a way I can get out of this?'

'I'm saying you're not asking the right questions. The right questions get the right answers.'

'And what are the right questions?'

Death laughed. 'Good try.'

One man had fallen to the ground and the other was taking full advantage, raining down blows until a young woman in denim hotpants intervened, pulling him away. He swung a final strike, his fist finding his opponent's temple.

'Right, that's our cue,' Death said, rising from its resting spot.

The hooded figure walked over, ignoring the screaming girl and bloodied man. He had his opponent – now limp – by the collar of his jacket, shaking him in a desperate bid to revive him. Death passed a hand over the unconscious man's face and a white mist vanished into its bony palm.

'Always such a shame when it's a blatant accident. It's the people who are left behind that suffer the most,' Death said as it passed Pétur and walked towards the main arcade.

'What games do *you* like?' Pétur asked, jogging to keep up.

'Now we're getting to the good questions.' Death marched on, holding back slightly to allow Pétur to stride in step. 'Well, it's not chess. I can tell you that for free. Have you noticed I'm often depicted playing bloody chess? I mean, I've played it a few times but it's such a boring cliché. Honestly, allow yourself to be painted playing it once, and that's you tarred for life. I enjoy so much more than chess.'

'Can we play a match so I can go back? Is that what you're getting at?'

'Oh, no. Sorry.' Death sounded appalled to have given false hope.

Ok, this was a good old-fashioned conversation. Pétur felt it would be best just to go with the flow. 'So, what is your favourite game – if it's not chess like most people think?'

'Oh God, where to start? I have so many, it's hard to pick just one.' Death laughed. 'Oh! There's one guy in Oklahoma, I've been playing with him for years. He's so clumsy, doesn't know what's he's doing half the time, makes stupid decisions. So I've been letting him get away with more and more. Last week he fell off his roof trying to fix his TV aerial and I let him get straight back up.' Death was giggling now, 'He's realised there are no repercussions. God, it's taken him long enough. I'll see how far I can push him, see what he does to test his theory and then BAM I'll lay it on him.'

Pétur stared open-mouthed.

'What? You don't see the fun in it?' Death asked.

'Not particularly. It sounds cruel.'

'Oh please Pétur! Death is my thing, what did you expect? You mortals are continually questioning me, pushing boundaries. Why can't I do it back? So many advancements in modern technology, it makes my job rather mundane to be frank. Fourteenth century – now those were the days...' said Death, wistfully.

'So you toy with us to pass the time?'

'I have to do something. I get lonely on my own.'

Pétur hadn't realised that Death had any human-like emotion. You learn something new everyday.

'Can't you do something else? Get a second job Up Top or whatever?'

Pétur swerved to avoid a couple coming towards them who had no intention of parting hands. In the distance, a siren wailed – an ambulance for the fallen fighter. Few people seemed bothered by its presence and most carried on queuing for the rides. Humans could be so heartless and disconnected when their own joy was at stake.

'You know I tried the job thing once. Can't remember what century. Time is so...' Death raised its bony hand, searching for the word, and drummed its fingertips into its palm with a staccato of clicks as it found the right turn of phrase. '...Forgettable. It all blends together, don't you find? I mean we've been at this fairground for God knows how long; anyway, yes I tried it. Didn't like it. I was a baker. Boring.' Death feigned an exaggerated yawn.

They were nearing the end of the busy strip and turned a corner on the edge of the attractions. The crowds thinned out as they walked.

Pétur looked at the sky and studied the stars; he'd never seen them so bright. Evening had turned to full night in a matter of moments. The big wheel continued to turn, its multicoloured lights looking even more magical against the dark backdrop. They walked further, the looping organ music from the rides growing fainter until it was barely audible. They were the only people daring to walk this far.

Or so he thought, until a couple exited a tent to their left. Laughing, joking and holding hands, this was different duo from the pair they'd seen at the hammer. This must be a popular spot for dates.

'Ah, here we are. Good timing too. After you Pétur.' Death motioned to the vacant tent. Pétur held back.

Beside the door, painted on what looked like the off-cut of an old duvet, was a crude sign reading *FORTUNE TELLER – only £5 to know your fate!*

'What's wrong? Why aren't you going in?' Death asked.

'I don't believe in fortune tellers.'

Death laughed and continued to hold the pose, motioning him in. Pétur sighed and made his way to the door. Chances were he wasn't going to get a choice anyway.

Pétur pushed the tatty vinyl flap aside and entered. The cold hit him like a slap in the face. Death stepped up alongside him and surveyed the landscape: blinding white virgin snow as far as the eye could see. Despite this, he could tell what the snow was hiding: by their feet was a dark, creaking lake. Unmistakable. Unforgettable.

'Do you remember this place?'

'Of course.' The lake where he'd almost drowned when he was six. How could he not?

A short silence followed (or, again, what felt short), while Death continued to take in their surroundings. The wind whistled around them and the lake's icy surface shifted. It was taunting Pétur, inviting him back.

Death sighed.

'Pétur, do you know what a Rube Goldberg machine is?'

'Yeah, one of those inventions where you set off a complicated chain reaction to complete an easy task.' He'd seen one online; a man dropped a marble that ran through a device with various contraptions and ended by flicking a light switch off. He didn't know if it was genius or a waste of time. Everything had to be just right to complete the circuit or the chain would fail. It must have taken days to plan and set up. Fun to watch, but the man must've had the patience of a saint to create it.

'Well, I guess that's the best way to describe one of my games. They can take generations to come to fruition,' explained Death. 'But it's so satisfying when you see each part tick off.'

'What does that have to do with us being here?'

There was the faceless smile again. Our first ever meeting happened here. I like to orchestrate little parts for myself. Call me vain but I like to be involved in the big bits, the life-changing moments. Don't you remember me?'

Pétur shook his head, deciphering what that meant. Death took his silence as a cue to continue.

'You see Pétur, there are three types of people in this world. I learned that a long time ago. I decided I'd set up a little game with the three types and see how it played out. Test my theory if you wish – heck, if I was wrong, it was a nice way to pass the time.'

'And what are they? The types?'

'You're getting better at asking the right questions. Ok,' Death held out a bony index finger. 'Number one – oh wait, I've forgotten to explain the first part.' Death laughed gingerly at its mistake. 'So, fortune telling. It's been my little catalyst for this machine. I've used other things before, but never this. I had to wait for the perfect first ball, the initial reaction to spark the chain. A person powerful enough to see everything I needed them to see, and to believe it. Those individuals don't come along very often you know.' Death nudged Pétur, who was shivering.

'Erica's mum,' he realised.

'Bingo! Lucy. She was really something you know. I've never known anyone with divination powers like that. Not sure I'll ever see it again.'

'Does this have anything to do with the outbreak?'

'I thought you'd figured that out already? I really am off with our place in the narrative. Don't you know? Maybe it's Erica that knows... Oh, you poor thing. I thought that was why you went to Misty. To end it all.'

'Tell me,' pleaded Pétur. 'I need to know. Misty didn't give me any answers. What did I miss?'

'Pétur, honey, it was you.'

'Me?'

'Yes, well, sort of. Teamed with the rest. Listen, are you going to let me do my three people speech or not?'

'To be honest, I'd rather talk about this.'

'Oh.' Genuine disappointment. 'It's really rather good. And it ties in with why you've fucked the whole thing up. Bear with, there's a conclusion – I promise.'

'Right,' Pétur sighed, 'go on then.'

'So, when you show people the future, they divide into three types. Number one,' Death counted them off on its skeletal digits, 'they do everything they can to make their vision happen. Number two: they forget about it, let fate run its course, see what happens. What else can they do, right? Number three: do everything they can to fight against it. Live life in an opposite way, to test reality. Who knows, will it happen anyway?'

'Which type am I?'

'I'd say a strong two, a one if pushed. You accepted quickly but it's hard to tell. You didn't give me long to evaluate.' Death sighed. 'It's a real mindfuck isn't it? It could go any way. For all you know, all three could have the same outcome. Makes life pointless, doesn't it?'

'You sound awful cheery about that. Listen, Death,' Pétur said, not knowing what else to call it. The name felt wrong as his words came out. 'Can we talk about this somewhere else? It's freezing here.'

'Call me Grimmy, all my friends do.'

Pétur blinked and found himself in the cave again.

'So what did I do wrong? Are you saying it wasn't a set course?'

'I'm not saying anything,' explained Death. 'But what I will tell you is, it's like that guy in Oklahoma. There's a hidden fourth option. Only for the idiots with a false sense of their own mortality. You let them think they're guaranteed a future and they push too far, believe too much, muck up the machine. You've stopped my chain Pétur. And now you're going to pay for ruining my game.'

E rica drummed on the steering wheel. Patience was never her strong point but this was beyond the pale. She'd been driving for days, surely?

She'd been close to losing it when she realised she needed petrol and had to call into the service station at Stirling. Granted, her car had been an absolute trooper this weekend, but this wasn't the time to be wasting precious seconds.

Standing at the pump, she'd become further exasperated by the constant product flogging. She wanted petrol and she wanted it as fast as bloody possible. No, she did not need a new pair of Himalayan yak wool gloves or a solar-powered lantern. Who the hell needed that stuff at a petrol station? She'd nearly ripped the cashier's head off when he asked if she wanted water, but she managed to keep her cool. *Only 20p, it goes out of date this week.* What the what? No. Actually, on reflection, yes. Some nice cool water was exactly what she needed in order to calm down. If only wine could have been an option.

Misty had called soon after Erica had fuelled up; concerned that Pétur wasn't coming round.

'You've definitely put it back in?' she asked, wondering if it was a 'turn it off and turn it back on again' scenario. Could you reboot a person?

P was breathing, and right now that was enough to stop her worrying and keep her going towards her goal of getting the bastard behind all of this.

Bill. Bloody bastarding son of a bitch Bill.

It had come to her in a flash. Little nuances, connections, throwaway statements, and forgettable sentences had collided to expose the truth. It was so bloody obvious when she thought about it.

Erica hit the steering wheel. Fuck, why didn't she see it sooner?

You gave yourself away by saving her, Tobias rightly said but wrongly accused. However, it wasn't until Erica (well, her subconscious) had put that together with what she'd noticed about both P and Misty's hands that it had clicked. P struggling with the thread, Misty with the bottle. Two able men who couldn't manage a simple task, and yet Bill with hands so gnarled he struggled to pass her a dressing gown had managed the complicated process of distilling a potion.

Bullshit.

Bullshit, bullshit, bullshit.

How did she miss the fact he'd had no trouble setting up the complex distillation equipment? Attaching its tiny tubes and tricky clamps, never mind opening the potion bottles. She was a damn fool.

Her arm ached as she slammed her fist on the steering wheel again. Her jumper sleeve sported a large blotch of crimson blood – she needed to give it a rest and stop hitting things.

Erica put the nearly out-of-date water between her thighs and twisted the cap off. She was at Callander's outer limits, the town's welcome sign announcing her arrival. Her fingers fumbled at the cap and it pinged into the passenger footwell. *Crap*, well it would have to stay there for a bit. She took a swig and composed herself. There was no sense in getting worked up; she needed her wits about her.

She felt relieved that P wasn't to blame for the outbreak. More than relieved – it was like the weight of the world had been lifted off her chest. Erica imagined Pétur wouldn't have been able to live with himself if he'd been responsible. He was a good guy, she could tell. Georgia already loved him. G was a shy girl who struggled to relax around strangers, but with P it was like she'd known him as long as Quinn or Holly. He was family.

He was also super hot. Bonus.

She turned on to Bill's street. Time to start psyching herself up. Was she going to barge in, metaphorical guns blazing or would she play it cool, drop the issue into conversation? Going slow hadn't worked with Tobias and he was a psycho she knew well. God, she felt so unprepared for this.

Erica parked in front of Bill's house and sat for a few minutes, sipping the water. She stared at the unassuming bungalow. It was tatty, worn, and neglected, complete with classic hints that an older person lived within its walls: the 'no cold callers' sticker alongside the doorbell, the white handrail by the door and net curtains hanging in the windows. Who would have thought a mass murderer could live here?

Twenty-eight years he'd been doing this. Hundreds killed across all continents. That's one hell of a run.

Erica took a last gulp of water before popping the bottle in the cup holder. *Time to rock and roll.* Taking one last deep breath, Erica forced herself out of the car and through Bill's lopsided gate. Her legs were moving of their own accord, but her head didn't want to be a few steps away from his door. It wanted to be at home, drinking wine straight from the bottle.

Her phone buzzed again. She hit the lock button and silenced it. If she stalled any more she would never do this.

With a shaking hand, Erica rang the bell. Shoving both hands in her back pockets and bouncing on the balls of her feet, she tried to look casual. Her efforts instantly failed as she caught the gaping wound on her arm just as Bill opened the door. She grimaced. She'd need to get that seen to.

'Erica, I didn't think I'd be seeing you again so soon. Are you ok?' queried Bill. 'You look like you're in pain.'

'Can I come in?' she asked, cutting to the chase.

He led her through to the living room. The cat was fast asleep on the couch but moved when she took a seat next to him. Perhaps he could feel the tension.

'Do you want a cup of tea?' Bill asked.

'No thanks. We need to talk.'

Bill looked concerned as he sat down in the armchair opposite. Erica pressed her palms together and stuck them between her thighs. *Where to start?* The words caught in her throat, heavy and glutinous. She couldn't believe she was going to have this conversation. She had a stuttering false start before finally making an attempt at a sentence.

'It's you, isn't it?'

Bill didn't ask what she was talking about. Instead, he swallowed hard and stared at his lap, hands resting on his knees. He took a few breaths before talking. 'I wondered how long it would take you. You're a smart girl. I knew I was in trouble when you visited,' he sighed. 'Oh well, I'm old. I guess it had to end sometime.'

She sat, open-mouthed and in shock. 'Is that all you have to say?'

'What else is there? I did it,' he admitted. 'You caught me. Game over.'

'Is that all this was to you? A game? People have died!'

'Oh, no, no. Much more than that.' He looked at Erica, searching for a way to explain. 'Are you sure you don't want a cup of tea?'

'Definitely,' said Erica. 'Bill, you do realise what you've done, don't you?'

'Of course. I might look old, but I'm not senile. One moment,' he said, pushing himself up from his armchair. 'I need to get something.' Bill steadied himself on his quad cane and shuffled off to the kitchen.

Was she safe? She wished Nick was here, he had a good understanding of wizarding capability. Plus she'd feel safer with someone who knew how to defend themselves magically. Fuck, Erica wished she had practiced more. Why hadn't she practiced? She'd been given a gift that thousands would kill for and had decided to ignore it and pretend it didn't exist. Where was the sense in that?

Erica could hear the clink of glasses from the kitchen. What was he up to? What if he was getting a knife? Or worse? He could have anything hidden among the stacks of crap. She readied herself for two scenarios: if it was a magic attack, she could conjure what she could or simply hide; if it was a physical attack, she'd have to Turn and fight back.

Bill appeared from the kitchen holding a glass filled with a generous measure of what Erica guessed was whisky. His hands gripped the glass with ease, not like the show he'd put on with the mug before. He lowered himself back into the chair.

'So you really do need the cane then?' she asked; interested to know how far the charade went.

'This? Oh God yes. Polio. Buggered up my hip and leg.'

'But your hands are fine?'

He smiled. 'Nothing wrong with them. That was an essential part of the plan though.'

'Care to tell me the rest?'

'Ok, but be warned – it's long.'

'It's fine, I've got time.'

'Well in that case, I'll start from the beginning.

'**P**ay?'

'I do hate disappointment Pétur. You stopped my fun; don't you think it's only fair that I pass the frustration on? Eye for an eye, et cetera...?' Death reasoned.

'Erm, not really... It was an accident. What do you mean by pay?' He looked around, searching for the flames of Hell. The cave remained unchanged.

'I'm still deciding. I am, sadly, particularly fond of you... Which makes this so much harder.' Death turned before adding, 'Well, part of you.'

Death, or Grimmy as Pétur been given permission to call it, disappeared into one of the cave's dark offshoots. Was he meant to follow? He chose to stay put.

Wrong choice.

'Come on Pétur, get trotting!' Death's voice hollered from the dark tunnel.

He'd expected light to appear as he got closer to the tunnel's entrance, or at least see an exit at the other end, but the pitch black only intensified as he got nearer.

'Come on, don't be scared!' Death called again. Its voice echoed.

'Coming!' Pétur shouted back, a quiver running down his spine. Who knew what was waiting for him in there?

He widened his eyes as he went further in, letting in as much light as possible. It was futile, the darkness consumed everything – Pétur couldn't see his own hands in front of him, never mind what might be lurking only metres away. He stretched his arms out, hoping they'd act as a crash barrier should he encounter a wall... Or worse.

'You there? Good.' A bony hand closed around his wrist.

Pétur blinked and found himself in an impossibly long, narrow room showcasing an infinite choice of white doors with gleaming gold knobs.

'What is this?'

'It'll take too long to explain. Hurry up and pick one will you? I have a meeting in thirty minutes.' Death looked at its watchless wrist. '...Whatever that means.'

'Pick one?'

'Yes, yes. And be careful. No swapsies, you're stuck with what you choose – that's you for eternity boyo.'

'What's behind the doors? Are they all different?'

'Not necessarily. And does that really matter? You get what you get. It's more the neighbours you have to think about,' Death explained. 'Some right noisy ones here.'

Pétur rubbed his chin, thinking. His mind was blank, it was a bloody big decision to make and he was being rushed to commit. His stomach clenched, panic setting in.

'Look, right. I've got an idea,' Grimmy piped up. 'What if I shove you in beside the mother-in-law? Give you chance to get to know each other better?'

'Mother-in-law? I don't have one.'

'What? Bloody hell, I'm really off with my timings here. Gimme a minute.'

Death turned and disappeared through an invisible door only to return a moment later. Pétur jumped at its sudden reappearance.

'Right, that's me caught up, refreshed myself, whatever. Ruddy hell Pétur, you've not got very far with it all have you?' It rubbed at its skull.

'How far with what?'

'With my plan. You've cocked things up more than I'd thought. It's not salvageable. Urgh.'

Pétur ignored this, not wanting to remind Grimmy that his punishment should be worsened. Doors would do him fine. Unless...

'Couldn't you send me back and I'll fix things? Tell me what I need to do and I'll make sure we get back on track.'

'Impossible,' revealed Death. 'Firstly, where's the fun in telling you? And secondly – no soul, no returns. Told you.'

'Ah, so you did. Bugger. No spare bits hanging about?'

'Let me check.' Death disappeared through the invisible door again. 'Nope, none in the back. Totally out of spare souls. Sorry.'

'What if I don't choose a door?'

'If you don't choose a door? Well, I don't know. No one's ever not done what I've asked.'

'Really?'

'No, that was a lie. Happens all the time. You mortals are so reluctant to die.'

'Keeps you busy though.'

'That it does, that it does. Look Pétur, this meeting's with the Big Man. Really can't be late. Can you just pick a door?'

'To be honest, I was hoping Misty would have put my soul back in by now.'

'Ah, well, you see. Bit pointless that – you're already here, there's no point trying to bargain with something you don't have. Plus you need a full soul to return,' it explained. 'This half nonsense you've been walking about with doesn't float here.'

'Fuck.'

'Yes. Sorry, I forgot you didn't know about that.'

'So, that's it then?'

'It would seem so. Sorry,' Death apologised again.

'You don't need to keep saying sorry. I'm the one who mucked up. But why do I need a full soul? I've lived my whole life with only half.'

'Hmm, that one's a bit complicated. You were born with half your soul, your human soul – your wolf one was dead.' Pétur nodded as Death continued: 'Well, you need a full human soul or both parts of your original to return. Those are the rules; you have to have a full one. You wouldn't survive the journey otherwise and I'm not one for sending vegetables back. Go back with half and you'll be in a coma forever more. Such a waste of a good conscience.'

'So there's no way to get round it?' Pétur raised an eyebrow and put on his best smile. There had to be a way.

'Nope, sorry. Contrary to popular belief, I don't make the rules about death. I'm just the taskmaster.'

'I guess I can't argue with that.' Well, he could... But what would be the point?

'Always a pleasure doing business with you Pétur. It's good to have the talking part of you, I often wondered – '

'The talking part?'

'Yes, look. I'm picking for you. If I'm late again, I'll be dead. Ha!'

Death opened the nearest door and pushed Pétur in. There was no floor, only icy water that pulled him under. He grabbed at the door frame. *Hell was real after all.*

'No, wait,' Pétur gasped. 'Tell me where I should have ended up. Was I the man in the diary?'

'Really? You're going to drag this out?'

Pétur nodded; the biting chill froze him to the bone, making it almost impossible to talk.

'Honey, why worry about it? You all die in the end.' Death slammed the door shut and Pétur let go at the last second. Underwater he went.

U p Top, Pétur was indeed in a coma, as Grimmy had promised.
For all intents and purposes, Pétur was alive. Had Misty
had the gumption to call an ambulance, he would be carted off and
put on life support. He had a pulse and was breathing, but that was
about it.

Further tests at hospital would have declared him braindead, but
that wouldn't be right. Medically speaking, yes – the doctors wouldn't
have been able to determine much more but, in a spiritual sense,
Pétur was very much alive.

His eyes wouldn't react to light or any of the other brain activity
tests he would most likely be subjected to, but Grimmy would rightly
point out that at the very very root of Pétur's subconscious there was
definite action. Meanwhile, the front of Pétur's brain was doing just
enough to make him aware of what was going on. He wouldn't
remember any of this, not even under hypnosis because it wasn't
being filtered or filed away (that part of his brain was on a definite
vay-cay).

The part keeping Pétur informed was usually deployed as the
annoying little voice that likes to pipe up at sporadic intervals. It's
most likely to start chattering when its owner is deciding whether to
have another piece of cake or go to the gym. It's not under our
control, but we're acquainted with it enough to realise that we haven't
suddenly developed schizophrenia when we hear it.

At first, Pétur was only aware of darkness as a buzzing in his ears.
His eyes moved for a fleeting second as though he was in a deep
sleep. His brain woke up, his half-soul swelling and filling out the
gaps it had left. If Pétur had been able to feel anything, he would've
felt tingling, but instead his head was filled with more a static
awareness than a conscious presence – a screensaver for the mind.

A short time went by and Misty began to make panicked noises.
Things weren't going to plan. That should've worried Pétur, but what
could he do apart from lie there in silence? The sensation of fingers

on his neck and the unmistakable presence of an ear to his lips were the only indicators that someone was checking for life. Misty didn't speak, but his quick heavy breath suggested he was scared.

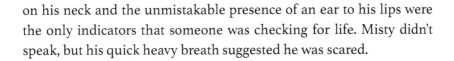

TIME PASSED. How much time, Pétur would never know. He was aware that Misty was talking. A one-sided conversation, so he guessed Misty was on the phone. His front brain was very happy at having made such a complicated and clever deduction. Who needed the other bits anyway?

'Bloody pick up, Erica,' said Misty, through gritted teeth.

MORE TIME TICKED BY. Pétur was drifting in and out of consciousness. He could feel the rise and fall of his chest as he breathed. Funny, he wasn't mindful of asking his lungs to fill with air. Have you ever become aware of your own breathing? It's an all-consuming realisation. Once you notice, it's hard to ignore. A bit like when you think about blinking. Awful.

His heartbeat was distractingly noisy. Was it always like that?

YET MORE TIME PASSED. Misty was back on the phone, but this time joined by Erica's distant voice. Speaker phone?

'Just put it back in!' she barked.

'I have. He's just lying there.'

'But he's ok? Breathing?'

'Yes, all the vital signs are fine, but he's not awake.'

'Well, how long does it usually take?'

'I dunno, I've never done this before. I told you.'

She groaned. 'Right ok, look. If he's fine then watch him like a hawk until I get back. I won't be long I promise.'

Silence.

....

....

....

There's a bar, in the Merchant City,' Bill explained. 'Strictly for occult folk.' It was there where Lucy had met Misty. Charismatic, charm-the-pants-off-you Misty. Which is exactly what he'd done to Lucy. Erica's stomach tightened. She felt repulsed, choosing to file that little nugget of info away and never think about it again.

It was through Misty that Erica's mum had joined The Clydebank Circle. This wasn't just any coven; this was the crème de la crème of covens. You really had to be somebody to join. For this reason, the circle was small, with only six of them in the group. Three of them being Misty, Bill, and Lucy. 'I wouldn't worry about the specifics of the rest; one blew himself up, one sent herself stark raving mad and the other moved to Morningside in Edinburgh,' Bill informed her.

He explained that they were a tight group and for the most part got on well – when Misty wasn't winding people up of course. 'Lucy was the heart of the group. It was a different coven after she joined,' he reminisced.

They met once a week, practised magic, shared spells, and had general chit-chat. Erica could remember her mother going to these meetings; right up to the week she died. Wednesday nights like clockwork. She doubted her mum ever missed one.

'It wasn't long before I fell for Lucy. I know I was a lot older than her, but this was over thirty years ago – when you're in your forties, age gaps don't matter so much. Or so I thought. I mean Misty's no spring chicken.'

'She didn't feel the same?' Erica asked.

He smiled, shook his head and downed some whisky.

Lucy's feelings for Misty were apparent, even after she met Raf, but she was intent on following her vision.

'Did anything happen between them after she was married?' The sickening idea of Misty being her real dad (who knew what he got up to behind that curtain?) flashed through her mind, which would make Nick her half-brother, but she was half-wolf so that outcome was off the table. No doubt about it, thank God.

'I can't say for sure. Only he could tell you.' His face changed when he spoke of Misty — his lips tightened, jaw set, and his eyes narrowed, darkened, and filled with anger. 'His advances were the last straw. I know he only pursued her to get at me.'

'You can't say for sure.'

'Oh believe me, I can.' He glared at her, wickedness in his eyes.

'Also, mum had a choice. And I'm sorry, but she chose him.'

'He can be convincing when he wants to be.'

Erica wasn't going to argue the case any more. Bill was set on hating Misty. He asked her to get the whisky bottle from the kitchen and she obliged, returning to top up his glass. At this rate, he was going to be pie-eyed before the story truly began.

'Misty was no good for her. Why she couldn't see that, I'll never know,' he said, rolling his eyes. 'And as for your dad... We'll get to him later.'

Her mum had friend-zoned Bill from the start, but he wasn't having any of it. He rambled for a while about how much better he would have been for her, how he would have treated her better than Misty or Raf. Lucy would still be here if she'd chosen him. He was obsessed.

Then it got interesting.

Bill revealed that Lucy had confided in him about her visions and had shown him her diaries. The fact that she trusted him with her secrets teamed with a shitload of misread signals led Bill to believe that he had some sort of chance with her.

We've all been there. Well, Erica hadn't – but ninety-nine percent of the population had. Unrequited love was human nature. You can't choose who you fall for, and there's a fifty-fifty chance they'll like you back. Another reason to keep your heart on lockdown.

Poor little lovelorn Bill hatched a plan to win Lucy over, plotting the ultimate move to prove she should turn her attention to him. He went full-on CIA and figured out who the recurring boy in her visions was, the Seelie she attributed all her bad luck to. Surely getting rid of him could win her over?

Erica had seen her colleague Sasha do similar when her ex had dared to cross her. Only that was in the age of social media and the internet – you could find answers on your lunch break. Bill investigated the old-fashioned way: word of mouth and reading. It took him months, but he cracked it. Otti Jóhannsson's second son was to blame. Bloody impressive detective work to be honest.

With his target identified, Bill set about eradicating him before he even got a chance to exist. What Bill didn't know was he a month too late. *And Erica thought she was unlucky.* P had already been conceived and the spell to make his mother barren hadn't gone to plan.

'I thought I'd messed up but then, as it turns out, it had swung in my favour.'

By this point her mother was with Raf and it wasn't long before word got to Bill about the outbreak. He could tolerate Raf better than Misty, but the fact he was a werewolf made Bill's blood boil.

'Neither man was good enough for her,' he spat.

Erica eyed his glass of whisky; she was going to have to cut off his supply. He was already halfway through this measure. Bill could drink.

'So how did you spread it? The virus I mean?'

'Well, your boyfriend was the catalyst for it all. He's the one that's been doing the spreading.'

So Nick had been right. *Shit.*

'It was an accident, I have to admit that, but when I heard about what had happened in Reykjavik, I knew it was my doing.' A disturbing smile spread across his face. 'It took me a while and a few guinea pigs but I got a similar reaction in ninety-one. It didn't last long though, so I set to work following Pétur to get a better idea of what he was spreading.'

'Did Mum know about this?' Erica was so shocked, her voice had reduced to a whisper. Bill showed no remorse.

'Of course not. When the hex didn't work, there was no point in telling her. And as for the virus, well, I doubt very much that it would've impressed Lucy.'

'So why keep going?'

He shrugged. 'I've never been one to look a gift horse in the mouth.'

Jesus, he did all of this to get my mum.

Erica was thrown by how calm Bill was. He may as well be sharing rudimentary stories of times past – not how he organised the deaths of hundreds of people.

Bill explained that he'd been able to follow Pétur by casting a binding spell and using divination water. He checked in sporadically to see if he was travelling; he would take notes and visit for samples. He revealed he was surprised that Reykjavik hadn't suffered another outbreak, but soon realised it was down to 'that stupid talisman necklace.'

Keep it on and P was fine, but removing it to wash would cause infected water to drain into the water system. The water cycle took care of infecting the Packs. Bill looked satisfied with how well this 'happy accident' turned out.

'I have to admit,' he conceded, 'it was complete luck.' It wasn't Erica's definition of luck, but each to their own.

He sat for a moment, swirling the whisky in his glass and watching it twist. The house was silent apart from the clink of ice in Bill's drink.

Erica's brain felt like the whisky. There were so many questions going round and round in her head, it was hard to grab hold of one and run with it. This whole thing was so surreal that her mind was struggling to keep up. Poor P was the unsuspecting weapon at the centre of it all. She reminded herself that he was an innocent party, to blame or not, Pétur wasn't doing it on purpose. It was Bill's doing.

A crash in the kitchen caused Erica to jump. She looked towards the open back door but Bill didn't even flinch. Two further thumps followed.

'It'll be the cat,' he said, not looking away from his glass.

'Don't you want to check?'

Silence, apart from the thundering rhythm of her heart as it beat fast against her rib cage.

'Your father deserved it. Your Pack deserved it. He was the Pack Leader. He had to pay for stealing Lucy somehow, he wasn't going to get out of it the easy way like he'd planned.' He chuckled. She didn't get the joke.

'What do the water and sweets have to do with this?' Erica asked. 'Tobias seemed to think – '

He cut her off. 'He figured that one out did he? I'm not surprised; I started leaving him little clues. It's taken him long enough.'

'How did you get them inside the Chambers?'

He sat up, straightening himself with excitement. 'That's where the hands came in.' He placed his whisky glass on the precarious book pile next to his chair. 'See, I knew I'd have to get around the handprint machine. It wasn't hard though – I simply had to play on the human nature of assumption. I'm no spring chicken, I've got a dodgy leg, so why would anyone question if I had arthritic hands?' He clawed his hands and showed them off before relaxing them. 'You'd be hard pushed to find anyone wanting to challenge an old bloke like me when they ask you to do the hand scan for them. A lady even did it for Pétur when he needed a hand... If you'll pardon the pun.'

'You were there?'

'I wanted to see how my virus was getting on. These things need to be monitored you know, can't let them run amok.'

How courteous of him to want to keep it in check.

'Why target children?' asked Erica, another question springing to mind. She couldn't believe she was having such a long conversation with this sicko. The truth was, she'd come ready for a fight, a showdown, but since Bill was so calm she was struggling to know her next move. She couldn't call the police, because this wasn't a Seelie matter. Erica realised she had to keep him talking while she decided what to do.

He smirked. 'Weaker immune systems, that's all. Children and the frail always fall first.' He downed the rest of his whisky and went to pour another. Erica swiped the bottle away.

'I think you've had enough.'

He narrowed his eyes at her but didn't protest. 'Pétur's virus had a habit of fizzling out. That's the problem with it being waterborne; it diluted itself when he was no longer there to reinfect.' He shook his head, unhappy with the flaw. 'So I figured out a way to replicate it, but it had to be administered in doses.'

'The sweets and water.'

'Exactly. I came up with a solution similar to silver nitrate but with the added kick of a few spells. Honestly, you have no idea how long it took to get it right. How on earth it appeared organically from Pétur, I'll never know.' Erica couldn't even muster a reply, but Bill ignored her silence and carried on, relishing his accomplishment. 'I began sneaking in hexed items after I'd started a frenzy in February. It wasn't hard to blend them in with the rations. To be honest with you, it was a bit of an anticlimax after taking so long to perfect it. I thought I'd get a buzz but I never got the satisfaction I expected. That's why I started leaving clues for Tobias.' He paused for a moment, before asking: 'Oh, by the way, is he dead yet?'

She avoided the question. 'Why did you save Georgia?'

He grinned, the toothy smile taking over his face. 'A momentary emotional slip, I'm afraid. I couldn't let Lucy's granddaughter die. Especially when she's so like her.'

Erica nearly said thank you, but caught herself before the absurd notion left her lips – she didn't want him to feel any gratitude for saving one out of hundreds.

'You think I'm a fool who did this to win your mother,' Bill said. His eyes looked glassy, no surprise given how much whisky he'd had.

'Is that not the case?'

'Perhaps in the beginning.'

'But not now?'

'I moved on from trying to impress her a long time ago.'

'Then tell me why you kept going. What was your motive?' Erica was running out of questions and didn't have a clear idea of what to do next. Going around in circles, she wondered if she ought to phone Tobias. *There's a sentence I've never uttered before.* There was an occult version of the police, The Guard, he'd know how to contact them. Surely?

'What more is there to say? You know how it started.'

'Well, what was the plan? To carry on indefinitely?' Her phone buzzed again. She pulled it out of her pocket, sent Misty to voicemail and turned it off.

When her gaze returned to the armchair, Bil was up, rummaging through a nearby pile. Not finding what he wanted, he moved to a stack behind the sofa.

'Oh no,' he said, answering her question. 'I knew I was going to get caught. Like I said, the game had to end sometime.' He paused. 'But all games have a climax, a prize at the end. The best part is just about to get started.'

Bill held a rag over Erica's face, covering her mouth and nose.

Darkness.

So this is it, Pétur thought.

With the door closed, it was impossible to know if it had ever existed. The freezing water stretched as far as the eye could see, only to meet an endless grey sky at the horizon.

Treading water for eternity. What a way to end up.

But what if he stopped? Can you die if you are already dead? Maybe this was the key to reincarnation and Grimmy was giving him a way out. What would he return as? He'd always loved dogs; one of those would be good. A shaggy retriever or a hip pug. That would be the life. Hopefully he wouldn't come back as a fly. On reflection, despite the fact that his parents were absolute bellends, his life hadn't been bad at all. Had he done everything he wanted? No, but he'd done *stuff*. Had he made a difference? Ok, no again – but give him a little more time and he'd make sure of it. God, what a magnificent thing hindsight was.

Pétur had spent his entire life avoiding water and yet, now he seemed to be in it for eternity, he wasn't all that bothered. Usually he would be a hyperventilating, sweaty mess but instead he was calm and collected. What was the point in being scared? He was already dead.

He stopped moving and let himself sink.

Further and further he travelled into the abyss, his surroundings becoming darker than the tunnel he'd just negotiated with Death. But humans aren't designed to sink like a stone, so it wasn't long before he came to a halt floating a few feet from the surface.

He held his breath (was that even a thing now he was dead?) and waited. And waited. And waited.

Nothing. His lungs didn't even protest. All in all it was boring.

What would happen to Erica now he was gone? Given Death's vague revelations he could only assume her mother's diary was in fact correct and the vision *was* of him. So not only had he potentially mucked up Erica's life – *be real Pétur, there's no* '*potentially*' *about it, you arse* – but he'd also snuffed out his son's. What a strange thing to realise. His mind wandered to the butterfly effect and how his son's nonexistence would bugger up the simplest of things.

Death had every right to be mad.

Pétur floated in the murky darkness like a man hung on a butcher's hook. This is what giving up looked like. If you weren't going to die drowning, why would you bother breaking a sweat treading water?

This was boring and he was only ten minutes into it. How was he going to survive an eternity like this? Pétur sighed, as much as you could when you were underwater with lungs that no longer needed oxygen.

All he'd wanted to do was help Erica. Little had he known that he was the problem in the first place, but how the hell was that true anyway? Grimmy was crap at giving details. He did have an eternity to figure them out though. God, what must Erica think of him? And Georgia? Jesus. She must hate him.

A hand closed around his limp wrist. Not Grimmy's bony fingers but flesh and blood. Whoever it was hauled him out and he found himself zooming towards an open door.

The action was over in a blur and he was soon lying on his back in the corridor where he'd last seen Grimmy.

He gasped for breath, natural reaction and all that. He was still getting used to not needing air.

'That's twice I've seen you do that,' an Australian accent announced.

He twisted on to his side, trying to compose himself. 'Who are you?'

'Shhh, don't worry about that for now. Let's get you somewhere dry before Grimmy comes back.'

The person helped him to his feet, hauling him up with a hand under his armpit. He couldn't see much of his female saviour apart from long, wavy blond hair and a colourful baggy jumper.

They didn't have to go far as she led him into the room next door, but his legs were heavy after being suspended in water; they refused to work as normal. She slumped him into an armchair.

His rescuer must have been well-regarded Up Top as her room looked much like the Scottish Chambers' library. Bookcase upon endless bookcase stretched as far as he could see, and in front of him was a roaring fire complete with a lazy dog soaking up the heat. She took a seat opposite him.

'Do you want a drink?' she asked, holding up a decanter. He was still finding his voice so she offered further details to fill his silence. 'It's Sauvignon Blanc. New Zealand, not Australian, but life can't all be perfect.' She winked.

At last he was able to focus and spotted something familiar. She had one brown eye, one blue eye.

'You're Erica's mum, aren't you?'

'Guilty as charged. I'm guessing you must be Pétur?'

'How does everyone know so much about me down here?'

'You've got yourself in a right mess.' she said, ignoring him. She looked as happy as Grimmy had.

Pétur lifted the glass on the table beside him. 'I think I'll take that drink, thank you,' he said. She poured, not breaking eye contact. 'You're mad aren't you?'

'I'd expected better to be honest.' She half-smiled. 'I mean not looks-wise, but Erica has gone so bloody long being single that I thought the guy who won her round would at least have some common sense. How did you end up here?'

'Misty.'

'Ah. Fair enough.'

'Really? I thought you'd be the one to defend him after what he did for you.'

'You'd be surprised.' She studied him, not hiding the fact she was sizing him up. He wasn't living up to expectations.

'Nice place you've got here,' he said, feeling the need to change the subject.

'Thanks, it's not bad I suppose. Not sure what I'd have done for the last eighteen years without books.' She sipped her wine. 'Sorry about yours. Looks like you've royally pissed Grimmy off.'

'Yeah, I've really screwed up.'

'You could say that.' Her jaw muscles tensed and, going by Erica's stories, it wasn't an easy task to make her mother angry. Pétur realised he wasn't creating the best first impression. Quick, time to backpedal.

'I was only trying to help,' he said, staring into his drink. Eye contact was difficult. 'I thought if I was the guy in your book it would be ok. I just wanted answers from Misty.'

'I know darling. We all make mistakes.' She finished her wine with astonishing speed. 'The only problem is that your mistake is going to muck up my granddaughter's life.' She rose from her seat, placing her empty glass by the decanter.

'What can I do? How can I fix this?' He was desperate.

'It's all too little, too late.'

'No, there must be something. I'll do anything,' he pleaded.

'Anything?'

'Yes, anything.'

'Isn't that what got you into this mess in the first place? I thought you would've learned by now.'

He smiled weakly. 'You'd think! But I don't want to hurt Erica and Georgia. They deserve to be happy. It's worth the chance.' She looked at him from her spot perched on the arm of the chair. 'Please,' he added, hoping that a display of good manners would be enough to push her over the edge. It seemed to do the trick as she got to her feet.

'I have an idea. Wait here.' There was a hint of a smile on her lips.

She disappeared behind a bookcase and Pétur did as he'd been asked. All he'd done over the past three days was obey Hutchinson women. His mind wandered to the unfinished friendship bracelet he'd been making with Georgia. He wanted to finish it. She'd be worrying about him; Pétur had said he was only going to the toilet. He hadn't wanted to scare her but that would be her final memory of him. Not ideal.

He tapped the side of his empty wine glass. Would it be rude to pour more? Yes. Don't do that. Instead he gave the dog a good scratch behind the ears. The mutt looked up from its slumber and Pétur was surprised to see it wasn't a dog at all but a white wolf. The animal eyed Pétur before falling back to sleep, unfazed by the uninvited attention.

He placed his glass on the nearest table, leaned back and waited.

PÉTUR MUST HAVE DOZED OFF, as he heard Lucy's calm voice guiding him back to consciousness. 'Pétur, darling,' she said, shaking his wrist to wake him.

He blinked a few times, his brain playing catch-up and remembering what was happening. *This was not a dream.*

Lucy's face was much rounder than her daughter's and she wore her untamed hair down past her shoulders. She looked like the type of lady you'd see at a folk music festival; knitted jumper over a flowing floor-length skirt. It was bizarre that she was only in her early forties; his head struggled to get round the tiny age gap between them.

Her smiling face came into focus.

'Sorry, I must have fallen asleep,' he said, rubbing his eyes.

'It's ok, you've had a tough day.' She sat down on the seat opposite, a large leather book resting on her lap.

'Can I ask you something?' he said, wanting to quiz her before he forgot again.

'Sure thing, fire away.'

'Why did you get us to burn the hut?' It had been bothering him all weekend.

She smiled; it was a good question. 'Well, if you know my daughter at all, you'll know that she never does what she's asked. It was the easiest way to let her discover her brother and the diary. Plus the hut needed to go – it's not like I need it anymore.'

'Clever.'

'Not if you know Erica. She's stubborn to the point of exhaustion. You have to create little workarounds with her.'

'You make it sound like she's trouble.'

'She is. The best kind of trouble though.' Lucy's eyes dropped to the book on her lap. She looked sad. 'If this works, can you do me a favour? Don't worry – no arson this time.' She smiled, the light coming back to her eyes.

'Sure, what do you want me to do?'

'Tell Erica I love her.' She let out a little laugh; he wasn't sure what the joke was.

'Can't you do that yourself?'

'I'm not exactly her favourite person right now. I thought she would've told you?'

'Erm, things have been a little complicated this weekend. I guess you could say we kind of fell out for a bit.'

'Oh really. How come?'

'Like I say, it's complicated.' Lucy narrowed her eyes, deciding if she wanted to follow up. She thought better of it and moved on.

'Right,' she said and opened the book. 'I'm not sure how this is going to work, or if it will work at all for that matter.' She flicked forward until she was at the right page. 'Of course, there'll still be the problem of you spreading the virus.' She trailed off, thinking out loud.

'Yeah, look, can you explain that to me?' asked Pétur. 'How am I to blame?'

'Details don't matter now darling. Forget about it.' She held a finger to her lips. She was reading, not paying full attention to him. 'Of course, once Bill's gone it'll be a different story.'

'Bill? What does he have to do with it?'

'Oh, he's the one behind it all.'

'You knew that all along?' Pétur barked.

She snapped out of her reading haze and looked him dead in the eye. 'Of course I knew,' Lucy declared, matter of fact. 'It's obvious when you look back on it, don't you think?'

'Why didn't you tell Erica on Friday and save us the bother of all this?' His eyes widened, a crucial fact hitting him. 'You could've saved me the bother of dying!'

She closed the book, keeping her place with a finger. 'Well, yes, true – but this weekend marked a major turning point for Erica. If I'd told you both whodunnit, it would take the whole learning arc away from her and the next four years of her life wouldn't play out right at all.' She paused, letting him take that in. 'It had to happen this way.'

'So you don't care that I frickin' died?' He was verging on hysteria and had to take a deep breath in an attempt to calm down.

'Que sera sera, Pétur. I know it's hard not to take it personally, but it's how it had to go.'

'Hard not to take personally? Oh my God.' He huffed, exasperated. He got to his feet and paced, rubbing his temple. *Was this for real?* 'I need some space,' he said, throwing his arms down. He didn't know where he would go, but he couldn't stay here any longer.

'There's no time Pétur. Sit down and let's get on with this before Grimmy gets back. You can be mad at me later.'

He didn't have a choice; she might as well have pushed him into the seat, her glare was disturbingly powerful.

SHE MADE Pétur move the seats and tables to one side, creating a sizable space for her to do whatever the hell she was doing. He watched as she drew a circle on the ground, her chalk squeaking over the wooden floorboards. Running a hand through her hair, Lucy surveyed the ring and muttered to herself. She nodded, her face deep in concentration.

'Can I help with anything?' Pétur asked.

Lucy ignored his offer and set to work marking out a five-pointed star – each point touching the circle's edge. At each star point she added strange symbols, kind of like ancient Greek letters. It reminded him of a stereotypical heavy metal band logo. Then the true meaning dawned on him.

'Are you summoning the devil?' he asked, fear creeping into his voice.

'Oh God, no,' she reassured. 'Common mistake. This is a pentacle – you're thinking of an inverted pentagram. Looks like horns.' She mimicked horns on her head with her two index fingers.

He remained unsure and couldn't hide the concern on his face. 'Isn't it just a matter of where you stand?'

'What? No. Totally different. Trust me. This will protect us from evil, not summon it.'

She produced a bouquet of dried herbs tied with string and placed it on a large shell. The scent sparked a brief memory of one of Langamma's friends saging their home when he was very young. He smiled. It was the smell of safety.

Lucy shut her eyes and said something under her breath before lighting the bouquet, careful not to produce an actual flame. It billowed smoke before she picked it up and wafted it over the totally-unsatanic-star. As she was doing so she quietly chanted 'Air, fire, water, earth. Cleanse, dismiss, dispel. Protect those of us in the circle. Grant us strength. Cleanse, dismiss, dispel. Shield us from evil.'

Not wanting to disturb what could be the only thing between him and the Lord of the Underworld, Pétur kept quiet until she'd finished. Once she'd placed the sage back on its shell he asked, 'Will it hurt?'

'Oh there's no pain here darling. That's more Hell's MO.'

'And what if it goes wrong? Will I be stuck here?'

She put a finger to pursed lips and thought before answering. 'Well, no, not really. If this goes wrong you'll cease to exist. Your conscience will be obliterated. Worth a try though, yeah? And better than being stuck here for eternity. Believe me, eighteen years has been hard enough.'

He wasn't sure he liked the sound of his conscience being obliterated. Surely it had to go somewhere?

'You're hell bent on making your vision happen, aren't you?'

She was placing candles at the star's points, around the outer edge of the circle. 'You could say that.' She straightened herself up after placing the last candle. 'I've always thought if it was important enough for me to see it, then it must be important enough to have to happen.'

'And it was definitely me in the diary?'

'Describe it for me. What bit do you mean?' she said.

'Erica with the baby, the guy with the accent, Trevor, that bit.' He circled his hand as he rattled through.

'Ooh. That bit. Not sure to be honest, I never saw the guy's face. Sorry darling.' She looked at him, thinking. 'Say a few lines. Let me think.'

He let out a long frustrated sigh. *Really?* Could he even remember what had been said? Time to adlib. 'How is baby Trevor?' he sounded as flat as he felt.

'Put some feeling into it darling.'

'How is baby Trevor?' Bit more upbeat this time.

'Once more.'

'How is baby Trevor?' He even threw in a smile for good measure.

'Hmm.' She thought, finger to lips again. Narrowing her eyes she concluded, 'You know, I'm not sure. I feel it was more – I dunno – bouncy?'

'Bouncy?' He could be bouncy.

'Yeah, it was so long ago it's hard to remember. You were in other visions if that helps.'

'I was? I never read any others which featured me.'

'That'll be because I had Lewis destroy them. Right, are you ready? Time is marching on.'

He wasn't, but the question was rhetorical.

'Where do you want me?'

'In the middle if you will. I'll light the candles.'

She lit the five candles, muttering under her breath as she went round.

'Do you think I'll remember any of this?'

'Ooh now there's a good question. I don't know. I mean, we've all heard of out-of-body experiences haven't we, near death and so on, but there are no white lights or pearly gates are there? Who's to say who's right or wrong?'

'You've never done anything like this before, have you?' Pétur asked.

'Never. It's fun to have an excuse to do proper magic again,' she grinned.

Pétur, you're doing this for Erica and Georgia. Be strong and focus on them.

'Ok, let's do this,' he said and positioned himself in the pentacle. He braced himself, fists clenched as if waiting for a punch.

'One more thing before we get started. Pétur, over you come.' She whistled as if beckoning a dog.

'I'm already here.'

'No, not you. The other you.'

He was confused until the wolf appeared from behind a bookcase. He'd forgotten it was there. It clicked.

'That's... That's my wolf soul?'

'Indeed. Good to finally meet each other...'

The majestic white wolf took a seat by Pétur's feet like a faithful dog. Its head was level with his chest and two dark eyes stared at him. *So this is my wolf form.*

'Right, time to begin.'

The two Péturs looked at each other. Was wolf him as nervous as human him?

'Do I have to do anything special?' Pétur asked, unsure what do with his hands, body, everything.

'No, no. As you are darling, stay still and I'll handle the rest.'

Lucy bowed her head and muttered while bringing her arms out like a bird ready to take flight. When they were at full span and level with her head she spoke in a low voice.

'Moirai, we call upon you today to help our brother Pétur. He has taken the wrong path and wishes to return to your chosen one. Please, do not let him be held back by his past indiscretions but instead let him learn, become wiser, stronger. Let him become more aware of the world around him and how important his decisions are. Let him become one again, his two souls reuniting as you intended them to be. May they come together in unity and live a long, fulfilling life. May you bind them together to be connected for eternity, never to part again. May they reawaken as one whole. So make it be. Thank you Moirai.' Lucy blew out the nearest candle. Pétur was expecting something epic but all that occured was a slight drop in temperature. He didn't know who Moirai was, but he

hoped she was some sort of Goddess of sweetness, light and everything nice.

Lucy spoke in a whisper as she made her way round, blowing out the candles in a clockwise fashion. Two, three, four down. Wolf Pétur watched him. They both looked at Erica's mum.

'Good luck Pétur. Godspeed.' She blew, the final candle extinguished.

Cold air hit him like concrete. Wolf Pétur felt it too as a howling whine echoed, his shaggy fur flapping in the breeze. The air around them was becoming foggy and it wasn't long before Pétur couldn't see Lucy any more. The air swirled like they were in the centre of a twister. He was getting dizzy just looking at it.

He moved closer to wolf Pétur and grabbed at his fur, scared they might become parted in the storm. The wind was picking up, the sound of it swirling around them was nearly deafening.

In the blink of an eye the candles ignited again and were lifted by the spiralling air. The candles flew around them once, twice, three times, before the whole twister became a mass of flames. He held the wolf tighter as the heat became unbearable. The swirling wind was now a ferocious roaring fire. Was he being sent to Hell?

Pétur's talisman was burning hot, worse than it had ever been, even hotter than when he'd visited a local kirk on a school excursion. It seared into his skin, he could feel it melting into him, becoming part of his chest. He wanted to rip it off but he didn't dare let go of wolf Pétur for fear of being separated.

The spinning inferno closed in and was nearly touching when a tentacle of fire reached out and batted at him. He ducked and avoided contact, bracing himself for combustion, to be burnt alive. He was sweating.

Again the tentacle reached out and swooped over the wolf's head. This time Pétur wasn't so quick and it pushed him, jabbing straight into the talisman with force. He staggered back and the cyclone picked him up, spinning him around his wolf, which looked up with a mix of confusion, fear, and anger.

A strange black mass was spiralling upward from his talisman, disappearing into nothingness above the swirling flames. It contorted and bucked, attempting to break free of the circle. Twice it hit the flaming sides before bouncing inward like a boxer off the ropes.

With a shaking hand, Pétur ripped off the poker-hot necklace, throwing it into the centre of the pentagram. A sickening shriek erupted from the mass as it was pulled downwards, into the talisman. It vibrated. Wolf Pétur backed away and whimpered.

There was nothing Pétur could do but watch as he spun inside the funnel of fire. He was helpless as the talisman continued to buzz, the tremor getting stronger and stronger until it was jumping from side to side. It had never done that before. It was thumping off the ground with such speed that Pétur was sure it would leave a dent. He was getting dizzy. Was this it? Was this the big spell that would take him home? It seemed unlikely. Whatever was meant to happen, it had better hurry up. He'd never been good on roundabouts.

A high-pitched wail stung his ears as the talisman exploded. Wolf Pétur hit the floor, a paw covering his face, ears flat to his head. Pétur couldn't take his eyes off the broken necklace as the black mass reappeared. It spiralled up like smoke from a campfire.

At six feet tall, it stopped rising and expanded outwards, sprouting arms and forming legs. Pétur's stomach sank. *What the hell have I been wearing all these years?*

The mass lumbered forward, ignoring wolf Pétur and focusing on its human prize. Its arms reached out, attempting to snatch Pétur as he hurled past. Missed. Wisps of black were whisked into the flames; swallowing most of an arm, before it retracted the shortening limb and sprouted a new one.

What is this thing?

The fiery twister was closing in, long tentacles reaching for the mass.

'Lucy, how long will this last?' Pétur shouted. He was going to be sick soon. No answer.

The whirlwind continued to close. Wolf Pétur was doing a good job of shuffling forward on the ground, too scared to go near the mass. He tucked his tail under to avoid the fiery fury behind.

Now that Pétur was in the fire it didn't feel so hot and he wasn't being burned alive. Odd.

But he did feel like he might pass out from dizziness. With the twister closing in, wolf Pétur had no choice but to join his human counterpart, or risk being engulfed by the black mass. After a few trips around the wolf leaned on its haunches, ready to spring. Each time Pétur passed, the wolf readied himself, judging when to go. Pétur's attempt to cross the stream in Balmaha flashed through his mind. He hoped wolf Pétur was better at leaping than him.

The wolf jumped. A mass of white fur and snarling teeth made for Pétur's face. He braced for impact.

BANG. The wolf collided with his chest.

Heat radiated to parts of his body he didn't know existed. His neck snapped back, veins and tendons protruding as his body endured a pain like nothing he'd ever experienced. It was like being set on fire while being crushed by a steamroller. But worse.

Pétur's mind buzzed and crackled. Images of war zones, battlefields, and destroyed cities flashed through his head. He was sure he recognised images from terrorist bombings, and the vision of an unarmed man being shot in the back lingered in his mind before whizzing off and being replaced by another battlefield scene.

Why was he seeing this?

The lake. His lake. He shivered, the icy wind so real it was like he was there.

He screamed, the pain was too much. His bones were as hot as lava and they were too big for him, fighting to push through his skin.

The mass grabbed for him again and let out a high-pitched screech. Something hot and wet was in his ears and trickling from his nose.

God, please just let me die.

PLEASE. LET. ME. DIE.

Pétur must have got his wish because the world went black and that was that.

W hen Erica came round her eyes were covered and for the second time today she found herself tied to a chair.

This time however, her captor had more sense and a better understanding of her powers. He'd used duct tape to bind her wrists behind her back. A strip of tape above her hips further hindered her; he'd stuck it straight to her skin rather than over her jumper. Apart from her head, she was immobile.

She was nauseous and her mouth was dry.

'Ah, you're awake,' Bill said, not far away.

She couldn't undo the duct tape. No knots to untie or zip locks to undo; she was stuck. He'd been clever in covering her eyes too – she couldn't see any objects to command, whether to free herself or to attack him. He knew her better than she knew herself.

She craned her neck, hoping there'd be the slightest hint at where she was. No luck. Whatever was over her eyes was on tight.

No one knows I'm here.

Footsteps told her he was coming closer. A rough hand grabbed her jaw. He moved her head from side to side, studying her face. 'So much of your father in you. But still...' She didn't want to know where this train of thought was going.

'What are you going to do to me?' she asked, forcing herself to sound strong despite fear taking over inside. He sighed. She could feel his hot breath on her face. The stench of whisky made her nose wrinkle.

'Before you get any ideas, I've got Wolfsbane here so you can't Turn. Sorry to ruin any plans you had for escape.' He laughed, sounding pleased with himself.

Wolfsbane. *Bloody Wolfsbane.* One of the few plants on Earth that could actually affect a werewolf. Depending on quantity, Wolfsbane would either stop her from Turning or severely weaken her wolf form, making the transformation pointless, if it didn't kill her on the spot. Wolfsbane was poisonous once in wolf form – even being in close proximity was a serious threat. It could kill a wolf in seconds.

His dry lips touched hers, she pursed them tight as he pushed into her, deepening the kiss. She recoiled her head, pulling away, but it was a pointless manoeuvre.

He pulled away but his saliva remained. The taste of him made her feel sick.

'You know, your mother's seen everything you get up to. I read your whole life story before you were even born.'

'And? You make it sound like I have something to be ashamed of.' Fear gripped Erica, tensing her every muscle and making her palms sweat.

'You're heartless, like her. Using men as pawns, we're just afterthoughts to your own happiness. Only you have no reason to be that way, apart from your own selfishness.'

'Heartless? When have I ever been heartless?' She wasn't a bad person by any account.

'Lucy sacrificed so much because she couldn't risk her visions going off track. That's all life ever was to her, a series of steps to get to the grand finale, not caring who she hurt or tossed aside.' Erica could hear him pacing. 'Well, guess what? It'll have been in vain because I'm stopping the story. This is the final chapter. All that work will have been pointless.'

So that's what this was – revenge for Lucy's rebuff.

Bill must have known he'd get caught and she would come here. The final part of his convoluted plan. *Shit*.

'What do you mean by stopping the story?' she asked. She didn't really want to know the answer. Screaming crossed her mind, but what good would it do? He could finish her off in a matter of seconds. It took a lot for a quiet village to react – neighbours were likely to hang back in the face of danger, and let someone else be the hero.

Bill was chuckling. 'Exactly what you think,' he explained. 'You've read the diaries, you know how the rest of your life turns out.'

'Why do you keep saying diaries? I thought there was only one?'

'It doesn't matter. It's not like you're going to live any of it out anyway.'

Every single entry in that diary had come true – bar the one regarding Erica's future son. Surely fate was rock solid, you couldn't write over it like a VHS. Her mother had seen the future and there was no changing it. Erica was going to survive, right?

Bill's footsteps moved to the other side of the room before returning to Erica's side. Another sickening kiss on the lips. She sensed him smiling as he pulled away – was he enjoying her repulsion? His attention turned to her arm.

'You've been through a lot today,' he noted, pulling at the blood-stained sleeve.

'I have a feeling it's going to get worse,' she said.

'Don't worry, I won't hurt you. Not today.' She didn't like the implications of that sentence.

Bill pulled Erica's sweater taut where the arm met her shoulder. Cold metal jabbed at her skin before she heard the unmistakable sound of scissors snipping through fabric. He cut the sides and around the arms to create a flap of fabric which he could lift off without disturbing his makeshift restraints.

The cold air clawed at her skin. She'd never felt more vulnerable in her life.

He fumbled with her bra strap, the back of the chair making it difficult for him to get at the right angle to undo it. Couldn't he have done this when she was unconscious? No, the sick fuck wanted her to suffer as much as possible, for as long as possible. As the hooks came free and the weight of her breasts released, Erica had a brainwave.

'Wait, there's something you should know.'

'Yes?'

'I had a bottle of water from Tobias's office today. The same one he'd had. I probably don't have long.' He was quiet. 'Honestly, it's in my car if you don't believe me. You can see it, in the cup holder.' Panic teased the edges of her words.

'Do you feel sick?'

'I can't feel my feet, if that's what you mean.'

Silence. He was thinking.

'Don't make a noise, or there'll be consequences,' he warned her as he made his way to front door.

Ok, think Erica. THINK.

She twisted her body, thrashing from side to side. There was no give in the tape. It wasn't worth Turning with possible Wolfsbane nearby. She needed a way to render Bill useless.

She took a deep breath and forced her brain to be rational. Easier said than done when you're tied to a chair about to be subjected to who only knew what.

Hopefully her bluff about the water would have some traction, or it would move this nightmare along a little faster. The front door slamming shut announced Bill's return and halted Erica's train of thought.

'I didn't think you were so stupid,' he said. Walking up behind her, he muttered dismissively: 'Never mind, I can knock up an antidote.'

His voice was further away, like he was in another room. She was getting a sense of her bearings. If he was working on an antidote he must be in his back room, meaning she must be in the middle of the living room, facing the kitchen.

'I thought you said it was a Mother's Love incantation?' she queried.

'Smoke and mirrors my dear. It would've looked suspicious if I'd miraculously produced the antidote.'

'So what is it?'

'Nothing more than an oral potion. Now, be a good girl and keep quiet while I make it.'

Good, this was buying her time. He'd want to keep her well for as long as possible. He had to be in control, not the virus.

I read your whole life story before you were even born, he'd said. So, what had her mother seen in place of what was happening now? Every decision she'd ever made had led to this moment. There was no way there could have ever been another outcome.

She afforded herself another deep breath and exhaled, counting to five as her lungs emptied. *Be logical.* You could get yourself tangled in a thousand different theories about fate. Everything led back to that stupid diary and the weight of knowing the future. Put knowledge and power in people's hands, and they go crazy.

Bill thought he knew everything. But what if he'd not been told the whole truth either? Maybe this was another stepping stone. Perhaps Lucy had shown him a curated version if she knew what he was going to do to Erica?

Now, there's a thought. People kept talking about the diaries, multiple diaries, expect the one they found was more like specific highlights. What was the significance of those entries? Why had they been put together?

'Won't be long now!' Bill called.

Think, think, think.

Right, slow down. The diary had a note for Erica. Lucy knew she would find it. Why those entries? What was she trying to tell her?

Focus on reading it in the pub, P's smirking face, the assuming American couple, and then being at home, reading in bed. Come on, calm down, you're back at home reading it, no pressure, just think.

So, the longest passages: there was her brother crying, the page P tore out, her asking the universe for a sign and baby Trevor.

If what I need was on that page P, so help me God I will make it my mission to haunt you forever more.

There was nothing special in those entries, aside from the fact they showed each of them at their lowest and a massive hint that a future existed for the trio.

Jesus Mum, why couldn't you just tell me how to get out of this?

Her mother was obsessed with things going to plan. There was no way she'd let Erica get into this situation without a way to get out.

She could hear the hiss of a bunsen burner as Bill heated the liquid for distillation. Erica didn't have long before he'd return. Cold sweat prickled on the back of her neck.

Ok, assuming her mother knew this would happen – what tools did she have to escape? Lewis had been shipped off to the fairies and honed his potion-making, a skill Erica lacked. There was a reason

Lucy didn't touch on this; they had more important things to learn. She knew her daughter didn't need to bother with the practice.

Why those incantations in particular? There had to be some hidden clue.

Footsteps came from behind, the thud of Bill's cane echoing his gait.

'Now, that won't take long to distil,' he said, leaning towards her. 'Then we can get you fixed.' His breath caught the sweat blooming on Erica's chest, sending a shiver down her spine.

Focus, Erica.

Bill's hands cupped her shoulders before tracing the shape of her collarbone with his thumbs. Her stomach twisted with his touch.

'You're not as curvy as your mother.' He sounded upset. 'Shame.'

What did she know? *Lumio, Telica, fairy magic and the ability to do simple spells.* Was there a spell that could freeze Bill? Nope, not that she knew. Fairy magic was no use, she'd still be stuck on this bloody chair and he could hurt her.

Bill lifted a bra strap and begin cutting. The thick elastic was harder to cut than her jumper and he was furiously hacking away with the scissors. He let out a sharp intake of breath as the strap parted and exposed her right breast. He liked what he saw.

Despite the blindfold, Erica shut her eyes tight, not wanting to think about where this was going.

He set to work on the other strap.

It's going to be ok. Mum put the last entry in to show there's a future. Don't lose faith; it's going to work out. Whatever this monster does, it won't last. This isn't the end.

The cutting continued. *It must be Lumio or Telica.*

She hadn't gone very far with Lumio spells, exploring nothing stronger than orbs or fire. Neither seemed suitable for this situation. She couldn't set the mad bastard on fire – not that she felt particularly sympathetic towards him, but she couldn't risk trapping herself in a burning building.

The strap gave out and Bill yanked away what was left of the bra.

'Please, don't,' she whimpered, finding her strength hard to muster as she felt his breath on her face again.

'It's just a little fun Erica. I'm not hurting you.' He pressed his lips to hers.

The kiss was slow and she fought the urge to gag. The fact she made no attempt to return it didn't seem to put him off as his lips moved over her clamped mouth. He pulled away and traced her breastbone, she could feel the sweat sitting on her skin as his rough finger glided over her.

FOCUS. Telica. How could she use it to buy some time? Usually she had to see an object to move it, but her lock-picking technique only required her to know what she was feeling for. If she could pinpoint a part of Bill to target she could, in theory, use the same premise.

His hand cupped her left breast, his thumb rubbing circles on her nipple; it stiffened at the mix of his touch and cold air. She pressed into the back of the chair in revulsion, but it did little to ease her misery as she could still hear the sickening sound of his heavy breathing.

Bill was standing close by, so kicking him could be a serious option. However, given that her legs were taped to the chair it wouldn't buy her the time she needed. He had to be incapacitated if she was going to have any chance of wriggling her hands free.

His breath skimmed her chest and his other hand found her right breast, his thumb flicking at her nipple. She swallowed in disgust as something hard rubbed against her leg. He was nearly eighty, how was this happening?

Oh God. He couldn't have my mother so he's going to have me, Erica's mind cried out, panic hitting like a tidal wave. She flinched as a hand rested on her stomach while he moved positions; he wasn't steady without his cane.

Satisfied he was distracted, she wiggled her hands. Her sweat was doing a good job of loosening the tape, she just needed the chance to go at it hands free, blindfold off. Then she could put an end to this.

She focused hard on the current task, anything to take her mind off what was happening to her body.

'What about my antidote?' she asked, hoping he would straighten up and get off her.

He answered without moving. 'Won't be ready for another ten minutes.'

'You sure?'

'I'm sure.' She could hear the glee in his voice. 'Don't worry, I'll let you know when it's ready. Plenty to keep you busy with until then.'

She ran through the scenario in her head, wondering where was best to aim for. She had a rough idea of how he was standing; it was just a question of what to grab.

The hand on her right breast creeped south before resting on the top button of her jeans. His clumsy hand fumbled to undo it but was hindered by his awkward angle.

Fuck it, it was now or never, this had already gone too far. If this didn't work, Erica would attempt to Turn and suffer the consequences. Anything was better than what this sick fuck was about to do to her.

She focused, letting the rage inside her swell. She had to harness this power to make the spell work. As he popped her button open she clenched her hand, envisioning his windpipe. The technique had worked on Tobias, why not Bill?

Great gasping breaths told her it was working.

'You wee bitch,' he spluttered. 'You're going to kill me.'

Intense pins and needles radiated up her arm. She'd never held on so tight for so long. She didn't want to kill him, but needed to get her point across. Release her or face the consequences.

'Untie me and I'll let you go,' she growled menacingly.

'You – ' Bill's body convulsed against her thigh. His muscles stiffened as he let out a disturbing cry. She'd never heard a human make a noise like that – it seemed to vibrate in the air and was a hiss and a bark all at the same time.

She relaxed her hand and let go of his windpipe. She'd gone far enough. He stumbled away from her.

'I think I'm having a heart attack,' he said, his breath heaving. He gave another monstrous cry.

'And what do you want me to do about it?' she asked, unable to hide the sarcasm. The manoeuvre had exhausted her. Her whole body ached, and had she not been taped to a chair it would have been a chore to keep herself upright.

He groaned again. Guttering noises hinted that he was trying to talk, but no distinguishable words came.

The sound of heavy panting startled her when the room stopped spinning and reality hit like a slap in the face. It took a second to realise that the panting was coming from her. Bill was silent.

Erica took a faltering breath before forcing her lungs to slow down. She then held her breath to listen for signs of life, feel movement nearby. Silence.

'Bill?' she called tentatively.

A familiar feeling shrouded the room, making the air feel thick and heavy. Once again, death had intervened.

'Sorry, can I just squeeze past?' the nurse asked, placing a hand on the back of Erica's chair.

'Yeah, sure, sorry.' The chair squeaked on the hospital's floor as Erica edged it forward, allowing the nurse to sidle through.

'You know, there shouldn't really be so many of you here at once,' Nurse Grimshaw smiled as she spoke, hopeful they'd guess she was joking, well half-joking at least. 'But I'm sure we can make an exception just this once.' That confirmed it and the worry etched on Quinn's face evaporated, back to smiles and laughter as she played snap with the children.

'Maybe get off the bed though, G. Come, back on my knee.' Erica ushered her daughter over, drawing her own cards to her chest as Georgia plonked herself down. 'No peeking mind.' She nuzzled into the child's neck and whispered something, making the girl snort with laughter.

The nurse suppressed a smile, the edge of her mouth only curling the tiniest fraction. It wouldn't do to show favourites.

She examined the chart at the end of the bed, running her finger down rows of observations. The doctor's scrawls and various numbers meant absolutely nothing to her but the part had to be played and this felt like the natural thing to do. Many a time Grimmy had stood and watched proper nurses and doctors do the same before stepping in and rendering their effort futile.

Nurse Grimshaw flipped the corner of the page up and pretended to read the sheet underneath. She nodded, feeling Quinn's eyes dart to her. A mother still worried everything could go wrong again, that her baby wasn't quite out the woods. There was no need to fret though, Samantha had a full life ahead of her. Erica on the other hand—she flipped the page back, skimming the rows of boring, meaningless numbers—Erica had, three thousand days, no, seven thousand, no. Urgh, it was too hard to think in this room. It was trivial anyway, Death would have Its way and win the game with Fate.

Everything had gone to plan. In fact, it probably couldn't have gone any better — Erica had Lewis replicate Bill's final antidote and administered it where needed. Pétur, despite a few threats of catastrophic divergence, had fulfilled his role perfectly. The deaths of those along the way were of little consequence, simply a day's work, it was what happened now that truly mattered. Like toppling dominoes, events were playing out in fantastic fashion, forever marching Erica towards her new Death Day. Fate was going to lose this bet fair and square.

'Do you want to play?' Georgia asked, thrusting cards towards the nurse and breaking Grimmy's train of thought.

'I think the nurse is busy just now, G,' Erica said, looking surprisingly sheepish that her daughter would be so bold.

Nurse Grimshaw grinned as she replaced the chart on the end of the bed before accepting the child's offering.

'Always time for one sneaky round. I do love a good game.'

ACKNOWLEDGMENTS

In no particular order, thank you to
    Claire
    My Mum and Dad
    Melissa
    And you, for buying this book.

You all mean the world to me.

ALSO BY EVE PEARSON

What Will Be

When The Shadows Call

The Secrets We Tell

Fancy a FREE e-book?

Join my reader's club and receive my free novella, Jimmy M'Lad. A light-hearted ghost story perfect for devouring in one sitting.

Visit evepearsonauthor.com to get your free book.

How hard can it be to get rid of a ghost?

Erica Hutchinson is on a mission to embrace her newfound title of Paranormal Investigator when an email drops in her inbox that she can't say no to. One of Glasgow's most prestigious hotels has a ghost problem, and they need Erica to solve it.

Having no experience with ghosts isn't going to dissuade her. After all, she's secretly a witch. Surely a ghost will be no match?

Join Erica as she tries her hand at exorcism and finds out the hard way that life and death don't always go to plan.

Printed in Great Britain
by Amazon